CATWOMAN™

SOULSTEALER

— DC Icons —

SARAH J. MAAS

PENGUIN BOOKS

PENGUIN BOOKS

UK | USA | Canada | Ireland | Australia
India | New Zealand | South Africa

Penguin Books is part of the Penguin Random House group of companies
whose addresses can be found at global.penguinrandomhouse.com.

www.penguin.co.uk   www.puffin.co.uk   www.ladybird.co.uk

First published in the United States of America by Random House Children's Books
and in Great Britain by Penguin Books 2018

001

Copyright © 2018 DC Comics.
BATMAN and all related characters and elements © & TM DC Comics
WB SHIELD: TM & © WBEI. (s18)
RHUS41175

The moral right of the author has been asserted

Set in 9.57/15.24 pt Berling
Printed and bound in Great Britain by Clays Ltd, Elcograf S.p.A.

A CIP catalogue record for this book is available from the British Library

Hardback ISBN: 978–0–141–38688–1
Paperback ISBN: 978–0–141–38689–8

All correspondence to:
Penguin Books, Penguin Random House Children's
80 Strand, London WC2R 0RL

FOR THE WOMEN WHO RAISE HELL
AND HAVE FUN DOING IT

BEFORE

CHAPTER 1

The roaring crowd in the makeshift arena didn't set her blood on fire.

It did not shake her, or rile her, or set her hopping from foot to foot. No, Selina Kyle only rolled her shoulders—once, twice.

And waited.

The wild cheering that barreled down the grimy hallway to the prep room was little more than a distant rumble of thunder. A storm, just like the one that had swept over the East End on her walk from the apartment complex. She'd been soaked before she reached the covert subway entrance that led into the underground gaming warren owned by Carmine Falcone, the latest of Gotham City's endless parade of mob bosses.

But like any other storm, this fight, too, would be weathered.

Rain still drying in her long, dark hair, Selina checked that it was indeed tucked into its tight bun atop her head. She'd made the mistake once of wearing a ponytail—in her second street fight. The other girl had managed to grab it, and those few seconds when Selina's neck had been exposed had lasted longer than any in her life.

But she'd won—barely. And she'd learned. Had learned at every fight since, whether on the streets above or in the arena carved into the sewers beneath Gotham City.

It didn't matter who her opponent was tonight. The challengers were all usually variations of the same: desperate men who owed more than they could repay to Falcone. Fools willing to risk their lives for a chance to lift their debt by taking on one of his Leopards in the ring.

The prize: never having to look over their shoulder for a waiting shadow. The cost of failing: having their asses handed to them—and the debts remained. Usually with the promise of a one-way ticket to the bottom of the Sprang River. The odds of winning: slim to none.

Regardless of whatever sad sack she'd be battling tonight, Selina prayed Falcone would give her the nod faster than last time. That fight . . . He'd made her keep that particularly brutal match going. The crowd had been too excited, too ready to spend money on the cheap alcohol and everything else for sale in the subterranean warren. She'd taken home more bruises than usual, and the man she'd beaten to unconsciousness . . .

Not her problem, she told herself again and again. Even when she saw her adversaries' bloodied faces in her dreams, both asleep and waking. What Falcone did with them after the fight was not her problem. She left her opponents breathing. At least she had that.

And at least she wasn't dumb enough to push back outright, like some of the other Leopards. The ones who were too proud or too stupid or too young to get how the game was played. No, her small rebellions against Carmine Falcone were subtler. He wanted men dead—she left them unconscious, but did it so well that not one person in the crowd objected.

A fine line to walk, especially with her sister's life hanging in the balance. Push back too much, and Falcone might ask questions, start wondering who meant the most to her. Where to strike hardest. She'd never allow it to get to that point. Never risk Maggie's safety like that—even if these fights were all for her. Every one of them.

It had been three years since Selina had joined the Leopards, and nearly two and a half since she'd proved herself against the other girl gangs well enough that Mika, her Alpha, had introduced her to Falcone. Selina hadn't dared miss that meeting.

Order in the girl gangs was simple: The Alpha of each gang ruled and protected, laid down punishment and reward. The Alphas' commands were law. And the enforcers of those commands were their Seconds and Thirds. From there, the pecking order turned murkier. Fighting offered a way to rise in the ranks—or you could fall, depending on how badly a match went. Even an Alpha might be challenged if you were dumb or brave enough to do so.

But the thought of ascending the ranks had been far from Selina's mind when Mika had brought Falcone over to watch her take on the Second of the Wolf Pack and leave the girl leaking blood onto the concrete of the alley.

Before that fight, only four leopard spots had been inked onto Selina's pale left arm, each a trophy of a fight won.

Selina adjusted the hem of her white tank. At seventeen, she now had twenty-seven spots inked across both arms.

Undefeated.

That's what the match emcee was declaring down the hall. Selina could just make out the croon of words: *The undefeated champion, the fiercest of Leopards . . .*

Her hand drifted to the one item she was allowed to bring into the arena: the bullwhip.

Some Leopards opted for signature makeup or clothes to make their identities stand out in the ring. Selina had little money to spare for that kind of thing—not when a tube of lip gloss could cost as much as a small meal. But Mika had been unimpressed when Selina had shown up to her first official fight in her old gymnastics leotard and a pair of leggings.

You look like you're going to Jazzercise, her Alpha had said. *Let's give you some claws at least.*

All sorts of small weapons were allowed in the ring, short of knives and guns. But there hadn't been any on hand that night. No, there had only been the bullwhip, discarded in a pile of props from when this place had hosted some sort of alternative circus.

You've got ten minutes to figure out how to use it, Mika had warned Selina before leaving her to it.

She'd barely figured out how to snap the thing before she was shoved into the fighting ring. The whip had been more of a hindrance than a help in that first fight, but the crowd had loved it. And some small part of *her* had loved it, the crack that cleaved through the world.

So she'd learned to wield it. Until it became an extension of her arm, until it gave her an edge that her slight frame didn't offer. The high drama it provided in the ring didn't hurt, either.

A thump on the metal door was her signal to go.

Selina checked the bullwhip at her hip, her black spandex pants, the green sneakers that matched her eyes—though no one had ever commented on it. She flexed her fingers within their wrappings. All good.

Or as good as could be.

Her muscles were loose, her body limber, courtesy of her old gymnastics warm-up, which she'd repurposed for these fights. Between the physical fighting, the whip, and the sheer acrobatics that she used both for show and to throw her heavier opponents off-balance, making sure her body was *ready* for these fights was half the battle.

The rusty door groaned as Selina opened it. Mika was tending to the new girl in the hall beyond, the flickering fluorescent lights draining the Alpha's golden skin of its usual glow.

Mika threw Selina an assessing look over her narrow shoulder, her black braid shifting with the movement. The white girl sniffling in front of her gingerly wiped away the blood streaming from her swollen nose. One of the kitten's eyes was already puffy and red, the other swimming with unshed tears.

No wonder the crowd was riled. If a Leopard had taken that bad a beating, it must have been one hell of a fight. Brutal enough that Mika put a hand on the girl's pale arm to keep her from swaying.

Down the shadowy hall that led into the arena, one of Falcone's bouncers beckoned. Selina shut the door behind her. She'd left no valuables. She had nothing worth stealing, anyway.

"Be careful," Mika said as Selina passed, the Asian girl's voice low and soft. "He's got a worse batch than usual tonight." The kitten hissed, yanking her head away as Mika dabbed her split lip with a disinfectant wipe. Mika snarled a warning at her, and the kitten wisely fell still, trembling a bit as the Alpha cleaned out the cut. Mika added without glancing back, "He saved the best for you. Sorry."

"He always does," Selina said coolly, even as her stomach roiled. "I can handle it."

She didn't have any other choice. Losing would leave Maggie with no one to look after her. And refusing to fight? Not an option, either.

In the three years that Selina had known Mika, the Alpha had never suggested ending their arrangement with Carmine Falcone. Not when having Falcone back the Leopards made the other East End gangs think twice about pushing in on their territory. Even if it meant doing these fights and offering up Leopards for the crowd's enjoyment.

Falcone turned it into a weekly spectacle—a veritable Roman circus to make the underbelly of Gotham City love *and* fear him. It certainly helped that many of the other notorious lowlifes had been imprisoned thanks to certain do-gooders running around the city in capes.

Mika eased the kitten to the prep room, giving Selina a jerk of the chin—an order to go.

But Selina paused to scan the hall, the exits. Even down here, in the heart of Falcone's territory, it was a death wish to be defenseless in the open. Especially if you were an Alpha with as many enemies as Mika.

Three figures slipped in from a door at the opposite end of the hall, and Selina's shoulders loosened a bit at the sight of the Latina girl who emerged. Ani, Mika's Second, with two other low-ranking Leopards flanking her.

Good. They'd guard the exit while their Alpha tended to their own.

The crowd's cheering rumbled through the concrete floor, rattling the loose ceramic tiles on the walls, echoing along Selina's bones and breath as she neared the dented metal door to the arena. The bouncer gestured for her to hurry the hell up, but she kept her strides even. Stalking.

The Leopards, these fights . . . they were her job. And it paid well. With her mother gone and her sister sick, no legit job could pay as much or as quickly.

The Leopards had asked no questions three years ago. They hadn't wondered if she'd deliberately picked that fight with the Razor girl in the block courtyard—and another and another, until Mika came sniffing about the hothead in Building C.

Mika only told her that pulling this sort of shit in the East End would get her killed pretty fast, and that the Leopards could use a fighter like her. The Alpha didn't ask who had taught her to fight. Or how to take a punch.

The bouncer opened the door, the unfiltered roar of the crowd bursting down the hall like a pack of rabid wolves.

Selina Kyle blew out a long breath as she lifted her chin and stepped into the sound and the light and the wrath.

Let the bloodying begin.

Her hands were so swollen that she could barely handle her keys.

Their jangling filled her apartment complex's hallway, loud as a goddamn dinner bell.

It took every lingering scrap of concentration to keep her hand steady enough to slide the key into the top lock. Selina refused to look at the three others beneath it—each as imposing as a mountain peak.

Too long. Falcone had dragged out the fight for too long.

Mika hadn't been lying about her opponent. The man had been

a fighter himself. Not well trained, but big. Twice her weight. And desperate to repay his debt. His blows had hurt. To say the least.

But she'd won. Not by brute strength, but because she'd been smarter. When the injuries had started to pile up, when he'd managed to snatch the whip from her hand, when she'd temporarily lost sight in one eye thanks to the blood . . . she'd used simple physics against him. Her science teacher would be proud.

If she showed up to class tomorrow. Or next week.

The top lock snapped open.

Against larger, heavier opponents, pure physical strength wasn't her greatest ally. No, her own arsenal was something different: speed, agility, flexibility, mostly thanks to those countless gymnastics classes. And the bullwhip. All things that she might use to surprise her opponents—to harness the speed of a two-hundred-pound man charging at her and wield it against him. A few maneuvers, and that blind rush at her would turn into a flip onto his back. Or a face-first collision with one of the posts. Or the bullwhip around his leg, yanking his balance out from under him as she drove her elbow into his gut.

Always aim for the soft parts. She'd learned that before she'd ever set foot in the ring.

Her left eye still a bit blurry, Selina surveyed either side of the grayish-blue-painted hallway, skimming over the graffiti, the puddle of something that wasn't water. None of it threatening.

The shadowy parts of the hall . . . Precisely why there were four locks on this door. Why Maggie was to open it under *zero* circumstances. Especially for their mother. And whoever her mother might have with her.

There was still a dent in the metal door from the last time—six months ago.

A large, round dent, right beside the peephole, where the sweaty man who'd stood beside her strung-out mother had planted his fist when Selina refused to answer the door. They'd left only when a neighbor had threatened to call the cops.

There were nice people in this building. Good people. But calling the cops would have made things worse. Cops meant questions. Questions about their *living situation*.

Selina turned back to the door, assured that no one had slipped into those shadows. In the shape she was in . . . She managed to open the second lock. And the third.

Selina was just starting on the final lock when the elevator grumbled down the hall. The dented doors parted to reveal Mrs. Sullivan, grocery bags in one hand, keys threaded like metal claws through the fingers of her other.

Their eyes met as the ancient white woman hobbled down the hall, and Selina gave her a nod, praying the hood of the sweatshirt beneath her jacket concealed her face. The bullwhip, at least, was hidden down her back. Mrs. Sullivan frowned deeply, clicking her tongue, and hurried for her apartment. The woman had five locks.

Selina took her time with the final lock, well aware the woman was monitoring her every movement. She debated telling Mrs. Sullivan that she wasn't lingering because she was thinking of robbing her. Debated it, and decided against it at the sneer the old woman threw her way.

Trash—that was the word that danced in Mrs. Sullivan's eyes before she slammed shut the door to her apartment and all those locks clicked into place.

Selina was too sore to bother being pissed off by it. She'd heard worse.

She freed the last lock and entered the apartment, quickly

shutting and locking the door. Lock after lock after lock, then the chain at the very top.

The apartment was dim, illuminated only by the golden glow of the streetlights in the courtyard outside the two windows of their living room/kitchen. She was pretty sure there were people in Gotham City whose bathrooms were bigger than the entirety of this space, but at least she kept it as clean as she could.

The tang of tomato sauce and the sweetness of bread lingered in the air. A peek in the fridge revealed that Maggie had indeed eaten the food Selina had bought for her after school. A lot of it.

Good.

Shutting the fridge, Selina opened the freezer and fished out a bag of peas stashed beside a stack of frozen dinners. She pushed it against her throbbing cheek as she counted those frozen dinners—just three. Their meals for the rest of the week, once the Italian ran out.

Pressing the frozen peas to her face, savoring the cool bite, Selina stashed the bullwhip under the sink, toed off her sneakers, and padded over the dingy green carpet of the living area to the hallway with the bathroom and single bedroom across from it. The tiny bathroom was dark, empty. But to her left, a warm glow leaked from the door left ajar.

The wad of cash in her back pocket was still not enough. Not between rent and food and Maggie's tests and copays.

Her chest tight, she eased open the door with a shoulder, craning her head inside the bedroom. It was the only place of color in the apartment, painted buttercup yellow and plastered with Broadway posters Selina had been lucky enough to find when yet another East End school had been shut down and cleared out its theater department.

Those posters now watched over the girl in the bed, curled up under some cartoon kids' comforter that was about two sizes too small and ten years too worn. So was everything in the room—including the glowworm night-light Maggie still insisted be left on.

Selina didn't blame her. At thirteen, Maggie had dealt with enough shit to earn the right to do whatever she wanted. The labored, rasping breathing that filled the room was proof enough. Selina silently picked up one of the several inhalers beside Maggie's bed and checked the gauge. More than enough left if another coughing fit hit her tonight. Not that Selina wouldn't rush in here from her spot on the living room couch the moment she heard her sister's hacking coughs.

After plugging in the humidifier, Selina crept back to the living space and slumped into a cracked vinyl chair at the small table in the middle of the kitchen.

Everything ached. Everything throbbed and burned and begged her to lie down.

Selina checked the clock. Two a.m. They had school in . . . five hours. Well, Maggie had school. Selina certainly couldn't go with her face like this.

She fished the cash from her pocket and set it on the plastic table.

Hauling a small box in the center of the table toward her, Selina looted through it with the hand that hurt only a fraction less than the other. She'd have to be smart at the market—the EBT funds only stretched so far. Certainly not far enough to cover herself and a sister with severe cystic fibrosis. Selina had read up on food-as-medicine on a library computer while waiting for Maggie to finish her after-school theater class. Not a cure-all, but eating healthy could help. *Anything* was worth a try. If it bought them time. If it brought Maggie any relief.

Cystic fibrosis—Selina couldn't remember a time when she hadn't known those words. What they meant: the incurable genetic disease that caused a buildup of mucus in several organs, but especially the lungs. The mucus clogged and blocked airways, where it trapped bacteria that at best led to infections. At worst: lung damage and respiratory failure.

And then there was the mucus that also built up in the pancreas, blocking the enzymes that helped break down food and absorb nutrients.

Selina had Googled it once: *life expectancy for severe cystic fibrosis.*

She'd closed the web browser and vomited into the library's toilet for thirty minutes afterward.

Selina studied the cash on the table and swallowed. The kinds of healthy foods Maggie needed didn't come cheap. The frozen microwave dinners were emergency meals. Garbage food. The fresh Italian meal Maggie had consumed tonight was a rare treat.

And perhaps an apology, for the fight Selina had left her sister in order to take part in.

"Your face."

The rasping words had Selina's head snapping up. "You should be asleep."

Maggie's curly brown hair was half wild, a pillow wrinkle running down her too-thin pale cheek. Only her green eyes—the single trait they shared, despite having two different fathers—were clear. Alert. "Don't forget to ice your hands. You won't be able to use them tomorrow if you don't."

Selina gave her sister a half smile, which only made her face hurt more, and obeyed, transferring the peas from her throbbing face to the split, swollen skin of her knuckles. At least the swelling had gone down since the fight finished an hour ago.

Maggie slowly crossed the room, and Selina tried not to wince at the labored breathing, the quiet clearing of her sister's throat. The latest lung infection had taken its toll, and the color was gone from her usually pink cheeks. "You should go to the hospital," Maggie breathed. "Or let me clean you up."

Selina ignored both suggestions and asked, "How are you feeling?"

Maggie pulled the pile of cash toward her, eyes widening as she began counting wrinkled twenties. "Fine."

"You do your homework?"

A wry, exasperated look. "Yes. And tomorrow's."

"Good girl."

Maggie studied her, those green eyes too alert, too aware. "We've got the doctor tomorrow after school."

"What about it?"

Maggie finished counting the money and neatly set the stack into the small box with the EBT card. "Mom won't be there."

Neither would Maggie's father—whoever he was. Selina doubted even her mother knew. Selina's own father . . . She only knew what her mother had said during one of her rambling monologues while high: that her mother had met him through a friend at a party. Nothing more. Not even a name.

Selina moved the frozen peas from her right hand to her left. "No, she won't. But I will."

Maggie scratched at an invisible fleck on the table. "Auditions for the spring play are soon."

"You going to try out?"

A little shrug. "I want to ask the doctor if I can."

So responsible, her sister. "What musical is it this year?"

"*Carousel.*"

"Have we watched that one?"

A shake of the head, those curls bouncing, and a beaming smile.

Selina smiled back. "But I assume we're going to watch it tomorrow night?" Friday night—movie night. Courtesy of a DVD player she and the Leopards had taken off the back of a truck, and the library's extensive movie section.

Maggie nodded. Broadway musicals: Maggie's not-so-secret dream and lifelong obsession. Selina had no idea where it had come from. They'd certainly never been able to afford theater tickets, but Maggie's school had taken plenty of field trips to Gotham City productions. Perhaps she'd picked it up at one of those outings, that undying love. Undimming, even when the cystic fibrosis battered her lungs so brutally that singing, standing on a stage, and dancing were difficult.

Perhaps a lung transplant might change that, but she was at the bottom of a long, long list. Even as Maggie's health plummeted with each passing month, she didn't move any higher. And the drugs that the doctors had hailed as breakthroughs that would add decades of life for some people with CF . . . Maggie hadn't responded to them.

But Selina wasn't about to tell her sister any of that. She'd never make her feel like there were limits to what she could do.

That Maggie was even willing to audition made Selina's chest unbearably tight.

"You should go to bed," Selina said to her sister, setting down the frozen peas.

"You should, too," Maggie said tartly.

Selina huffed a low laugh that made her aching body protest in agony. "We'll go together." She winced as she stood, and chucked the peas back in the freezer.

She'd just turned around when frail arms wrapped carefully around her waist. As if Maggie knew that bruises now bloomed on her ribs. "I love you, Selina," she said quietly.

Selina kissed the top of Maggie's head through the riot of curls and rubbed her sister's back, even as it made her fingers bark in pain.

Worth it, though—that pain as she held her sister, the fridge a steady hum around them.

Worth it.

"I don't understand how our copay the last time was so much cheaper."

It was an effort to keep her voice steady, to keep her hands from curling into fists on the counter of the hospital's checkout desk.

The aging woman in pink floral scrubs barely glanced up from her computer. "I can only tell you what the computer tells *me*." She pointed with a long purple nail to whatever was on the screen. "And this says you owe five hundred today."

Selina clenched her jaw so hard it ached, glancing over a shoulder to where Maggie waited in one of the plastic chairs against the white wall. Reading a book—but her eyes weren't darting over the page.

Selina kept her voice down, even though she knew Maggie

would just lean forward to eavesdrop. "Last month, it was a hundred."

That purple nail tapped against the screen. "Dr. Tasker did tests today. Your insurance doesn't cover them."

"No one told me that." Even if they had, Maggie *needed* those tests. Yet the results they'd received . . . Selina shoved the thought from her mind, along with what the doctor had said moments ago.

The woman finally looked up from her computer long enough to take in Selina. The swelling had gone down on her face, the bruises concealed with some expert makeup and artful arranging of her curtain of dark hair. The woman's blue eyes narrowed. "Are you the parent or guardian?"

Selina just said, "We can't pay that bill."

"Then it's something to take up with your insurance company."

Yes, but Maggie would need more tests like the one she'd had today. The next one in two weeks. The third a month from now. Selina did the math and swallowed the tightness in her throat. "There's nothing the hospital can do?"

The woman typed away, keys clacking. "It's an issue for your insurance company."

"Our insurance company will say it's an issue for *you*."

The clacking on those keys stopped. "Where's your mother?" The woman glanced around Selina as if she'd find her mother standing a few feet away.

Selina was half tempted to tell the woman to take a stroll through an East End alley, since that was the only place their mother would be, dead or alive. Instead, she plucked up the insurance card that had been left on the counter and said flatly, "She's at work."

The woman didn't seem convinced. But she said, "We'll send the bill to your house."

Selina didn't bother replying as she turned and scooped up her sister's heavy backpack. Slinging it over a shoulder, she motioned for Maggie to follow her to the elevator bay.

"We don't have five hundred dollars," Maggie murmured while Selina punched the elevator button harder than was necessary.

No, between the food and rent and today's tests, the money from the fight wouldn't stretch far enough.

"Don't worry about it," Selina said, watching the elevator floors light up one by one.

Maggie wrapped her arms around herself. Not good—the news had not been good.

That crushing tunnel vision again crept up on Selina. Those five hundred dollars and those stupid tests and that bland-faced doctor saying, *There's no cure for CF, but let's try another route or two.*

She'd almost asked, *Before what?*

As Maggie continued to hold herself, her blunted, rounded fingertips—their shape another *screw you* from the disease—dug into her thin arms hard enough to make Selina wince.

Selina pried one of her sister's hands free and interlaced their fingers.

Squeezing tightly, neither sister let go the entire trek home.

The neighbors were really at each other's throats.

Barely five minutes after Selina had turned on the movie, the shouting and screeching had begun filtering in through the wall behind them. Curled up on the sagging, stained couch that also served as Selina's bed, her sister tucked against one end with her feet in Selina's lap, Selina half listened to the drunken fight unfurling next door and the musical on the ancient TV in front of them.

Carousel. The music was fine, even if everyone was a bit too judgey and smiley and the dude was a total controlling loser-douchebag. Still, Maggie's head swayed and bobbed along.

The aroma of cheap mac and cheese clung to the air. Selina had offered to buy Maggie a real dinner out, but Maggie had wanted to just go home—tired, she'd said. She hadn't lost that grim-faced expression since the hospital. And there was enough of a nip in the air that Selina hadn't tried to convince her.

Not that they had the money. But after the doctor's not-so-sunny prognosis, what difference did thirty bucks make?

Selina eyed her flip phone sitting on the coffee table she'd propped her feet on. Mika and the other Leopards knew not to call on Fridays. Knew tonight was the only night Selina wouldn't show up, no matter the job or the threat.

But if Mika called right then, saying Falcone was hosting another fight and it'd pay big, she'd take it. She'd take three fights in a row.

Yet—no. She had to be smart about it. If she was hurt badly, the hospital social workers would come sniffing. Ask where their mother was, and likely recognize the tattoos inked down Selina's arms. Tattoos she kept covered year-round with long sleeves. Even with Maggie, she made sure to dress in the bathroom and never to roll her sleeves up too high while washing her hands.

But in the ring . . . those tattoos were on full display for her opponents. *Look how many have fallen*, they snarled at all who saw them. *You're next.*

The wall behind them thudded, rattling the two framed pictures. The bigger one: a photo of her and Maggie from two years ago—the frame stolen, the photo a cheap printout off the school library printer. They'd been sitting on a bench in the park on a glorious fall day, the trees bright as jewels around them, and Maggie had asked a passing businesswoman to take the picture on her phone. The quality of the image wasn't great, but the light shining from Maggie's face was still undeniable.

And the second: a photo of Selina five years ago, midair as she executed a perfect backflip on a balance beam. One of many gymnastics competitions she'd participated in. And won. Her instructor at the Y had tried to convince her to keep going after those initial three years, claiming that she was remarkably gifted. But Maggie's illness had been getting worse, their mom had just bailed, and the time and money it would take to train and compete . . . Not an option. So Selina had stopped going to gymnastics class, had stopped picking up the coach's calls. Even if she still used everything she'd learned in her fights.

The crowds loved it, too. Perhaps more than the bullwhip. Their favorite: a back handspring into a backflip—right onto her opponent's shoulders. Where gravity and a squeeze of her legs around the throat did the work in bringing a man to his knees.

A string of curses shot through the apartment, and Maggie leaned forward to grab the remote off the table and punch up the volume. "This is the big number," her sister explained, eyes fixed on the screen. "The most famous song in the musical."

The controlling douchebag had indeed launched into a seemingly endless monologue.

"He's just found out that his wife is pregnant, and he's having a total freak-out."

"I'm watching," Selina said, brows lifting.

Maggie smiled, shaking her head. "You were listening to the neighbors."

Guilty. Selina gave her sister a wince of apology, and focused again on the musical.

Musing and brooding and gloating about the son he'd have, utter macho nonsense. "They're really putting this on at your school?"

Maggie hushed her with a waved hand. The song shifted, the jerk now mulling over what it'd be like with a daughter, more macho nonsense and misogynistic crap.

Selina slid her attention over to Maggie as the music shifted, rising. Her sister's beautiful green eyes were wide and bright. "This is the part," she whispered.

The music exploded, and her sister's lips moved, mouthing every word.

Mouthing, because those failing lungs couldn't hold enough air to make the sounds, and the latest infection in them had ripped away any chance of holding a note in key.

Maggie silently sang on, not missing a word.

Selina looked to the screen. To the crashing ocean and the man belting out every note, every dream to shelter and clothe and keep food on the table for his child. To attain money in any way he could, whether by theft or by making it honestly. His only alternative: die trying.

And for a moment, it seemed that even the neighbors quieted to hear it. The entire complex. All of the East End.

When Selina glanced back to her sister, Maggie was staring at her, mouth closed. Eyes bright with tears.

And it was the understanding on her sister's face, the way Maggie's damp eyes flicked to the bruises on Selina's own . . .

Selina made herself stay seated for another minute. Two. Five. Ten.

Maggie went back to watching the movie. The neighbors went back to screaming and cursing.

Then Selina casually rose, gently setting Maggie's blanket-wrapped feet on the couch before padding for the bathroom. She wondered if her sister saw her scoop up her phone.

Selina shut the bathroom door and ran the sink faucet on full blast.

She managed to close the lid on the toilet, at least, before she slumped onto it and covered her face with both hands, breathing hard between her fingers. The room pushed in, and she couldn't get air down fast enough, deep enough—

Her hand slid to her chest, as if she'd somehow will her lungs to open up—her lungs, and Maggie's lungs, wrecked and failing. *There are countless other desperate patients waiting for lung transplants*, the doctor had said this afternoon. *I would not count on it as an option.*

Unless you were rich enough to buy your way up that list. Or to buy yourself a pair on the black market.

Selina took gulping mouthfuls of air, hands shaking so badly she lowered them to her knees, gripping tight. They were fighting for twenty years at best. At worst . . .

The rate at which the disease has progressed and Maggie's resistance to the drugs are cause for concern, the doctor had gone on, speaking more to his flock of interns than to them.

Maggie hadn't asked him if she could be in the musical. Her sister had known. She'd known that this thing that made her come alive with joy, that gave her whatever slim shred of hope. It didn't matter how many fights Selina fought for her. How many stores she looted with the Leopards. The blood and the bruises and the cracked ribs could not buy her sister a new set of lungs or a cure for this disease or a chance to stand on that school stage and belt her heart out.

Sobs threatened, shuddering beneath each breath.

Selina covered her face again, as if she could hide it—the tears that rose up within her like a tidal wave, that she pushed back and back and back.

Hands trembling, she grabbed the phone off the narrow sink counter, fingers shaking so wildly she could barely text Mika: *I need another fight. ASAP.*

Mika replied a few minutes later, *If you need cash, I've got you covered.*

Tempting, but too many complications. She wouldn't be able to repay Mika. And though she trusted her Alpha, this was the East End. Everyone needed cash, and Mika might be ruthless in getting it returned to her.

Fights are fine. Then, after a heartbeat, *But thank you.*

Mika's response came instantly: *Anything I should be concerned about?*

Not because she cared, but because if it was something that threatened the Leopards, she needed to know.

Just personal shit.

Whether the Leopards knew her sister was sick, she wasn't sure. She had never told them, and Mika wasn't the type to ask.

Mika replied, *You healed enough from last night to do it?*

No. *Yes.*

Selina blew out a breath, tears sinking back into her. Shutting off the faucet, she listened. The musical continued on—along with the neighbors' fighting.

She could steal the money, of course. Had done it in the past with the Leopards. Even enjoyed the puzzle that some burglaries offered: how to break inside a place, how to ease past the guards or security systems, how to avoid leaving a trace. But to go it alone . . . She hadn't done that yet. Wouldn't risk jail, not with fighting as a relatively safer option.

Mika only said, *I'll ask Falcone.*

Selina flipped her phone shut and flushed the toilet. Mercifully, her hands had stopped shaking by the time she emerged into the living room, where her sister was still bundled on the couch.

Maggie picked up the remote and paused the movie. Looking Selina over with eyes that missed nothing, not even the cell phone clenched in Selina's hand, Maggie asked quietly, "Can't you just ask for the money?"

Selina didn't care to guess how Maggie had figured it out as she slid her phone into her back pocket. "No."

She and the Leopards were often sent by Falcone to those in his debt. Either to remind them of the money owed or to exact punishment when the final warning had been ignored. It was ugly and dirty, and over her dead body would she be in his debt.

"But—"

"No."

Maggie opened her mouth again, green fire lighting her eyes, but a knock sounded on the door.

They froze. Not good. At this hour.

Another pounding knock. *"Police!"*

CHAPTER 2

Shit.

Selina had cataloged every possible exit from this apartment. She looked toward the window at the other end of the room. Could her sister make it down the fire escape fast enough to slip away?

She'd carry Maggie if she had to. Selina winced as she shot to her feet, lingering pain lashing through her body.

Maggie threw the blanket off her legs as the door rattled again. "What do we do?" she breathed.

If this was about the Leopards—

"We're looking for Maria Kyle," the officer said.

Selina blew out a breath that Maggie echoed. Thank God. They'd dealt with this in the past. Several times.

Hide, Maggie mouthed. The cops would surely start asking questions if they saw her bruises. Selina shook her head. But Maggie stood and pointed to the bedroom in a silent order.

Another pound on the door.

Selina limped over and confirmed it *was* two thickly built GCPD officers standing there, one dark-haired and the other balding and mustached, before heading for the bedroom closet.

A reliable hiding place in the past, a pocket of it tucked back far enough that she could remain hidden. Or put Maggie in there. Selina was just climbing in around the tightly packed clothes when Maggie opened the front door, locks clicking free.

Ears straining, Selina heard her sister say quietly, the portrait of sleepy confusion, "My mom didn't come home tonight."

One of the cops asked, "Can we come in?"

"I'm not allowed to let in strangers," her sister said. "Even cops."

A pause. Then a woman's voice asked, "What about social workers, Maggie?"

Selina's heart stopped dead.

There hadn't been a woman outside when she looked, no mention of social services—

Maggie stammered, "Why? M-my mother isn't here."

"We know," the woman said calmly but not gently. "She's down at the precinct."

Hangers rattling, Selina shoved out of the closet, pain barking down her body as she stepped over neatly folded piles of clothes, the room now a minefield keeping her from getting to the hall.

She stumbled into the living room, where Maggie stood before the open door, the two towering cops, and a small, fair woman in an ill-fitting suit. They all looked at her, the cops' eyes narrowing as they beheld the bruises, the woman's face tightening in disapproval.

"Good. I'm glad you're here, too" was all the social worker said.

Maggie backed up to Selina's side. The officers and the social worker pushed into the apartment, shutting the door behind them.

Selina knew the neighbors were likely listening through the walls as the social worker went on. "We picked up your mom earlier tonight. She's not in good shape." A glance around the apartment. "But I'm sure you know that."

"We do," Selina said evenly.

"You're not in good shape, either," the woman added.

"I'm fine. Just fell down the stairs yesterday."

"Must have been some fall," one of the cops said, crossing his thick arms. A gun, a billy club, and a Taser hung from his heavy belt.

Selina said, "We can't make her bail."

The social worker had the nerve to laugh quietly. "We're not here for that." A glance between her and Maggie. "We're here to bring you two in."

"Maggie's innocent," Selina said, pushing her sister behind her.

"And what about you?" the second cop said, brows rising on his meaty face.

Selina ignored him, meeting the social worker's stare. There was a grand stashed in the box taped under the kitchen sink. If they wanted to be paid off—

"Neither of you is in trouble, Selina Kyle," the social worker said, the embodiment of a bureaucratic, rule-abiding worker bee. "But as you're both underage and living here alone"—a glance around the apartment said the woman was well aware they'd been on their own for years—"we need to find a better living arrangement for you both. There are two very nice spots in homes waiting for you right now."

Foster homes. *Separate ones.*

The room, the sounds, her body . . . they all started to feel a bit distant.

"This is our home," Maggie said softly. "We're fine here."

"State doesn't think so," one of the cops said, his sandy mustache yellow against his pasty skin. "Two little girls living alone in *this* building?" The man walked over to the kitchen and began opening cabinets.

Selina's heart pounded with every groan and thud of the wood. And her hands began to shake as he stooped, opening the sink cabinets, and peered in. A rip of tape, and he chuckled as he stood, cashbox in his hands.

Flipping open the lid, he smiled at the money inside. Lifted the wad of bills and fanned them. His partner let out a low whistle of approval. "Been working on the side?" he asked Selina.

The way his eyes raked over her, she knew what kind of work he thought she did. "No" was all she said.

He'd known exactly where that box might be hidden. Perhaps he'd anticipated drugs instead. She should have been better at hiding it, figured out a smarter place for that money—

The social worker said, "You have a record."

"It was from three years ago." Selina's voice came out surprisingly even.

"You have two strikes," the social worker continued. "No judge will let you stay here." She gestured to their bedroom. "Go pack your bags. Bring enough stuff for a week or two."

Maggie shook her head. "I'm not going."

Selina watched as the mustached cop smiled at her and slid that grand into his pocket. Her stomach dropped to her feet, her pulse pounding through every battered inch of her.

Two corrupt cops were in her apartment. And an unsympathetic social worker. Not good. Not safe.

"Maggie," she murmured to her sister, "go pack your bags."

Her sister refused to move.

Selina turned to the woman, who had now crossed her slender arms. "My sister has a serious medical condition. A group home in some filthy house is not what she needs."

"Every foster home in our system is constantly inspected for cleanliness and safety. Any home she goes to will meet her needs."

Bullshit. She'd heard from girls in the Leopards that those homes were roach palaces at best.

"And as for Maggie's special needs," the woman said, patience running thin as her words turned clipped, "living with a sister who has a criminal record does not seem so safe, either."

Maggie snapped, "You don't know *anything.*"

Selina shot her sister a warning look. "Go pack your bags."

Maggie shook her head, brown curls bouncing. "I'm not going."

"It's nearly one in the morning," the social worker coaxed. "Let's get you settled somewhere safe."

"I'm safe *here,*" Maggie said, voice hitching.

At the sound of it, the way Maggie's voice broke with fear, Selina's blood started roaring.

Stay calm. Stay focused. Selina tried again. "If it's so late, then why don't we sleep here? You can pick us up in the morning."

"And come back to find you've skipped town?" asked the dark-haired cop who hadn't pocketed her money. "Not a chance. Get your stuff. Now."

No options. No choices. No way to figure this out.

Selina put a hand on Maggie's too-skinny arm. Medications. Maggie would need to bring all her medications with her—

The touch seemed to snap some leash in her sister.

Maggie bolted.

Not for the bedroom but for the apartment door.

For a moment, the world slowed and bent.

All Selina saw was her sister, so frail and small, sprinting past those cops, hair flying behind her. All she saw was the closest cop, the mustached one with their money in his pocket, lunging for Maggie, his enormous hand reaching for her delicate arm.

And as that hand closed around Maggie's arm, as her rasping inhale of breath, of *pain* at the tightness of that grip, filled the apartment, the world . . .

Selina exploded.

The dark-haired cop went down first. Uppercut to get his head up, then elbow to the nose to put him on the ground. He was unconscious before he hit the carpet.

The social worker screeched, but Selina was already on the mustached cop, now whirling toward her, that meaty hand still on Maggie's arm.

Selina barreled into him. He dropped Maggie immediately, both of his hands grappling to shove Selina off as they slammed into the wall, cracking plaster.

"You little—" His spat words were cut short as Selina ducked out of his grasp, dodged the fumble he made to grab her again, and her fist connected with his face.

Her body sang in agony, wounds ripping open, bruises bleating.

"Run," she managed to say to Maggie.

But her sister remained frozen. Gaping, terror draining the color from her face.

Slim white hands wrapped around Maggie's arm again. The social worker. "She's not going anywhere."

And those hands, those hands and that cold, hateful face—

Selina shoved the woman. Hard.

Hard enough that the social worker went careening into the table, chairs scattering.

Maggie screamed, and Selina whirled, fists up, knees bending.

Too slow. The mustached cop had risen to his feet. She didn't have time to try to dodge before volts of pain tore through her. Before his leering, bloody face smiled as he dug a Taser right into her neck.

Agony barreled in—then the world tilted.

Then nothing.

The humming of the fluorescent lights was what awoke her.

Her tongue was a dry, thick weight in her mouth, her head a pounding mess, her body . . .

Sitting in a chair. Handcuffed to the metal table before her.

Precinct room.

Selina groaned quietly, surveying the space. Tiny. No one-way mirror. No speakers or cameras or anything.

She tugged on the cuffs linked to the table to see if they were secured.

They were.

Maggie—

The metal door hissed open, and Selina braced herself.

It wasn't the blond social worker in her cheap suit. Or the cop who looked at her a little too long.

A tall, slim woman with night-black hair and skin like golden honey entered instead.

Selina had seen enough of the various businessmen who Falcone liked to associate himself with to know that the white pantsuit was high quality. And from her work with Mika, she knew that the simple, elegant gold jewelry at her neck and ears was real and expensive. The manicured nails, the silky sheet of hair cut into stylish layers, the full mouth painted red, were all markers that screamed *money.*

This was no social worker.

Those crimson nails tapped against a thick file in her hands as she approached the table and the empty chair before it. *Selina's* file.

Not good.

"Where's Maggie?" The words were a low rasp. Water—she needed some water. And aspirin.

"My name is Talia."

"Where. Is. Maggie."

Keeping her head upright took every bit of effort thanks to the Taser bruise that still radiated pain down her neck and spine.

"*Your* name is Selina Kyle, and you are seventeen years old. Three weeks away from being eighteen." A click of the tongue as she slid into the metal chair across the table, opened up that fat file, and began flipping through the pages. The table was too long for Selina to see what the woman examined. "For someone so young, you've certainly accomplished an impressive amount." *Flick, flap, hiss.* "Illegal betting, assault, robbery."

Shame and pride warred through her. Shame for the fact that if Maggie ever heard this, the unvarnished truth of her crimes . . . Selina knew she couldn't endure the look she'd see on her sister's face. Pride for the fact that she *had* done this, had survived in the best way she could, had given her sister what she could as well.

But Selina managed to keep her voice cool, bored, as she replied, "I was never convicted of the last two."

"No, but the charges are on here," Talia countered, tapping a red nail on the paper. "What you *will* be convicted of in a matter of days is aggravated battery of two police officers and a state worker."

Selina just stared at the woman from beneath lowered brows.

No way out of this room—this precinct. And even if she did make it, then she'd have to find Maggie. Which would be the first stop the cops would make, too.

Talia smiled slightly, revealing too-white teeth. "Did the police give you those bruises?"

Selina didn't reply.

Talia flicked through those papers again, scanning for something. "Or are those bruises and split knuckles from the fighting you do for Carmine Falcone?"

Silence. Leopards didn't talk. Selina hadn't the first two times she'd been here. She wasn't about to now.

"Do you know what it means to be three weeks away from eighteen in Gotham City?" Talia leaned forward, resting her arms on the metal table. There was a slight accent to her words, some rolling purr.

"I can buy lotto tickets?"

Again, that hint of a smile. "It means you will be lucky if the judge tries you as a juvenile. It's your third strike. You're looking at bars no matter what. The question is whether it's kiddie prison or the big girls club."

"Where. Is. Maggie."

The question was a roar in her blood—a screaming, thrashing demand.

Talia leaned back in her chair and slid a paper-clipped file toward Selina. "Your sister is at a group home. In the Bowery of the East End."

Oh God. If their apartment complex was garbage, then the Bowery was the entire dump. The gangs in that area . . . Even Falcone didn't mess with them.

Selina set her bound hands on the file Talia had pushed over, the photo of a grimy, cramped bedroom atop it. Maggie's *new* bedroom. She turned the paper over, fingers curling.

"Lord knows who is running that home," Talia mused, flipping through the rest of Selina's file.

"Are you trying to piss me off so they can add assaulting a grade A asshole to my rap sheet?"

The question was out, low and growling, before Selina could reconsider.

Talia laughed, a light and silvery sound. "Do you think you could do it? Handcuffed?"

A faint click sounded in answer.

Rotating her free wrist, Selina dropped the straightened paper clip onto the metal table. A sleight of hand—turning over that photo of Maggie's foster home to distract the eye while she palmed the paper clip. And then used it and some careful angling to spring a handcuff free. She'd bought a pair a few years ago to use for practice, to learn how the locking mechanism worked. For precisely this sort of moment.

Talia smiled again, full and wide, and let out a satisfied hum. "Clever girl." She jerked her chin toward Selina's free hand. "I'd suggest putting it back on. You know how uptight the police can be about such things."

She did. And she knew that even if she unlocked the other cuff and pummeled this woman's face in, she still wouldn't make it out of this holding room or the precinct.

Selina clicked the handcuff back around her wrist. Leaving it loose enough that she could free herself again, should the need arise.

Talia watched every movement, head angled to the side, dark hair shifting. "I'm here to offer you a bargain, Selina Kyle."

Selina waited.

Talia closed her file. "I run a vocational school for young women like you. Physically skilled, yes." A nod toward the cuffs, the bruises on her face. "But *smart* most of all." She placed a hand on the file. "I've got chart after chart of your grades. Your exam scores. Do your little kitty-cat friends know you're top of your class and that you aced all statewide exams?"

"I don't know what you're talking about." She'd made sure the Leopards never heard about it as well. Being good in the ring with the bullwhip and gymnastics was about as much talent as she'd let show. Selina leaned forward a bit. "Acing tests doesn't win fights."

Another laugh, this one low and sultry. "You know, if your frequent absences didn't bar you from graduating this year, you might have been able to have your pick of scholarships."

College wasn't a possibility. Not with Maggie to look after.

"This school of mine, though," Talia said, tracing a nail over the surface of the file. Like a long red talon. "It would be a new start. And a better fit than juvie. Or prison."

With every passing minute she spent in here, Maggie was in that disgusting home, breathing in filth and dirt.

"The catch, before you ask, is that my school is located in the Dolomites of Italy. And your sister cannot come."

Selina blinked, processing what the woman had said. A school in Italy. No Maggie.

"If you come with me," Talia went on, "I can make this record"— a tap of the hand on the file—"vanish. Forever."

Selina studied the file and then Talia's beautiful face. These offers didn't come without major strings.

"I don't give a shit about the record," Selina said. "I want Maggie out of that house."

Talia blinked, the only sign of surprise.

"I want my sister put in a single-family foster home. With good people who are willing to adopt her. Somewhere in a cushy suburb. No gangs, no violence, no drugs."

Silence.

Selina added softly, "And I want you to make sure my mother is never able to get her hands on Maggie again."

The lights above hummed. Talia's hand scraped over the rough surface of the file folder as she slid her hands into her lap. "You're in no position to make demands."

Selina leaned back in her chair, refusing to break the woman's dark gaze. "If you want me so badly for your human-trafficking club, you'll do it."

Talia burst out laughing. There was no joy in the sound.

Selina rolled her shoulders and waited.

Talia chuckled once more before tossing her sheet of hair over a shoulder. "I'll make it happen."

Selina didn't let her shock show.

"There is one more condition," Talia said, rising from the table.

Of course there was. Selina monitored her every breath.

"We leave tonight," Talia said. "And you will not get to say good-bye."

For a moment, Selina didn't hear the words, or the hum of the lights, or the click of Talia's beige heels as she strutted for the door. She heard that damned *Carousel* song.

And Selina was still hearing it as she said, voice thick, "Take off the cuffs."

*   *   *

The tarmac of the private airport was empty.

Empty save for the sleek white jet idling just off the runway, its steps already lowered to reveal a near-glowing wooden interior.

The perfect match to the Aston Martin that Selina had just vacated. Talia was already striding toward the plane.

Rubbing her wrists, Selina stalked after the woman, glancing toward the glittering city skyline to their left. The eastern horizon was just beginning to lighten. Dawn.

Her body ached. Everything ached. Not just bone and flesh.

Selina shoved down the thought as she took in Gotham City. The light and the shadow.

A cool wind whipped at her face, dragging strands of her hair free as she caught up to Talia's side just before the woman began to ascend the steps into the private plane. A flight attendant waited at the top of the stairs, a tray with two glasses of champagne fizzing in her hands.

"Is this your plane?" Selina asked as Talia braced a hand on the stair rail and set a well-heeled foot on the first step.

"It is."

This school, then . . . Selina again glanced toward the city's horizon. To where she prayed Maggie was being shuttled through the streets to the trees and open air and quiet of the suburbs.

She swallowed, trailing Talia up the narrow steps of the plane. The private plane.

"Are you a Wayne or something?" The Waynes did plenty of charity work, and a fancy Italian school for wayward young women didn't seem beyond them.

Talia let out a low laugh and didn't bother to turn as she reached the top stair, swiped a flute of champagne from the flight attendant, and said, "No. My family name is al Ghūl."

TWO YEARS LATER

CHAPTER 3

She was a ghost. A wraith.

Selina reminded herself of that little fact as she stood atop the stairs of the private jet, squinted into the blinding midday sun glinting off the hangars of the exclusive airfield, and got a faceful of late-August Gotham City stink.

That, at least, hadn't changed in the past two years. But as for Selina herself . . .

The four-inch beige heels that clipped so nicely against the steps as she descended were just the start of the changes to her. The long golden-blond hair, the manicured nails, and the suntanned skin were the next. And then there was the perfectly tailored cream-colored linen suit, steamed for her by the flight attendant thirty minutes before landing. The portrait of unthreatening, carefree money.

No sign of the girl who'd ascended the stairs of this plane two years ago, bloody and battered. No sign of the girl who'd clawed and fought to keep her sister safe, keep her as healthy as could be expected—especially with Maggie now well cared for, living in a pretty house in the suburbs.

No sign of that girl at all.

Indeed, the resources of the League of Assassins had made these first steps back into Gotham City so much easier, clearing a path for all she'd arrived here to do. The League was bigger, more lethal, than any criminal organization in this city. A near myth. They answered to nobody and nothing, a veritable force of nature. Their goals were so much larger than financial profit. No, the League dealt in power—the sort that could alter countries, alter the world. The smart criminals were the ones who got out of their way. The smartest were those who bowed.

Selina took a slow, bracing breath, flexing her fingers against the slight tremor that rippled down them. No space for fear, for doubt, for hesitation. Not with so many eyes watching.

Photographers sporting long-range cameras snapped photos through the nearby chain-link fence.

Selina shoved away any lingering trace of nerves and offered a sultry, sly look in their direction, her broad-brimmed black hat— the crowning piece of her ensemble—blocking half her face. She did the photographers an even bigger favor and removed her sunglasses as she stepped off the stairs and turned toward the awaiting black sedan.

And just because she was finally back in this shit-hole city, finally back in this place that had been both hell and home, she flashed them a wave and a smile white and bright enough to light up the Gotham City skyline.

Snap, shutter, snap.

Had those photographers even thought to question the anonymous tip about socialite Holly Vanderhees coming to town after a lengthy stay in Europe? Or were they too afraid of looking foolish to ask *who* this person was who'd just descended upon Gotham City?

The information she'd leaked through their computer systems had been brief but detailed. Her family had investments everywhere. Old money. Parents: deceased. Siblings: none. Net worth: billions.

Selina reached the sedan and the driver holding the door open for her. It took years of training to hold back her nod of thanks, to make herself ignore the urge to meet his eyes in a minimal greeting.

He didn't dare introduce himself. Didn't do anything. Well trained not to be a presence but an instrument.

Even now, after all she'd been taught and instructed to do, it made her stomach churn.

A lie. This is all a lie. The East End bred me, raised me. The words sat on her tongue as she ducked into the car. *This is all a lie.*

But she didn't need to speak a word to him: he already had the address of the Old Gotham City penthouse *Holly* had leased for the as-yet-unknown length of her stay. Likely through gala season, she'd informed the real estate agent, who'd nearly fainted at the commission of a lifetime.

Butter-soft leather cushioned her when she slid into the rear seat of the car, the driver making sure her waxed golden legs were fully inside, Birkin bag nestled in the seat beside her, before quietly shutting the door. Air at seventy degrees, two chilled bottles of water in the lowered tray beside her, a smart tablet anchored to the back of the front passenger seat, packets of lemon-scented face towelettes tucked into the mesh netting beneath.

Not that she'd use them. Why ruin the makeup she'd carefully applied before landing? The barely-there foundation, matte dove-gray eye shadow with a swoop of eyeliner, and bold flamethrower-red lips.

She'd refused to acknowledge the slight trembling in her hands while she'd done it—the hands she'd had to shake out multiple times before they were steady enough to precisely apply her eyeliner and lipstick.

Being nervous before a mission didn't help anything. She reminded herself of that over and over. Even if she'd already gone through every breathing technique she'd been taught.

The driver got in, turning on the radio to the station she'd requested: classical. As a soon-to-be patron of the Gotham City Opera, she at least had to appear interested in it.

Appear to be many things, since the driver was sure to talk. Just as the flight attendants on the plane were sure to talk. Money bought nearly everything, but silence was never a guarantee. In Gotham City, loyalty was bought and sold as fast as any stock on the market.

Loyalty couldn't exist in a place like this. She'd learned that, too, these past few years.

The car pulled out of the private airport, the heavy gates parting to let them through. Selina stroked a hand down the silky-smooth leather of the Birkin beside her. The bag, the shoes, the clothes, the jewels—all were loaded symbols. Literally. And also passports, veritable golden tickets into the circles of society who dwelled above those eking out a living on the streets of Gotham City.

Nature is all about balance, Nyssa al Ghūl, her mentor and personal instructor during her time in Italy, had once purred to her. *Tip too far in one direction, and it will always find a way to right itself.*

Gotham City had been tipping too far toward the rich and corrupt for a long, long time. She'd come home to right it once more.

The car wove through a grid of streets before merging onto the highway that would cross the Gotham River and take them downtown. As they sped over the Brown Bridge, the southern tip of Gotham City spread before her, packed with the glittering highrises that pierced the cloudless summer day like lances. And lording above them all: Wayne Tower. Every citizen of the city could likely sketch the building from memory. A symbol of welcome, the postcards claimed.

That tower was a symbol of anything but.

And when she was finished here, the world would see that, too.

She peered out through the gaps in the steel beams of the bridge toward the muddy-blue waters of the Gotham River. How many bodies would be swimming in it by the time she was finished here?

Gotham City was primed to fall. All it would take was a little encouragement.

What fortunate timing that the sanctimonious Batman was currently gone—no sign of him for weeks now. And that Batwing, along with a few others, was barely holding back the tide of lowlifes seeking to take advantage of that absence.

She snorted softly. What ridiculous names they gave themselves, these vigilantes.

Selina lifted her gaze from the river to the shining metropolis approaching with every heartbeat. To the darker, shorter buildings of the East End smudging the horizon.

Home. Or it had been. She hadn't let herself consider it her home in a long while. Refused to contemplate where home might be, if such a thing could ever exist for her now.

The brutal training at the League of Assassins had taught her many, many things. Had killed that street-raised, desperate girl, leaving her somewhere at the bottom of a ravine in the Dolomites. Had drained that girl away into nothing, along with the blood of the men who Nyssa and the others had taught her how to bring down—how to punish.

You will bring empires to their knees, Nyssa had once sworn to her after a particularly grueling demonstration on how to get men to talk. A kernel of promise while she'd puked her guts up afterward.

No, *home* did not exist anymore. But it was worth it. She'd come here to make sure it had all been worth it—the training, the unspeakable cost. She would not fail. Not this most vital mission.

So Selina loosed a settling breath and beheld the sparkling city as she reclined in the cushioned seat of the car.

And finally, at long last, she allowed herself a little smile.

Let Gotham City enjoy its final days of summer.

CHAPTER 4

―――――――

The nightmare was always the same.

Blinding sun, heat so dry it choked the air out of his lungs, and a flat plain of sand and scrub spreading to the horizon.

And then the roar. The screaming. The exploding sand and metal.

The blood and chaos. Gunfire.

A world away—a different world, different life. A different hell.

Because for Luke Fox, hell wasn't fire and brimstone. It was friends he'd laughed with in the morning at the canteen winding up in body bags by lunch.

Night after night: this dream, this moment.

A year had passed since he'd returned to Gotham City, and Luke was still crawling back toward who he'd been before.

Whoever that person had been. Whoever had been ripped apart that day, along with the flesh of his ribs, where the Kevlar hadn't been covering him. As if the enemy they'd been dispatched to put down had known precisely where to strike with the IED that went off beneath the tank lumbering ahead, sending shrapnel tearing through the air.

Through him—and his soldiers.

Had it been worth it? The grueling training and the three years in the Marine Corps. Had he made a difference?

They were the questions he asked himself over and over. That haunted every step, every breath. The questions that drove him each night into the streets of Gotham City.

Luke blew out a breath, his muscled chest rising and falling as moonlight leaked in through the windows, highlighting the jagged line along his ribs, the scar stark against his brown skin. He scanned the sky, his penthouse apartment offering an unobstructed view of downtown Gotham City.

No bat-shaped sigil lighting up the night.

Luke couldn't decide if he was disappointed or not.

He glanced at the clock beside his bed. Only two hours ago, he'd crept back into his apartment after a quiet night of patrolling. Apparently, the August heat had made even the worst of Gotham City decide to stay indoors.

Luke snorted, imagining some of the usual suspects opting to seek out an air-conditioned movie theater instead of terrorizing the streets.

At least he still had his sense of humor. Sort of.

Bruce Wayne didn't have one. Or hadn't revealed one in the months Luke had been training with him.

It had been his dad's idea. Right after the family's annual Fourth of July fireworks barbecue at the beach house last summer. After the Incident.

Luke had been standing among the crowd gathered on the back

lawn, beer in hand, when the fireworks had exploded over their private beach, as they'd done every summer that he could remember. But unlike all those summers before, as those initial fireworks bloomed and *boomed* in the dark sky, his body had gone absolutely haywire, as if it had been programmed like one of his gadgets. He'd been unable to get a breath down, to control the undiluted terror that swept through him. Pushed in on him, as if the ground were about to swallow him up, as if he were again in that blood-soaked desert, and his nightmare was all playing out again.

His first full-blown panic attack. In the middle of his family's annual party.

Bruce had been standing next to him when it happened. And had instantly noticed the symptoms and gotten Luke's father to help discreetly escort his son back into the house.

When he'd finally been able to breathe, when the world had crept back in and the desert had faded away once more, it had all come spilling out: he hadn't been able to save them. His team. He told them he had no idea if he'd made a difference that day, or any day in his life. His father and Bruce had sat with him, just listening. Like they had nowhere else to be.

The subsequent diagnosis: post-traumatic stress disorder, triggered that particular night by the crackle and boom of the fireworks, by the flashing lights.

And then the treatment: group therapy once a week and private sessions every three days. That was fine—that was good. Necessary. *Vital.*

But his dad's suggested treatment had been just between him and Bruce and Luke. A visit to Wayne Manor a week later. To a secret chamber beneath it. If Luke wanted to make a difference, Bruce had said, perhaps there was something he could do about it.

Luke had learned a lot in the thirteen months since. About himself, about what haunted him, and about the man who lived in Wayne Manor.

Giving up on sleep, Luke swung his legs out of the bed and padded onto the balcony. Even at four in the morning, the air hung hot and sticky against his skin. He again scanned the city, listening for sirens. Anything to call him out of bed, out of his penthouse apartment. Anything to do in these final few hours before dawn when he knew sleep would no longer come.

Nothing. Only muggy heat and silence. Even the stars seemed small and faded, the constellations he recognized as well as family members blurred under the blanket of heat. Their names rattled through his head, more instinct than intentional thought: Lyra, Sagittarius, Hercules . . .

Luke rubbed a hand over his short hair. He'd let the sides grow in a bit but still kept it military-short.

Movement to his left caught his eye.

Every sense went on alert as his body slipped into a loose fighting stance.

Being thirty floors up wouldn't keep the more creative criminals from finding their way here to loot the troves of one of Gotham City's richest.

A flash of gold at the corner of his balcony.

No, not his balcony, but the edge of the balcony for the penthouse that shared this top floor, the corner of which was just barely visible from where he stood. Along with the source of that gold: long blond hair, slightly curled at the ends.

There were only two apartments up here; the other had been sitting empty for months. Until yesterday, he remembered. The apartment had been leased by some socialite—old money, the gossip sites said when he'd checked them in the evening for any hint of trouble ahead. Holly Vanderhees.

Luke peered over the rail, craning his neck to see more of the owner of that luxurious blond hair he could just barely make out.

A neighbor was an inconvenience.

He should have bought the apartment next door just to keep it empty.

A stupid mistake. A rookie mistake.

He'd have to be careful now, coming in and out of the apartment. Might have to account for his odd hours if she was a snoop. Especially if she was a gossip. Most socialites were. He'd developed a healthy respect for them. He'd seen socialites take each other down with words and rumors far more efficiently than insurgents had with bullets and IEDs.

His new neighbor vanished along the wraparound balcony. As if she'd been pacing it.

First night in a new city. Perhaps she hadn't been able to sleep, either.

For a heartbeat, he debated crossing the small hallway they shared and knocking on her door. Introducing himself.

But he couldn't afford another mistake. Building bonds invited questions. And if Holly Vanderhees had no idea who she was living next to, if she never saw or heard from him, so much the better. Easier to be unaccounted for.

He didn't know how Bruce did it: juggling the man the world believed they knew with the vigilante who fought to keep Gotham City safe. Luke had asked him throughout their training, but Bruce hadn't been forthcoming.

It was one of the few things Bruce hadn't taught him.

Luke had known plenty about fighting, about building clever, useful things, before they'd begun. Even before enlisting in the Marines, he'd been as keen on honing his body as he was on sharpening his mind.

A rare combination, his mom often said, beaming at him. *Brains and beauty*. Luke always laughed at her, waving her off. Even if the brains part was officially true. He'd been declared a genius before finishing high school. A lot of good that had done him overseas.

He certainly wasn't doing much with it these days as the millionaire playboy the world believed *him* to be—son of Lucius Fox, the CEO of Wayne Industries, granted a cushy job in Applied Sciences at the company.

What the job actually did was allow Luke to roll into Wayne Tower, go down to the restricted sublevel seven, and mess around with his suit, his gear, his various gadgets that helped him round up Gotham City's worst. Luke sometimes even modified Bruce's gear, since his colleague was always game for a new upgrade. They'd bonded over it—their interest in tech.

Watery gray light began to bleed into the eastern horizon. He had another boxing match tonight. He'd make sure not to mention it to his mother at brunch in a few hours.

You shave years off my life with every match, she complained to him and his dad.

It's only semiprofessional, his dad often said, coming to his defense. Knowing that the boxing, which Luke had done for years before he shipped out, had always steadied him. Settled his mind. And in the year since he'd returned, he'd picked it up again. As part of his ongoing, endless recovery.

But only semipro, as his dad said. As was befitting a socialite of Gotham City.

Even if he didn't lose. Ever.

Not a single fight.

What his mom didn't know, what she couldn't know despite how much he wanted to tell her, was that he and his dad had decided the fights would not only balance him but help explain away any injuries that might arise during his nocturnal activities. His real job.

Batwing.

He'd come up with the name himself, in part to honor the training he'd done with Bruce, but mostly as a nod to his favorite part of the suit. The part he'd worked the hardest on, and got one hell of a kick out of surprising lowlifes with. Nothing like a pair of retractable wings, capable of gliding over long distances, to make criminals wet themselves.

And to land easily on the roof before slipping back inside the building. A task that would now be infinitely harder with his new neighbor.

Luke frowned toward Holly's balcony before turning back inside and sealing the door shut, the AC instantly icy against his skin.

He'd figure out some way to make sure she thought he was as boring as possible.

Luke headed into his closet, lights flickering on automatically. He glanced to the wood panel that held a full-length mirror. A hidden touch pad would reveal the extra closet concealed behind it, chock-full of his various mechanized suits, weapons, and gear.

But he opted for gym shorts and an old Marines tee, sliding on his worn sneakers before striding from the room. A full-service gym was open 24-7 a level below. It'd be empty at this time of the night. Day. Whatever four-thirty a.m. was classified as.

Luke caught a glimpse of himself in the mirror as he left. His skin was still shiny with sweat, his cheeks a bit hollowed out. His mom would worry at brunch—she was too damn smart not to note everything. Especially if he didn't get rid of the empty, glazed look in his eyes.

A year, and it was still there.

A year of trying to adjust to civilian life and managing his PTSD so that he could finally do *something* of value to keep this city from falling into ruin. To honor the good men and women who hadn't returned home—at least not outside of a pine box—and the families they'd left behind.

Luke shouldered his way through the gym door, the fluorescent lights a clang to his senses, all the TV screens above the machines set to various news channels. Even they were full of nothing, filler stories because the truth of the world—that didn't sell ad space. And Americans watching didn't really want to have their oversized houses and wasteful lifestyles called into question when faced with the poverty most of the planet lived in. The despair, the ugliness of it.

Hell, they couldn't even stand to look too long at the East End in their own damn city.

His mom knew that. Fought against that every day. He supposed his mom's ball gowns and well-tailored suits were another kind of armor—that she, too, had masks she used to fight against the injustices of the world, especially as a black woman in the upper echelon of society. He wished he could tell her that. Wished he could explain that he was honored to follow in her footsteps, even if the fighting they did each night was different. Hers took place at galas and in boardrooms, winning over Gotham City's richest to contribute to her charities with that charm and wit of hers. His fights, beyond those in the ring, were in places few dared to venture.

Luke picked a treadmill that enabled him to see anyone who

entered the gym—another lesson from Bruce: always be on guard—and climbed on, punching in his preferred speed and incline. His body was a tool. A weapon. The same as any he'd fought with overseas.

And even as Luke launched into a run, even as sweat again slid down his body and his lungs burned in his broad chest . . . he still couldn't feel it.

Himself.

As if his skin, his bones, were as distant as the high-tech suit he donned every night.

The sun began to rise over Gotham City, the wall of windows offering an unparalleled view of the city skyline.

Another day.

He'd make it count. For the friends who hadn't made it home, for the people living in this city . . . He'd make it count.

CHAPTER 5

Silence lay heavy throughout the Museum of Antiquities.

In the darkest hours of the night, the quiet that permeated the marble chambers was as tangible as the muggy heat outside the sprawling complex. Only the occasional whisper of the air conditioner or the jingle of a drowsy guard's keys provided any interruption.

Certainly not Selina. Her black boots didn't so much as scuff against the white floors as she crept through the wings and halls of the behemoth building, her helmet providing a steady read of the tangle of alarm sensors.

It was a puzzle—and not a particularly clever one.

Her helmet's scanner gave her a constant stream of information, tailored to her specifics. The helmet's ears, the overly large eyes . . . She'd taken one of the standard helmets—Death Masks, they called them—that the League of Assassins gave to all their acolytes, and modified it.

Kitten, they'd taunted her. *Kitty-cat*. Acolytes and assassins alike whispered and hissed and growled it during training sessions, in the eating hall, down the walkways. One look at the spots inked on her arms, and the taunts had begun. Her fists had done the talking at first—though all it had earned her was Nyssa's disdain. *Control is vital. Control is everything.*

So Selina had taken control. Of the taunts, the hated nickname.

All while improving her Death Mask. Tinkering through the quietest hours of the night, deep in the science labs of the Sanctuary. She'd shocked herself a few times, sliced up her fingers while cutting the wires, but in the end Nyssa had given her a rare smile of approval when Selina had come to training one day wearing her modified helmet. The audio receptors shaped like cat ears. The large eyes. And the dagger-sharp claws at the tips of her black climbing gloves.

The taunting had stopped after that.

Especially when she'd ripped open the side of Tigris, one of Nyssa and Talia's fiercest assassins and trainers, and settled things between them.

And that was before Nyssa had started letting her officially train with the bullwhip.

Head to toe in black, her breathing barely elevated, Selina paused before the entrance to the famed Egyptian Wing and surveyed the labyrinth of shimmering lasers.

It was outright cliché: the web of lasers nearly invisible to the naked eye.

Without the helmet, she might have resorted to an aerosol to reveal them. Even more cliché.

Yet despite the helmet's map of the various pitfalls and suggested routes, Selina found herself studying the lasers. Gauging the angles, the landing space, the possible disasters.

The relic was displayed only fifty feet away. A straight shot down the arched marble corridor. Even at night, the small bronze cat statue was lit up in stunning relief, tribute to Bastet, the feline-headed goddess of warriors. Protector of children and cats.

No larger than a bottle of shampoo, the thirty-two-hundred-year-old statue was in flawless condition. That, along with the gems embedded in its collar, made it nearly priceless.

Nearly priceless. Someone had, in fact, slapped a price on it.

A price that made Selina smile beneath her helmet and begin.

Setting her weight onto her left leg, she lifted her right and eased it through the largest gap between the shimmering sensors.

Balance was key. The beam had been her best and favorite event in gymnastics. She had no idea why. Most of her teammates had dreaded it, feared it. She'd sometimes wondered if that fear had been a poison, making their balance worse.

Selina eased the rest of her body through the initial gap between the sensors, landing in a small island of open air. She'd tucked her bullwhip in tightly for this heist—had triple-checked that it wouldn't fall loose from its place at her left hip while she moved.

The guards didn't rotate into this wing for another ten minutes. It was all the time she needed. Especially when she'd taken the liberty of jamming the camera signals with a simple *Computer Error: Contact Provider* message. One with a fake phone number that would keep the guards on hold for a good fifteen minutes.

Arching smoothly into a bridge over the next sensor beam, the world tilted upside down for a heartbeat as her gloved hands met the marble floor. A push of her legs and pull of her abdominal muscles had her feet rising up and over, her landing as smooth as silk.

A dance. These movements felt like a dance. One she'd learned to enjoy.

Just as she'd enjoyed taking that diamond from the Gotham Museum three days ago. And that trove of jewels from a shop five days before that. Little dances—little tests.

Tonight would be another step. A bigger one.

Considering those two burglaries had proved . . . disappointing.

Sure, she'd made off with what she needed. But no one had even put up a fight. A challenge. And no one had come looking for her afterward.

Selina slid to the marble floor, slipping beneath a low-hanging beam.

She'd make sure tonight was different.

A larger expanse of space opened before her, leading to a more intricate web of sensors. The last stretch before the statue's glass display case in the center of the hallway.

She could make it with a few careful dips and ducks.

But where was the fun in that?

She'd been devoid of fun for most of her life. Had found it only in rare moments. And even then it had been overshadowed with fear and dread. But tonight . . .

She'd learned to take the things she wanted. Including her own amusement.

Sucking in a breath, again checking that the bullwhip was secure, Selina launched herself forward.

The motions were muscle memory, the calculations sharp and precise. Glorious.

Front handspring into a twisting backflip, followed by a high-soaring tuck, right into a somersault that sent her into a neat tumble over the final alarm sensor. And right up to the glass of the case.

Breathing loud beneath her helmet, Selina grinned at the Bastet statue.

She could have sworn that ancient bit of bronze seemed to smile back. Seemed to say, *Go on. Take it.*

So Selina did.

A claw of reinforced steel slid free from her black glove. Perfectly honed. Perfectly ready to slice a circle through the thick glass.

Selina caught the panel of glass in one palm as her other hand slid into the case and wrapped around the figure.

And just as she'd planned, the alarms began blaring.

Selina was gone before GCPD arrived.

But she was not done.

The Bastet statue tucked into a satchel at her side, Selina knelt at the edge of a high-rise rooftop and adjusted the focus on the scope of her rifle.

She didn't use guns on people. Ever.

She'd allowed Nyssa to teach her how to wield them, but she'd kept her thoughts on the matter to herself. Never mentioned how she'd seen them used to such detrimental effect and destruction, how she'd seen them bring such pain and sorrow into the lives of those in the East End.

So it was a good thing Nyssa wasn't here. And a good thing Selina had so many other weapons in her arsenal.

But for this task . . .

Selina counted down the seconds. Knew it was coming.

Her finger shifted slightly on the trigger as she aimed the rifle at the top of the eleven-story GCPD precinct building. The most important building in this city, by her account.

The door to the precinct roof flung open, and two men rushed out.

Selina allowed them to get close to the object they sought. The giant spotlight.

She allowed them to turn it on, the beam of light spearing into the sky, the bat icon dark against the bank of clouds. She allowed them that one moment of calm before she fired.

The rifle's kickback was a punch to the shoulder, but the shot was a whisper thanks to the silencer. The crack of shattering glass and metal and the shouts of the two officers were not.

Selina fired again a heartbeat later, her careful planning and the scope's night vision allowing the bullet to fly perfectly.

The glowing power source on its lower left side shattered before the bullet embedded in the brick wall of the stairwell entrance.

More shouts and cursing from the men, now whirling in her direction.

But Selina flicked the safety back on the rifle, shouldered the weapon, and prowled for the stairs, little more than a shadow against the night.

This time, someone would come looking.

Hopefully, they'd want to play.

CHAPTER 6

Luke had been surprised to see Alfred's name light up his cell at three a.m.

Mostly because they'd never once called each other, though Bruce had given Luke his butler's number in case of emergency. The sort that involved Bruce either never coming home again or needing a discreet pickup. Thankfully, Luke had never had to make a call, but if Alfred was calling . . .

The call, like the man on the line, had been polite but firm.

"Hey, Alfred," Luke said, instantly awake and sitting up in bed.

"Good evening, Mr. Fox," came the dry British voice at the other end.

Luke set his feet on the cool wooden floor. "Is Bruce all right?" Better to get down to business. Alfred, at least, seemed just as disinclined to make small talk.

"Yes. His mission is going well."

He knew the butler would say no more than that. Luke scanned the city skyline beyond his bedroom windows, struggling for the right response. "Glad to hear it."

A lengthy pause. Luke winced a bit. But Alfred just said, "Commissioner Gordon sent a message through the usual channels to say that he needs to speak to *one* of the Bats flapping around this city."

Luke wasn't stupid enough to ask if the phrasing was Gordon's or Alfred's. "Anything to worry about?"

"The commissioner claimed that it was an urgent matter."

That didn't sound good. There was a private line between Gordon and the Batcave precisely for these sorts of situations. A line that now forwarded to Alfred's own inbox while Bruce was away on a mission of such secrecy that he hadn't even told Luke what he was up to.

Their goodbyes were as quick as their hellos, and Luke had found himself relieved when the phone call was finally over.

It had been a quiet night until now. Too quiet. He'd even headed to bed early for once. He certainly hadn't filled the night with a date with one of the women his mom was constantly trying to set him up with. No, he didn't date at all. Not when he was still climbing back toward the person he'd been; not with all the responsibilities Batwing bore. And then there were the inevitable questions, along with the threat he'd pose to anyone associated with him if the truth about his identity ever came out.

Five minutes later, he'd donned the comfortable weight of his suit and slipped through the streets of Gotham City while a thunderstorm unleashed itself overhead.

And now, as he dripped water onto the tiled floor of Gordon's dim office, the pale, middle-aged GCPD commissioner frowned up at him, his auburn mustache twitching. Not at all surprised to see him emerging from the shadows. "Good of you to join me."

Luke waited, his face hidden beneath his mask. The low light danced on the bluish silver of his armor, the bat-symbol across his chest glowing faintly.

Alive—the suit he wore hummed and ticked faintly with life, each inch of it made by Luke in that lab, designed and modified and tweaked to his liking. Full of hidden surprises for Gotham City's worst.

"Where's the other guy?" Gordon said at last, brown eyes narrowing beneath his thick-rimmed glasses. "Haven't seen him around for a while."

Luke approached the desk, his suit clinking softly. Bruce had been the one to suggest the particular metal—his father the one to supply it. "He's on a covert op." No need to let Gordon know that he had little idea what it entailed.

"Is he now."

Luke angled his head, the single sign of his impatience. Yeah, Bruce and Luke worked with Gordon. Had an agreement to make sure the GCPD locked up the criminals they nabbed, and provided backup when needed. But they didn't answer to the police. Luke himself still chafed when he had to work with the GCPD. What he'd seen just now after slipping through the precinct's roof access had only reinforced that sentiment. He'd nearly made it through the halls unnoticed when he'd spied the black kid, no older than fifteen, handcuffed to a bench in the corridor outside the holding area. Soaked through, his clothes clinging to his thin frame. The kid's face was carefully blank, even if the tapping of his foot on the tile floor revealed the nervousness undoubtedly coursing through him. Rightfully coursing through him, considering the words Luke heard a second later as he ducked into a shadowed alcove.

What'd you nab him for? The question had come from an officer passing by.

Unaware of Luke's presence mere feet away, the cop who had undoubtedly brought the kid in had answered, dabbing at the sweat on his ruddy face. *Pot possession.*

Caught in the act? the first cop had asked, pausing.

The ruddy-faced cop had smirked. *Does it make a difference?*

The question, the cop's words, had Luke's blood roaring in his ears.

His parents had explained to him from a young age that the world wasn't always fair, had explained how—regardless of their wealth—there was a very specific way he needed to interact with the cops. They had told him it was for his own protection. That sometimes the police got ideas in their heads that had nothing to do with him but affected him anyway. Him and kids who looked like him.

Like the kid on the bench. As Luke snuck another glance at the boy, he wondered if the kid had been taught the same.

Luke emerged from the hall shadows and walked over to where the boy was seated.

The cops, almost at the end of the hall now, halted. Swore as they spotted him. He and Bruce never revealed their presence inside the precinct. Never.

What would those officers say if they knew the color of the skin beneath his suit? It hadn't escaped Luke's notice just how many of the guys behind bars looked like him, but he knew that the real criminals—the ones who truly posed a threat to Gotham City—those guys didn't look like him at all.

Luke had made sure to calm his raging heartbeat, the anger simmering in his veins, before he said to the kid, *You good?*

Slowly, the kid's head lifted. He scanned Luke from head to

toe, starting to shake a bit, his jeans dripping onto the floor, but he said nothing.

So Luke asked again, signaling he was a friend, especially with the cops gawking and yet not daring to come closer. *You good, bro?*

The boy still said nothing. But his eyes went wide—wide as saucers as the question settled in. Luke gave him a slight nod.

He turned to the cops at the end of the hall. *Get this boy a blanket. He's soaked through.*

The cops blinked at him, the ruddy-faced one's skin going white as death. Then he hurried away. Luke waited until he returned, blanket in hand. Until it was around the kid's shoulders.

Luke had marked the man's badge—his name and ID number—as he ran past. And as Luke finally left the hall, he dialed up one of the best lawyers in the city, who just so happened to be one of Luke's old prep school friends. She asked no questions, only promised to be at the precinct in twenty minutes.

Luke was still trying to shake off the encounter, to steady himself, as he asked Gordon, "Why not use the signal tonight?"

"Because it's gone."

Luke blinked, even though Gordon couldn't see it. "Explain."

Gordon stiffened a little, the older man sweeping his sharp gaze over Luke.

He'd stood in front of his own damn mirror enough to know how he appeared in the suit: more machine than man. Especially with the eye lenses that glowed the same pale blue as the bat-symbol across his chest. No sign of the human beneath—the way he preferred it. No way to guess who he was, who he loved. And against his enemies . . . The *Jaws* effect, he'd decided: it was way more petrifying *not* to get a glimpse of what lurked beneath the surface. To let the mind imagine the worst.

Gordon laid a metal tray on his desk. An object rolled and hissed within its borders—a bullet.

"Someone shot it out tonight. Right as we went to signal to you."

Luke approached the battered, paper-covered desk and plucked up the bullet. "What was the crime they didn't want me involved in?"

Gordon's jaw tightened. "We don't know for certain that they're connected, but the Museum of Antiquities was hit tonight. Someone stole an Egyptian cat statue, valued at one-point-three million. We arrived within five minutes of the alarms going off, saw no trace, went to light up the signal, and then . . . out of nowhere. Two shots fired, sniper-style. One to the light, the other to the power source."

Luke held up the bullet to the light on Gordon's desk. "I'd bet the burglary is tied to whoever stole the half million in jewelry last week. And the ten-carat diamond from the Gotham Museum." He rolled the bullet between his fingers. "But those two jobs were done without triggering an alarm."

Gordon removed his glasses and cleaned them on his askew tie. "And?"

Luke opened a panel in his left arm, revealing the command pad of his suit. He punched in a few orders, and the lenses on his eyes shifted, magnifying the bullet in his palm, giving him a read of irregularities and dimensions. "And," he went on, "tonight they triggered the alarms. And then left a calling card behind." He lifted the bullet between two fingers. "Self-made. ID-less. Sleek." He dropped the bullet in the tray with a faint ping. "Fired by a far more elegant weapon than the usual suspects."

Gordon put his glasses back on. "It doesn't match any of the ammo used by the main gangs. Harley Quinn is skilled in ballistics—she's got a sniper's aim. But not access to this kind of ammo." Luke nodded, and Gordon mused, "Poison Ivy doesn't use traditional weapons, and we haven't heard a whisper from the Riddler in months." The man scratched his head. "You think someone new is in town?"

Luke glanced toward the rain-lashed windows of the empty precinct office. He did. "A jewel and art thief. The first two crimes were in plain daylight. It's almost as if tonight's burglary . . ." He again picked up the bullet, weighing it in his hand.

"Was their way of saying that we weren't catching on fast enough and they were dumbing the game down for our benefit?" Gordon finished.

Luke snorted. "Yeah."

Which was . . . interesting. He'd seen the reports on the thefts. No one harmed. Just obscenely expensive things being stolen. And if they'd shot out the Bat-Signal, then they knew precisely what sleeping dragon they were poking.

Or sleeping bats, he supposed.

"Can I take this?" Luke held up the bullet.

Gordon adjusted his glasses. "Sure. We've run our tests. Keep it." Gordon jerked his chin toward the door in silent dismissal. Luke bristled at the order but leashed his temper. "And besides," Gordon added, dragging a hand through his silver-streaked brown hair, "I'm not so convinced they wanted to get the attention of the GCPD."

Exactly.

Dusty, long-sleeping parts of his brain started to fire up. He'd been a ballistics expert overseas, and this bullet, this new thief . . .

Come find me, the bullet seemed to say.

And maybe it was the lightning in the air, or the end-of-August heat, but Luke was inclined to take up the invitation.

* * *

Selina leaned against the carved oak doorframe and watched the antiquities dealer jot down another calculation on his pad of paper.

He'd been examining the Bastet statue for twenty minutes now, the golden lights of his ornate office dim save for the spotlight of the examination lamp over the statue. She'd lingered at the doorway of his office for the entirety of that time, dressed head to toe in black, her face obscured by her Death Mask and the low-hanging hood of her sweatshirt.

Such dramatics, the man had said when he let her in the back door.

She'd said nothing, opting for the power of silence and the bullwhip hanging from her side to convey any threats she might need to make. It had been minimally difficult to find the dealer, even considering how so much of the antiquities market existed in murky zones of ownership. A statue stolen outright from the Museum of Antiquities was a different matter, of course, but she'd done her research. Knew this man would find a way to make sure the statue vanished and money appeared in its place.

The man at last lowered the loupe from his eye, pulled off his latex gloves, and ran a hand over his bald, pale head. "Well, it's certainly real."

Selina crossed her arms over her chest, waiting.

His dark, beady eyes narrowed. "You do realize I'll have a great deal of trouble hiding the trail if I'm to sell it. That sort of discretion won't come cheap."

"Name your price." Even with the helmet's voice modified, she kept her voice low, raspy. Her sister might have been the one who loved the theater, but Selina had picked up some tricks of her own these past few years.

The man scanned the statue again, then her. "Nine hundred thousand."

"It's worth far more than that."

"I told you: discretion comes at a cost. There are ownership documents to forge, private methods of shipping to a buyer. . . . Those things add up."

Selina didn't flinch. "I'll take one-point-two."

The man straightened in his green leather seat. "You'll take nine hundred, since you'll be hard-pressed to find another dealer who'd even *touch* a stolen item like this. Especially one so publicly taken." Another sweeping glance, as if assessing whether *she* had done the stealing or not.

She didn't offer him any clues. Only braced her feet slightly farther apart on the blue Aubusson rug and countered smoothly, "You'll be hard-pressed to find another piece like this anytime soon, since the Egyptian government has cracked down on the antiquities market."

The man interlaced his fingers and set them on the antique wooden desk. "One million."

She met his stare. "One-point-two."

"One million, and that's the best you'll get."

Selina prowled toward the desk, her steps swallowed by the thick rug. She folded up the statue in its velvet wrappings and placed it into the slim wooden box she'd brought with her. "We'll see if the London dealers agree with that statement."

She turned on a heel and strode for the office door, beginning a silent countdown.

Five. Four.

She neared the arched doorway. *Three. Two* . . .

She stepped one foot over the threshold.

"Wait."

She made sure the money had been wired into the offshore account before she left the man's shop.

It was more money than she'd ever dreamed of having—had never even *considered* having that much money. But it was still not enough, not for all the plans she'd crafted.

Selina didn't immediately head back to her cold, clean penthouse.

As if her feet had some magnet of their own, she stalked through the quiet, rain-slicked streets, keeping to the shadows. It wasn't hard: as she neared the slums, the streetlights became few and far between.

It was in one of those pools of shadow that she finally stopped, gazing at the dark labyrinth of buildings ahead.

There was no point in striding into the maze of streets of the East End. In going all the way toward that apartment complex.

There was no one living there worth seeing, anyway. And certainly no home left to visit.

For a heartbeat, something in her chest tightened. Something that she'd buried down deep.

The money now in that offshore account seemed to rise up and loom over her shoulders.

What that money could do for so many dwelling here. What lives it might change. Save.

Later. That would all come later. This game was only in its opening movements, and there was much left to do.

Still, Selina lingered on the edge of the East End for a while longer.

CHAPTER 7

The next morning, Luke's dad picked up on the second ring.

It was Friday, which meant Lucius Fox was currently sitting at his shiny CEO's desk, in his shiny CEO's office, working on notes for Monday's board meeting before heading out early for a quick nine at the club.

"Luke," his dad said by way of greeting.

Walking through the private parking lot beneath his apartment building, Luke smiled. As he always did, likely always would, when he heard his dad's dry tone. "Morning, Dad."

He could practically hear his father taking a sip from his daily green smoothie. *Brain food*, his mom called it. She insisted his father drink one every day. And she'd tried to make Luke start, too, going so far as to buy him a juicer. He hadn't the heart—or nerve—to tell her that in the three months since, he hadn't taken it out of the box.

His dad asked, "Will I see you at the office today?"

"On my way over now." Luke unlocked his gunmetal Porsche

72

911 with a click of the key fob. He waited until he was sealed in the plush interior before saying, "I wanted to see if you had an hour or two free before you get too busy."

"New experiment?" He could *also* practically see his father sitting up in his leather chair. It had been an honor—and a much-deserved one—to have Bruce tap his dad to be CEO, but Lucius made little secret that his true passion would always lie in the Applied Sciences division.

Luke set his phone in an empty cupholder, buckled his seat belt, and switched the call over to the car's Bluetooth. "Unfortunately for you, no."

A long-suffering sigh.

Luke grinned, revving the engine and backing out of his spot. "I've got a bullet that I need analyzed—is that machine still there?"

"Might be a bit dusty, but it should be."

"Good. Could you—"

"Already asking maintenance to have it sent to seven."

What the people who worked in Wayne Industries saw when they entered level seven . . . Luke knew his father paid them well. But he also knew that loyalties were bought in this town, which was why level seven mostly appeared to be an empty concrete chamber. Until a few buttons revealed it wasn't.

"Thanks, Dad," Luke said, pulling up the garage ramp and into the morning traffic that would likely make his two-mile drive an eternity.

He expected his dad to ask him about the bullet, so the next question caught him by surprise. "Will you be at the party on Sunday?"

"What party?"

"Our Labor Day party." His dad added quietly, "No fireworks.

Even from the neighbors. I made sure the town enacted a noise ordinance on behalf of the local wildlife."

It meant more to him than he could say that his dad broached the subject for him and had gone to such lengths to make sure he was taken care of. So it filled him with no small amount of guilt as he said, "I can't. I gotta work."

His dad knew what he meant. "Even for one night?"

"Did Mom tell you to guilt-trip me?" Luke avoided the urge to honk at a car that idled in the left-turn lane while the green light came and went. Even with the Fox name attached to him, it didn't erase certain realities. Like the fact that he'd been pulled over by a pair of cops last month, even when he'd been going the speed limit.

He could still see the two officers flanking his Porsche. Still feel the way the seams on the steering wheel dug into his palms as he kept his hands in clear sight, gripping hard against the fury seething in him. Still feel his pulse raging throughout his body as he spoke as clearly as he could, keeping his temper on a tight leash. He'd made sure to slowly, so slowly, reach for his wallet and registration.

But the moment the cops had seen his name and address that afternoon, their eyes widened. The officer on the driver's side had gone brick red, his mouth tightening before he muttered an apology as if every word tasted like sour milk.

It had taken Luke a few hours to shake the tremors and simmering anger, so fierce his hands shook. Even now, it set his teeth on edge. And not just for himself.

"I am certainly not trying to guilt-trip you," his dad said drily, "but I know precisely how sad your mother will look when *I* have to tell her you won't be there, and I'm trying to avoid it."

Luke sighed. "I would—but with Bruce away . . . I can't."

"Bruce came to the party last year. So did you. Who looked after Gotham then? Alfred?"

Luke clenched the steering wheel. "Why is it so important I go this time?"

A lengthy pause. "We might have invited a few young ladies who—"

Luke groaned. "Jesus, Dad. Really? Again?"

He loved his parents more than anything in the world, knew he was tremendously lucky to have them, but . . . they had been trying to set him up from the moment his boots had touched the tarmac at the airport. They often conveniently forgot his no-dating policy, too.

His dad chuckled.

Luke winced. "There's been a string of high-end burglaries. Labor Day weekend seems like the perfect time to strike, with half the city away at the beach. Especially the rich ones."

"Oh?"

"You don't sound disturbed."

His dad hummed. "The possibility of certain individuals being set loose from Arkham Asylum disturbs me. Someone robbing a few places? I'll take that any day over the alternatives."

Luke would, too. Major shit had gone down in Gotham City while he'd been overseas. He had no idea how Bruce had dealt with it alone.

"I'll make it up to you   and Mom."

"By going to the Gotham Museum Gala next week."

Luke groaned again. "You have this all figured out, don't you."

His dad laughed. "I'm not CEO for nothing, you know."

Luke managed about twenty feet of cruising down the broad

avenue before traffic brought him to a standstill again. "Tell Mom I'll go to the gala."

And an event like that . . . An idea sparked, making his brain go rapid-fire more than any cup of coffee. Oh, an event like that might have some interesting *opportunities*.

"Good. Your mother and the young ladies will see you there."

Despite himself, Luke laughed. "Fine, fine." He grimaced at the traffic. "I'll swing by your office in twenty."

"Bring me a hot dog, will you?"

Luke's brows rose.

His father said, "This spinach smoothie tastes like cold garbage."

Luke chuckled all the way to Wayne Tower.

He didn't find anything on the bullet. Not a trace. A ghost bullet.

And nothing—absolutely *nothing*—happened over Labor Day weekend. As if the criminals had gone to the beach, too.

Had *everyone* left town?

Luke felt like a jerk for even thinking it, but a week later, as he rode up the elevator of his apartment building, tux freshly pressed and in the garment bag dangling from his hooked fingers, the *last* thing he wanted to do was go to the annual Gotham Museum Gala in a few hours. The first event of gala season—the flashiest and most publicly broadcast.

But he had his reasons to be there, ones he prayed paid off, since the thief had been quiet this past week as well. But with an item so tempting laid on the table, perhaps that would change. Luke smiled to himself as the elevator doors opened, revealing the sunny penthouse hallway.

And the knockout blonde walking down it.

She was young—probably somewhere around twenty, just a few years younger than him—and she stopped short as she beheld him. Luke mastered himself enough to offer a half smile as he stepped off the elevator and kept the door open for her with an extended arm.

"New neighbor?" he asked as she resumed approaching, a small smile curling her mouth.

Yeah, *knockout* was an understatement. Long, lean legs not at all hidden by the workout gear she wore. And her light exercise jacket that also displayed a tapered waist. As she stopped before him, he got a look right into those green eyes, and . . . Wow.

"I was wondering when we'd meet," she said, her voice low and cool. Not a trace of an accent—likely from European boarding schools. Swiss, if he were to put money on it. She extended a tanned, manicured hand to him, palm down—the same way he'd seen his mom and the other fancy ladies of Gotham City do. As if it wouldn't be unexpected for him to kiss it. "Holly Vanderhees."

The light calluses on her palm were unexpected, though, as he opted for a quick shake. She probably did CrossFit. Even with the long sleeves of her jacket, he could see the strong, sleek shape of her arms. "I know who you are," he said with a hint of a smile that usually made ladies go red or start giggling.

She only angled her head, that mass of golden hair tilting with her. "I suppose you have the upper hand, then." Not a giggle or blush in sight. A woman used to handling men—or making *them* blush. Interesting.

So he went for option B: the roguish grin. "Luke Fox." The elevator started beeping, an incessant demand to get out or in.

"You can let it go," she said, and the tone . . . A woman definitely used to giving orders. And having them obeyed. Definitely old money—maybe even some Old World titles to go with it.

Luke let go of the elevator doors, and they slid shut. "I'm sorry I haven't come over to say hi." He lifted the garment bag for emphasis. "Been a busy summer."

Holly flicked those killer green eyes over him once. "Are you attending the museum gala tonight?"

Only for work purposes, he was tempted to say, but Luke tapped the garment bag. "Just heading in to get ready."

She arched a brow—darker than her blond hair. "You need three hours to get dressed?"

Luke choked on a laugh. "And if I did?"

"I'd offer to bring over some face masks and make it a party."

Luke chuckled this time. "Are you going?"

A nod. "Any tips for a newcomer?"

Many. Starting with never getting involved in the gala circuit. But she'd likely been born and bred for this sort of thing. A bit of a disappointment, if he was being honest with himself.

"Avoid the raw bar after Jaclyn Brooksfeld arrives," Luke said. "She picks up every shrimp and then puts the rejects back."

Holly laughed, a husky sound. "Disgusting." She glanced over a shoulder toward his door. "You live there alone?"

"My parents are at their place out in the suburbs."

"Your parents, hmm? Do they get you a babysitter while you're in the city?"

He rolled his eyes. "Funny."

Holly let out that low laugh that rippled down his body, then leaned past him to push the elevator button.

He asked, "Where do your parents live?" *You look young enough to still be in college.*

He knew it was the wrong question when she stiffened. "They passed away years ago."

Luke winced. "Sorry," he said. "I'm so sorry for your loss."

He couldn't imagine it. Even with all he'd gone through. That loss . . . He'd never recover.

Holly studied the rising elevator floor numbers. "Thank you."

Silence fell, heavy and awkward. So he found himself asking, "You need a ride to the gala later?"

"No, thank you." Again, that little smile returned. "I have my own ride."

He blinked at her. Normally, they said yes. Normally, they asked *him.* "What brings you to Gotham?"

Holly examined her manicured nails for any flaws—a bored expression growing on her face that he'd seen a thousand times, from prep school to galas to brunches. "Europe got boring."

Only someone with too much money and too little to do would say something like that. Someone who'd never been hungry or frightened or bothered to think how the rest of the world lived.

Or what they could do to help it.

He might have grown up with the world at his feet, but his parents hadn't. And they'd made sure he never took any of it for granted. Working as Batwing, being in the Marines, had only reinforced that awareness and gratitude. And made Holly's lack of it even more apparent.

Any sparkle in his blood simmered out.

"No job to entertain you?" he asked tightly, hoping she'd prove him wrong.

Again that bored look. "Why would I ever bother to work?"

He'd heard enough. Seen enough. He'd met her kind a hundred times. Had grown up with them. Why bother to work? Why bother to volunteer at a charity when money could just be handed over and bragging rights gained? Donations were more for tax purposes than kindness—how often he'd heard *that* notion. Holly was no different.

Luke lifted his tux in farewell. "Well, I hope we entertain you." He strode down the hall, aiming for his door.

He felt, more than saw, her turn to watch him.

As the elevator doors opened and he slid his key into the lock, Holly said, "See you later, Luke Fox."

He heard the promise in her voice and debated telling her she was now the last woman in Gotham City he'd bother letting through this door.

But he opted for ignoring her, knowing it'd rile someone of her ilk more than any insult.

He threw a glance over a shoulder at her as the elevator doors slid shut.

But she was already studying her nails again, frowning at whatever flaw she found.

A disappointment and a waste.

Gorgeous but spoiled.

CHAPTER 8

Arrogant and well aware of his charm.

That's how Selina decided she'd describe Luke Fox.

It had been disappointingly easy to deceive him. To make him believe the pathetic, spoiled words that came from her mouth. He was the same as the rest of them, who saw what they wanted to see.

And what he wanted, she'd read in about two heartbeats. Someone to entertain *him*.

Oh, she'd known what mark she was hitting with the *Europe got boring* and *Why would I work?* comments. Knew she was playing into what he hated, what he likely was trying to escape from so badly that a new neighbor seemed interesting, but . . . Selina was willing to admit she'd been hoping he'd be a *little* more suspicious. A *little* more aware that the nails and hair and non-accent were fake.

Sometimes it felt as if there were nothing left of Selina Kyle at all. As if she were well and truly gone, her body now little more than a shape-shifter's skin. *Holly's* skin. To be donned and wielded.

The thought clanged through her, hollow and cold.

None of Gotham City's richest, in the two weeks she'd already been here, had noticed that she was an imposter, either. Show up at the right restaurants, the right fund-raisers, and the invitations pour in. Flush with foreign cash, Holly Vanderhees was well on her way to being the socialite of the season.

She wondered if the idiots would ever realize that the same parties she'd attended were ones where people had gone home to find an emerald bracelet or a Rolex missing.

But those little thefts were just to make them uneasy. Start questioning each other.

She'd learned most of the sleight of hand when she was a Leopard.

Selina still remembered that first robbery, though. Still thought of it often.

Her hands were shaking.

It was all she could think about as she sat on the park bench in the midday sunshine and monitored those passing by. How her shaking hands would get her caught. Thrown into jail.

People streamed by her, and she sorted through their faces, clothes, attitudes. Elderly people, kids, and anyone who seemed poor were instantly dismissed. She hadn't told Mika about the rules she'd created, but she doubted the Alpha would care. As long as Selina brought back something worth selling. Something that proved she deserved a spot here.

Selina slid her trembling hands into the pocket of her ancient gray sweatshirt, her backpack on the bench beside her. She'd been sitting on this bench for an hour now—had arrived just prior to the lunchtime rush of people desperate for a few minutes of fresh air before returning to their soul-sucking jobs in the offices towering high above the small city park.

She'd get a cut of the money, Mika had told her. From whatever she stole—she'd get a cut of the money. Maybe enough to get Maggie a decent dinner. Maybe even dessert.

A man in a suit approached from beneath the towering oaks. Selina avoided the urge to sit up as he strode down the busy park walkway, his head bowed over his phone as his thumbs typed away at the screen.

Expensive-looking suit. Polished shoes. Slicked-back hair. And a total lack of interest in or fear of his surroundings.

She scanned his pants. No sign of a wallet in the front pockets, but . . . she noted the way one side of his suit jacket seemed to sway a little slower—heavier—with each step nearer to where she sat.

She scooped up her backpack over a shoulder, pulling out her flip phone and letting her thumbs start tapping at the buttons as she launched into a swift walk.

Right into him. Hard.

The man cursed, phone falling to the concrete, and Selina's backpack went flying, spilling the pens and dented notebooks across the asphalt path. She let out an oomph as she hit him, clutching at him.

A beat of guilt went through her as the man twisted to steady her, opting for her well-being over that of his phone. But he only gave her a passing glance before looking to the debris now scattered before them, his phone among it.

Selina's heart pounded so loud she was surprised he didn't hear it as she said, "I'm so sorry—"

She pulled away from him, the wallet he'd tucked into his interior jacket pocket sliding away with her carefully positioned hand. Selina waited for him to notice the lack of weight. To notice that she'd deposited his wallet into the pouch of her sweatshirt.

But he was too busy scowling as he rushed to pick up his phone. "Watch where you're going, moron," he snapped as he realized his phone's screen had splintered.

Asshole. And the way he sneered at her, noting her worn jeans, her frayed sweatshirt . . . He deserved to lose his wallet.

Selina maintained her feigned blinking at him as she began scooping up the contents of her bag, which she'd left half unzipped. "Sorry," she murmured again.

He shook his head at the phone, the mess, at her, and strode off.

Crouched on the ground, Selina watched him go for a heartbeat. Waited for him to pat his jacket and figure it out.

He didn't, too busy being angry about his destroyed phone to care. Selina finished gathering up her things, slung her backpack over both shoulders this time, and headed for the opposite end of the park. Mika was waiting there, Ani in tow.

Selina cast a searching glance around the park, the streets, for any signs of uniforms or patrol cars. Found none.

She slid the man's wallet over to Mika, who gave her a firm, approving nod.

As they launched into a casual walk that would take them quickly away from the area, Ani said, "I thought you were supposed to be some kinda gymnastics freak."

Selina said nothing. She'd been with the Leopards for three weeks now and she already knew to keep her mouth shut.

Ani just chuckled, clapping her on the back. "Next time, do some flips and shit."

"Not exactly covert," Mika countered.

The Leopard's Second only shrugged. "Yeah, but it'd look cool."

A week later, Ani had gotten her wish. They'd robbed an electronics store that required some careful, flexible maneuvering to disable the alarms and cameras. And as the only gymnast among them, Selina wound up assigned the task.

And wound up with two hundred bucks when the night was done.

Those first robberies had been over five years ago now. She'd learned as much from Mika and Ani as she'd learned through her own trial and error.

But once she'd gone to the League, Nyssa and Talia had taught her far, far more.

Bring Gotham City to its knees.

The burglaries would begin that process. That undoing. And the cash was a wonderful addition. A bonus, as it were. All hers.

And tonight . . .

The universe had a sense of humor, Selina decided as she went to the gym to limber up, a combination of her old gymnastics warm-ups and what she'd been taught at the League. Because the big prize tonight . . . Well, its owner lived across the hall from her.

She'd picked the apartment for its proximity to one of Gotham City's richest and most popular. No one could question her credentials when she was Luke Fox's neighbor.

In the East End, she'd often witnessed the substandard treatment endured by so many black people in this city—and part of her wondered if Luke himself had ever faced any. Yet from all she'd seen and heard, everyone treated the Foxes like royalty.

To her, Luke seemed like nothing more than a pretty boy used to getting what he wanted. Who probably had those muscles just to admire them in his mirror. There was no shortage of those types here in Gotham City, and now that the summer had ended and gala season had begun, all the trust fund brats and titans of industry would be returning to the city from their beach estates. Starting tonight.

Selina strode into the gym, smiling at the news reporter on the screen above her favorite treadmill, the one that allowed her to keep an eye on the door. The news was reporting live from the museum's red carpet in anticipation of the gala in a few hours.

Where that ten-million-dollar painting, no larger than a sheet of paper, had just been loaned to the museum—courtesy of Luke Fox's private collection.

Selina smirked as she stepped onto the treadmill and tied back her ridiculous blond hair into a heavy ponytail.

Luke Fox could afford to lose it.

Selina had been to the Gotham Museum of Art before.

This week, obviously, had been one of those times, while she'd scoped out the entrances, the skylights, the various windows and surrounding streets under the cover of darkness. To anyone passing by, she would have likely only appeared as a gargoyle crouched on the lip of one of the nearby buildings, or as a ripple in a deep shadow of an adjacent alley.

Five days now, she'd monitored the museum—five days of marking the guards' rotations, their physiques, the weapons they carried. Five days of constructing her plan, as if she were sliding pieces on a chessboard into place.

The other League assassins relied on their tech, their fancy devices, to help them. But those things could fail. And while she'd certainly use them tonight, once the gala guests had left and Holly Vanderhees slipped into something more comfortable, Selina wanted to be able to navigate every inch of this museum blind.

The planning was as much of a high as the heist itself. Had always been. Figuring out a way in, figuring out the puzzle of alarms and security and exits . . . It sparked something in her. Even now, after her training had been so thorough that it was mostly muscle memory.

A low thrill was still coursing through her as she let the CEO of one of Gotham City's biggest hedge funds waltz her around the ornate, cavernous grand hall of the museum.

Step one of the plan: let Gotham City see Holly here, believe her to be one of them—while she took these hours to get a first glimpse at where the painting had been displayed, how they'd guarded it. They'd waited until just before the party to set it up in an adjacent hall, where revelers might drift, champagne in hand, to admire the work of art in solitude and reflection.

Or some ridiculous reason like that. But it made it easier for her to get close enough to casually assess the painting. Which she'd do as soon as she finished charming the preening idiot dancing with her.

Life on the East End had been brutal—but there, at least most people had been real. None of the labyrinths of lies and illusions these people spun with words and sparkling wealth. Yes, there had been people just as untrustworthy, but . . . She'd still take the East Enders over these people any day of the week.

The CEO spun her, the world blending into a living band of color and glitter and marble. So different from how she'd first seen the grand hall of the museum, with its swooping staircases on either side, the mezzanine overlooking the entire space, the quiet, looming sense of mystery—of sacredness in every inch of this place.

She'd been here on a seventh-grade field trip and had focused more on keeping her growling stomach from being overheard in the whisper-filled galleries than on the art itself. Then, she'd been in clothes scrounged from the donation piles, not in a golden wrap dress that cost more than the poorest of Gotham City made in a year. With matching heels.

Those shoes now traveled across the parquet floors, the embroidered tulle and silk-crepe dress glinting in the lights of the chandeliers above and the countless candelabras throughout the packed space.

"You'll be going to the Save the Children Gala, I presume?" The CEO wasn't bad-looking—for a man old enough to be her father. Too bad everything about him, his life, repulsed her.

Selina forced her red-painted lips into a smile. "Only if you are."

A gleam of interest in the man's eyes—the same gleam that she'd spotted across the hall and then encouraged with frequent knowing glances. Until he strode up to her and asked for a dance.

Disgustingly easy. Ridiculously predictable.

The hand the CEO had braced on her waist shifted a little southward. It took every ounce of effort to keep smiling and not to rip that hand off her. "Oh, I'll be there, Miss Vanderhees."

She was beautiful, loaded, and young. Precisely this man's type.

Too bad his two-hundred-thousand-dollar Rolex was more *her* type.

Picking him out of the crowd had been simple. No wedding ring, and he strutted around like he owned the place. He'd already known who she was, thanks to Holly's frequent appearances at Gotham City's finest restaurants and stores these past two weeks. And more than that: her own established source of income offered an automatic in.

The cliché of rich men marrying their secretaries or flight atten-

dants is gone, Talia had drawled during those early lessons. *The rich only trust the rich.*

Nyssa taught her the blades and the discipline. And Talia taught her everything else. About society's masks—about the rules. How to slip past them.

Rich men now want to marry their equals, Talia had explained. God, she'd loved to hear herself talk more than anything in the world. *Other CEOs, heiresses. To consolidate power—amass more. So you must learn to play the part.*

Selina had. And that training had been just as hard as Nyssa's.

Nails, hair, skin, body, makeup—the first signifiers, Talia had ordered as they'd sat before her dressing table in the compound. She'd examined Selina's short, rough nails. *You will wear gloves while training and grow these out. Not too long, though. And no hangnails.* She'd handed over a small pink-and-silver compact full of a pale rose cream. *For the cuticles—and your lips. Apply morning and night.*

Then had come the regimen of creams and gels and masks for her face. Her hair.

Makeup should be light but skilled. Not for the men but for the other women, who will notice immediately. Suspect you. It is to emphasize, not draw attention to yourself. If you go bold, do it sparingly. Lips or eyes—pick one.

A different sort of armor from the ones Talia's half sister, Nyssa, had been showing her. A different way of breaking into locked rooms than a pick kit.

Nyssa and Talia: two sides of the same dark coin. One trained for bloodshed and battle, the other for politics and strategy. Together, they ran the League's headquarters in Italy, overseeing the training of the young women they recruited.

These are the weapons and passports they use against each other, Talia had purred, dusting Selina's face with golden highlighter. *So we will use them as well.*

Selina let the CEO's hand drift a little lower, let a little corner of her mouth lift. So many eyes upon them now. Curious about the new socialite in their midst. The waltz rose, turning frenzied as it neared its end.

She knew his attention was focused on the location of his hand. She even arched her back a little bit, as if enjoying it—encouraging his inappropriate groping. Even while her stomach turned over, her blood simmering to a near boil.

You will learn to talk, walk, and dance like them. When you speak to the other acolytes in the dining hall, I expect you to use the same phrasings you would when speaking to a baron. When you walk to your lessons, I expect you to float as if you were in the midst of a ball.

And the dancing? Selina had asked.

Talia had taken her to Venice three nights later. To the Grand Masquerade Ball at Carnevale. Selina had brought a simple black gown whose back draped open dramatically. She'd also brought the black-and-gold mask Talia had given her. Just in case.

But Selina shoved the thought of that ball from her mind as this waltz drew to its close. As the CEO's hand brushed even lower, her own hand grazed his thick wrist.

She held his gaze while she did it, allowed him to be too distracted by her heavy-lidded stare, her pert red mouth, to notice the watch she slid off his wrist as she pulled out of his touch. She said to the CEO, voice low and wicked, "I certainly hope I see you before then."

A wry little smile emphasized the words, the promise in them, as she turned away, leaving the CEO on the floor. She wished she could wipe the feel of his hands off her body, wished she could purge his musky cologne from her nostrils.

There were indeed lowlifes here, just as despicable as any in the East End. Selina supposed these ones just dressed better.

It certainly made the Rolex now in the hidden pocket of her dress all the more satisfying.

She counted her steps as she approached the open marble bar, a vacant smile on her face. But no shouting followed—and a coy look over her shoulder revealed the CEO still staring at her, even while he danced with his new partner.

Dazzle and distract. No different from that first robbery in the park.

But so much more fun.

With a private smile to herself, Selina leaned forward to the bartender and said—

"Champagne—two glasses." The deep male voice cut across the bar.

Selina glanced sidelong at the man who'd come up next to her.

Clad in a Marines dress uniform that fit him like a glove, Luke Fox gave her a tight smile.

Selina gave one right back. Like hell he'd jump ahead of her in line. "Make it three," she said sweetly to the bartender. The man nodded and swept off.

Selina twisted to watch the waltzing crowd in the center of the room, the mingling guests now chatting, with the formal meal over. "I stayed away from the shellfish," she said to Luke.

He lifted a dark brow. "Wise choice." The two words held little invitation for further conversation. Especially as he threw down a few bills for the bartender and took his two flutes of champagne in his white-gloved hands.

Selina scooped up hers, not daring to glance at the artfully hidden pockets in her dress—to make sure the lump of the Rolex was hidden. And the Cartier bracelet from the woman she'd bumped into in line for the raw bar. And the Harry Winston ring from the witch who'd looked down her nose at Selina when they'd shaken hands.

Selina jerked her chin toward Luke's second glass of champagne. "For your date?" Good. Perhaps his girlfriend would console him when he got the news his painting was gone.

He motioned with his glass toward a striking older black woman across the dance floor, chatting beside a black man she immediately recognized as Lucius Fox and an elderly white couple. Both ladies were bedecked in jewels—but the woman she was guessing was Luke's mother wore them tastefully, paired well with her deep sapphire ball gown. "For my mother," Luke countered, his tone still clipped and distant. He took a step forward. "Enjoy the gala."

So her little comment about boring old Europe earlier had irked him.

Unable to help herself, Selina purred, "Aren't you going to ask your neighbor to dance?"

Luke swallowed a mouthful of his champagne before turning back. Buying himself time to come up with an excuse, no doubt.

Selina watched him beneath her fake lashes and added wryly, "Though I suppose a dashing soldier is already spoken for."

"I promised someone else a dance" was all he said, back stiff. "Sorry." He didn't sound that way in the least.

It was entertaining enough that Selina added, "Considering how happy you look to be here, I'm surprised you came." Because that was one hell of a scowl as he surveyed the crowd.

"I owed a lady a favor."

"The lady whose champagne you're holding." Only a son who truly adored his mother, she supposed, would drag himself here to please her. She made a note of it—his devotion and loyalty. A fact to be used later. Perhaps.

Luke shrugged, his broad shoulders shifting within his immaculately tailored uniform. "I enjoy these parties." Another lie. From the tightness of his jaw, he either *hated* being here—or hated Holly Vanderhees. He began striding toward his parents, and Selina sipped her champagne.

"If a dance opens up," she drawled to him, savoring the parting shot, "let me know."

Another glance over his shoulder. A bit of wariness in his eyes now.

Gold-digger, she wanted to tell him. *That's the word you're tossing around now. Wondering if someone with money going after another person with money counts as being a gold-digger.*

From the tight smile he gave her again, Selina knew Luke had arrived at a conclusion. One that involved keeping far away from her. One that cemented Holly as someone to avoid.

Perfect. The last thing she needed was a nosy neighbor.

And she highly doubted he'd be coming over to ask for a cup of sugar anytime soon.

Another task now off her hands and her path cleared a bit more.

Selina sipped her champagne again and surveyed the bejeweled crowd. Sensed the men circling like sharks, debating how to approach her now that Luke had yielded her attention.

People will see what they want to see, Talia had told her. *Give them the illusion. Become the illusion. And never let them know, even when you are long gone. Even in your triumph.*

Selina watched a young trust-fund-looking man decide to close in on her. She offered him that little smile, draining her champagne and setting it on the bar behind her.

The young man sauntering up, a haughty angle to his chin, wasn't much to tempt her. But the Piaget watch glimmering in the low light, just peeking out from beneath the dark sleeve of his tux . . . oh, that was a beauty.

Rich men and their watches. Another thing Talia had made her study. She'd never asked Talia how she'd learned herself. Who'd taught her. Talia had never volunteered it, either.

So Selina had learned the status symbols that women wielded and the ones men used to declare to each other that they were as wealthy as kings.

But that twenty-thousand-dollar watch on his wrist was nothing compared to the ten-million-dollar painting that waited for her in this museum.

Luke Fox would certainly need a lot more champagne before the night was through.

Luke could barely focus on the conversation he was having. He kept scanning the room, listening for any whisper of alarm. Nothing.

His two prep school friends—Elise and Mark, now running their own joint hedge fund—were debating the merits of which reality TV show was the worst to watch. Luke drowned it out, as he often did when their conversations skewed toward the absurd. A skill both Elise and Mark took pride in. Enjoyed.

But half listening to their banter was better than his dad not-so-subtly sending Luke to the bar to get his mom champagne, hoping he'd run into at least *one* of the young women of which his parents had approved.

At least he'd avoided the few older women who stared at him like a piece of meat, whose devouring glances he'd never been able to stomach or grow used to.

Still, he'd never ordered a drink faster—only to wind up next to Holly at the bar.

He'd seen that creep CEO she'd been dancing with. They'd match perfectly.

He'd given his mom her champagne, then made a beeline for his friends, standing together by the window, as they usually did. As the three of them had done at every school party and event while growing up.

Their own little unit, inseparable. Even if Mark, who he'd known since seventh grade, had been secretly in love with Elise for years. But Elise, who was likely the closest thing Luke had to a best friend, had no idea.

Elise, golden-skinned and dark-haired, smiled at him as he approached, but didn't pause her arguing with Mark.

Mark, however, seemed unaware of anyone else in the ballroom with Elise in front of him, only occasionally breaking his focus to drag a hand through his blond hair.

That focus, however, finally broke when Mark turned to Luke. "You're quiet tonight, man." A frown crossed his face, his brown eyes fixing on Luke with a piercing intensity different from the way he'd been looking at Elise. "Everything okay?"

Elise sipped from her champagne, watching Luke over the rim of the glass. While Mark was usually direct, Elise knew when to observe, when to wield silence as effectively as words.

After a heartbeat, she said to Luke, "You kind of look the way you did that time in junior year English when Mr. Bartleby said we had to compose love sonnets for the midterm paper." Genius, Luke might be; poet, he was definitely not.

Mark tipped back his head and laughed. Luke smiled, throwing Elise a grateful look for the deflection as he admitted, "It was the worst grade I ever got in my life." A sorry C-minus. "I think Bartleby deliberately marked it down *because* of the face I made when he announced the assignment."

"You and me both," Mark said, nudging him with an elbow. "Though I still think I deserved more than a C. My poem was epic."

"You both deserved exactly what you got," Elise retorted. "For writing a poem about your love of *donuts*," she said, jerking her chin at Mark. She then pointed at Luke. "And a sonnet about your love of *not* writing sonnets."

Luke and Mark rolled their eyes. "We were robbed," Mark declared. Elise, of course, had aced the assignment.

Luke surveyed his friends. Mark and Elise had been the only ones who'd really supported him when he'd declared he was enlisting. When Luke had said he didn't want to go to college, to deal with more of the same in the Ivy League circuit, and instead wanted to *do* something. Wanted to serve.

Even when their other friends had pretended to understand, even when Luke knew they thought he was making a bad choice, Elise and Mark had encouraged him. When he was overseas, they had written to him and video chatted.

Both had been there the day after he'd come back. Mark had cried when he saw the still-healing wound slashing down Luke's ribs. Elise had taken out her phone and started to research physical therapy treatments.

They never asked about the PTSD, but they knew. And though he wasn't ashamed of it, he remained deeply grateful they let him bring it up on his terms. That it mostly remained out of their friendship dynamic for now. Glad to have some semblance of things being the same.

"Things are fine," Luke said, meeting Elise's weighing stare. She seemed to read the truth in the words, and gave him a slight nod. Luke gave Mark a grin. "One gala into the season, and I'm bored to tears."

Elise put an affronted hand on her chest, gold bracelets and rings glittering. "You mean to tell me that our highly intellectual debate about the top ten reality show breakups isn't enough to entertain you?"

Mark scowled at them both but couldn't hide the amusement from his face.

Neither could Luke as he said, "If you two were *at* every event, it wouldn't be so bad."

"You couldn't pay me to go to more than three of these a year," Mark said. Elise murmured in agreement. "I'm all for giving to charity, but does a party have to be involved as well? My parents don't even bother to go anymore." He waved a callused hand to the sparkling room around them. Mark had always been into crew—still took out a boat at least once a week on the Sprang River. "They told me this summer that *I* had to go now. That they'd done their time, and now it was my turn to represent the family." *And deal with the socialite crowd*, Mark didn't need to add.

Luke and Elise cringed in sympathy. Her own parents weren't here, but that was because her mother, heiress to a fishing empire in Venezuela, had business to attend to. If the Marvez family was in the country, however, they attended all of these events, right alongside Luke's parents, who had become good friends with them over the years, actually.

"Poor baby," Elise said, patting Mark on his broad shoulder. "Such a hard life, dressing up and drinking other people's booze."

"Such a hard life," Luke joined in, chuckling, "eating free food and going home with a fancy gift bag."

Mark flipped them off. Elise and Luke returned the gesture.

Behind them, a cluster of old ladies gasped as they passed by. Mark only lifted his champagne in salute.

They waited until the horrified women had passed before stifling their laughter.

"Never changes," Elise said, watching them go, her dark eyes bright.

But Luke found Mark studying him again. While Luke might have counted Elise as his closer friend, Mark had been the one who'd often shown up to physical therapy in those initial weeks, and then accompanied him to the PTSD therapy whenever Luke wanted company. The offer was always there: on hard days, when Luke didn't want to make the trip alone, one call to Mark and his friend would pick him up.

"But you're doing good, though?" Mark asked again.

"If he says he is, then he is," Elise countered. Mark waved her off, refusing to take his attention off Luke.

They'd always looked out for each other, but since he'd come home, Mark and Elise had taken being protective to another level. It warmed something in Luke's heart—made enduring their bickering worth it. "I'm doing well," Luke said to his friends. "I really am."

Mark seemed satisfied this time, and fell back into arguing with Elise about which reality contestants were likely to break into a brawl on the current season of their favorite show. Luke listened for a minute, smiling, and drained his second glass of champagne. His last.

He needed to be sharp tonight. There had been a number of small robberies these past few weeks. Gotham City's elite who'd all lost valuables while out in public at dinners and parties.

Luke was willing to bet his inheritance that the city's newest thief would be here. That the thief was already among them, the season kickoff gala too big of a payday to resist.

He prayed it was true. If they didn't arrive, it'd mean going to the next gala. And the next. To watch for a pattern. Note the faces and names of attendees.

He had set the trap. And it would only be a matter of time before the thief fell for it.

CHAPTER 9

Selina had only risked five minutes with the painting during the gala.

On the arm of a beautiful oil executive, she'd strolled into the long hall where the painting of a nondescript bowl of fruit hung on the far wall. It had been roped off, with a bored-looking security guard a few steps away to make sure no one took photos or got too close.

The oil exec actually knew a thing or two about art, and she'd rattled off various techniques the artist had used. Selina had nodded, leaning in as though she were studying the details. Instead, she'd been eyeing up the size and weight of the small painting.

Her heartbeat had pounded through her, but she'd managed to subtly suggest to the woman that perhaps they could return for another viewing of the painting in a day or so. And the exec had turned to the guard and asked just how long this painting would be on display.

Only through the weekend, ma'am.

Confirmation that Selina had to move tonight.

She had made sure that more than a few people, a frowning Luke Fox included, saw her swaying precariously as she headed to the bathroom toward the end of the night. And never emerged. At least not in that golden dress.

The security guards, tired and eager to head home, quickly checked the bathrooms upon leaving. None bothering to look *up*, at where she'd stretched herself out over the top of a stall.

Only when silence had fallen, and she had given enough time for even the few remaining security guards to have settled into heavy boredom, did Selina slip from the bathroom.

Stashing her bag with her League suit and matching helmet in the bathroom's utilities closet had been the hardest part—the riskiest.

She'd done it during a daytime visit yesterday, hauling them inside with an oversized tote, waiting in the bathroom nearest the gala hall until it was empty and she could pick the lock on the closet door. She'd buried both helmet and suit at the bottom of a giant box of toilet paper, tucked it beneath *another* box of the stuff—surely they wouldn't go through *all* of it in twenty-four hours—and sent up a prayer to whatever ancient gods were watching that the janitors wouldn't find it.

They hadn't. And now, the museum dark and quiet as a tomb, Selina slipped through the shadows of the various galleries, a thrill creeping through her veins with every movement.

Ancient statues watching on, she filtered the sounds that the receivers on her helmet picked up: a coughing guard five galleries away, a gurgling fountain in the center of the Egyptian hall, birds' talons scraping on the fogged glass roof.

The glass panels of the built-in goggles gave her perfect night vision, turning the world into greens and yellows. Nothing but art and shadows. Each of these paintings was valuable, but stealing one of them was not the *statement* she needed to make.

But first: the security system.

She'd hacked into the museum's network to draw up the blueprints for the building—had memorized them meticulously. Knew that there was a centralized room, in sublevel one, that controlled every switch. Knew it was staffed by two guards at night, thanks to a memo she'd found in the email servers, each with panic buttons on hand.

Too risky. And shutting down the entire security system increased the risk of a guard in another part of the museum noticing the lack of little red lights.

So she'd picked her grid. Combed through the blueprints to find where the alarm wires ran through the building and the carefully hidden hubs where one might access them.

Another clever puzzle to solve. One that set her blood thrumming.

Selina silently eased through the hallways of the museum, counting her steps to the nearest locked wall panel. She'd easily cleared half a million in valuables tonight. But that ten million from the painting . . . one hell of a payday.

Scanning the halls around her, Selina stopped before an almost invisible panel built into the wall. She'd eyed it twice now while walking through here at the gala, using each step and glance to figure out its lock.

Selina pressed on a section of the utility belt slung across her hips, a little compartment opening up to reveal an assortment of lockpicks and clever, useful things. Selecting one, keeping an eye on the hall around her, she slid the pick into the lock.

Idiots—for leaving this panel here. Though it made her life easier.

With a click, the panel swung open, revealing a network of switches and wires. Her helmet scanned them, providing her with the feedback she needed to narrow in on the wire to disable.

No cutting. That'd trigger the entire system.

But rerouting the alarms . . . Selina pulled another device from her belt—a cord with a USB on one end and a smaller port on the other. She fitted the latter end into the small slot at the base of her helmet, then slid the USB end into the security panel itself.

Instantly, data whirred by. Security feeds, routes . . . Her Death Mask sorted through it all. And began creating a false loop of data for the several halls ahead. So that even when she entered it, crossing over trigger beams, the loop of old data would keep playing for the main computer. Along with the video footage from the mounted cameras.

When it was done, she unhooked the cord and closed the panel.

One guard lay ahead. Stationed just to the left of the open doorway down the hall. She'd seen him these past two nights. Half asleep, nodding off at least twice an hour.

A crack of her bullwhip would wake him up. She smirked at the thought.

On silent feet, Selina approached the hall, flexing her clawed fingers.

She would disable him—not kill him. The man wasn't involved in this. Didn't deserve anything worse than a headache.

Taking a small, bracing breath, she neared the corner. The inhale before the storm.

Quiet as death, Selina swept around the corner, angling for the guard who she knew would be standing just two feet to her left.

But her fingers closed on open air.

The man was already down. Unconscious. No sign of injury except for some sort of shimmering green powder on the lapels of his uniform.

Selina whirled, knees bending, a hand going for the bullwhip at her left hip while her goggles scanned the room—

A soft female laugh flitted from a darkened corner. The corner where the Fox painting would be.

"You know," the stranger said, stepping into a shaft of moonlight leaking in through the glass roof above, "I was hoping you'd be a woman."

Selina rose to her full height and kept her claws unsheathed as she stalked toward the young woman standing on the other side of the gallery.

In the dim light, the woman's red hair was blood-dark, her skin moon-pale. A pretty face smiled above a green bodysuit with countless pockets. Young, around Selina's own age—nineteen or twenty.

"Happy to please," Selina said, her voice raspy and warped thanks to the League's standard voice-modifier. She jerked her head to the small painting the stranger was standing in front of. "But I think that belongs to me."

"Technically," the stranger said, vibrant emerald eyes flickering with amusement as she gestured to the painting a few feet behind her, "it belongs to Luke Fox." Her hands were covered with dark green gloves. No—*vines*. Those were closely wrapped, thin vines all along her fingers. *Organic, living organism*, Selina's helmet supplied.

Impressive.

The woman angled her head, her heavy curtain of red hair slipping over a slim shoulder. Small white flowers seemed to be woven throughout. "And technically, I was here first."

"You only got here first," Selina said, sliding the bullwhip free and letting it unspool to the marble floor, "because I was disabling the alarm. It's mine." She hadn't used that tone since those days in the East End. Enforcing Mika's rule.

The stranger snorted; some of the flowers in her hair *closed*. As if they were alive, too. "Do you know that there's a species of dung beetle that just waits for other beetles to create their reserves and then takes them? It happens all the time in the animal kingdom, actually. It's called kleptoparasitism."

Selina smiled, even though the stranger couldn't see. "You're Poison Ivy."

With the living plants on her, there was no one else the stranger could be.

Selina had heard and read the rumors: mad scientist who specialized in plant-based weapons and toxins. That she had no allegiance to any criminal organization, had outright refused to be recruited, and only sought to save the planet. By whatever means necessary. The more outlandish stories claimed that Ivy had become plant-based herself.

Perhaps reality wasn't so far from the myth.

The vines around Ivy's wrist began writhing, as if they were small snakes, readying for a strike. "And you are?"

She'd dealt with posturing plenty, both in the Leopards and at the League. So Selina prowled across the parquet floor, aiming right for that painting. Getting a sense of whether the other woman would hold her ground, whether she'd cede direct access to the painting. "No concern to you."

Selina got within three yards of Ivy before the young woman sidled a few feet away from the painting. And the reach of Selina's bullwhip.

Still, Ivy lifted her chin and said tartly, "I'll be taking that painting, thank you."

Brave woman. Selina snickered, halting three feet from the painting. "To fund your save-the-rain-forest bullcrap."

A low hiss—one that sounded like it came from something *other* than Ivy's mouth. Selina's helmet ran another scan and only the same generic readout: *living organism*. Ivy demanded, "You know how much money was at that gala tonight? For what? This museum? These dead, lifeless *things*?" Ivy gestured around them, vines shifting.

"So sad," Selina clucked, knowing precisely what beast she was prodding. Or plant, she supposed. "Just awful." She studied the fruit-bowl painting, hardwired to the wall. Exactly as it had been earlier. Separate from the alarm system. It'd start shrieking the moment she touched it. Selina sheathed her claws but kept the whip clenched in her left hand. She'd planned three escape routes, anticipating the guards' layouts. But Ivy added another variable.

Selina asked without looking over at Ivy, "You buy that exterminator-at-the-ball getup at the Halloween store?"

Ivy chuckled, drawing Selina's attention to her left. Ivy's head bobbed as she surveyed Selina's League battle-suit, the night-vision lenses, the receptors on her helmet. "Yeah, but now I wish I hadn't passed up the sexy cat costume."

The corners of Selina's mouth twitched upward.

First rule of disorder: find some interesting company.

Ivy kept within range of the painting even as Selina stood directly before it. "You allied with any of the gangs or bosses?"

"I answer to no one."

Ivy hummed in approval. "Why'd you come to Gotham?"

"Curiosity."

"Doesn't that sort of thing usually not end well for your kind?"

Selina huffed a laugh, the sound devoured by her mask. Not much time. Every second delayed was a risk, a potential disaster. Yet she said, "Things have been quiet—and the money is easy picking."

Ivy yielded her spot to the left of the painting and approached Selina's side to face the painting directly.

Selina unsheathed the claws on the hand she had tucked behind her, monitoring Ivy's every breath. Ivy said, "You sound like a cyborg with that helmet."

Selina bit her lip to keep from laughing again.

Ivy pointed with a green-wrapped finger to the painting. "Here's the deal. We split it fifty-fifty."

"Ninety-ten. Be grateful you get a million out of capitalizing on my hard work."

Ivy shook her head, red hair catching in the moonlight, some of those blossoms opening once more. "Sixty-forty."

"Eighty-five, fifteen, and stop wasting my time."

Ivy opened her mouth. And then the shouting began.

Selina's Death Mask offered an analysis of how long it'd take the museum guards to approach: one minute.

"I thought you disabled the alarms," Ivy hissed, the vines along her hands now roving up her arms.

Selina scowled beneath the helmet, shifting her bullwhip to her right hand. "I did."

Someone had been waiting, then. Anticipating this robbery. Her mouth dried out, though something like lightning shot through her veins.

"Seventy-five, twenty-five, and that's it," Selina said, tossing the whip over her shoulder and lunging for the painting. Alarms screamed as she hauled the small frame off the wall, yanking out a piece of canvas from the folded satchel tucked into her utility belt to carefully wrap around the century-old painting. No point in stealing the damn thing if she destroyed it on her way out.

Selina tucked the painting into her satchel, nestling it amid a cocoon of padding. Another reason why she'd picked this painting: it was small enough to be easily transported. Her lenses picked up a flurry of movement. Not from the hallways beyond but from Ivy in front of her. Selina lifted her head in time to duck—

Unnecessarily.

Ivy snickered as she lobbed a gold-rimmed purple flower to the nearest archway, the blossom the size of a softball. Pale green smoke rippled out from its center.

"Fancy," Selina told her.

Ivy's grin was a slash of white. "Better hope that mask has a gas-filtration system."

It did. Selina only pointed to the small staff door tucked into the corner—unlocked, no doubt thanks to Ivy's own entrance. "If you run like your mouth, we'll get out of here in one piece."

Ivy didn't bother to reply as she turned toward the staff-only door and bolted.

Selina sprinted after her, satchel bobbing at her side, the bull-whip in one hand while she glanced back. Right as the guards came barreling through the spores leaking from that flower, coughing—

She lingered at the door for a heartbeat. Just in time for them to get a glimpse of her, the suit, and the empty spot where the painting had been. Just in time for Selina to sketch a bow—right as the guards inhaled that green smoke, likely custom-made by Ivy in her lab from whatever combination of plants, and collapsed onto the parquet floor.

Fancy and effective, Selina admitted as she shoved through the door and charged after Ivy into the labyrinth of staff passages.

Nyssa and Talia would approve.

Sirens cleaved the night, but Selina's suit fed her the intel she needed: heading toward the museum, not after them as they escaped into the nearby quiet, posh neighborhood, full of embassies and old-money residences. The last place any sane criminal would flee to, considering the security cameras mounted on every building, the guards posted at every other entrance.

Which was why they kept to the rooftops.

Ivy had no issue scaling the building behind the museum using the fire escape—and apparently, no problems with cardio or heights as she kept pace with Selina, leaping without hesitation over the distances between buildings.

They made it three blocks before a particularly large gap appeared. Large enough to merit careful consideration on how to take the jump. Selina slowed, panting lightly—lungs barely needing to push themselves. Ivy's breathing was heavier, her eyes bright.

Selina studied the gap, the cop cars that had just arrived at the museum illuminating the night sky behind them in flickers of blue and red. The lights cast Ivy's hair in varying hues of deep crimson and purple, the silky strands ruffling past her face in the cool night breeze. No sign of the little flowers, as if they'd ducked into the safety of her hair. "Too far," Ivy observed around gasps for air, studying the gap. "Take the drainpipe down."

That would take too long and take them too far from where she needed them to be. So Selina shook her head, flicking her wrists to free the claws in her suit.

Ivy flinched, backing away a step. Her left hand went to a pocket in her bodysuit with curling pink petals poking out of it. Selina didn't care to find out exactly what that flower could do.

She gestured with her claws to the gap. "For climbing," she said, and wriggled her fingertips.

Strange, to have to explain herself, her methods. Strange, Selina realized, to have become something, someone, who required explaining.

A wraith—a ghūl. She'd given up everything to wear that title, that skin. She hadn't realized just how far it might separate her from others. That she might become *other* herself.

But Ivy blinked, hand lowering from the botanical surprise she kept in her pocket. "You can't make that jump."

"I've cleared worse." Not a lie. Selina backed up on the roof, calculating the distance, the speed she'd need to clear the gap and land safely.

She'd never considered that those long, all-out runs she'd done for the vault in gymnastics might be a training of another sort. Not until the League.

Selina stopped at the farthest edge of the roof and glanced to Ivy. "You want in, then you'd better learn to keep up."

Then she was sprinting toward the roof edge, body falling back into muscle memory, into the training she'd had pounded into her bones, her breath.

"Show-off," Ivy groused as Selina sprinted past.

Arms in formation, legs eating up the distance, body bracing for the leap—

Clear the ravine.

A cold, unruffled order.

Selina had glanced between Nyssa al Ghūl and the ravine that cleaved the two granite mountains. All around them, the unforgiving towers of the Dolomites watched as unfeelingly as her teacher. The five other acolytes, mercifully, seemed to hesitate.

Nyssa only lifted a tanned, scar-flecked hand and pointed to the narrow ledge—and a path—across the ravine. "The way home lies over there. The path behind you is closed." A hard, brutal smile. The opposite of the sleek, coy smirks of her elder sister, Talia. "Clear the ravine, or live here."

Or die at the bottom far below.

Selina's palms turned sweaty, her breakfast churning in her stomach. The other acolytes, all of them in the League's black battle-suits, began sizing up the gap, the angle. The wind.

She'd learned as much about the other girls as she could: their movements, their reflexes, their height and weight and favored weapons.

The real details, the ones that mattered . . . None of them shared that information: where they came from, what life they'd led that had brought Talia al Ghūl to come knocking.

All Selina knew was that they hailed from all over the world. The boys, apparently, were trained elsewhere. And Anaya, the acolyte standing beside her, had come from India. She spoke even less than Selina, though she had been here for two months before Selina arrived at the sprawling, luxurious compound deep in the mountains.

If Selina had anything close to an ally here, it was Anaya. She was the only one who ever sat beside Selina at the mess hall or paired with her in classes. Never through any voiced request or invitation, but just a silent, steady presence. That often made other acolytes think twice before pushing either of them.

"When the sun sets," Nyssa went on in English, her accent lilting, "the temperature will drop below freezing. I have no plans to be here when it does." But you will be, *she didn't need to add.*

Then Nyssa launched into a sprint, her slim body eating up the rocky ground, black hair tied back in a tight braid from her face. Not a pretty face, not like Talia's. Where Talia's was marble-hewn in its perfection, Nyssa's had been carved from granite.

And like the granite peaks around them, Nyssa's stride never faltered, never showed any sign of emotion beyond that cool brutality. It was set in the same expression as she hurtled for the ravine ledge—and leapt.

No ropes, no equipment. Nothing beyond icy will.

The acolyte from Eastern Europe swore in some Slavic language. Serbian, perhaps. Recognizing the languages of the world: another course of instruction.

Nyssa soared over the gap, body arcing perfectly. The only bit of beauty the al Ghūl half sister would ever have, in the precision of her movements.

She made it look easy. Landed with a crunch of rock and a smooth roll that flowed into a standing position.

Selina couldn't help the half smile that curved her mouth as Nyssa leaned against a boulder, crossed her arms—her battle-suit dusty from the landing—and waited.

Selina didn't look at the other opponents, didn't engage in the silent battle of who would go first, of whether it would be foolish to do so or if it would earn them a kernel of Nyssa's respect. Or if the one who went last would be deemed cowardly or smart to study the others' mistakes and learn from them.

Selina turned, stalking back to the exact point from which Nyssa had launched herself into that run. Gave herself a few more feet be-

yond it. She studied the faint path of footprints Nyssa had taken. The angle of the jump. Beside her, Anaya did the same.

And her sort-of ally murmured, too softly for the other girls to hear, "They might try to spook us when we run."

She was right. Likely by shouting, maybe even stepping into their path. And no one would punish them for it. No, Nyssa would likely reward them. Another bit of training—not to lower your guard, Nyssa would say. They were all merely instruments to carry out the League's mission. Better to weed out defective ones before sending them into the field.

Survival of the fittest. Biology had been one of her favorite classes. It seemed the League took Darwinism to another level.

Nyssa still waited, arms crossed over her chest. Someone had to make a move.

Even from the distance, Selina could have sworn the woman's eyes met hers. Full of challenge. And invitation.

She'd jumped and run across rooftops with the Leopards, hauling TV sets and other stolen goods. Then, the drop had been thirty feet, not three hundred. But no less lethal.

And perhaps it was the thought of those Leopards she'd left behind a month ago, but Selina murmured to Anaya, "Go. Now. I'll block for you."

Warning flared in Anaya's rich brown eyes, her long black hair fluttering in the fierce wind roaring through the peaks. A test of trust.

Selina only held the other girl's gaze, steady and calm. "Now," she repeated as the four acolytes began to approach, smiling faintly.

Yeah, they'd try to spook them. Trip them.

With a shallow nod, Anaya sucked in a breath and launched into a sprint.

A blond acolyte moved first. Scooped up a small rock to throw, discreet and tiny enough to go unseen as her arm cocked back—

Selina grabbed another stone, slinging it out. Slamming right into the blonde's arm. Forcing her fingers to splay and drop the rock that had been aimed for Anaya.

Anaya hurtled down that narrow path. The acolyte from Serbia moved next. Lunging toward Anaya's path, to force her to dodge sideways, to lose traction.

Selina was on her before Anaya could register the movement.

The Serbian acolyte let out a grunt of pain as Selina stomped down on her foot. The acolyte's body arced downward, as if she'd grab her own foot, right into Selina's awaiting elbow.

She'd done the move a thousand times in the fighting rings. Always followed by her next move: locking the Serbian acolyte's arm and hurling her toward the other two approaching acolytes, as if they were no more than the ropes of the ring. Sending the three of them staggering back.

Selina didn't wait. Didn't give them a moment to recover as she whirled and ran.

Anaya soared through the mountain air, the breeze shoving her to the right—

But she landed, barely, and scrabbled her way onto the ledge, where Nyssa didn't so much as look at her.

No, because Nyssa was watching Selina as she thundered down the narrow path toward the ravine as the acolytes recovered enough to realize her plan and look for retaliation.

She didn't have as much space as Anaya had to make that jump. With the attack, she'd yielded twenty feet.

But Selina raced onward, the ledge nearing, the drop beyond beckoning.

Pain flared on the side of her head, a starburst of agony. She stumbled a step but kept going, kept going as more hurled rocks landed behind her. She didn't care where the other acolytes had come from, but she knew where she'd been born. Where she'd been raised.

She wondered if the others knew, if Nyssa knew, that the pain was secondary. The pain was an old friend. Introduced long before those fights, before the Leopards. Introduced courtesy of her mother.

So the blow to the head did not stop her. It had never stopped her, that kind of pain.

And as Selina cleared the ledge and leapt, throwing herself a bit farther left to account for the gusting of the wind, she only heard the screaming air and the roughness of her breathing, only felt the bitter cold and the warmth of the blood trickling down the side of her face.

The opposite ledge was too far. Still too far.

Every nerve in her body came screaming awake as she slammed into the edge of the cliff, half on, half off. Gravity hauling her down—

Anaya lunged for her, but Nyssa held out an arm. Blocking her path.

Selina's nails broke and screamed in agony as she dug them into the rock.

But where Nyssa had refused to help, Nature threw her a bone.

A rise in the stone with enough of a jutting lip that her hands latched on. And held.

And held.

Nyssa made no move to help Selina as she hauled herself up, arms trembling, head pounding.

And when Selina at last had solid ground beneath her, when her temple was dripping blood onto the gray stone as she crawled, panting, from the ledge toward Nyssa, she looked up at her instructor.

Nyssa glanced between her and Anaya.

And Selina could do nothing as Nyssa shoved Anaya over the cliff edge.

Anaya did not scream. There was only silence. And then a thud that echoed over the granite peaks.

Selina couldn't move. Couldn't do anything other than stare at Nyssa, her dark eyes so cold.

Nyssa offered no explanation.

None.

Selina cleared the leap between buildings, claws finding purchase in the stone. Metal shrieked and sparked in their wake.

But she didn't hear the thud of her body on the metal roof. She heard that thump and crack of Anaya on the ravine floor. And the police sirens were little more than the howling wind through the Dolomites.

She uncurled to her feet and looked back toward where Ivy watched, head angled. "Not bad for a cat," Ivy called.

Selina just blew the dust off her claws.

She'd added them to her gloves after she'd returned to the League compound and had the blow to her head cleared by the physician. She'd gone right down to the lab, head still throbbing, insides still utterly numb and quiet, and helped herself to the assortment of blades and metals in the room. Left there for acolytes to tinker with.

Selina had selected the hardest steel she could find, and began to work.

Selina gestured to Ivy, reining in the thrill coursing through her. "Head down, limbs in as tight as you can get—"

But Ivy backed away a step, surprise and fear lighting her face. Selina whirled, hand going to her bullwhip.

Leaning against the roof doorway behind her, cloaked in shadows . . .

Selina smiled beneath her mask.

Ivy called from across the way, "Keep the painting." She pointed to the man waiting behind Selina. "Good luck dealing with him . . . cat-woman."

Then Ivy was gone. Running for the door that would lead her down through the building.

Selina's Death Mask sized up the male before her.

Six-three. Jacked. Or at least his bluish-gray metal suit was.

And glowing across his broad chest, an emblem in the darkness . . .

A bat.

Selina inclined her head in greeting. "I was wondering when you'd show up, Batwing."

CHAPTER 10

Luke observed the woman standing before him.

Head-to-toe black suit, made from some high-tech material. Confident, athletic, skilled.

And with the helmet on . . .

Cat-woman was a good way to describe her. The ears on the dark helmet, the oversized lenses, the claws that she'd just retracted after that spectacular jump . . . Even her steps toward him oozed feline grace.

The bullwhip, however, promised pain.

She was highly trained. He'd realized it from that jump, from what he'd seen when she escaped the museum guards with Poison Ivy. *That* was a pairing that made him wince. This stranger before him was bold. Fearless. Utterly unruffled by his appearance as he pushed off the wall and they stopped perhaps ten feet from each other.

The thief he'd been hunting for.

"Return the painting." He pointed to the small satchel at her right hip.

"Say 'please,'" she crooned, that helmet of hers making her voice low, raspy.

His suit fed him the details: *her* suit was equipped with surprises. But cloaked—as if the material itself was built to avoid scanning. A stealth suit.

Only the bullwhip was made of natural materials, unequipped with anything but what met the eye.

A signature weapon, no doubt. Definitely no signs of any affiliation with Gotham City's criminal organizations.

Luke braced his feet slightly farther apart, centering his weight better, before he demanded, "What's your name?"

Her head angled. She remained silent.

"You clearly know mine," he said, adding a hint of charm to the words. "I should know yours."

She was slender but stood with a sturdiness that spoke of iron-hard muscle beneath. She'd made the jump without any assistance from her suit beyond those claws.

Metal-shredding claws. God.

"Let's use Ivy's little nickname," she drawled, and Luke could have sworn he heard laughter in her voice. "Every good criminal in Gotham has a call sign. Let's add this one to the mix." She examined her claws as if she were looking over a manicure, her bullwhip swaying in the wind. "Catwoman. Has a nice ring to it."

"Give back the painting."

She patted the satchel at her side, then asked, "Where'd you come up with *Batwing*? Was it because *Batman* was already taken?"

"This can go one of two ways. Either you—"

"Give back the painting right now, or you take it from me?"

A sound that might have been a click of the tongue. "Isn't it wrong for a big, tough man to threaten to hurt a woman?"

Holy hell. "I think you lost the right to ask that question when you took the painting."

"A girl has got to eat."

"Find another profession."

She stalked toward him, a few steps. Certainly closer than most of Gotham City's worst dared get. Close enough for him to make a grab for that satchel if he could brave the reach of the bullwhip.

Exactly why she did it. A taunt.

"If you want stealth," she observed mildly, "then that night-light on your chest isn't very helpful."

Luke ground his teeth, the sound amplified in his helmet. "It's a symbol."

With every word, he sized her up, calculating the space of the roof, the way he'd seen her move, the weight of the painting in that bag.

"And symbols have power," she recited. "I forgot how boring you self-righteous do-gooders can be."

Luke released a slow breath, counting backward from ten. Temper. His temper was his downfall, Bruce had said. Controlling it was key.

Well, Bruce wasn't here.

As she stretched out her free hand and touched the tip of a claw to the center of the glowing bat-symbol on his chest, Luke lunged.

Or he tried to.

He'd aimed for her arm, intending to whirl her around and pin her to the brick facade of the doorway into the building below. But her arm wasn't there.

Fast. She was so fast. And she let her arm and the bullwhip be a distraction while she swept her leg.

The world tilted—

Luke hit the roof but rose instantly—

Metal on metal clanged through his head, the night.

A one-two combination right to his face, those claws now retracted. His head snapped back, and he managed to throw all of one jab before—

She used the same maneuver he'd intended for her. Grabbed his outstretched arm, locking it, and *slammed* him to the ground.

His suit cushioned much of the blow, but however he'd anticipated this night ending, it hadn't been like this. Knocked on his ass.

He surged upward, his suit sending him a whirl of analytics on her technique, her calculated moves based on what it had already observed.

But she was gone.

No, not gone. She'd moved to the corner of the roof. And was now peeling from a pole what looked to be a *camera*—

She wouldn't dare. She wouldn't have *dared* to record this encounter.

But the stranger, this Catwoman, lifted the camera in salute as she leapt over the edge of the roof.

By the time Luke had scrambled for it, ego smarting more than his body, she was gone.

The next morning, however, proved that the video footage was not.

Striding into the gym at dawn and surveying the neat piles of newspapers along the greeting counter, Luke scowled at the headline blaring above the photo on the front page.

When the Bat's Away, the Cat Will Play

And there he was—or Batwing was. The shot, he would admit, was brilliant. She'd likely picked a frame from her footage.

The photo showed him in the middle of falling, Catwoman's body the portrait of conquering queen as she sent him to the ground.

Luke swiped up the newspaper and chucked it into the gym trash bin to land among empty cups of water and cleaning wipes.

Not good. Not good at all.

The message it would send to the other criminals in Gotham City was precisely why she'd leaked the photos.

Luke knew it'd be futile to go to the newspaper to ask who'd sent them. They had an anonymous tip line. And they had clearly struck gold last night. No way they would reveal their source. Even if they could.

Luke stepped onto a treadmill, punching it up to a flat-out run.

He had to get her under control—and fast.

Before the underworld of Gotham City started to stir.

CHAPTER 11

Selina didn't mind the name: Catwoman.

And the papers seemed to adore it, too, granting her the front-page banner.

She was still smiling about it two nights later, especially the little tidbit about how the Fox heir had lost his painting. Maybe she'd swing by her neighbor's apartment later to see how he was coping with the loss.

After she completed this job, of course. She'd nearly finished hacking into the cavernous jewelry store's security system to reroute the video cameras to play the same footage on a loop.

If only her old social workers could see her now: a different sort of poster girl for the efficacy of Gotham City's At-Risk Youth Program.

Selina's smile faded as she stood in the small security office in the back of the enormous, multilevel store that occupied half a city block, the alarms disabled courtesy of a few careful snips from her tiny wire cutters.

A broken system—that's what it was. What it had always been. Maggie had only gotten out because of whatever strings or cash Talia had handed over that night. How many other kids never got that chance?

Too many. Too damn many. And while the wealthy in this city swathed themselves in jewels and cloistered themselves in penthouses that looked down upon those very slums, kids like Maggie went to school hungry, wore secondhand clothing, and knew, deep down, that no one was coming to help them.

These are the things that you might change, Talia had told her during her weekly one-on-one sessions with each acolyte. *What you will return to upend.*

And so she had.

Not a whisper of trouble arose while Selina prowled over the shining gray floors of the dark store, passing beneath the crystal chandeliers dangling from the arched ceilings, and headed down a level into the fairly plain catacombs below.

Navigating the warren of halls was easy; she only had to follow the path of the heavy, grated metal doors.

But even mapping out her plan mentally didn't prepare her for the sheer *size* of the vault as she passed through the last of the metal doors and into the small chamber where it lay. The sole occupant of the room.

Hands on her hips, Selina surveyed the sealed vault set into a solid wall of concrete, the puzzle before her.

Try it, it seemed to whisper. As if some great, sleeping dragon lay curled behind the vault. *See if you dare.*

The low hum that had been coursing through her veins earlier turned into a full-throttle electric current.

The store had been smarter than the museum about keeping its blueprints and receipts off any kind of database. Holly Vanderhees, of course, had visited this store only yesterday afternoon, but asking too many questions about the vault would have led a trail of bread crumbs right back to her. Which meant going into this robbery more blind than she'd like, but that was part of the thrill—this moment of finding a way in. Outsmarting them. As she had from those initial years in the East End.

Selina studied the looming vault, studied the solid wall of concrete it had been built into, an empty duffel bag dangling from her hand.

"I'm going to do you a favor and avoid a joke about the cat being out of the bag," Ivy drawled from behind.

Selina arched a brow beneath her Death Mask. "Following me?"

Ivy smirked as she approached, clad in the same getup as the other night. "I want my twenty-five percent."

"You'll get it when the painting goes to market," Selina said, turning back toward her metal opponent. "Give it a week or two."

"Nice spread in the morning paper," Ivy said, coming to survey the vault at Selina's side. "You didn't seem the type to self-promote."

Selina closed the distance to the vault and ran a gloved hand over the smooth metal of the door. Diamond-brushed steel. At least six inches thick. "The media is just another weapon to wield," she murmured. They certainly hadn't asked questions when an anonymous email account had sent the footage of Batwing being laid out flat on a rooftop *and* losing the priceless painting in the process.

Ivy hummed. "I'm sure Batwing's humiliation was just a pleasant side effect."

Selina gave Ivy a sidelong glance, though the woman couldn't see it with the helmet on. "It was."

Selina didn't tell her that it was the message to *other* criminals that had mattered. The invitation. Instead, she asked drily, "Why, exactly, are you here?"

Ivy tapped a gloved hand—one that truly seemed wrapped in *vines*, not cloth—on the brushed metal of the vault. "I want in."

"I work alone." Selina set her small bag on the floor, crouching to open it and yank out a tiny electromagnetic pulse machine. She'd built it herself in one of the League's labs—had designed it to be tiny enough to haul with her.

She'd never tested it in the wild, though.

Ivy leaned against the wall beside the vault, examining what appeared to be a small pink flower growing out of the material of her glove. Interesting. "Think about it: we team up, split the profits, and take on Gotham City's finest."

"You ran when you saw one of Gotham City's finest." Selina positioned the black rectangular box of the pulse machine by the vault door.

"How was I to know you'd hand his ass to him?"

"So his suit filters out your plants' chemicals, then."

"Let's just say that I make a point to stay out of his way." Ivy waved a hand. "You, though . . . Think of what we could accomplish together."

"What's in it for me?"

"You'd have someone guarding your back. We could hit up bigger targets. Make more."

"To fund your eco-terrorism plans to save the trees."

"To help put an *end* to the destruction before it's too late, before this planet is nothing but a wasteland. Do you know that both our state *and* federal government have an overwhelming majority of people working there who believe climate change is a hoax?"

"And you think attacking them is going to change that?"

"They can't vote to defund agencies and open up pipelines if they're not around to do it."

Selina frowned up at Ivy. "Or you could make martyrs of them."

Ivy's mouth tightened, her flowers winking out. "They've already done enough damage to the earth that there might not even be a chance to turn back. Entire ecosystems—*gone*. Who fights for them? Who makes sure that they get justice?"

The same could be said of people, children especially, in the East End.

Selina made a show of considering. "It seems like *you* benefit more from being around me than I do with you."

A flash of irritation. "I'm making you an honest offer. Less risks involved in these robberies when you can just gas the place instead of bringing the guards down."

"Then why don't I just get myself some canisters of it?" Selina stepped back from the electromagnetic pulse charger.

"Because they don't sell my special blend at the store, honey."

"Oh?"

Ivy smiled down at the vines encasing her hands, and without so much as a flicker of movement, they slithered up her wrists.

Selina blinked. Once. Twice.

"My toxins are organic compounds," Ivy explained. "All plant-based, hybridized, and weaponized. Made by yours truly in my lab." She pulled what looked to be a pink orchid from a pocket. "A signal from me, and this beauty will send you right to sleep."

Well, damn. Selina gave herself a moment to stifle any hint of awe in her voice before she said, "I heard a rumor that you didn't need to bother with fancy flowers. That you can emit those toxins on your own."

Ivy was quiet for a heartbeat as she pocketed the flower once more.

Then a pale emerald smoke began to drift from her—as if it leaked from every pore. It slithered and floated into the air, wending around Selina. "A friend thought throwing flowers might be a cool touch," Ivy said as that green mist swirled between them. "But I like to do it the old-fashioned way every now and then."

Selina reined in a curse. How Ivy had done it, why she'd done it—this wasn't the time for those questions. Or the right place. "It sounds like I'll never be able to take off this helmet with you, then. Not exactly an ideal working relationship."

Silence. Ivy's smoke faded as quickly as it had come.

Beneath her Death Mask, Selina smiled. And let Ivy work for it a little more as the woman went on, "There's never been a duo of ladies to take on Gotham City. All the bosses are male."

"That makes it sound like they'd want to put us down the moment we step onto their turf."

"You beat the shit out of Batwing." Those vines slithered down Ivy's wrists to wrap around her hands again, as tight as any glove. "They might think twice."

Selina again made a show of considering, fingers hovering over the dials on the machine's top. "All right," she said slowly, and Ivy grinned. "But I want one more member."

Ivy's deep red brows rose.

"I want Harley Quinn." Selina hit the button, a low electric hum surging through the room, hollowing out her ears, even with the suit. Metal groaned.

Ivy's pale face went even whiter. "Why?"

Selina set down the control box and strode over to the now-ajar vault door. "Because we won't last long without her."

The flowers on Ivy's living gloves snapped shut again. "Harley can be . . . unstable."

Selina hauled open the vault door, revealing stacks and stacks of cash. Beautiful. "Harley is not only daring when it comes to tactics, but she's also skilled with firearms and explosives."

"I know," Ivy said quietly.

Selina pretended not to have anticipated that softness in her voice. "But what Harley *also* offers is her relationship history."

Ivy's eyes turned to chips of ice. "You mean the Joker."

Selina began dropping stacks of cash into her open bag and asked innocently, "Is there someone else?"

"No." Ivy added tightly, "But he's locked up for life in Arkham."

"Along with some of his most notorious cronies."

Ivy stormed up to her side as Selina kept depositing stacks of cash in the bag. "You're out of your mind if you're thinking of tangling with the Joker—"

"I'll be tangling with Harley. And her status as the Joker's main squeeze"—again that ripple of cold anger on Ivy's face, the tightening of those vines on her hands, perhaps to the point of pain—"will make any other criminals in this city think twice before crossing us. I don't have the time or interest in dealing with their petty bullshit."

Ivy blinked. But she began helping to haul stacks of cash into Selina's bag. After a moment, she said, "Harley's always game for a little anarchy."

"You know her personally, then?" A casual, calculated question. And a total lie. She'd read up on both of them—their fraught relationship, their history. More than friends, yet not. The particulars of it—who wanted something more than friendship and who didn't, whether Harley's former relationship with the Joker played a role in that—remained murky.

She doubted it was information either of them publicly shared. Knowing where to strike emotionally, what to manipulate, was another weapon in her arsenal. Especially when it came to assembling the team she needed. Despite Harley's history with the Joker, she operated on her own now. Ivy, too—precisely the sort of criminals she required.

Independent, unafraid. Why the League hadn't recruited them yet was beyond her.

"It's none of your business," Ivy grumbled. Exactly as Selina had predicted. Ivy scowled and went on. "Harley's been restless since Batman, Batwing, and all those other do-gooders threw half of Gotham's criminals behind bars." Including the Joker. "But she won't join our little crime ring without some sort of . . . enticement."

Selina knew that. Had anticipated that. Selina squeezed one last wad of cash into the bag before zipping it shut. She slid another bag toward Ivy in silent offer—it was hers to fill. "I'll make her an offer she can't refuse."

Ivy began filling her own duffel and asked tightly, "Which is?"

Selina slung the bag over her shoulder, letting her balance adjust to its weight. "I'll get the Joker out of Arkham."

A greenish pallor overtook Ivy's face, and Selina doubted it had anything to do with the fact that she was partially plant-based herself. "That's impossible."

"Some would have said making a fool of Batwing was impossible."

Ivy shoved cash into her duffel. "The Joker *needs* to stay behind bars." Selina could have sworn Ivy's hands trembled slightly. "His kind of anarchy isn't the kind that . . ." She shook her head, red hair flowing. "It's not the kind I like. Or want."

"He doesn't care about the trees?"

Ivy cut her a glare. "He's a bad man."

"People believe the same of us."

Another fierce shake of the head. "I want to *help* the planet. He . . ." She went back to shoving cash into her duffel. "There are no lines for him. He's soulless."

"Well, you'd better get off your high horse, because if you want a cut of the millions we stand to make"—Selina jostled her cash-heavy duffel for emphasis—"I'll only do it with Harley as our third."

Ivy stared her down for a moment. "Where did you even *come* from?"

A neighborhood two miles north. But Selina just shrugged and said, "Some might ask the same of you. You graduated from college at nineteen—just last year. A prodigy at botany, toxins, and biochemical engineering."

No pride in Ivy's face at the words. No shame, either. Just wariness.

So Selina asked, "Why'd you decide not to go to grad school?"

Ivy finished with her bag, zipped it up, and strode out. "Some things happened that made it impossible for me to go."

The icy, distant tone offered no space for questions.

Selina stepped out of the vault, listening for any signs of alarms, of the police. Nothing. She asked carefully, "How'd you get into science, anyway?"

Another hesitant pause. But then Ivy said, emerging from the vault, "My mom was a scientist. Dad, too. Before they both got offered mega jobs and fat paychecks by a drug company. Turns out their love of science was as shallow as the rest of them."

Wealthy, emotionally distant parents—how had they even produced someone as passionate as Ivy?

Together, Selina and Ivy stalked up the stairs, the bag of cash weighing heavily on Selina's back. "What sort of science did they study before they changed careers?"

"Plant regeneration. They met in the lab. Called me a lab baby thanks to it." A slight smile. "It was only a matter of time until the drug companies came sniffing. They sold their work to the highest bidder and never once looked back. At the science stuff or at me."

Selina could think of quite a few countries that might be interested in that sort of science, too. "I'm sorry." Brutal—no matter the training that had been instilled into her, it didn't lessen how hard it must have been, and still was, for Ivy.

Ivy shrugged, as if it could somehow erase the weight of her past. "My aunt basically raised me after they sold out. She encouraged me to take all the science classes that I wanted. But it got boring, even in college." A short pause, as if debating what to say. How much to say. Selina kept still and quiet, giving her space to decide. Ivy pulled out a flower—a yellow bloom this time—and studied it. "So my last semester in college, I signed up to work with a scientist on a more . . . radical experiment regarding the human connection to plants."

Selina had a horrible feeling she knew where this was headed.

Ivy pocketed the flower. "Turned out, *I* was the test subject." Her green eyes turned hard as stone. "To explore the possibility between human-plant hybrids."

"What happened?" Selina's question was a push of breath.

Ivy's smile turned a bit cruel. "*I* happened. And the lead scientists learned *exactly* what someone like me could do once they applied their *sciences* to my body. Their first and last successful experiment." Ivy studied the vines on her hands. "I realized soon afterward that as awful as it was, maybe it had happened for a reason. Maybe it had happened so I might use these . . . powers"—she stumbled over the word—"to help our planet. Try to right it from its current collision course."

Selina didn't shy from the mirror she now saw before her. Two clever young women, taken and molded into something else. Something worse.

But she wouldn't tell Ivy that. Not yet. Instead, Selina said, "So the life of crime beckoned."

"*Life* beckoned," countered Ivy, following Selina toward the back door she'd used to slip inside. "I was nineteen and had never gone to a party, had never kissed a girl I liked, had never done *anything*. And they had taken it all away from me."

Understandable. Completely understandable. Selina asked wryly, "And now you do all that?"

She heard, more than saw, Ivy smile. "Definitely the girl-kissing part."

Selina snickered. "Priorities."

She quietly shut the metal door as they stepped into the alley behind the behemoth store, the street in the heart of the shopping district near-silent on either end.

Ivy lifted a brow at the shut door. "You going to leave a calling card, or should I?"

Selina flicked out the claws on her glove.

Screeching metal and two slashes of her nails down the back door was her only answer. Claw marks.

Ivy studied Selina's handiwork. "Simple but efficient."

Selina sheathed her claws. Motion down the alley triggered her helmet's warning system, and she whirled—

Night-bright eyes, silent feet, an upright tail came into view around a sagging cardboard box. Ivy followed Selina's line of vision and snorted. "Relative of yours?"

Selina smiled beneath her helmet and crouched as the small alley cat approached, her gray coat blending into the shadows. Selina extended a gloved hand, and the cat sniffed at it, whiskers twitching.

"You're too thin, friend," she told the cat, ignoring Ivy's question, and scratched the cat under her little chin.

"I feel like I should be taking photos of this," Ivy said.

The cat pulled her face away, and Selina ran a hand down her slender spine, the cat arching into the touch. "I thought you loved animals."

"I do," Ivy said. "But I didn't expect *you* to."

The cat, satisfied by the attention, scampered off into the alley. Selina rose, watching the cat disappear into the darkness. "I always wanted a pet. Never had one."

"Why?"

She couldn't answer that. Not when it required explaining so much. Too much. Secrecy was vital, another weapon. Even among allies. "I moved around a lot. Was never settled enough to get one."

Not entirely a lie. But she'd had her hands full those years, and a pet, no matter how much Maggie had pleaded for a cat, was another mouth to feed. Vet bills could add up. It hadn't been responsible to get a pet. Still wasn't.

"We should go," Selina said, scanning the dark skies above. "I disabled the alarms, but someone might spot us."

Ivy pointed a thumb over her shoulder, down the alley. "I'm that way."

Selina lied and pointed with her chin in the other direction. "I'm that way."

Ivy nodded once. "How do I get in touch with you?"

"You've been stalking me for two nights. Seems like you have no problem finding me."

Ivy laughed again. "Use this number to give me a heads-up on your next target." She pulled a piece of paper from one of her bodysuit's pockets. "It's a burner phone, but I'll have it for a few more days."

Selina took the paper, gloves scratching. "Get Harley on board. Or don't bother to show up."

Ivy gave her a mocking salute and lifted her heavy bag. "Thanks for the payday."

Selina didn't leave until Ivy had vanished into the shadows, her steps fading away.

A long night ahead. And she was just getting started.

CHAPTER 12

Seated in bed, bracing for another sleepless night, Luke stared at his phone like it was about to bite him.

Bruce: *Everything all right over there?*

He'd seen the headline. Bruce might be on a vital mission, but there was no way he wasn't keeping tabs on his city. Their city.

Luke slid the phone over to himself, unplugging the charger, and typed back, *Nothing to worry about.*

He conveniently forgot to mention that tonight he'd found himself staring at two slash marks on a jewelry store door, the cache of money and jewels stolen. Wiped clean, except for some of the lesser-priced pieces. Someone with a discerning eye.

Or oversized lenses.

No one harmed, at least. But when the frantic store owner had seen the claw marks, he started shouting at him about why someone hadn't put a leash on this Catwoman.

Bruce's typing bubble popped up. *Let me know if you need anything.*

Luke wouldn't. Not just because Bruce was on a mission but because he wanted to handle this on his own.

He typed back. *Will do.*

Luke debated asking how the mission was going, but . . . he and Bruce had never really engaged in small talk. Hadn't been the sort of friends who watched a game together, though they certainly had shared a few drinks at various galas they were obligated to attend as sons of Gotham City.

Sometimes Luke felt as if they were both already old men. Weary and jaded and worn at the edges.

So Luke set down his phone, plugged it back in, and switched off the light.

The piece of art Catwoman had stolen was insured, but the fact that she'd not only evaded the trap he'd laid but had done it so publicly . . . He gritted his teeth.

He'd find another way to snare her. And learn who was beneath that helmet.

Selina bustled out of her apartment around eleven in the morning, as befitted someone with nothing to do with their time, the shopping bags dead weights in her hands. Considering that the shoe boxes stacked inside were full of cold, hard cash and jewelry, she was praying they didn't break on her way to her safe-deposit box at the bank.

The door across the way opened. Selina debated turning right back around and pretending to be coming *in*, when Luke Fox appeared.

She instantly settled into Holly's persona, tossing her hair over a shoulder. He was the portrait of casual, graceful money in his white fitted polo—immaculate above gray slacks. A pair of sunglasses shielded his eyes, but he politely lifted them atop his head as he surveyed the bags. "Coming in?"

Was that a note of hope she detected in his voice? To avoid riding in the elevator with her?

Selina gave him a simpering smile. "Going out," she clarified, lifting the bags, the tissue paper covering the boxes rustling. "Need to return and exchange a few things."

He gave her a look that said it seemed she had a *lot* of things to haul with her, not a few. But ever the gentleman, he asked, "Can I carry your bags to your car?"

She was tempted to say yes, because Holly certainly would, but if he was as smart as everyone claimed he was, then he'd no doubt realize that the weight of the bags didn't add up to a few pairs of shoes. "I've got it, thank you." She made a show of hefting the bags. "Good workout."

He gave her a bland smile before striding for the elevator, pushing the button in silence.

She followed him, trailing at a casual pace. "Are you going to the Save the Bees Gala tomorrow?" Seats started at ten grand a plate.

Luke glanced sidelong at her as the elevator shot up the building. "Maybe."

Oh, he *really* didn't like her. She gave him what she called her Holly Smile: coy, aware, self-obsessed. "And will you turn me down again if I ask you to dance?"

"Maybe."

"Is that the only word you know now? *Maybe?*"

Something close to humor danced in Luke's eyes as he met her gaze head-on and drawled, "Maybe."

Perhaps not as completely arrogant as she'd thought. Despite herself, Selina laughed quietly. Her fingers were starting to go numb from the weight of her bags, and she was grateful for the ding of the elevator as the doors opened and they strode in. She leaned against the railing, setting the bags down lightly—to avoid the clunk that was sure to sound if she dropped them.

"I heard about your painting being stolen," she said, unable to resist. "I'm sorry."

Luke slid his hands into his pockets. "It's fine. Worse things happen to people in this city every day."

She avoided the urge to blink. Definitely not the answer she'd expected.

"You were in the Army, right?" A vapid, light question, if only to get them back on equal footing.

And an entirely wrong question to ask, from the way his back stiffened. Sore subject, then.

But Luke said, "The Marines."

She batted her eyelashes. "Is there a difference?"

His jaw clenched. "Yeah. There is." She knew there was, and part of her writhed under the vapid, inane weight of being Holly.

They reached the basement, and Luke was truly enough of a gentleman to hold the elevator doors while she swept out, aiming for the black Mercedes her driver had left for the weekend. A click of her fob had the trunk opening, revealing a pristine interior.

Luke headed toward the gray Porsche beside her car. He paused as he opened the door, as if the manners drilled into him yanked on his leash. "Enjoy your shopping," he said tersely.

Selina waved a manicured hand. "Enjoy your . . . whatever you're doing."

He slid into his car. "Brunch with my parents. A Sunday tradition."

Another surprise: it didn't sound like a chore when he said it.

For a moment, she debated telling him that he was lucky—luckier than he knew—that he had parents who loved him, wanted to see him.

She debated scratching her key deep into the side of what was surely his beloved car, just for the fact that he *had* parents who gave a shit.

She hadn't bothered to look her mother up once. Didn't want to know. Even with the League's resources, she didn't want to know what her mom was doing. Where she was. If she was even alive.

And her father was a dead end. She sometimes wondered if he knew that he had a daughter. And if he did, would he even care?

At least Maggie was safe, cared for, in her new home in the suburbs. Even if all of this, what Selina was doing in Gotham City, meant that she had to stay far, far away from her sister.

It didn't make it any easier, though.

Pathetic. She was absolutely pathetic for thinking such things. For that quiet, distant ache that still lurked deep in her chest. For the rage that made her want to put on her League gloves, flick open those claws, and start shredding.

Luke turned on the car, its thunderous roar filling the garage. It sounded an awful lot like the bellowing in her head.

Selina kept her face neutral as she slid into her own front seat and found him waiting. Stalling.

It took her a moment to realize Luke was waiting for her to leave. To make sure she got out of the garage safely.

A bit of an arrogant rich kid, but still a gentleman. She gave him another inane wriggle of her manicured fingers before backing out of the spot. Carefully—like how a rich woman unused to driving herself might maneuver the vehicle.

Not the graceful swoop her muscles screamed at her to do. The driving lessons on the deadly S curves of Italian roads had been one of Selina's favorite parts of training at the League.

She inched along, out of the garage, Luke finally pulling his Porsche out to follow. He rode on her tail, as if he could barely keep the car from containing its impatience.

She debated letting her own vehicle roll back to tap his as she ascended the ramp onto the busy, sunny street, but it'd mean a delay in getting the money to the bank, *and* the possibility of getting her trunk opened up.

So she merely turned right while he went left, watching him vanish around a corner in her side-view mirror.

Perhaps she'd have to do something about him. Make sure his apartment became *unavailable* to him. Because having someone around asking questions, especially if he was a trained Marine, was not good.

She'd think about that later.

The alley in the Coventry district that night was quiet. Secure.

Selina had arrived early to ensure that. She'd bought her own burner phone today to contact Ivy, giving her the time and place. Nothing more.

Gotham City was stirring again. The rich were uneasy and the underworld was sitting up, paying attention.

Look. Look how easy it is, she'd been purring to them these two weeks, with each robbery. *While you cower and run, look how I make out.*

Her plan was coming together. Not as fast as she wanted, as she needed, but . . . it was weaving together. Talia would be proud. Perhaps even Nyssa. In the muted, cold way both of them expressed such things.

She'd often wondered whether the sisters had been born that way or if they'd had all traces of warmth and humanity trained out of them.

Footsteps sounded down the alley.

Selina's helmet scanned the approaching person and found nothing.

She could see the female figure slipping from the darkness, but the suit's normal feed of intel provided her with more: heart rate, height, weapons . . . nothing.

And Selina knew. Before the woman fully emerged into the dim light of the alley, Selina knew that it was not Harley or Ivy.

But a wraith.

A ghūl.

Sent from the dark heart of the League of Assassins to kill her.

CHAPTER 13

———

Shrike.

Selina had not seen the assassin in months. Nyssa and Talia had dispatched Shrike to Tokyo for an assignment, and Selina had deemed it a small mercy.

As the small-boned, beautiful woman prowled out of the shadows, clad in black and her own Death Mask, Selina remembered why.

She wasn't holding guns—no, that wasn't Shrike's preferred way to kill. Shrike enjoyed causing pain. Savored it. A sadist with a dagger in each hand.

That was how one of Nyssa's most notorious assassins liked to end her targets. Slow, deep cutting. Carving you up.

Selina had been granted the pleasure of being Shrike's target practice more than once. Of being cornered in a shadowed hallway of the compound and feeling that knife in the assassin's right hand press into her throat as Shrike had purred in her ear, *Where are your claws now, kitten?*

Shrike paused about twenty feet away. Selina flicked her wrists, claws sliding free, trying and failing to master her thundering heart. Knowing Shrike could detect every frantic beat.

Shrike's battle-suit had been modified to fit an assortment of daggers. Her Death Mask helmet was painted with strokes of bone white, which looked like nothing up close, but from where Selina stood . . . they formed the face of a skull.

Selina calmed her breathing. Took in every bit of the alley: the brick walls, the dumpster to her right, the trash piles, the doors and lights.

She waited for some explanation for why Shrike was here.

Why those knives were out.

Shrike offered nothing.

Absolutely nothing as she hurled one of her daggers right at Selina.

Selina ducked, rolling to the side, already avoiding Shrike's countermove: the second knife that the assassin sent her way, anticipating Selina's dive to the right. But Shrike didn't foresee the dumpster that Selina slid behind. The dagger clanked against its side, burying itself deep.

Selina had three heartbeats to unsheathe the twin short swords artfully hidden in the back of her suit. Standard for all League suits. The bullwhip would do nothing against someone with Shrike's training—not unless Selina wanted it chopped into pieces.

Sucking in a breath, Selina whirled from behind the dumpster just in time to catch the glint of a third dagger. A swing of one of her blades had the dagger skittering to the side, the reverberations biting through her skin, even with her gloves.

Then Shrike was there, two longer daggers in hand. Slashing low and high.

Selina parried one, met the other.

A twist of Shrike's foot and it was hooked behind Selina's knee. Selina spun out of the way, using the momentum of her fall to avoid being gutted by Shrike's left dagger.

Not fast enough.

Metal screamed, and Selina yanked her head back, narrowly missing Shrike's blade as it instead carved a line down her helmet. Glass splintered in her left lens. Another strike and it'd go right through.

Selina swept with her blade for Shrike's back, but the assassin turned with her, fast as an asp.

Calm. Fear will get you killed. Calm your breathing, your heart.

Nyssa's lessons whispered through her mind. But there was no way to catch her breath as Shrike unleashed herself upon Selina, landing blow after blow onto her swords.

Forced to retreat, Selina knew she was being herded to wherever Shrike wanted her, had assessed for herself what would be the prime place to end her.

Her helmet's left lens was cracked enough that the vision in that eye was worthless. She might as well be fighting with the eye closed.

Shrike used that weakness to her advantage. Kept her blows coming from the left, in Selina's blind spot, then switching to the right, knowing her concentration lingered on the opposite side.

They danced through the alley, steel striking. The longer it went on, the less likely her chance of walking out of this. And Selina had come home, she'd come to this city to *do* something, and if she failed—

Shrike got past her guard.

A shallow swipe of a dagger to her thigh had Selina going down. She swallowed her scream, knowing it would draw the wrong attention. But as she hit the filthy asphalt, warm blood leaking through where even the suit's protective material hadn't held up to those daggers, Shrike began her death blow.

One dagger, poised to slam right through that broken eye piece and into Selina's skull beneath.

A crack boomed through the alley.

It was near deafening with her audio receptors turned high. Louder than thunder.

One moment, Shrike was lunging for her face.

The next moment, Shrike was on the ground.

That skull helmet shattered. Blood splattered on the shards.

A large ax lay on the ground nearby. A perfect throw.

And as pieces of the helmet fell away, revealing the pale-skinned, dark-haired Russian woman beneath . . . Shrike's face was the portrait of surprise.

Selina wiped the blood off the lenses of her helmet as she looked up to the building flanking the alley.

A ghostly white, platinum-blond woman peered down at her, leaning against another enormous ax, a braid sliding over the shoulder of her two-tone motorcycle jacket.

Ivy appeared at her side and cringed at the carnage.

"Catfight?" was all Harley Quinn said as she grinned at Selina.

In this hellhole part of town, the loud thunk of Harley's ax against metal wouldn't trigger any calls to the cops—or anyone snooping around. Which was partially why Selina had picked this place to meet, but now, with Shrike's cooling corpse leaking blood into the pavement, they needed a change of plans.

Through the one good lens of her helmet, Selina monitored Ivy and Harley's approach. The former was in her usual green bodysuit, the top buttons of her collar open to reveal green whorls and swirls of some tattoo beneath.

Harley strode up with hair in twin braids down to her chest, one side's tip dyed blue-black, the other cherry-red. Matching her motorcycle jacket. The ax was strapped across her back, shifting with each step, its clacking against the bandolier of knives across her chest barely audible over the thud of Harley's black combat boots. A throwing knife was strapped to her muscled thigh, over worn black jeans, and a third was definitely holstered beneath her jacket, judging by the way the fabric bunched.

"Friend of yours?" Harley asked with a raised brow as she and Ivy halted a few feet away. She studied Shrike, the face forever etched in shock.

No. Never.

"Good throw" was all Selina said, grateful for the voice-modifier of the mask. The way it hid the slight tremor as she saw, over and over, Shrike's head crack apart like a melon.

Selina pushed the image down, shoved it into a box.

Harley didn't pick up the discarded ax lying nearby. Instead, she sized her up, and Selina pretended to do the same. She'd learned enough about Harley to know who she was dealing with. That her aim just now hadn't been accidental, and she'd likely walk out of this alley utterly unfazed by Shrike's demise.

"My girl Ivy said you requested my services?" Though Harley's voice was sweet, almost childlike, the gleam in her sapphire eyes . . . anything but.

Another one of the girls who this city had made grow up too fast, too hard. Only Harley hadn't found the Leopards. No, she'd found the Joker and his merry band of psychopaths.

Selina leaned against the wall, ignoring the blood on it, and crossed her arms. "I heard you were a free agent now. We need a third to fill out our little group."

Harley glanced between Ivy and Selina, the former still grimacing at Shrike's body. "To do what?"

Selina ticked the items off on a gloved hand. "Robbery, mayhem, notoriety . . . What else could a girl want?"

Harley tossed the black-tipped braid over her shoulder. "Ivy said you could get the Joker out of Arkham."

The thought of that man being loose made her want to puke, but Selina shrugged. "What about it?"

Harley took two stalking steps closer, Ivy on her heels, wide eyes darting between them. Fear for Harley's safety or fear of this little cadre falling apart? "How are you going to get him out?" Harley's makeup was too light for her skin tone, her eyeliner too heavy. It made her look ill—macabre.

Selina pushed off the wall. She'd dealt with enough questioning these past few years. Her entire life. She certainly wasn't going to let Harley Quinn start doing it. "Are you in, or out?"

"How are you going to get *him* out?"

As she stepped over Shrike's body, Selina was grateful for the helmet covering her face. "When the time is right, Quinn, I'll tell you."

A hiss. "You think I'm just going to say okay based on that?"

Ivy cut in. "I've seen her in action, Harley. If she says she can, she can." She again glanced to Shrike.

A slight tremor shook Ivy's hands as she brushed her red hair back.

She'd stood there beside Harley just now. Watched Harley hurl that ax with deadly accuracy.

Ivy asked, her voice thick, "Who was she?"

Selina glanced over a shoulder at Shrike and cringed at the pool of blood that was slowly spreading. "I don't know," she half lied. She knew who Shrike was, but the things that mattered, the *vital* things . . . Selina didn't know them. Only Talia and Nyssa did.

They locked up the secrets and truths about their cabal of assassins as if they were jewels. More valuable than jewels.

Selina faced them once more, bracing her hands on her hips, and asked Harley with as much cool bravado as she could muster, "Don't you want your own mountain of cash to sit on when your sweet ex-boyfriend gets out? To know you don't have to answer to him—to anyone?"

Harley's eyes flashed. "You got something to say about my ex?"

Selina rolled her eyes beneath her helmet. "It never hurts to have financial independence. Surely you got into this lifestyle because you wanted something similar."

"I got into this *lifestyle*, kitty, because it was freedom from *everything*."

"Is that what they're calling anarchy these days?"

Ivy casually stepped between them. "It'll be fun, Harley," she said with a charming grin. "I need the cash, even if you don't. Think of all the rain forests I could save."

Some edge in Harley's eyes soothed at Ivy's teasing words. An answering smile tugged on Harley's mouth, but she turned to Selina. "You drag me along, you back out of your promises, and I'll make what I did to her"—a nod toward Shrike's body—"seem like heaven compared to the hell I unleash on you."

Yeah, yeah, yeah. Selina snorted. "Fine." She turned, walking toward the alley exit.

"That's it?" Harley demanded. "You haul us here for that?"

"Yes," Selina said without looking back. "I'll provide our targets and meeting spots the morning of." She waved a hand over her shoulder. "Come dressed to impress."

Harley let out a low growl. "Who does she think she is, coming to *my* town—"

"You are exactly where I was a few nights ago," Ivy said with a low laugh as Selina continued out of the alley. "Trust me: the feeling passes."

"You said that the last time we got dollar tacos."

Selina bit down on her laugh as she kept walking away, though Ivy didn't. "I'll never live that down, will I?"

"Never. Not even when we're little old ladies knitting on a porch."

By the time Selina reached the alley exit, their voices had dropped to murmuring. Gentle, sweet words passing between them.

Loving words.

Tiny, pale flowers bloomed in Ivy's hair like fallen stars.

Tucking that tidbit aside, Selina vanished into the shadows.

There was no sign of her. Two hours out here, and there was no sign of her.

Luke couldn't tell if that was a good or bad thing. He racked his brain for any sort of alternative for where she might be, but with a city this big . . . she could be anywhere.

His night had been nice enough before now. He'd gone to dinner with Elise and Mark, who bickered with each other the entire time, when they weren't asking him about his work at Wayne Industries. He'd even managed to get to his boxing gym for a few hours before that, to spar with an up-and-coming middleweight who needed some seasoning.

He loved the gym, especially its outreach to at-risk teens in this city. His mom oversaw the charity that funded it, and she sometimes even jumped into the ring herself for a few practice sessions.

He often wondered if the joy in her eyes when she did it was the same in his own. Whether she might have held her own in the ring if she'd been given the right training when she was young. His temper, his focus, that driving thrum in his blood that pushed and pushed him . . . all of that came from her.

There were other vets at the training hall. One was an Army captain who attended his group therapy session. Luke never mentioned therapy at training, and she never really talked to him beyond a quick hello and a nod, but it was nice to see familiar faces from the other parts of his life. Beyond the prep schools and galas. The military had been full of people from all backgrounds and walks of life. He was still getting reacclimated to how little variety existed in the upper echelons of Gotham City.

Overseas, they'd been too busy fulfilling commands and working their asses off to protect this country to bother with caring about where someone came from. What had mattered was whether the person next to you had your back when it counted. He'd only met a few people in this city of whom he could say the same.

He and his mom had been talking for months now about doing an outreach program for vets at the gym. She was already taking meetings with therapists, vets, and boxing pros about how to make it work. And taking meetings with investors and government officials for how to get funding. Of course, his family could fund it indefinitely, but his mom savored this: wrangling companies that made ungodly profits to do something in turn for the community. Getting people involved and caring.

Standing atop a three-story building at the edge of the dark, glittering band of the Gotham River, dawn still hours away, Luke rotated his shoulders, keeping loose, limber. He was about to turn away from the water, the glowing city around him, when motion caught his eye.

Not who he was looking for, but . . . Luke smiled.

"Dumping a body in the river. Real original."

The three men whirled as Luke sauntered up behind them, the body landing with a splash off the rotting docks.

His suit had a video camera, and he made sure it was recording, marking their faces, the van that they had just driven up, even the body now bobbing in the river.

"Should have weighed that package down," Luke supplied, stalking closer.

Two of the men pulled guns and fired.

The sound ripped at him, trying to haul him back into his memories, but Luke focused on his breathing, the shift of his body as he rolled to the side, the docks groaning beneath him.

Clumsy, panicked shots. They fired and fired, and Luke's suit whirred and then pulsed. A wave of ear-ringing sound rippled out.

The sonic pulse stopped the bullets dead. The men fired again, though their bullets fell to the wood, pinging and thudding against the force of the sonic waves. They emptied their clips within seconds.

Then silence.

The third man—the one who hadn't fired—leapt into the river. Trying to swim away.

Luke smirked as he got to his feet. Surveyed the two men now clicking away on the triggers of their Glocks. The bat-symbol on his suit flared, primed and ready to unleash more surprises.

"This really isn't going to be your night" was all Luke told them.

Twenty minutes later, Luke lurked at the edge of the pedestrian overpass, watching as Gordon and his men hauled away the three low-level cronies, including the soaked one.

He'd had them tied up in five minutes.

Less than five minutes. He'd waited longer than that for GCPD to arrive, making sure the murderers didn't escape their bonds.

As soon as Gordon shoved the last of them into the police van, slamming shut the door, Luke loosed a long sigh and turned.

And found the so-called Catwoman leaning against the opposite railing of the bridge.

CHAPTER 14

———————

Her figure cut a dark shadow against the railroad tracks illuminated below.

His helmet's night vision told a different story. A cracked lens now marred the left side of her helmet. And blood. Even with her suit's stealth keeping him from any further readouts, there was no mistaking the organic material splattered over her helmet, her chest and shoulders.

Yet she appeared steady. Unfazed.

"Are you responsible for the body they were dumping?" His words were low—rough. He sized up the weapons on her: two blades sheathed down her back, built right into her suit. That bull-whip at her left hip. Nothing else.

She let out a quiet laugh. "No. Whose men are those?"

None of her business. "Why are you here?"

"I thought you might be bored, so I came to say hello."

Luke couldn't help but make the analogy: a cat playing with its dinner.

"Why is there blood on your suit?"

"Want a DNA sample?"

Yes. He hadn't gotten a call from GCPD that anything was amiss, that anyone was down. "You came to brag about it?"

"I came to give you a little warning."

Luke kept his arms at his sides, in easy reach of his weapons, even though he had the urge to cross them. "About what?" he ground out.

She was so still. It was an animal's stillness. Even Bruce, trained and lethal, never stood with that sort of stillness. Like she might blend into a shadow and never emerge.

"Far bigger players are coming to Gotham."

A chill skittered down his spine. "Is that who landed a punch tonight?" As he said it, his suit zoomed in on the damaged helmet, lighting it up. A long, wicked-looking scratch sliced down one side of it, straight through the cracked glass. That had to have been made by one hell of a blade. And a shallow wound sliced across her thigh, the blood caked on too thick to get a glimpse at the skin color beneath.

She gave a little nod. "More are coming."

"At your invitation?"

A pause. "More are coming," she repeated. "Worse than any of the criminal factions here. More powerful—and with a deadlier agenda. Keep your eyes open."

"Why warn me?" he demanded.

That stillness settled over her again. "Because this city won't survive them."

"And that's not what you want?"

She looked him over. Or he thought she did. "There are good people in Gotham. Protect them."

It surprised him enough that Luke couldn't think of a reply. Didn't need to.

Because one of the cop cars still parked at the docks below exploded, the boom and fire and shouting filling the world.

And then he wasn't in his body, wasn't on that footbridge anymore.

He was in sand and sun and blood; he was on the side of a road. He was cut up, body screaming, but not as loud as his men, his friends—

He had the dim sense of slamming to the ground. Of being unable to breathe, of his suit going haywire and sending a frantic feed of internal assessments: heart rate too fast, breathing rapid, blood pressure spiking—

Not here. Not here and now.

"That asshole," he heard someone—heard *her*—hiss. In another world, in another life.

He had to move, had to get up, had to get air into his lungs—

"You're not hurt." A quiet observation.

He reached for the overpass railing to pull himself up. Tried and failed, his hands shaking so hard that even his suit couldn't stabilize them.

He hadn't had a reaction like this in months, and the last time, Bruce had been there to help get him away, but now—

A different matte-black helmet filled his vision. Lifted his head for him.

It wasn't a real face. Wasn't human. As inhuman as the people who'd set that roadside bomb—

The lenses slid upward into her helmet, revealing a pair of shadowed emerald eyes. Bright. Steady. Human.

"A car exploded," she explained calmly. "A device set off by Harley Quinn."

He knew that name. In his other life, new life, beyond the desert, he knew that name.

"It was a message—to me. The car was empty; the cops aren't hurt."

Cops. Harley.

She scanned his face, the helmet he himself wore. Cunning and calm. "PTSD," she murmured.

He refused to acknowledge it. She'd tell the others. This sort of information would be worth a ton of money.

Grab her. He had to grab her *now* and bring her in before she sold him out.

She let go of his face and backed away to the opposite railing, limping slightly. A horn wailed through the night.

Move. He had to move, had to apprehend her.

His body refused to obey. Refused to uncurl, refused to stand.

She climbed onto the railing, graceful despite the injury on her thigh. As if she had been born balancing on a few inches of steel. And while she stood on the rail, flicking her broken lenses back down over her eyes, she said, "It does me no good if you're dead. Your secret is safe."

Before Luke could find a way to get his body to cooperate, to get a full breath into his lungs, she leapt.

His heart stopped. Until the train swept past, barreling toward the tunnel beyond.

He spotted her atop it, a lone, dark figure. Looking back, as if to watch him, the light from the burning police car dancing on the silver train.

As the train neared the tunnel, she smoothly slid onto her back and vanished into the underground.

A queen returning to her underworld.

Shadow and light flashed and eddied overhead, the train car beneath her a rumbling, thunderous rocket shooting beneath the earth.

Selina lay on her back, hands tucked behind her head, watching the tunnel pass by.

She'd meant what she said to Batwing. His secret was safe with her.

If League assassins were converging on Gotham City, he was perhaps the only other person who might stand a chance against them. Keep them occupied until she'd finished her mission.

She knew precisely what they were after—why they thought they could come to claim what was hers.

Nyssa and Talia often set their assassins against each other, gave them the same, competing missions. To keep them on their toes. To see who might survive. This was no different.

Selina wondered who Shrike had pissed off to warrant being dispatched here. If Talia and Nyssa had bet on who would walk away from their fight. They often did.

But Batwing's PTSD was interesting. Terrible for him, but an interesting piece of the puzzle.

Taking on Gotham City's underworld would no doubt inflict some serious internal scars, but to have his reaction be *so* debilitating . . .

Whatever he'd witnessed, it must have been . . . Selina tried not to imagine it. Even if he was her opponent.

Harley had no clue—Selina was certain—that her little pyrotechnics would trigger that reaction in him.

No, the explosion had been a giant middle finger to Selina. She'd probably tracked Selina here, seen the cops, and blown up the car as a warning to Selina not to double-cross her and Ivy. A little indication of what Harley was capable of if provoked.

A loose cannon. But one Selina would manage. Somehow.

Yet seeing Batwing on the ground like that, shaking . . . For a moment, she hadn't been on that footbridge. For a moment, she'd been in a marble-and-gold bathroom, hurling her guts up, a waltz trickling up through the shining floor below. Because what she'd done minutes earlier . . .

"It is a simple movement," Talia had purred in her ear, resting her head on Selina's shoulder as they peered at the aging, overweight man paralyzed on the plush bed.

His eyes, however, were wide with terror as he watched the young woman he'd led up here, to his bedroom, while his masquerade party went on below.

"You know what he likes to do," Talia said, her ice-cold hand wrapping around Selina's wrist. The dagger held there. "Make him pay for it."

Selina had given him a choice. At least, in her head she had. A secret, silent choice: to be a better man than his file suggested and not invite her up here. To avoid this moment, to let her find some way to get out of it, to spare his life and convince Talia that it was too risky to kill him. She'd piled up a list of plausible excuses, had been prepared to sneak into a bathroom and trigger the sprinklers, but then he'd invited her here.

And when he'd shut the bedroom door, when she'd pretended to study the art on the walls and had used the mounted antique mirror to watch him dump the contents of a tiny vial into the glass of champagne before he handed it to her, he'd chosen his fate.

A kiss—a kiss that had nearly made her gag—had transferred her own drug to the man's lips. Into his system when he'd licked his mouth afterward. By the time it had entered his bloodstream, he'd been on the bed, unable to move.

Talia had slipped in a moment later, her ivory mask concealing her face. Selina's own half-mask remained in place, black as night.

A level below, Venice's wealthiest glittered and danced, the Carnevale revelry soaring toward its peak. This masquerade ball was an annual tradition. Hosted here, by this man.

She'd read his file on the drive down here from the mountains and as she dressed tonight, preparing her body the way Talia had shown her, adopting the speech and mannerisms. Gone was the clawing back-street girl. Gone was the sullen, stone-faced fighter.

Talia moved Selina's wrist upward, holding the blade for them both. Dim light danced on the steel. No guns—not for this first mission. This rite.

The first kill must always be a blade. *Nyssa had told her before she left. So she could feel it when she ended someone's life. Guns were too impersonal, too distant. With a knife . . . she had to mean it. Had to be close.*

"You have practiced," Talia whispered in her ear, pantomiming the movement with Selina. "Now show me what you learned."

The man's private guards would not interfere. They had been trained to ignore any shouts of pain from this room. To stay away.

She knew Talia had picked this target specifically for that. For the victims who Selina had seen, one photo after another. A corrupted lesion on society, *Talia had said. One that had to be excised to cleanse the ruling order. Men who were shielded by their power, their money.*

Talia let go of Selina's hand.

The blade remained upright.

And Selina reminded herself of those victims. Of their faces, their corpses. He likely wouldn't have killed her, not when she oozed money and class tonight, but he'd have given her that drugged champagne, taken what he wanted, and predicted that she would be too ashamed and afraid to speak out about it. The others . . . they hadn't been given the armor of privilege. Lost, forgotten souls that no one would miss or fight for.

A cold, rippling sort of rage settled her. Spread through her, crackling like hoarfrost.

The system is broken, *Talia had said.* We are its cure.

The dagger did not tremble as Selina brought it slicing home.

She made it out of the room, down the hall, slipping past the unaware guards, Talia on her heels. She made it to another hallway, near the back exit of the palatial home, and then stumbled into the nearest bathroom.

The small window was open to the night air, the canal a glittering thread, the revelry across the city blending with the music playing below.

Blending with the sounds of her retching as she fell to her knees and hurled up the contents of her stomach.

Talia strode in behind her, silently shutting the door. Watching as Selina vomited again and again into the toilet.

Talia handed her a pile of paper napkins. "Wipe away any trace and flush. There's bleach in the cabinet below the sink."

Hollow and numb, Selina obeyed.

She didn't speak to Talia as she cleaned. As she wiped away any trace of herself.

As the last of who she'd been swirled down that toilet and out into the Laguna Veneta.

Selina blinked, the train beneath her slowing as it headed into a station.

Time to go.

She felt distant, far from her body once more, as she slid off the car and to the murky tunnel floor below, her aching thigh protesting.

She wondered if Batwing would sleep as poorly as her tonight.

CHAPTER 15

———

Standing atop the shadowed roof of the twelve-story Hotel Devon two nights later, her Death Mask repaired and the shallow wound to her thigh healed enough that walking was no longer painful, Selina surveyed Ivy and Harley from head to toe.

They grinned back at her.

Pacing a few steps, Selina said quietly, "Where are all the weapons?"

They said nothing, their grins faltering.

"Where," Selina repeated, "are the *weapons* I told you to bring?"

They glared at her. Selina glared right back. Even if they couldn't see it through the helmet.

Nyssa and Talia would have a collective heart attack if any of the League assassins came so unprepared to a job. And then peel the skin from their bones.

Selina had seen the punishments doled out for disobedience. Done not by Talia, who never dirtied her immaculate hands, or even

Nyssa, who relished such things, but by the League assassins themselves. So they realized what, exactly, would be done to them if they similarly failed. Precisely the sort of lesson the sisters loved to give.

Leaning against the metal door that led to the hotel below where the Save the Gotham City Landmarks Gala was well under way, Harley patted the holster at her waist, the twin colorful orbs hanging there. Strapped across her chest, intersecting her baseball tee that read *Gotham City Sluggers*, a bandolier of smaller ones, no larger than Christmas ornaments, hung as well. She cocked her head, pigtails bobbing with the movement, almost in time with the band playing ten levels below. "Isn't this enough?"

Selina pointed with the coiled-up bullwhip clenched in her hand—clenched *hard*, to keep from throttling them. "I told you to bring *weapons*. Not toys."

Harley took a step forward, her bright-red-and-black boy shorts catching the dim light over the roof door. Her fishnets did nothing to hide the tattoos inked on her thighs, flowing right into her calf-high combat boots. Animals, ranging from a roaring lion to a monarch butterfly, covered her skin. She thumbed free one of those orbs. "Just wait and see what *fun* these toys will bring to the boys and girls down there," she said, a wicked smile on her mouth.

They were *bombs* strapped on her. Small, and likely not enough to bring down any major structure, but disruptive enough to cause some chaos.

To make a statement.

Selina smirked, irritation fading away. "I stand corrected." She turned to Ivy. A utility belt hung at the waist of her emerald bodysuit, those vines again covering her hands. A larger vine of blooming orchids snaked across her middle, as if it were the sash on a beauty queen.

Selina lifted a brow beneath her mask. "No magic flowers to-night?"

Ivy ran a hand over the vine down her chest. "I thought I'd display them this time."

Clever. A bandolier of the weapons, the botanical twin to Harley's own ammo.

Selina hummed. "You got anything else to fight with?"

Ivy's answering grin was the definition of *wicked*. "Maybe."

"I don't operate on *maybe*."

Ivy muttered to Harley, "I feel like I'm being scolded by the principal."

Harley snickered. Selina gritted her teeth, even if they couldn't see it.

"Wouldn't this whole plan be easier if I just gassed them?" Ivy asked, patting the vine across her torso.

"No." Selina surveyed the pouch at Ivy's hip. That seemed to *move*. "We want them to know who's doing this."

"Who is 'them'?" Harley demanded.

"Everyone." Selina stalked up to Ivy's side. "What's that?"

Ivy winked at her. "A little experiment."

Harley grinned. "Killer vines."

Selina lifted a brow. "For real?"

Ivy flipped open the pouch, revealing a swirling mass of green inside. Twining about itself like a snake. "Plants can remember—feel things."

Ivy would know better than anyone, Selina supposed. Indeed, a touch of sadness seemed to soften Harley's eyes. As if she realized it, too.

It faded as Ivy dipped her hand into the pouch and a tendril of green hemp-like vine wrapped around her forearm. Almost lovingly.

Holy crap.

"I raised this one from seedling to what it is now," Ivy said, stroking a hand down the vine that curled up her forearm like some living bangle. "It works like that whip of yours." A nod toward the bullwhip still gripped in Selina's hand. "Except it likes to squeeze. Tightly."

Harley stroked a finger down the vine, tracing its curls. Selina could have sworn both plant and Ivy shuddered—in pleasure.

What Nyssa and Talia would give for a weapon like that.

"Right," Selina said, surveying the roof door. "You remember the plan?"

"Yes, Mom," Harley quipped.

Selina ignored her. "Bags ready?"

Harley and Ivy held up matching duffels.

"All set?"

The flowers on Ivy's bandolier seemed to shimmer in confirmation. But Harley reached into her duffel and pulled out two ribbons, one red, one black. With deft fingers she tied one to each braid.

"You matched the ribbons to the underwear?" Selina blurted.

"You've got the cat costume," Harley drawled, adjusting the bows. "I've got my colors."

Ivy chuckled. "Micromanage much, kitty?"

Selina chose to ignore that, too, and slung the whip over a shoulder. "Go for the watches over wallets. Jewels over purses." Selina opened the roof door, rotating her wrist to limber it up.

Harley's smile was a crooked slash of white beneath her red lipstick. "Talks like a lady, acts like a thug."

She didn't know the half of it.

* * *

Luke was about to fall asleep midconversation. The Landmarks Gala was the worst so far, the music and people and floral arrangements bleeding into all the other parties he'd been dragged to these past few weeks. He'd already searched the faces of every woman here for any hint of an injury, but nothing. No jewelry reported missing, no woman in a battle-suit.

He'd danced with all the young women who'd approached him, including his neighbor Holly, who'd been just as vapid as he remembered. Full of idle snobbery. But denying her a dance for a second time—not an option. She lived across the hall from him. He didn't want to spend *years* of peeking into the hallway to make sure she wasn't there before leaving. Not worth it.

Perhaps coming to this gala hadn't been worth it, either. Hours in and no sign of Catwoman. Mark and Elise were off on a company fishing retreat in Vermont, and his parents hadn't come tonight.

His mom had laughed—literally howled—at brunch when he'd said he'd accepted the invitation. *You're in for a night of architects boring you to tears*, she'd said.

She was right.

Luke drained his water. He'd driven himself, and stayed away from the booze because of it—and to keep his senses alert. But even if he spotted nothing, had no need of the suit he'd hidden in a large gym bag at the coat check, he'd made sure his Porsche had been left out front by the valet. Perfect for a quick escape. Not from Catwoman, but from the socialites.

Like the two older-looking ladies who had just spotted him across the crowded space.

Luke tried to pretend he hadn't seen them, twisting back toward the glass bar. The ballroom was on the second level of the

Hotel Devon, its enormous windows overlooking the southern edge of Robinson Park.

Honestly, some small part of him was grateful when the wooden doors to the ballroom were kicked open.

He had expected her to be there. Expected the battle-suit and helmet, expected the bullwhip in her hand as she strutted forward, the music halting. People shrieking or falling quiet.

But the other two behind her . . .

Shit. *Shit.*

Poison Ivy, clad in an ornate bodysuit, bearing a duffel in one hand and some sort of vine *moving* over her other arm. Not to mention the gloves on both hands that seemed to be in *bloom.* Or the vine of orchids she wore like a bandolier.

And Harley Quinn, clad in nothing but fishnets, boy shorts, and a baseball tee, armed to the teeth with what seemed to be an arsenal of small bombs.

Luke hadn't yet had the pleasure of dealing with them, but Bruce had. Through the keen-edged cunning Harley possessed, she'd managed to avoid capture and incarceration while working with the Joker. Bruce had warned Luke of her unpredictable moods—and her lethal aim.

Apparently, she'd ditched the Joker and his henchmen for more interesting company. As for Ivy, Luke had read Bruce's file on her arsenal of toxins.

This did not bode well. Not at all.

Everyone in the ballroom went still. No one dared move.

Harley lifted an arm over her head, pointing with one of those small, deadly orbs to the ceiling as if she were only stretching, and said, "Who's ready to party?"

The trio paused near the doors. Luke sized up the obstacles and casualties in their way. As a vet, he could interfere as Luke Fox. He would be *expected* to interfere, but if he had his suit, he could do more. Save more people. It'd take him five minutes to slip out to the coatroom and return as Batwing.

Catwoman snapped her wrist and the bullwhip answered. A crack, wild and wicked, cut through the room.

People murmured in alarm, stepping out of the range of that whip.

Luke began edging through the crowd. Thank God his parents hadn't come.

"Here's the deal," Catwoman said, her voice low and raspy. "You drop your jewelry, your watches, your cash into the bags. And we don't hurt you."

"Trick or treat," Harley said, lifting the empty duffel at her side.

Ivy only strode up to a nearby man, a pale purple smoke leaking from her. The man's eyes went glazed, his white face slack, and then he handed over his watch into Ivy's awaiting duffel. His wallet and cuff links, too. The woman nearest him began doing so as well, her face equally slack. Entranced. Bruce's file hadn't exaggerated.

Luke reached the small service entrance just as the crowd began to remove their jewelry and personal belongings in a flurry of glittering gems and flashing gold. He'd bet the security guards were likely unconscious, knocked out by Ivy's cloud of toxins.

Seven people stood nearby, a mix of staff and guests, all fixed on the unfolding scene. Luke motioned subtly to them.

Out, out, out, he conveyed with mere gestures. The group wasted no time obeying, ducking low and hurrying through the door.

The trio had yet to kill anyone. In fact, they seemed averse to killing those merely caught in the crosshairs.

At least they had that going for them.

Luke followed the small group of people, pointed them toward the back stairs, and sprinted for the coatroom, where the attendants were tied up at their posts with red-and-black-striped zip ties. Harley Quinn's colors. Four minutes—he'd be ready in four minutes.

He prayed all hell didn't break loose before then.

Selina's bag was growing heavy as she prowled through the crowd.

Where she moved, jewels and watches followed.

The security guards remained down in the halls, courtesy of that living whip Ivy had wrapped around their throats—rendering them unconscious.

Just people doing their job, Ivy had said when Harley demanded why she hadn't made it fatal. Selina had agreed, earning an eye roll from Harley.

Wimps, Harley had sneered, then asked Ivy, *If you balk at dealing with them, what are you gonna do when it matters? When you go after those politicians?*

Ivy had stiffened, but said nothing.

Selina had spoken up in her defense. *She'll deal with it. Just as we are now going to deal with this gala.*

Harley had clicked her tongue, striding ahead. But Ivy had given Selina a small, grateful nod.

Selina had tried to ignore the slight warmth that kindled in her chest. The answering smile that bloomed beneath her helmet.

But now, standing in this ballroom . . . Those were sirens wailing in the distance. She had to get them out of here.

"We need exit music," Harley said to the dead-silent crowd. She pointed toward the band standing motionless on the stage against the far wall. "Can I make a song request?"

The bandleader was pale as death as he nodded. Selina chuckled, holding her duffel in front of an aging woman she'd chatted with merely thirty minutes ago. *So good to see more old money here,* the woman had trilled.

It had been nearly impossible to keep from throwing her drink in the woman's face.

It didn't stop Selina from now being rougher than necessary as she plucked the woman's ruby tiara off her head and shoved it into the duffel.

No sign of Luke Fox. Perhaps he'd already left. He'd seemed bored to tears when they'd danced earlier. But perhaps that was Holly's effect on him.

"'Don't Stop Me Now' by Queen," Harley ordered the bandleader as the couple in front of her shed their jewelry like a snake with a second skin.

Ivy clicked her tongue, her toxins continuing to leak out and ensnare those before her. They handed over their jewelry without a blink of fear. "Good choice."

Selina was inclined to agree. And hid her laugh as the band struck up the song immediately, the piano player missing the first few notes as his hands shook, but then settling into it. The singer was no Freddie Mercury, but what he lacked in range, he made up for with sheer bravado.

The audio receptors on her helmet gave Selina an update: two minutes until those cop cars got here. SWAT team, likely.

Harley was dancing to the music, braids swinging as she

bounced through the crowd. Ivy was swaying along, too, that vine of hers slithering whenever someone seemed to notice her lack of gun and contemplate attacking.

"Playtime's over," Selina said to them, zipping up her bag. Two echoing zips sounded.

"Gimme a drumbeat," Harley ordered the band.

And holy hell, the drummer gave it to her. Right as the band paused, the singer putting enough attitude into the lyrics that Selina finally laughed as she faced the enormous windows overlooking the street below and park beyond. She motioned the crowd back against the far wall.

Harley hurled one of those colored balls right at the window. A blink, flash, and then—

Glass slid to the floor, shattering into countless shards. Someone screamed.

The singer didn't miss a single beat.

The band was enjoying it, Selina realized as Harley whistled and chucked one of those orbs to her. Catching it in one hand, Selina grinned and lobbed it at the chandelier in the center of the room. Perhaps the band was as sick of these rich pricks as Selina was. There was no way of faking that shredding guitar solo, not faltering as the chandelier came crashing down. Blocking access to the open window as Selina broke into a run, Harley and Ivy already a few steps ahead.

The two launched out the window, people screeching over the music and crashing glass.

As Selina reached the window, the main doors blew open again.

Batwing appeared between them, glowing like he'd been freshly forged, arm raised to fire some weapon from his suit.

Selina leapt out the open window, twisting as she fell. Turning back midair to meet Batwing's gaze from across the room.

And give him the finger with both hands.

Free fall sang to her for two heartbeats before she hit the awning below, bouncing up to catch the hotel flag jutting out a few feet away. She wrapped her legs around it, slithering down. Right into the convertible where Harley and Ivy were already waiting, duffels overflowing with jewels. Right into the driver's seat.

Batwing reached the window as Selina punched the ignition, popped the clutch, and floored the gas pedal. His roared curse was sure to make some well-bred ladies behind him faint as Selina, Harley, and Ivy sped off in Luke Fox's Porsche.

CHAPTER 16

They'd gone too far.

He didn't care about his car, top down and parked out front all night, keys left in it by the valet. No, that was the least of his concerns when people had been outright robbed and terrified. It didn't matter what level of society these people existed in, or whether or not they could afford to replace their valuables. This sort of thing could not, *would not* happen on his watch.

Luke glanced behind him to the panicked, stunned people still in the ballroom, the band that was now making a quick, guilty exit.

He said to the room, to anyone listening, "I'm on this."

"She took my diamonds!" a woman shrieked, pale face livid. *"Get them now!"*

Luke reined in the urge to roll his eyes, reminding himself that he was doing this to protect *all* of Gotham City as he launched himself out the broken window.

He'd haul all three of them into the GCPD precinct.

Starting with Catwoman.

Selina hit sixty, seventy, eighty, the car opening up beautifully as they cruised through Robinson Park's empty, curving road.

Her roaring blood was a song inside her, sweet as the warm night air around them.

No rules. No barriers. Nothing to hold them back.

Selina leaned into the feeling, savoring it.

Harley was cackling, draping herself in pearls and bracelets, and throwing a few over Ivy's head.

Behind them, red and blue lit up the night sky. Selina pushed the car faster, the engine a velvety purr rumbling through the trees.

They rounded a curve, Ivy oomphing as Harley slid into her, jewels and pearls clacking against each other. Selina checked the rearview mirror, assessing those sirens and how close their lights were in pursuit.

A black shadow cut across the sky.

"We've got a bat on our tail," Selina called to them.

Harley and Ivy fell silent, whirling around in the back seat.

Harley swore, scrambling for her bandolier of explosives as Batwing soared toward them with his wings—*bat wings*—spread wide.

"Creative," Ivy muttered, that long, deadly vine at her hip now dangling from her hand.

"His suit is reinforced armor," Selina shouted. "Go for the wings." The retractable, mechanical wings that allowed him to glide long distances.

A gamble to order them to shoot him down, but telling the

women *don't kill him* would involve too many explanations and questions.

A long strand of opera pearls streaming behind her, Harley unhooked one of those smiling orbs and hurled it toward him with the skill of a pitcher.

Batwing swerved, nimbly avoiding the ball as it exploded right where he'd been.

If it triggered anything in his PTSD, it didn't slow him.

Harley lobbed another one, a third on its heels.

Batwing again soared upward, dodging her shots. Gaining on them.

"He's still out of range for my vine," Ivy called over a shoulder as Selina held the car steady. "If you hit the brakes—"

Batwing lifted his arm, firing his own shot.

Some sort of arrow aiming for the back tires.

Selina swerved. Harley cursed, slamming into Ivy, whose vine wrapped around Harley to steady her.

The arrow went wide, ricocheting off the asphalt.

"This dude needs a *major* attitude readjustment." Harley pouted, trying to free herself from the tethers of Ivy's vine. Batwing raised his arm again, preparing another shot to their tires.

Ivy pushed Harley off her, her vine sliding free. "I think you're right," Ivy hissed, and lifted her arm. "He's gotten close enough."

Selina couldn't agree more.

"I'll line up the shot for you," Selina called to Ivy, taking another curve, then soaring over the small bridge spanning the Finger River, which cleaved Robinson Park in two. "Face forward and get ready." She ordered over her shoulder, "Seat belts *on*."

She veered to the left as Batwing fired another steel arrow. Ivy and Harley grinned and saluted before they obeyed.

And as they hit a long, straight bit of road, Selina slammed on the brakes.

The seat belt bit into her, even through her suit. Harley swore behind her.

Batwing zoomed overhead as they slammed to a stop. Exposing his back to them.

Ivy unclipped her seat belt and leapt into the front seat, balancing her forearm on the windshield. Within a heartbeat, she fired two long green vines, spearing through the night. One to the left, one to the right. Explosives and gases, Batwing had no doubt expected. But a living *thing* launching at him?

It seemed the element of surprise was on Ivy's side as his wings flared, trying to halt and pivot him. Too late.

Both of Ivy's vines hit home.

And whatever indestructible material Batwing's suit was made of, his wings were not.

The vines ripped through metal and wiring like a hot knife through butter, sending Batwing tumbling toward the towering oaks.

Harley whooped, bouncing in her seat as she clapped Ivy on the shoulder. Ivy only grinned, small flowers blooming on her gloves.

"Brilliant," Selina breathed, risking a full glance over her shoulder. She found herself answering Ivy's grin beneath her mask. "Absolutely brilliant."

Ivy sketched a bow—or as much of one as she could in her seat.

Still grinning, Selina adjusted the clutch and slammed on the gas, the Porsche shooting like a star into the night.

They ditched the Porsche on a side street, then took the subway back to the East End. When Selina stalked out of the car at a graffiti-covered aboveground stop, Harley and Ivy followed. They'd made sure to grab all the jewels from the convertible, the duffels they each bore now zipped up and nondescript.

Save for their outfits. People had outright moved off the train the moment the trio entered the car. Whether the passengers had called the cops on them wasn't a problem. They'd be gone before any patrol cars could arrive.

Harley had been too busy on her phone to notice and remained so now, walking down the platform, Ivy steering her out of the way of the steel beams and benches. "You should *see* this," she declared, pale makeup illuminated by the light of her screen. "We are *everywhere*."

Selina paused by the station stairs as Harley held up the screen to show them the video that someone had filmed inside the gala. It showed the three of them prowling into the ballroom, armed and smiling. Or Harley and Ivy were, since their smiles were the only ones visible.

"And look at this one," Harley said, lowering her phone to scroll to another video.

And there she was, leaping out the window, the footage in slo-mo, revealing Selina's midair twist, her middle fingers raised to Batwing, to everyone in that gala.

Selina blinked. She'd never seen herself . . . in action.

For a heartbeat, that old picture of her flipping on the balance beam at that gymnastics competition flashed through her mind. How much had changed, and yet how little. She pushed away the quiet weight that threatened to drag her down.

Ivy laughed as she studied the picture, nudging Selina with a hip. "Kitty has a fun side after all."

Selina nudged her back. "Let's go. There are security feeds

here." She nodded toward a mounted camera monitoring them a few feet away.

Harley tossed a small bomb.

Bye-bye, camera.

Selina chuckled. "Well, that's one way to deal with it."

Ivy fell into step beside her as they strode down the filthy steps and toward the street below. "When's the next hit, ladies?"

"Three days," Selina said.

"Why not tomorrow?" Harley demanded, eyes bright with excitement.

"Because we want those videos to get broadcast everywhere." Selina nodded toward the phone Harley still held in one hand. "We don't want the robberies to bleed into each other."

They reached the quiet, run-down street, their steps eating up the pavement. Ivy declared, "We'll lie low until then. I've got some stuff to do at my lab, anyway."

"Good." Selina paused. "That trance you put people into," she said to Ivy. "Why not use it on us?"

Harley lowered her phone at last. Ivy held Selina's stare. "One, your helmet makes that impossible. But two . . ." Ivy shrugged. "It's against my code. Well, part of it."

"Which is what?" Selina couldn't help the question.

Ivy ran a gloved finger over one of the orchids across her torso. "Don't screw over your allies." Her green eyes lifted, bright and intent.

Selina nodded. Warning received. And time to go.

She'd have to take a long, winding way home to avoid cameras picking her up. "I'll give you the details on our next hit in a few days."

The two women halted their walking, frowning.

Ivy asked, "What's your name?"

She wasn't sure she even had one anymore.

Names meant coming from somewhere, someone. And those things had either been erased for her, or were things she was glad to leave behind.

"Catwoman is fine," Selina said blandly, even as the question settled deep in her.

Harley clicked her tongue. "Secrets, secrets are no fun. . . ."

Selina waved a hand in cool dismissal. "Three days. Be ready."

She glanced behind in time to see Harley loop her arm through Ivy's. "Your place or mine, sweetstuff?"

Ivy's face flushed, but she said, "Mine." Definitely more than friends, then. Even if it seemed they did not define whatever lay between them.

As Selina melted into the shadows, something tightened in her chest.

She'd never known what it was like—to have someone she could be like that with.

It didn't really matter now, not with all that glorious chaos she had planned for Gotham City, all the upending of its corrupt ways that she would do, but still . . . she wondered what it would be like.

CHAPTER 17

They'd gotten away. Outmaneuvered him, then sped off into the night.

Luke was so mad he couldn't sleep that night. Or the next.

Which he supposed was better than his usual nightmare. But it didn't help that the video footage kept playing on the news. The shot of the three of them strutting in, the shot of Catwoman leaping out the window, flipping him off.

The image of all those frightened people in the ballroom who he'd failed to protect.

Deep in sublevel seven, Luke growled as sparks flew from the second hole he was repairing in his suit's wings. Ivy's shots had been precise.

And he'd lined himself up like a goddamn clay pigeon for them.

The vines had withered and died before he could bring them back to the lab for analysis. But from the way they'd *moved*, how Ivy had commanded them . . . Jesus. Maybe the rumors were right:

she *wasn't* fully human. Bruce had never been able to confirm it, not in the one brief encounter he'd had with Ivy, but it had been listed as a possibility in the Batcave's file on her.

Luke didn't want to consider what powerful forces might covet those abilities. Hone them into something worse than what Ivy had already become.

The buzzer sounded, blaring over the hum of the welder, and Luke turned off the machine, propping his welding mask on his sweaty head. "What's up?" he asked the speakers built into the walls and ceiling of the empty room.

"A Miss Vanderhees is here to see you."

Luke cringed.

His administrative assistant clarified, "In your eleventh-floor office. I informed her you were busy, but she said she'd wait."

Luke let out a low groan. What the hell did *she* want?

"Tell her . . ." If he said he was too busy, she'd probably come back. Or start looking for him at home, which might lead her to hunt for him at odd hours, which might lead her to start wondering where he *went* all the time.

Luke sighed. "Tell her I'll be up in fifteen. Thanks." He was covered in enough sweat and grime that it merited a shower. He had one in the bathroom down here, along with a change of clothes—a good suit, in case his dad called him into a meeting.

"Will do, Mr. Fox."

Luke made it upstairs in twelve minutes, his charcoal-gray suit a bit tight across the shoulders. He'd packed on more muscle these last few months; he'd have to take it to his tailor.

He was straightening the cuffs of his pale purple shirt when he strode into his corner office and found Holly waiting in one of the chairs before his immaculate desk.

He'd made sure bland company memos and party invitations were the only documents stacked on the side of his desk, the surface adorned with photos of his mom and dad, Mark and Elise, and a shot of him after his first boxing victory at fifteen. Everything else, anything important, was locked down in sublevel seven.

"Holly," he said by way of greeting, edging around his desk. "Good to see you."

It was training and instinct to note the details of her appearance— the appearance of anyone who came his way: her salmon-colored blazer, set over a matching dress and navy pumps. Nothing out of the ordinary.

Except for the hint of a smile. That gave him pause.

If only because her smile also held a hint of a sharpness that he'd never noticed before. Her eyes . . . keen.

That was the only way to describe her eyes. Keen and cunning. She might be an insufferable snob, but he had a feeling she wasn't as shallow as he'd first thought. That she perhaps pretended to be, to her own advantage.

"To what do I owe this pleasure?" Luke asked, settling himself behind the glass desk. And finding himself strangely glad for the barrier between them.

She flicked those green eyes over him. "I wanted to see how you were. I heard about your car."

It was the least of his concerns.

The Porsche had been tracked down, thanks to the tracing system he'd installed. A broken shell of a beautiful beast. He'd gladly handed it over to the GCPD for evidence.

"I'm fine," he said, waving a hand. And even though this conversation was the *last* thing he wanted to be having, especially with his suit still needing a few hours of repairs, Luke surveyed Holly again, the way her hands were white-knuckled on the chair. "How are *you*?" She'd been there two nights ago.

She brushed a hand over her collarbone, as if she could feel the jewelry that she'd no doubt been forced to give away. "Shaken, but fine."

He knew a good number of people were still saying that, too. His fault—that shakiness, that fear. If he'd been faster . . .

Luke said softly, "It was just a couple of criminals. They'll be brought in soon enough."

A glimmer of something in her eyes. "Those weapons were serious."

They were.

"Our building has good security," he said. Some part of him wondered if she'd come here, to him, for some sort of reassurance. "And every gala from now on will have armed guards." He offered what he hoped was a calm, if grim, smile, unable to suppress that part of him that still sought to reach out, to comfort and protect. The part he'd never been able to turn off. "They'll be apprehended soon. I promise."

Apparently, that was all she needed to hear. She nodded, rising to her feet. Luke stood with her.

Holly's attention drifted to the busy street behind him, a stunning view of the city visible from nearly every angle of his office. "I don't have any friends in Gotham," she said at last, her voice softer than he'd ever heard.

He wasn't surprised. But Luke said politely, "Oh?"

His mother would be so proud.

Holly studied the cityscape for another heartbeat. "I heard that you and your mother are starting a nonprofit to help veterans by teaching them boxing."

Each tick of the crystal clock on his desk was audible.

She shrugged with one shoulder. "I would like to help out."

Luke blinked at her. He cleared his throat. "That's very generous of you."

"No," she clarified. "I—I mean . . ." He'd never heard her stumble before. "I mean, I'll give you money, of course." Was that a faint hint of color on her cheeks? "But I'd like to help out. With my time. Volunteer, I mean."

The offer stunned him. And for the life of him, he couldn't detect a sign of anything but genuine feeling. The first he'd seen from her. Perhaps this was the person beneath the society-bred armor.

But why now? Why after this robbery? The question must have been on his face, because Holly said, "I heard you helped sneak some people out of the ballroom the other night. Got them to safety." He didn't ask how she knew, who'd told her. "I realized . . . maybe we got off on the wrong foot."

An extended olive branch. And enough of a glimpse into who might lurk beneath the web of status symbols she used to navigate their world, to defend herself against it, that Luke found himself considering.

He was sure he or his mom could find something for her to do. So he said carefully, "We're not official yet, still in the planning stages. But I'll keep you posted." He added quietly, "Thank you."

Holly's brows furrowed for a heartbeat. As if seeing him. *Really* seeing him. Something about it tugged at his memory, his chest. She shook her head a moment later, sunlight catching in her blond hair. "Of course. I'll see you later."

She pivoted on one of her towering stilettos and aimed for the door.

Luke knew it had nothing to do with his mother's etiquette

lessons, nothing to do with the fact that he needed to appear normal and make her think twice before wondering why he sometimes didn't return home until late, as he took a step around the desk and asked, "Do you wanna come over for some takeout tonight?"

Holly paused on the threshold. Luke realized the woman probably had never eaten takeout in her life, and opened his mouth to suggest an alternative, but she surprised him. "Pizza?"

There was enough hope, enough relief in the question that he smiled. "Seven o'clock. Bring whatever you want to drink." He only had beer and scotch, and he doubted she was the sort to drink either.

Holly gave him a grin, so unlike any he'd seen from her before. "Thanks. See you then."

And as he watched her stride out, her steps smooth and unfaltering, Luke wondered if he'd opened a door he might not be able to shut.

She'd needed an alibi for tonight.

There was no party or dinner where Holly Vanderhees might be seen and noted. After the events of the other night, all the other galas had been postponed until further notice.

So she'd gone to Luke Fox's office in part to check in on him after stealing his car, and in part to remind him and the rest of the gossips that she'd been at the gala two nights ago, and had been terrified and so scared and blah blah blah.

Selina certainly hadn't expected to be caught off guard by his genuine consideration and gratitude for Holly's offer of help. By looking at him, in that tailored suit, and realizing he'd indeed gotten people out of that room the other night.

The size of his bank account had nothing to do with it. He hadn't stopped serving the people of this country since coming home.

She certainly couldn't say that about herself.

Selina knocked on his door at seven, her heartbeat a little more elevated than she'd like. Especially when he opened the door, wearing a tight navy T-shirt and jeans.

Luke gave her a smile as he beckoned her in, his expression warmer than any she'd seen before. She'd opted for expensive yoga pants and a long-sleeved shirt and workout jacket. Casual, but the quality nice enough.

"Any preferences for pizza?" Luke asked as he strode for his phone on the glass dining table.

His apartment was nicer than hers. Warmer.

She scanned the exits and windows. It was the same open concept as her own place: one massive room that contained a kitchen, living room, and dining area—all contained within floor-to-ceiling glass windows that opened onto a wraparound balcony. To her right, past the dining area, was a long hallway, the mirror to her own, that no doubt contained the powder room, master bedroom, and two other guest rooms, each with its own bathroom. The walls were painted varying shades of gray, his leather and chrome furniture offset with thick, warm rugs and gently curving lamps. A gas fireplace flickered beneath the enormous flat-screen TV, currently playing the intro to *Jeopardy!*

If the plans were mirrored, then the safe would be in his closet, anchored into the wall.

Not that she was planning on stealing anything else from him.

"Nice place," she said, following him to the open kitchen, bedecked in Carrara marble and black cabinets. "And—um . . ." The last time she'd had pizza . . . She couldn't remember. It certainly wasn't the kind they made in Gotham City. No, it had been the thin-crust, simple pizza in Italy, so good that you could cry. Before that, her favorite had been a dollar-slice shop in the East End—the memory of it still enough to make her mouth water. Not that she could tell him that. "Plain is fine."

"Mind if I get half with sausage and pepperoni?"

She watched him dial the number. "Only if you get the whole thing with that instead."

Luke cut her a wry, amused look and then ordered. "Twenty minutes," he declared.

She nodded, sliding her hands into her jacket pockets.

"You didn't bring a drink."

"I'm not a big drinker," she admitted. She wasn't, not as Selina or Holly. She'd seen what it did to her mother. And though she sipped champagne at the galas and mimosas at the brunches . . . never too much. Never enough to make her out of control.

"Fair enough," Luke said. "Neither am I." Another mark in his favor, she had to admit. He opened his enormous fridge, surveying its contents. "Soda? Juice? Water?"

"Water is fine." She took a seat at the marble island, watching the TV across the room.

Trebek asked, "After England, more Shakespeare plays are set in this present-day country than any other."

"What is Italy?" Selina answered as Luke set the glass of water in front of her.

The contestant provided the same answer. Luke raised his eyebrows but said nothing.

Another question. "The last Grand Master of the Knights Templar."

Luke and Selina said together, "Who is Jacques de Molay?"

She smiled at him, the expression not feigned at all.

"I wouldn't have pegged you for a *Jeopardy!* fan."

"Being well dressed means you can't know some things?"

Before he could reply, Trebek asked another question. "It's the largest country in the world without any permanent natural rivers or lakes."

Selina answered just as Luke did: "What is Saudi Arabia?"

Correct.

Luke smiled slyly. "Loser pays for dinner," he offered, light dancing in those dark eyes.

Different, she realized. He was so different from the arrogant rich boy she'd assumed he was. No bravado, no need to flaunt that he was a true hero. He was gentle—kind. She'd known few men like him, she realized.

So Selina, despite herself, clinked her water glass against his. "You have no idea what you've just started," she purred.

They tied. Answering a few questions even the contestants didn't know. It was no surprise to Luke, since that occurred nearly every time he watched the show, but Holly's own mastery of the trivia had been a delightful surprise. She'd answered all the questions correctly. By the time the pizza arrived, he was assessing her again.

Had he assumed too much about her? But she'd done a damn good job of seeming like a bored, soulless heiress. But the person he'd seen in his office earlier . . . It had been a glimpse. Into this.

There was no sign of those refined manners, either, as she devoured three pieces of pizza, downing them all amid gulps from her water. Luke could barely keep up.

Jeopardy! moved on to *Wheel of Fortune*, and the competition began anew.

By the time they'd finished, tied again, she was smiling at him. A real, quiet smile. The smile that he doubted the press and the who's-who ever saw. It made her younger—prettier.

Holly rose to her feet, both of them having moved to the L-shaped couch before the fireplace and TV thirty minutes ago. "Thanks for dinner," she said, stretching her arms.

"I'm shocked I managed to get any slices for myself."

Holly let out a low laugh. "We'll order two pies the next time."

Next time. The words hung like an invitation.

And as Luke escorted her to the front door, he found himself saying, "Next time, then."

He closed the door, listening for the sounds of Holly going into her own apartment and locking the door behind her.

A few hours later, as he slipped into his suit and into the awaiting night, Luke was still smiling. Just a bit.

CHAPTER 18

"Hurry," Ivy urged from halfway down the bank's basement hall, frowning as Harley set the charges along the vault door.

"I'm going, I'm going," Harley muttered. "One wrong move, babycakes, and *we're* toast."

Ivy tapped her booted foot on the marble floor. "I know how explosives work."

"Then why don't *you* do this?"

"My vines would at least crack through that concrete faster than you're moving right now."

Selina stood near the steps that led upstairs, ignoring their playful bickering as she monitored the sounds of the darkened bank a level above. The alarms had been cut, avoiding triggering the heavy metal door at the top of the stairs. Ivy had downed the night guard with her flowers, and now . . . nothing.

Selina lifted a camera in her hands as Harley strode back over to where Ivy waited, then set it on a tripod she'd carefully positioned. "Ready?" Selina asked the two of them.

Harley only slung an arm around Ivy's shoulders, both of them grinning like fiends for the camera. Selina positioned herself a few inches away and crossed her arms as she said, "Now." Light flashed before and behind, the camera snapping away as the vault exploded open.

Well, a small explosion. Something akin to Selina's own electromagnetic pulse machine—a secret formula, Harley had declared when Selina asked about it. And then started to tease about cats and curiosity, and Selina had blocked her out entirely.

Small doses with Harley. She could deal with her, enjoy her, in small doses.

"You really think the paper will want this photo?" Ivy asked as the smoke cleared, waving away the gray cloud with a gloved hand.

Selina scooped up her duffel, striding into the lingering smoke.

"Who wouldn't want it?" Harley said.

Selina scanned the dim vault, night vision kicking in. No word had reached the press about Shrike. She couldn't decide if that was a good or bad thing.

She wondered how soon Nyssa and Talia would hear about it. Start to ponder.

Send someone else to test her.

"The papers," Selina declared, striding to a safe-deposit box, easily picking the rudimentary lock, and dumping the jewels right into her bag, "will eat this up. And even better, the fancy folk of Gotham will think we've moved on from their parties to banks, and they'll start up the galas again."

Harley frowned, waving away the smoke. "I could use another tiara."

Selina unlocked another box and snickered. "What about this?"

A glittering emerald necklace draped from her hand.

Harley's eyes went wide as saucers.

Selina chucked it to her. "For getting the vault open."

Harley caught the necklace. "My mom would love this," she breathed.

It was the first she'd mentioned of her mom. And even though questions might lead them down a rocky road, Selina couldn't resist asking, "You two close?"

Harley pocketed the necklace. "She's my favorite person in the world." A wink toward Ivy. "Aside from you, Vee." Harley jerked her chin toward Selina, pigtails swaying. "You close with your mom?"

No. Never. Not once. Selina shrugged. "She's not worth mentioning."

It was the truth. Harley's eyes softened, the expression unbearable.

Sparing Selina, Ivy cut in, hauling wads of cash into her duffel, "So we'll be hitting up more parties after this?"

Selina wished her helmet weren't on. If only so she could give Ivy a grateful look. But she only said, "Don't sound too disappointed." Selina moved from box to box, leaving the papers and random junk, scanning for any hint of jewelry. "Poor Batwing won't know where to hunt us."

Ivy hummed. "What do we do about him? No way we downed him for good."

Selina kept her voice mild. "We can deal with him when the time calls for it."

"We should use his insides to hang him from a lamppost," Harley added, going back to picking the locks and hauling valuables into her bag. Selina didn't think she was exaggerating.

"We should use him to find out who Batman is," Ivy mused, zipping up her own bag. "They work together. He might tell us."

"Torture? Nice," Harley said.

"I have methods that might convince him to talk," Ivy clarified quickly. "*Without* resorting to waterboarding." Those natural toxins that had gotten the people at that gala to hand over their jewels, no doubt.

But Selina cut in before they could travel farther down that road, "He's not part of our plans. We avoid him."

"Why?" Harley's smile slipped into something a little dangerous.

"Because he'll take care of the other bosses and gangs for us. Keep them out of our way. Bring him down, and we'll have every gang and boss crawling out of the sewers to stake their claim on Gotham. But if he continues to hold back the tide . . ." She shrugged. "He saves us a headache while we continue to sweep the city of its valuables."

Harley didn't look convinced as she zipped up her bag. But Ivy said, "What if he shows up at our next target?"

Selina smiled beneath her mask. "Then we keep playing this game of ours: evade and vanish."

"But—" Ivy challenged.

"Believe me," Selina interrupted, shouldering her duffel, "toying with him, driving him nuts, is far more satisfying than killing him."

Harley opened her mouth, but Selina held up a hand as her helmet began blaring. "We're about to have company."

Footsteps. Not guards—no jangling keys or the usual indicators.

Ivy pulled two baseball-sized flowers from the belt at her hips, the golden petals unfurling. Waiting.

Selina freed the bullwhip at her side as the helmet continued to give her a feed.

"Eight individual gaits—heavy," Selina murmured to Harley and Ivy. "Likely male. Coming as a group, not in a line. Entering the room in—"

"Look what the cat dragged in," sneered the tall, reedy man in the center of the group.

All wore stained dark clothes that had seen better days. Criminals. No doubt from some low-level group. She could pick up on no signifiers of their allegiance.

"An oversized fern," the man said, stepping into the chamber. Ivy stiffened, flowers opening wider. A leer toward Harley. "And a washed-up skank."

Selina ground her teeth, reining in her temper. If Ivy could knock out a few of them with those flowers, and Harley could detonate those small bombs . . . it'd even the odds.

Not great, but she could deal with the remainders. Even if taking down a group of some gang boss's men might be a complication in her plans.

Despite the insults, Harley stepped forward, pouting. "Is that really how you're going to be, Ralph? I haven't seen you in, what, a few months, and suddenly you gotta call me names? And my new friends, too?"

Ivy remained fixated on the men, flowers and vines at the ready. But Harley cut Selina a swift glance, the words clear in her blue eyes.

Trust me.

Trust her to do what? Get them killed? A few minutes, and they'd be sprinting out of here. If the cops didn't get here first.

Harley took another step, throwing that glance Selina's way again. *Trust me.*

It went against every bit of training, every instinct.

She didn't remember the last time she'd trusted anyone. Other than herself.

Ivy warned Selina, the words barely audible, "Follow her lead."

Selina sized up the men. Harley's welcoming grin.

Harley knew who these men were—well enough to understand that violence would either not work, or land them knee-deep in shit.

Trust me.

Her heartbeat a staccato, Selina did.

Ralph sneered at them again. "You and your new friends haven't been paying up. Makes some of us . . . mispleased."

"Not a word," Ivy muttered under her breath. Harley made a slicing *Shut up* motion behind her back.

Harley twirled the end of a braid around her finger. "Honeypie, you *know* we've just been waiting to accumulate enough good stuff to hand over our due."

Oh hell no. Like *hell* she was giving these creeps her money, *this* money—

"Boss wants it now," Ralph said. The other men behind him pressed in. He pointed at Selina. "He wants her to kneel."

Selina's hand didn't stray from the bullwhip. Harley shot her a warning *Be quiet* look before turning that grin on Ralph again. "Then why don't we head over there?" Harley patted her duffel. "I'll make the delivery in person."

Ralph considered.

"Come on, Ralphy," Harley crooned. "Your girl and I go way back." She pointed with a thumb toward Selina. "Kitty's new in town. She doesn't know the rules."

Selina bit her tongue. She knew their rules. And she was making her own now.

"Give us the bags, and we'll head over."

"You'd better be sure to tell Falcone I say hi." Harley pouted.

Falcone.

The name cracked through Selina.

These men . . . they were Falcone's?

They had to be new, because she didn't know their faces or names.

Ralph pointed a handgun at Harley. Ivy tensed, those vines writhing.

"Tell the freak," Ralph said, snarling toward Ivy, "to keep her plants away."

Harley began walking toward him. Toward the gun. "Here's the goods." She handed over her bag to the man beside Ralph. "Let's get going."

To Selina's shock, the men parted a path for Harley. A curl of her fingers at her back was her only sign. *Follow. Hurry.*

Shouldering her heavy duffel and snatching up the camera and tripod, Selina trailed her, Ivy at her side.

More guns pointed toward them as they walked up the stairs.

"Do you know what's the worst part of living a life of crime?" Harley asked as she got to the top of the stairs that would lead into the main hallway, turning to peer down at the men following with guns aimed at their backs.

Selina reached her side, Ivy a moment later. Just in time to see Harley punch the red button next to the stairwell door.

"Not knowing who to trust," Harley said, and the six-inch-thick metal door slammed shut.

Sealing the men inside.

The gunfire against the door was muffled, the shouts of the men Harley had trapped inside distant.

"And this was better than fighting?" Ivy demanded, backing

away from the heavy door and the red panic button that had saved their asses. The flowers in her hands had sealed again, and she swiftly pocketed them.

"It was, if you consider the fact that Ralph had a bomb with him that could have wiped us out."

"No, he didn't," Selina said, turning toward the hallway that would take them to the back exit. "I would have seen it." She tapped her helmet.

"Trust me, he did. Those clothes? Just to mask the hi-tech cloaking material Falcone stole off the black market. One throw and we would have been toast. He's probably debating using it on this door. We should hurry."

Falcone had such things in his arsenal now.

Unacceptable. On so many levels.

But . . . Harley had saved them. Selina shouldered her way out the back door and into the empty alley. Not even a lookout. Falcone needed to recruit smarter cronies.

"Thanks, Harley," Ivy said quietly.

Harley waved it off. "Falcone will be furious when he gets word of what we did."

Selina stalked down the alley, sirens already wailing in the night. Falcone had grown in power. Not anywhere near the global network and bottomless resources of the League, but enough to potentially grow beyond a local menace. "We'll deal with Falcone," she said, more to herself than them. But added after a moment, "Thanks, Harley."

Harley only grinned.

CHAPTER 19

Three weeks later, Selina was just entering her apartment building, trying not to limp at the ache in her leg.

One of Harley's little devices had been a bit *too* successful tonight and Selina had taken a chunk of concrete right in the thigh. The suit had kept the shrapnel from breaking the skin, but she'd bruised bone, likely. Ivy had said as much after she'd insisted on checking the injury. Even Harley had apologized for it.

But Holly Vanderhees didn't limp, and as Selina rode up the elevator from the basement parking garage, she gritted her teeth at the way her heels made every part of her injured leg throb. There was no way she could have entered the building wearing her battle-suit, and even though peeling it off in the alley to change into her current long-sleeved dress had been an effort of will . . . she'd done it.

The elevator paused at the lobby, and Selina plastered a bland smile on her face, hoping whoever was getting on wouldn't notice the sweat dampening her hair at one a.m.

She saw the bruises first. The swollen eye and lip. And within the span of a heartbeat, she was reaching for Luke Fox.

She halted before she could touch the sleeve of his gray zip-up athletic jacket. Luke blinked with his good eye, his every movement pained and tired, and stepped inside the elevator.

"What happened?" she demanded. If one of Gotham City's petty criminals had hurt him—

"I had a fight tonight."

"Who attacked you?"

Luke leaned against the wall of the elevator, his face utterly mangled—looking worse, no doubt, in the fluorescent lighting. "No. Boxing. Semipro."

It was her turn to blink. He hadn't been attacked, then. "Who won?"

A low, rasping laugh. "I did."

So the muscles truly weren't all for show. She didn't want to imagine the bruises beneath his clothes. Selina swallowed. "Why do you fight?" He had more money than God, and if she hadn't been near starvation all those years ago, she *never* would have set foot inside a ring.

"It . . . helps," he said, and refused to clarify.

Helps. He'd been in the Marines. Maybe the fighting helped him with whatever he still needed to sort through. She half wondered if Batwing himself had been a soldier, too. If he fought crime for a similar reason.

The elevator reached their floor, silence settling between them.

She'd gone overseas as well. And while Luke had been fighting for this country . . . she'd been learning how to break it.

Was here to do just that, to destabilize and undermine.

A heavy, hollow weight settled in the pit of her stomach, but she kept her steps slow as they walked out of the elevator. "Can I help you get cleaned up?"

He shook his head, but winced at the movement. "I'm fine."

She scanned his body—the sweatpants, the jacket that hid his battered body. "Let me get you some ice."

She'd stolen his car, his painting, lied to his face. . . . It was the least she could do. If he hadn't been a rich boy, she would have said he was a good man. A rare man.

Luke said, "Thank you."

And for a heartbeat, she was back in that dirty, dangerous hallway—as he tried and failed to pull out his keys.

His fingers were bloody, swollen. She caught the keys before they could hit the ground, saying nothing as she fitted them into the lock, opened the door, and flicked on the lights.

"Ice pack is in the lowest drawer on the left side of the freezer," he managed to say before slumping onto his couch, his knuckles smearing blood onto the dark leather.

Selina readied the ice pack, leg protesting with every movement, and brought over some paper towels to wipe up the blood. He leaned back against the cushions, pressing the ice pack to his eye, saying nothing while she dabbed at the leather.

Only when she rose, jaw clenched so tightly to keep in her grunt of pain, did he say, "Why were you out so late?"

"I had a date," she lied.

He went still. "With whom?"

Props for good grammar. She tossed the bloodied paper towel into the trash under the sink. "I get the feeling that the moment I tell you, you'll use that Wayne Industries database to look up his records, so . . . pass."

"That's assuming I care enough to do so."

Well then.

"Feel better," she said a bit tightly, heading for the door.

"Holly—"

But she was already gone. Even though she hated herself for it, Selina lingered by her own door for a moment longer than necessary, just to see if he'd come after her.

He didn't.

"Let's blow up the stage where they're hosting that kiddie beauty pageant."

"Jesus *Christ*, Harley!"

"What? Not while the kids are *on* it, obviously. But those contests are gross."

Selina wasn't sure how she'd gotten here. She'd given Ivy a call to say that tomorrow they were hitting up another target, but instead of agreeing and hanging up, Ivy had invited her over. To hang.

So here she was. Wearing her suit and helmet. In a lab teeming with plants that Ivy had constructed in the mammoth greenhouse adjacent to the abandoned grand hall of Robinson Park.

The entire place was something out of a dream: Trees grew from the floor itself, rising right through the glass ceiling, their thick leaves providing a roof. Paths lined with blooming flowers wended between the dense underbrush of dangling vines, ferns, and trickling streams. A few birds called sleepy good-nights to each other.

Selina could have sworn that some of the zoo animals they'd freed the other week during one of their Merry Band of Misfits adventures now lurked between the trees and oversized roots, eyes gleaming in the dark.

The air was sweet, warm—not quite comforting. The scent of fresh earth all around. A beautiful, if unsettling, place.

A lab-slash-apartment, apparently, from the little open grassy area tucked against a far stone wall that they now sat in, a rare spot of the greenhouse that hadn't been overwhelmed. Ivy and Harley sprawled on what seemed to be a sofa constructed of velvety moss, Selina perched on what she could have sworn was an oversized toadstool.

But at least the living furniture all faced the ancient TV screen currently playing some slasher flick.

How Ivy managed to create electricity *and* get cable out here was the least of her concerns.

"If there are children at the pageant," said Selina, wincing as she rotated her still-aching leg before her, going through a few of her gymnastics warm-ups that she could do while sitting down, "we don't risk it."

Harley rolled her eyes. "Aren't you going to take off your helmet?"

"No."

The two women swapped glances. "You ugly or something?" Harley said, eyes full of challenge.

Selina had dealt with enough Harley Quinn types in the Dolomites. "No," she simply repeated.

Harley snorted but turned back to the TV.

Ivy asked, perhaps deflecting, "Why do these idiots always run *upstairs* when the killer comes?"

Selina shot Ivy a grateful look that the woman couldn't see.

Harley stretched out her tattooed, fishnet-covered legs on the flower-speckled grass. "Because they're not good with explosives and don't have an army of killer plants to bring with them everywhere they go?"

Ivy chuckled and flicked Harley's white-painted cheek. "Smart-ass."

Harley batted her away and went back to watching, though Ivy's green eyes lingered on Harley for a moment longer. Tenderness filled them—and longing.

Ivy noticed Selina's attention and gave her a tight smile. But Selina only inclined her head. Secret safe. If Harley didn't want anything beyond what they already had, for whatever reasons of her own, then it wasn't Selina's place to say that it was obvious Ivy felt differently.

Ivy's smile widened into a wicked grin. "It really is weird—to only call you Catwoman. If we guess at your name, will you tell us if we're right?"

"Maybe." They'd never think of Selina. She asked before Ivy could start guessing names, "How long did it take you to make all of this?" She gestured to the lab, the teeming forest around them. The little fireflies, late for the outside world, that bobbed between the trees and flowers.

"Two years."

"You live here even in the winter?" With the holes and cracks in the glass, it'd be brutal.

Ivy shrugged, though she shifted on the moss couch. "I don't have many other options. And I like it here. This is more my home than any other place."

Selina understood that feeling too well. Not that she'd ever really had a place that was solely hers, that *felt* like home. No, Maggie had been her home—if home could be a person.

A familiar, old pain started to swarm her, so Selina asked, "No alter ego with a nice apartment and a cushy job?"

Harley cut Selina a warning glare, pigtails swinging. "Why so many questions, kitty?"

Ivy only said to Selina, "No. What you see is what you get." She added a tad softer, "And I have no one . . . no one who would need to be protected. By keeping my identity secret."

Harley's red-and-black-painted nails dug into the mossy couch arm, but she continued watching the TV.

Selina noted the reaction. Reined in the words that sought to come out of her. *I know—what it is to have that weight. To need this helmet. To keep them safe.*

She had no doubt that Harley wouldn't appreciate it. Would see it as a threat toward whoever she protected with the fake name, the makeup, the costumes. Her mom, definitely. But who else?

Ivy asked her, "What's your favorite food?"

Selina blinked. "I—don't have one."

She didn't. Food had been so scarce that she hadn't been given the luxury of finding a favorite one. But at the raised brows they both gave her, she amended, "Pizza. I guess."

She asked, just because she didn't know what else to say, "What's yours?"

"Raspberries."

"She's vegan," Harley said in a mock-whisper. "Don't ever let her cook for you."

Ivy nudged her with an elbow. "You said you liked those seitan tacos."

"With the fake cheese and fake sour cream and fake meat? Mmm. *Delicious.*"

Selina chuckled. "I'm with Harley on that one."

Ivy flipped them both off. Harley blew her a kiss.

Strange—to sit here in this exotic wonderland, with these women, and just . . . hang out.

Do nothing but talk and relax.

It sounded pathetic, probably *was* pathetic, but she'd never had friends. The Leopards hadn't counted. They weren't affectionate, their loyalty having more to do with survival and protocol than anything from genuine feeling.

And at the League, things like friendship hadn't existed. Loyalty did—to Nyssa and Talia and the Cause. Fervent, bone-deep loyalty to the two women determined to bring this world to rights, no matter the cost.

They had taught her well.

And yet . . . It was nice, Selina decided as Harley and Ivy began bickering over the stupidity of the movie's hero, to be around other young women, friends or whatever they were. Especially when they were so equally dedicated to not giving a shit.

Selina opened her mouth to explain how *she'd* escape the killer in the film—rather, how she'd hunt the creep down. But she didn't have time to.

Something smashed through the ancient glass, rolling onto the soft, thick grass between them and the TV.

Selina had a heartbeat to realize what it was.

Grenade. Homemade. Lethal.

Harley shouted, but Ivy moved, so fast Selina barely had time to contemplate lunging for the bomb.

A flash of green, a snap—

A thick vine that Selina had mistaken for a root in the grass plucked up the grenade and hurled it back toward where it had come from.

It barely cleared the greenhouse before it exploded.

Selina threw herself over both of the women as glass shattered and rained down.

Then silence.

"Shit," Harley panted beneath her. "*Shit.*"

They had to move. Had to get out *now*—

A heartbeat later, something heavy thudded into the grass.

The vine lunged again, but it froze.

Even from a few feet away, the message written around the brick was clear enough:

This was a warning. The next time, there will be more. You three bitches are done.

A warning. The grenade had been a warning.

Selina's body, still sprawled over Harley and Ivy, didn't seem to agree. Seemed to keep screaming, *We need to run. We need to go on the offensive. We need to get outside.*

She took a breath to calm herself. Another. It seemed the other women were doing the same.

"You hurt?" Selina asked them when her heart had steadied enough for her to stand and brush the glass off herself. None had pierced the suit, but the two of them . . .

Ivy was bleeding. Long scratches down her bare arms and legs. Where Selina's body hadn't reached.

But both of them were staring up at Selina. As if they'd never seen her before.

"You jumped in front of us," Harley said.

"I'm in this suit" was Selina's only answer. She pointed to Ivy. "We need to clean that up."

Harley straightened, noting the blood on Ivy, the glass. Her already pale face went ashen.

Ivy gritted her teeth, hissing at the leaking wounds. "There— there's some salve and bandages in the cabinet next to the sink," she said. "It'll help. I—made them."

Harley lunged into motion, half running toward the indicated cabinet.

Selina stalked for the greenhouse wall behind them, scanning the dark. Nothing. Not a sign of whoever had sent that little bomb and nasty message. "This location is compromised," she declared as Harley hurried over with the salve and bandages. "You need to move."

"Not until she's cleaned up," Harley said, falling to her knees in the grass to examine the long cut in Ivy's pale leg. No indication of glass in the wounds, Selina's helmet told her. She said as much. Harley ignored her, smearing that salve onto the scratch.

By the time Harley reached for the bandages, the skin had started to knit together.

Selina blinked. "How—"

"Nature has an answer for everything," Ivy said, still shaking. Harley just kept working, pigtails swaying with her steady, efficient movement.

Selina said again, "That message could have come from anyone."

"Batwing?" Harley asked without looking up.

"Not his style," Selina said. Too cowardly for Batwing. No, he would have faced them directly and put them in jail alive. "And GCPD would have done a raid. This was some criminal lowlife not appreciating us encroaching on their territory." Selina surveyed the beautiful lab, the haven Ivy created. "I'm sorry. You need to move. Now. GCPD is likely getting reports of an explosion in the park. And if someone tracked you here—"

"She gets it," Harley snapped. "Instead of talking, why don't you help?"

Selina stiffened, but strode for the moss-made couch, brushing off glass before she pulled off her gloves, dipped her fingers into the jar of milky salve and smeared some on Ivy's upper arm.

"It could have been anyone," Ivy said as Harley finished up one leg and started with the other. "Falcone, for what we did to his men a few weeks ago."

Selina considered. "It could be. And that's why when we retaliate, we'll do it wisely." Because that gleam in Ivy's eyes . . . revenge was burning there. In Harley's, too. The hateful message on the brick in the grass behind them seemed to glare as brightly as a neon sign.

"Then what do you have in mind?" Ivy demanded, surveying her plants, the lab she'd made. Her home, Selina realized. This was truly Ivy's home.

A pang of jealousy went through Selina, odd and cold.

She jerked her chin toward Harley. "I want names. Three names, for three of the Joker's petty cohorts. Lowest of the low—the kind that are definitely behind bars."

That lethal gleam in Harley's eyes sharpened. "Why?"

Selina went to Ivy's other side to tend to her right arm. "Because we need to send a few messages of our own."

"How will you get them out?"

"Leave it to me. Just bring explosives that can take out concrete and steel."

Selina finished on Ivy's right arm, and reached for her gloves on the other side of the woman.

"What's that bruise?" Ivy reached toward the hint of black-lining-purple just peeking out from beneath Selina's sleeve.

Selina smoothly slid on her gloves. "Nothing."

The Leopard tattoos.

Talia had wanted to laser them off. It was the one thing Selina had defied her on. She'd given up everything she was, everything she loved. But the tattoos . . . Talia would have to skin her alive to remove them if she wanted them gone. Selina had told her as much.

Talia had merely shrugged and drawled that petty attachments to the past would interfere with her ability to do what was necessary to further the League's cause.

Talia didn't know the half of it.

Ivy gave Selina a look that said she didn't believe her, but Harley sighed, shooting to her feet, pigtails bouncing. "You can crash with me, Vee. Get whatever shit is most important, and let's go."

Ivy swept a long look around the paradise of her own making—yeah, that was sorrow there. These plants . . . her friends. Her family.

But a glass house was definitely not the place for someone to live when they were throwing quite so many stones.

CHAPTER 20

———

Luke knew he could be an asshole.

But he'd really, truly been one last night, when instead of thanking Holly, he'd said some things that he really hadn't meant. But he'd been pissed off, still raging after three weeks of hell, chasing after Catwoman and her cohorts.

Three weeks and six robberies. Banks, jewelry stores . . . It was a shock there was any money or valuables left in Gotham City thanks to Catwoman and her merry band of criminals.

Then there were the little explosions—cargo boxes at the docks destroyed, animals freed from the zoo and circus. . . . There was no rhyme or reason to their attacks. Some for cash, some just for hell-raising.

And worse than all that, Gordon had told him last night, right before Luke had gone into his boxing match: some criminals were even pledging allegiance to Catwoman. Thanks to those leaked photos in the papers. The footage of their unchecked rampage.

A new Queen of the Underworld, the papers and petty criminals called her.

So he'd gone into his fight mad. Unfocused. He'd won, but he had taken one hell of a beating for it.

So when Holly had come in, when his body had been aching and his temper already on edge, and she'd casually mentioned her *date*. He'd reacted poorly.

And he would have gotten up to apologize, but his battered body had refused. Literally refused to get up from that couch. He'd slept on the damn thing. When he'd awoken and knocked on Holly's door the next morning, she hadn't answered.

He didn't have her cell, or he might have texted her with a request to meet up—not an apology. He owed her those words face to face.

But the day passed, and he spent it sleeping on and off, watching whatever football games were on TV. He staggered to knock on her door around lunch: nothing. Dinner: nope.

If she was ignoring him, he didn't blame her.

Luke was still lying on the couch as night fell, wondering how the hell he'd get into his suit, right as the football game cut to live footage. Of Blackgate Penitentiary smoldering under the night sky. Luke swore as he read the headline on the bottom of the screen, then bolted for his bedroom.

Three of Joker's Henchmen Freed from Prison,
Catwoman Suspected

———

Selina strode into the small bar at the docks, Ivy and Harley trailing her. The Joker's three henchmen, still in their orange jumpsuits, two steps behind them.

Everyone packed into the dark, wood-paneled space went dead still. Even the raging rock music from the speakers cut out.

She'd waited until now, weeks after that encounter at the bank, for a reason. Had picked this bar for a reason. Knew it was a hangout for people like Carmine Falcone, people who answered to *many* of the bosses in this city and came here to meet on neutral ground.

The grenade at Ivy's place had just propelled Selina to act a little faster.

Cops didn't come here. They didn't dare. Even the crooked ones.

Ivy and Harley stood tall beside Selina as she surveyed the room: the polished oak floors, the original 1800s tiled ceiling, the displayed photos of bosses both old and present, the globes of golden lights mounted on the paneled walls. For a group of criminals, they'd taken care to preserve the original character of the space.

And all of them now stared their way, some with drinks in midair.

Selina said to no one in particular, "Here are the rules."

Her claws slid free of her gloves, glinting in the dim lights. At her side, her bullwhip was a weight, begging to be used.

Not yet. Not yet.

"You stay out of our way, you assist us when asked, and the rewards will be . . ." She strode to the three chained men. A brutal slice of her claws had their shackles snapping free. One after another. "Plentiful."

The Joker's henchmen grinned, rotating their wrists.

"You decide to get in our way," Selina said softly to those assembled as she prowled for the man seated nearest to them at the ornately carved oak bar, "you try to screw us over, and the punishments will be . . ." The man trembled on his red velvet stool as she gently ran a claw down his stubbly cheek. Then the other. She rumbled a soft laugh. "Plentiful."

She turned, nodding to Harley and Ivy.

"Bitch," someone spat from the back. Selina rolled her eyes.

Yet—she knew that voice.

Selina halted.

The room was silent as a tomb.

Her mask identified the speaker, though she didn't need the intel. An aging, overweight Italian man seated at a table near the dartboard.

Carmine Falcone.

Precisely who she'd come to see.

He still looked the same, still wore his too-tight tailored suits, still had that slicked-back hair and sneer permanently on his pale face. The burst capillaries all over his hawkish nose. She wondered if the Leopards still answered to him. If Mika had broken free yet.

Selina stalked toward him. Ivy murmured, "You've done it now, asshole."

To his credit, Falcone didn't flinch.

He only smirked at her and took a swig from his beer. No one had ever made him tremble. No one had *ever* defied him.

There was a first time for everything, Selina supposed.

She thumbed free her bullwhip and let it sing.

One crack had Falcone's beer shattered in his hand.

The second had the whip wrapped around his neck, and him hauled over the table, thrashing like a lassoed pig.

Four of his men leapt to their feet from nearby tables, guns out.

Only to find Ivy and Harley with their own personal arsenals already aimed at them, the Joker's henchmen flanking the women, eager for the fight.

In Ivy's hand, a blood-red flower glowed in the golden lights of the bar.

I made a new model after the bank heist, Ivy had said when she showed Selina earlier. Flowers that were capable of taking out *many* men, not just the one closest.

But Ivy hadn't stopped there. Around her other hand: that vine. Its tip now equipped with slashing thorns.

The man closest to Ivy was cringing at the swirling plant around her wrist. The crony before Harley had blanched at the small metal ball in her hand, painted like a child's toy.

Selina tightened her grip on the bullwhip as she stalked closer, Falcone trying and failing to free it from around his bulging neck.

Selina swiped her claws down his back, opening up his suit and the checkered shirt beneath. A hairy, sweaty slab of flesh greeted her. "The East End is mine," she said quietly.

It always had been.

And despite the whip around his neck, Falcone screamed as she ran one claw down the column of his spine, skin splitting, blood gushing.

With a flick of her wrist, the bullwhip sprang free.

Falcone was shuddering and groaning.

Selina only said to him, "Be grateful that wasn't your tongue."

Then she strode for the door, Harley and Ivy backing out with little smirks, weapons still trained on Falcone and his men.

"Tell them good night, Ivy," Selina said, strutting out the bar door, the Joker's three henchmen following her like well-trained dogs.

Ivy chuckled, soft and sweet. "Good night."

A petal-soft thump on the floor, a hissing noise beginning, and then—

Shouts and roars.

By the time Harley and Ivy were swaggering out into the night to meet Selina, the bar had fallen silent. They'd all have one hell of a headache when they woke up. And realize that she hadn't called GCPD on them while they were knocked unconscious.

She only wished she could see Falcone's face when he regained consciousness. When he understood his reign was at an end, especially after that humiliation.

Harley half skipped down the cracked sidewalk ahead; Ivy linked arms with Selina. "What happens next?"

Selina gazed toward the northern horizon. "They kneel."

Gordon held his officers at bay long enough for Luke to study the site of the prison break at Blackgate for an hour, his suit's tech analyzing everything from the gas Poison Ivy had used to bring down the guards to the explosives Harley had set in the concrete walls. All orchestrated by Catwoman.

Out of hand. Completely out of hand.

Within the prison, the inmates were rattling the bars, taunting him as he passed by on his way out, Gordon in tow. Some spat on Gordon, but the man ignored it.

"They've gotten away with everything so far," Gordon said tightly. "Now they're just trying to see what the limit is."

Luke knew it. But Catwoman had warned him that worse was coming to Gotham City. Her words still lingered. "If she's bold enough to do this, then it might be an indication she'll go after Arkham itself."

"No one is that dumb."

"She's working with Harley. She freed three of the Joker's cronies tonight. She might very well be preparing to free the Joker, either as a gift to Harley or to curry favor from the man himself." Luke's blood chilled at the thought.

Gordon shook his head and opened the sealed door to let them out into the prison's main waiting area. Cops filled the space, all sizing up Luke as he passed. As Batwing passed—his armor like blue lightning in the fluorescents overhead.

"We can't let that happen," Gordon said, pausing at the doors to the prison.

Far beyond, out by the border fences, cameras flashed and reporters jockeyed for the best angle to catch his exit. Luke pushed a button on his suit, prepping his wings for flight. Soaring up and out was his best way to escape the reporters—and their questions.

"I've got it handled," Luke said, shouldering his way through the heavy front doors. "Trust me."

Gordon didn't look convinced, but he nodded.

Luke took three running steps into the night before flaring his wings and launching skyward.

He'd handle it, all right.

"I need you to host a gala," Luke said to his dad the next morning, bracing his hands on his father's desk. "Please."

Lucius Fox raised an eyebrow as he set aside the document he'd been reading. "Do I even want to know?"

Luke ran his hands over his head. "It's a huge favor, I know. I promise you—*promise you*—that no one will get hurt. But I need you to hold a gala in three nights. To raise money for the circus, the zoo, the jail—the public targets that have suffered from Catwoman and her criminal friends."

"I assume we will also be displaying an expensive object to be auctioned off for charity?"

"Exactly." Luke slid a pile of papers toward his father. "Ask Mom to invite all the people on this list." It was a mirror of the guest lists of every gala he'd attended where Catwoman had appeared.

His father idly scanned it. "Your mother worries enough about your readjustment to civilian life that she'll be thrilled—regardless of the inconvenient time frame."

"If anyone can put together a party in three days, it's Mom."

"She is indeed a wonder."

For not the first time, Luke wished she knew—about Batwing, about Bruce. About all of it.

Luke crossed his arms, pacing through his father's plush office.

"She's really gotten under your skin, hasn't she?"

Luke knew his father didn't mean his mother. He gave his father a long look. "She's taken it too far."

Way too far.

"Be careful, Luke. Making yourself the bait . . ." His dad sighed. "Just be careful."

Luke had no intention of doing so, but he nodded nonetheless.

CHAPTER 21

The Fox estate had been transformed into a twinkling garden, the halls and ballroom bedecked in bursting white flowers and candles, slender birch trees filling the corners, and cream silk streamers draping across the domed ceiling.

It was the prettiest place Selina had ever seen. The Venetian palaces hadn't compared to this. Not even Talia's luxurious personal quarters held a flame.

It wasn't just the signs of wealth—it was the sense of home, even in the ballroom, that radiated from each inch of it. Each room full of places where she'd love to spend an afternoon curled up. Tasteful, elegant, and welcoming.

A band played at one end of the giant domed space, the dance floor already full. Far more than usual, but the band was better than usual, too.

But even better: the diamond-and-sapphire necklace displayed in a glass case on the opposite side of the long, rectangular ball-room from where the band played.

She'd barely looked for Luke, even if it was his house. She'd spotted him by an archway, greeting almost every guest, when she arrived. All of them had seemed grateful for the security at both of the gates along the drive, stationed at every door.

Selina had seen it as a challenge.

Fifteen million dollars. That's how much the Fox necklace was worth.

Taking it when there was so much security? An added bonus.

Clad in a long-sleeved red dress, Selina had quickly surveyed the initial details of the ballroom, bypassed Luke, and greeted his mother instead. She could barely bring herself to look too long at the kind, glowing woman who had welcomed her into this house, the woman who she'd be stealing from. At the tall, handsome man at her side, the spitting image of Luke in a few decades, who greeted each guest as if they were a close friend.

So the hellos had been quick, before Luke could finish greeting the guest before him and turn their way, and Selina had headed into the crowd, letting the swish in her hips do the talking for her.

They hadn't seen or spoken to each other since that night, though he'd knocked on her door twice. She hadn't felt like answering.

In the past two hours, she'd felt him watching her, though. As she danced with countless men, as she drank and ate with the various ruling ladies of Gotham City. And now, as she danced with an aging business titan, a coy, bland smile on her face, she felt Luke's stare from across the room.

He was in the middle of a conversation with a truly ancient old man—good. The old man seemed to be talking his ear off, and though Luke seemed to be truly listening . . . Selina ignored the glance Luke cast her way. Perhaps she was being unfair, perhaps a bit sensitive, but . . .

She could still hear his cold words. About how he didn't care what she did. She didn't care if he apologized or not.

It had been her mistake. To hope for a different reaction.

The song rolled to a close, and Selina stepped out of her current partner's embrace, offering a smile to the old man. Before she'd made it a step, a deep voice said from behind her, "Mind if I cut in?"

The old man only gave a charming bow before backing away.

Selina stared up at Luke. He stared back at her.

"Hello," he said, his voice a bit hoarse. He was in his Marines uniform, dashing as ever.

Causing a scene by walking away would only draw attention to her presence. With the necklace in the balance, her best chance of remaining undetected lay in being seen here, but not really *noted*.

"Hello," Selina said, offering up a hand for him to take.

Luke kept silent, sliding a hand around her waist as he took her hand and led her into the next song.

Selina cringed a bit as a sweet, old jazz melody filled the ballroom.

Not this song. Anything but this song.

It wasn't the song from *Carousel*, but . . . How many times had she heard Maggie play this, singing along as best she could? How many times had she slow-danced with her sister in their kitchen to this song?

Her body turned distant, the dress stifling. Every beat and note a stab to the gut. She could barely look at Luke, at anyone.

Fighting the pain rising in her chest, Selina fixed her gaze on a spot over his shoulder.

Luke made it through the first verse and chorus before he asked, "Not a fan of jazz?"

The question pulled her out of the fog of memory long enough to look at him. It was another life ago. Another world. And this new world she inhabited . . . "I love jazz, actually." It was the truth.

"Then why the grimace?"

She could never explain. Not really. "Someone I . . . They loved this song." She shook her head. "Old memories." It was as much truth as she could offer.

Luke swallowed. "I'm sorry for how shitty I acted the other night."

Selina stiffened. "It's fine."

Luke frowned. "It's not. I'm never at my best after a fight, and with the pain and exhaustion, and when you mentioned your date—"

"Oh, so it's my fault you snapped at me?"

An older couple whipped their heads toward them. Luke led her a little farther away, voice low as he said tightly, "I didn't say that."

"Yes, you did." Her jaw clenched as she looked away, searching for an escape route off this dance floor that wouldn't raise any eyebrows.

He cleared his throat. "I reacted badly. That's what I'm trying to say."

"What do you even care?" The words were cold, flat. Not at all the lilting drawl she wielded with Holly.

"I thought we were friends," he said carefully.

Again, she looked at him, no light or amusement in her voice. "I don't have friends."

A muscle flickered in his jaw. "Well, I'm trying to change that." Selina said nothing. He went on, "And I'm trying to apologize to you."

She only watched the band behind him, her face a mask of calm cold.

"Holly," Luke said.

She hated that name. Was growing sick of that name.

He loosed a breath. "I'm sorry. I mean it."

He sounded sincere.

Slowly, Selina met his earnest brown eyes.

She didn't bother to keep her wariness from her stare. Wariness and . . . exhaustion.

Holly. He thought he was dancing with *Holly*.

It didn't matter. Not when she had so much to do to bring this city to its knees. Not with the weight of her mission pressing on her. It had been pressing on her for longer than she could remember.

Luke said, his voice rough, "Some days, I feel like I'm still back there. Overseas. Most nights, my body and mind can't tell the difference. And most days, I feel . . . half here." He swallowed, as if unsure where he was going with this. "I'm still learning how to return to being normal again. If such a thing exists."

Selina let his words sink in, his honesty.

She scanned his handsome face. "Being normal is a trap."

He blinked.

Selina whispered as the song came to a close, "Don't let it cage you."

The last of the guests had been taken home by their drivers two hours ago.

His parents had headed to bed thirty minutes after that, and Luke had feigned exhaustion as well.

But as the clock struck two, he remained cloaked in the shadows of the ballroom, the light on his suit dimmed as he watched the necklace across the room glint in the moonlight streaming in through the wall of glass doors leading onto the veranda.

He'd been waiting for over an hour now. Had listened as the estate workers turned off the lights and either left or found their own rooms in the sprawling house.

She hadn't come during the party. A small disappointment.

Perhaps she'd deemed the added security not as a challenge, but as suicide. Luke had sent them packing. He didn't want her to see the whole thing for what it was: a trap.

Two-ten.

Two-fifteen.

Then—

Luke kept as still as one of the statues flanking him as she appeared.

She slipped through the glass doors from the veranda without a sound. She'd disabled the house's alarm system, then. Interesting.

Catwoman moved across the parquet floors, little more than a shadow herself. Every movement fluid and graceful. Calculated and controlled.

She halted before the glass case on the pedestal—studied the necklace glinting within.

Her claws slid free.

Luke's muscles tensed, every instinct telling him to spring.

Yet he still watched as she scratched a claw in a circle around the glass. As she held out her awaiting palm right beneath, catching the disk before it could shatter on the floor. Expert, swift work.

No sign of Harley or Ivy. The slate veranda beyond the glass doors was empty, save for a few potted boxwoods, the manicured lawn glistening with dew in the moonlight.

Perhaps she didn't want her friends getting a cut of tonight's prize.

Catwoman again scanned the ballroom—as if listening for something. But Luke kept pressed into the shadows, the pillar in front of him hiding any sign of his body, his armor.

She returned her attention to the case, the necklace within. Her hand slid into the circle she'd opened up, claws glinting as she reached for the jewels.

Luke sucked in a breath. He had the evidence he needed, re-corded on his suit's camera. Proof of intent. His knees bent, ready-ing to lunge.

The attack happened so fast it took Luke a heartbeat to realize what was going on.

Not from him.

The attack didn't come from him.

A slim female figure, clad in loose black clothes, pounced from the shadows. From *above*. From the windows lining the wall right below the domed ceiling.

And as the woman landed on silent feet, sending Catwoman leaping back, slamming into the stone base of the case as she went, Luke got one look at the tan-skinned woman's face, half hidden beneath a black hood and scarf over her mouth, and knew who she was.

Tigris.

One of the most notorious and deadly members of the League of Assassins.

CHAPTER 22

A League member—a powerful one—had arrived in Gotham City. Luke had read Bruce's file on Tigris, on all the known assassins for the League.

The woman had killed her way across the world—and those kills were often ugly.

The perfect representative of the League itself, the organization that was larger, wealthier, and far more dangerous than any of the criminals in Gotham City. Mercifully, the League had yet to try to expand into this city. Luke's blood iced over at the thought of Tigris being just the start.

Catwoman rolled, claws gouging deep lines in the wood floors to steady herself as she jumped to her feet.

They stared at each other for a long moment; in her black hood, only Tigris's eyes were visible.

Far bigger players are coming to Gotham, Catwoman had said. She'd *warned* him.

Worse things than the Joker and his cohorts. Worse things like the League of Assassins.

And if the League had set its sights on Gotham City after all these years . . .

His parents were in this house. Sleeping upstairs.

Luke had a heartbeat to decide: to warn them to get to their panic room, or to join the fight to stop Catwoman and Tigris.

Catwoman moved before he could pick. She charged right at Tigris.

The assassin braced her feet apart.

Catwoman feinted left, then bolted right. Right through the open door from the veranda. Avoiding the crash of glass that might send his parents or employees investigating.

Catwoman made it twenty feet onto the slate tiles of the veranda before Tigris was after her.

Luke sprinted outside and halted dead in his tracks as the assassin launched herself upon Catwoman.

It should have been over immediately.

But Catwoman did not go down.

They fought in a black whirlwind, no weapons. Just fists and feet and limbs. Neither went for the weapons on them; even Catwoman's bullwhip hung untouched at her hip.

Fast. So damn fast he could barely track them.

Catwoman, even on the defensive . . . she held her own.

Where Tigris would have knocked her feet from under her, Catwoman nimbly dodged the blow. Where Tigris would have slammed her fist into Catwoman's helmeted face, the punch was blocked. Strike, move, block—over and over.

Luke had no words for it.

He'd never seen *anyone* fight like that.

When Tigris landed a brutal blow to the ribs, she took it. Didn't stumble. Kept moving. And the punches that Catwoman threw were deadly, like Tigris's, but he'd seen that style before. Whatever training Catwoman had gone through, boxing had been a part of it. And no small amount of gymnastics, from the ease with which she bent and moved.

She danced on her feet, weaving beautifully. She'd taken whatever she'd learned in the ring and modified it. Amplified it. Luke stopped naming the techniques and maneuvers after he recognized six of them.

After Catwoman began to push back—again and again. Punch, jab, duck, kick—

They held nothing back.

And as Catwoman took the offensive, while Tigris was forced to yield step after step, he knew who was going to win.

Tigris fought beautifully, like a blade made flesh.

But Catwoman fought like she meant it. As if her fear of losing wasn't death, but something else. Something that fueled her, focused her.

Luke saw it coming: the blow that would end it.

Tigris threw a punch—the strength behind it enough to shatter someone's ribs—its form utter perfection.

Catwoman let her think the blow was going to land. And as it neared her stomach, she whirled.

One hand locked onto Tigris's exposed arm. The other went around her back.

With a grunt that even Luke heard, she flipped the assassin right over her shoulder. Slammed Tigris onto the three steps leading down from the veranda.

Stone cracked; bone crunched.

Tigris lay there for a heartbeat—stunned. Or broken, Luke didn't know.

Catwoman was on her instantly. And this time, a blade came out.

She'd pulled a short sword from a hidden sheath down her back. He hadn't even known one was built into her suit. The blade glinted brightly in the moonlight as she lifted it.

Time to move. Luke fired a steel bolt from his suit's arm.

And as that blade came down, his bolt met the center of her sword.

Catwoman cried out in surprise as her blade went flying into the grass. She whirled toward him, the lenses of her helmet seeming to glow with irritation.

Luke approached, realizing that Tigris wasn't moving because Catwoman had broken her *spine*, and said, "Don't."

Catwoman remained where she was. "This doesn't involve you."

Luke pointed his next bolt toward Catwoman's face. "She might have valuable information."

"I'm sure she does," Catwoman said. "But it doesn't matter to me."

"You'll kill her for stepping on your territory?"

Tigris let out a low laugh. "You're dead," she said in a thick accent.

Catwoman turned back to the assassin, head angling in that way he knew meant trouble.

But faster than either Luke or Catwoman could move, Tigris brought her hand up to her mouth, grimacing in pain at the movement, and—

Poison.

Catwoman lunged, as if she'd rip the capsule from Tigris's mouth—

The assassin's chest rose and fell rapidly. "You're a dead woman walking after what you stole." She laughed at Catwoman.

Then—nothing.

Her dark eyes went still. Unseeing.

For a long moment, Catwoman stared at Tigris's body. She was a body now. A corpse.

"Shit," she breathed.

"You were about to kill her anyway," Luke said coldly, his helmet deepening his voice.

Catwoman stood, pushing off Tigris's broken, limp body, and retrieved her sword from the grass. A smooth motion had the blade again sheathed and hidden down the back of her suit. "I was going to give her an injury that would keep her out of my way for a while."

"The broken spine wasn't enough?"

He could have sworn she winced. "That was a mistake."

He couldn't quite process it. There was a corpse between them as Luke remained atop the steps, Catwoman in the grass.

Catwoman at his *parents' house*, his childhood home. On the lawn where he and his parents had played soccer, where his mom had pitched him baseballs, where they'd had picnics and parties, where he'd gone sledding down to the pond.

She did not belong here. In this place. With his parents sleeping only a floor up—

His parents. If his mom found a body on the estate grounds, if she even *heard* about it, she'd demand answers. Ones he wanted to keep her far, far away from.

And it would be such a profoundly shitty way to repay them for their help tonight.

Not that Catwoman knew. Not that she had any idea that the man standing before her was the same billionaire's son she'd stolen from twice now and had tried to rob a third time.

Luke said, "We need to move the body off the grounds for the cops to find."

"No handcuffs for me?" A sly, husky question.

"She attacked you and then killed herself. But if you want to go to jail, sure."

Silence.

"Consider this a favor. I don't arrest you, and you help me get this body off the grounds."

"Why?"

He pointed to the house. "Because the Fox family is one of the few decent ones in this city, and I'm not going to risk the League sniffing around here for information about their prized killer." The thought of the League coming here, grabbing his parents, was enough to make him nauseated.

"So noble," she snorted, but moved to Tigris's booted feet. Picked them up. "Well?"

Luke grimaced beneath his mask, debating. Drained from her fight and with her hands occupied, she'd be an easy target, and he had all the evidence he needed to bring her in, and yet . . .

She had kept the fight silent. Had moved it outside. Perhaps to keep the risks, the casualties, contained. And whether that was because she also knew that his parents were good people, Luke appreciated it.

He stepped up to Tigris's head and slid his gloved hands under her shoulders. "There are some woods by the road, just beyond the property border."

Luke realized within seconds that while Tigris appeared slender, beneath the loose black clothes, her body was packed with dense muscle. Heavy muscle.

He and Catwoman didn't speak as they hauled Tigris's corpse between them, across the lawn, past the formal gardens, through the dense thickets, and finally over the property border and into the woods beyond. He could have navigated it blind, but made sure to stop every now and then, as if assessing some mental map of his surroundings.

And only when they were perhaps a quarter mile into the pines did Luke say to her, "Here is good. The road isn't too far off."

To his surprise, Catwoman laid the assassin's feet down gently.

He blew out a breath as he did so as well, the sound gobbled up by the cool night winds dancing in the trees around them, making the pines sway as if they were drunkenly dancing.

She stared at the assassin. Long enough that Luke opened up a panel in his suit's arm to send a covert call to GCPD. He punched in the first two numbers, and then—

Soft, whispered Arabic filled the space between them.

At first, he thought Tigris was still alive.

But then he realized the lilting, beautiful words—they were coming from her. Catwoman.

Her Arabic was almost perfect.

He hadn't heard it spoken so well since he'd returned. There was a slight American accent, the same as his own when he spoke it.

He said nothing, lowering his hand from the panel in his arm. Terminating the call.

She finished, kneeling to close Tigris's open eyes with her gloved fingers.

When Catwoman rose, she stared at the woman's corpse for a long moment before she said, "She trained me at the League."

Every thought eddied out of Luke's head.

She'd been trained at the League, trained by Tigris herself. Which meant—

Catwoman's head lifted, the moonlight illuminating the lenses over her eyes. "I am a ghūl—as she is. Was." She flexed her gloved hands, as if shaking the feel of the assassin from them. "It's what League assassins call themselves. When our training is complete, our final task is to dig our own future graves and recite our own final prayers. We lie in them from dusk until dawn. And when we emerge from the earth afterward . . . we are ghūls. Wraiths."

He didn't ask how many of them ever made it back to their gravesites to fill those holes in the ground.

She wasn't just some skilled jewel thief.

A trained killer.

From the League of Assassins.

"The prayer," she went on, more to herself than him. "It was her final rite. What is owed to any wraith."

"Yet you didn't want to kill her tonight."

Even though Tigris had come here to kill *her*—for something she'd stolen.

Silence.

Luke demanded, "If you're in the League, why are you working with Harley and Ivy?"

She studied him as if debating her answer. "I left."

Luke took a moment to process those words. "No one leaves the League."

"I did."

Hence the assassin after her. "Why?"

"Nyssa and Talia al Ghūl have always striven to follow in their father's footsteps." An ecoterrorist maniac—not like Poison Ivy's desire to save the planet, to coexist with plant and animal. No, the man wanted the earth wiped clean of *all* human life. Catwoman shrugged. "I found I no longer fit in."

Hence the warning the other week. That worse was coming, either as part of Nyssa and Talia's agenda, or . . . to hunt the woman before him. "So you left," he said.

A slight nod.

He wanted to see her face. Wanted to know who he was speaking to, who had fought like a black wind tonight, who had dared walk away from the League, dared defy it—

"And as for why I'm working with Ivy and Harley . . ." A shrug. "Since I am no longer a part of the League, I need money to establish myself in Gotham."

Luke blinked, jaw clenching. Right. *That.*

She went on, "I stole something valuable from Nyssa when I left." Tigris's warning echoed in his head. "I've been weighing options for potential buyers. But until I sell it, I'm low on funds."

"What about just getting a *job*?"

She laughed quietly. "You're terribly naive to say that."

Luke stiffened. But instead of lunging for her, he lifted his forearm and finally dialed the GCPD. He gave a clipped explanation that a body had been found at this specific location, hung up, and growled at her, "Don't even think about running."

Because he was going to arrest her. Right now. He hit a button on his suit, the tech powering up, readying for the chase. His Bat-Cuffs clicked free from his Utility Belt.

Another soft laugh. "Oh, I don't think so."

His suit detected two others beside her. Right as Harley Quinn clenched two of those small circus-ball explosives—one in each hand—a gas mask covering her face. And Poison Ivy thumbed free one of the orchids from the vine snaking across her torso. Smoke rippled from it. Not to take him down but to cloud their escape.

"Hi, handsome," Ivy drawled. Harley grinned.

Something sparkled at Catwoman's fingertips.

The necklace. The Fox necklace.

When Tigris had slammed her into that case the second time, she must have swiped it. Too fast for even him to see.

The diamonds burned with blue fire in the moonlight. "Thanks for this," Catwoman said, and took a step back.

Luke said tightly, "I have it on good authority that necklace is a fake."

He'd had a replica made yesterday. Cubic zirconia and painted brass.

Total worth: a few hundred bucks.

Catwoman let out a low laugh, the sound echoed by twin rumbles. Motorcycles. Parked on the road a few feet away. She stepped back into the smoke. "Oh, I know."

Then vanished.

Luke lunged through the smoke, dodging trees before he reached the quiet road.

She sped off into the night on the back of Harley Quinn's motorcycle. Too fast for him to follow, even with the wings.

He should have grabbed her. Should have handcuffed her to

Tigris and waited until the cops came. Should have . . . He had no idea.

A League assassin with a conscience.

Here to sell something that the League would kill for and Gotham City's underworld would line up to buy.

His stomach turned. But even as it did, Luke recalled the way she'd fought. That low laugh. That frank, cool openness with which she spoke to him.

And the heat that rose through him, stretching his skin tight over his bones. An aftereffect of battle, of adrenaline. Even though he hadn't thrown a single punch. Even if he'd stood there, gawking, while she fought. Beautiful, graceful, and utterly off-limits.

Trouble. He was in big, big trouble.

CHAPTER 23

━━━━━━━━━━

Selina had been on the run for a month and a half.

She'd taken money from Nyssa. Broken into the safe in her office and swiped her bank card out of her wallet, minutes before Selina had headed off on a mission for the League. She'd walked out of the compound right through the front doors.

She didn't know how long it had taken them to figure out who had done it. Probably Talia herself had pieced it together. But by now it would be clear that Selina had taken a train not to Greece like she'd been ordered, but to Switzerland, where she withdrew all of the account's cash, set up a fancy new Swiss bank account, and became Holly Vanderhees.

The hair, the nails, the clothes. The shoes, the bags, the jewels. The cars, the residences, the private plane. The last one was leased, of course, but all of it—the identity she'd built—purchased with Nyssa's blood money. She only wished she'd had time to grab Talia's, too.

And what Selina had brought along with her, the payoff from *that* . . . Worth it. Utterly worth it.

"So all of this trouble tonight," Harley said over the motorcycle's roar as they sped off into the night, "was over a *fake?*"

Selina had known it was a trap. Whether Luke Fox and his stupid apologies knew his family had been used, she had no idea. Didn't care.

But it was interesting that Batwing cared about the Fox family. She stored that information away to puzzle over later.

Batwing himself was a problem. Mostly because she liked him. He definitely filled out that suit, but she . . . she just liked him. That relentless drive to protect the innocents in this city, no matter the cost. To fight past his own demons to do so. Which meant he was absolutely lethal for everything she was working toward.

And though she could tell he was equally intrigued by her, and could certainly use that to her advantage . . .

"He threw down a challenge," Selina said. "We couldn't let it go unanswered." Hence why she'd had Ivy and Harley remain behind. Going in for a fake necklace hadn't been worth the risk. So they'd waited here, on the outskirts, to retrieve her.

Tigris showing up had been unexpected.

Oh, Nyssa and Talia must be mad. Furious. And with Shrike and Tigris now dead . . .

"Get up, you pathetic worm." Tigris's burning dark eyes were barely visible beneath her hood. "Do you think our enemies give us breaks to catch our breath?"

Always words like our *and* us *were used here at the compound. Despite the brutality, the competition, there was an* us *vs.* them *mentality to the very way the instructors spoke; all designed to include. Indoctrinate.*

We. Us. Ours.

Lying on the mats of the training center, barely able to breathe around the stitch in her side, Selina focused. Tried to calm her raging heart and get up.

"Too slow," Tigris hissed, and launched herself upon Selina.

She had enough time to raise her arms, to bring up her knees. Enough time to roll up and out of Tigris's path, but not enough to avoid the sweeping kick that knocked her down again. The blow to the throat that truly ripped the air out of her lungs, then the blow to her stomach that knocked her down for good, curling around herself.

"Pathetic." Tigris had laughed at her then. Laughed and walked away.

Selina had hated her ever since. Hated her more when she'd seen some of the other acolytes not be able to walk away. Or breathe. Permanently.

Nyssa and Talia had never punished Tigris for it—for *killing* acolytes during training. Nyssa had only declared it natural selection. Talia had just stroked Tigris's dark hair.

Selina had imagined ripping out Tigris's throat more times than she could count.

Tonight she'd known that Tigris would savor killing her. Luckily, Tigris's confidence had been her downfall. She hadn't been prepared for Selina's show of skill, for Selina to *want* to win, and it had made the assassin *furious* to realize she had to go on the defensive. To realize that Selina had been sneaking in extra training at the League, had been studying Tigris herself during every encounter.

Yet when Selina had slammed her into those steps, accidentally breaking her spine . . .

That dark, shredded part of Selina had savored it, too. That blow. The repayment. For all of them.

Selina did not mourn her. She'd uttered that prayer because . . . She didn't know why. Perhaps out of some fool's idea that if she herself had fallen, she'd want someone to do the same for her. To at least mark that she'd existed—that *Selina Kyle* had existed.

But Selina didn't want to think on it. Think too long on the pieces inside her that were so blood-splattered.

"We should have ended him when we had the chance," Harley spat. "Made it look like he and whoever that was killed each other." A pause. "Who *was* that woman?"

"A crony of some boss," Selina half lied. Tigris *did* answer to Nyssa and Talia.

Ivy called over her bike's engine, "Definitely should have killed him, then."

Selina didn't answer. It had been hard enough to keep the two of them at bay, keep them from seizing their chance to bring down Batwing. They didn't understand that if the League was closing in, they needed a hero. *She* needed him. To keep the League away for as long as possible.

Limited time. She was on limited time.

She knew how Nyssa and Talia hunted their own. She'd helped them do it in the past.

First the vanguard: Shrike.

Then the test of abilities: Tigris.

And the next step . . .

There was not much time left before the next step.

And she would need an army to face it.

Selina looked up at the stars barely visible with the glow from the distant city lights.

Armies required money. And a healthy dose of fear.

* * *

"Remind me why we're sitting up on this rooftop in the cold?" Ivy's breath curled from her mouth as she sat beside Selina and studied the alley below. Summer was finally yielding to autumn's chill. A small mercy, to at last say farewell to the heavy heat.

"Because I need you to cover me while I have a little chat with some lowlifes in a few minutes."

Ivy only yawned, rearranging her colorful assortment of shimmering flowers on the roof tiles before them. Her little vine friend was tucked into the warmth of her pocket. "Plants don't like cold."

"Well, you're still technically a human, so it doesn't apply."

"Some days," Ivy admitted, "I don't feel like it."

Ivy had no idea how much Selina agreed with that sentiment. But mentioning it opened the door to too many questions.

So Selina picked up the newspaper she'd brought with her, telling Ivy when she'd asked that it was for the wait.

She'd already done the crossword puzzle, Ivy leaning over frequently to interrupt or snatch Selina's pen to fill in an answer.

Selina snapped the paper, flipping through the international headlines.

An inquiring *meow* sounded across the roof, and Ivy made a small sound of delight. Lowering the paper, Selina smiled at the little gray cat who padded over to them. "Stalker," she told the cat as she brushed against Selina's shins, wending through her legs.

Ivy leaned over, stroking the cat's back. "Do you know that free-ranging domesticated cats are responsible for the death of billions of birds and mammals each year? Our little fur-baby here is a stone-cold hunter."

Selina smiled, scratching the cat's whiskery chin. "I'm shaking in my boots."

Ivy frowned down at the cat. "So are the birds."

The cat blinked up at Ivy, as if scowling herself, and scuttled off into the dark.

Selina snickered, picking up the paper again and flapping through it.

Ivy smirked. "You pretend to be serious and broody, but beneath that mask, I know you're smiling all the time."

Selina waved her off, snapping the sagging paper upright. She paused at the Science section, sighing as boredom set in, and tapped the article on the front page. "You think this stuff is all just hocus-pocus?"

Ivy leaned over, skimming the article. "Ley lines?"

Selina shrugged, glancing to the alley below. All clear. "'Naturally occurring pathways of energy that run across the earth like highways.' Sounds fake to me."

Ivy hauled the paper toward herself. "Oh, they're real, all right. They've done tests on them—some of the energy is so strong that if you find a ley line on a hill and put your car in neutral, it can move the car uphill for you."

"That's got to be a hoax."

Ivy frowned at her over the paper. "This is the Science section. They don't publish *hocus-pocus*, as you called it." Ivy paused for a moment, as if weighing some internal debate. Selina held still as she did. At last, Ivy nodded, more to herself than anything, and said, "There's a ley line outside Gotham."

Selina scanned the rest of the page. "That's not in the article."

"That's because no one knows it's there. I mean, those of us in the science community do, but . . . we don't blab to the press. I'm sure some evil corporation is probably going to find a way to destroy the ley lines."

"Probably." Selina neatly folded the paper and set it aside. "Want to take a drive out there? See the car trick in motion?"

Ivy considered, then jerked her chin to the alley below. "What about them, though?"

Selina snorted as two figures entered the alley at last. "This won't take long."

She launched herself over the brick wall of the roof, down the drainpipe, and right into the path of the two midlevel cronies of Carmine Falcone.

By the time Ivy's toxins slithered over the roof edge, knocking the men out cold, Selina was grinning.

It would only be a matter of time before the two of them reported to their boss what she'd deigned to warn them: the League was coming to steal what Catwoman was selling to Gotham City's underworld. And that the League would raze the city to the ground before they left. They had no interest in alliances, in money.

Because what Selina was selling . . . it was that valuable. And to get it back, to avoid it falling into the wrong hands, the League would make sure that every lowlife and criminal in Gotham City was swept away in the bloodbath that would soon be unleashed on the city.

If the underworld did not prepare. If they did not ready to strike back. If they were content to continue being grunts and worms.

Gotham City would fall—but not to these foreign interlopers. It would fall to *her.*

* * *

"I'm assuming this car is stolen." Ivy frowned at the Range Rover's black leather interior. She perched on the leather as though she couldn't stand to have it touch her skin.

"It is," Selina said mildly. She'd swapped out her helmet for an onyx domino mask that revealed the bottom portion of her face, her hair hidden beneath the hood of a heavy black sweatshirt. Ivy, surprisingly, had said nothing when Selina emerged, car in tow, with her helmet stashed in the back seat. It seemed that silence was about to end, however.

"Do you know what sort of evil the leather industry does on a daily basis? The slaughter?"

"Hence you being vegan," Selina said.

Ivy watched the city passing in a blur. "You're not going to laugh about it?"

"It's your life. Your choices about food don't impact mine."

Ivy studied her. "You really need the mask?"

Selina snorted. "Little steps."

Ivy shrugged, monitoring the dark road ahead. The ley line was forty minutes to the west of the city, most of that drive down a single-lane road with no trees or anything to surround it. Only a flat, barren plain. "This used to be a forest." Ivy motioned to the hints of grass the headlights revealed. "It was cut down in the early 1900s to fuel the expansion of Gotham."

"Never grew back?"

"Obviously not."

Selina frowned. "The city should have planted new trees."

"Back then, no one gave a shit. Still don't."

Selina considered. "What would it cost—to replant the forest here?"

"A lot. And it'd take a long time for anything to grow."

There was enough sorrow in her voice, enough resignation, that Selina said, "Well, maybe some of our profits . . . Maybe it can go to that." More green spaces were never a bad thing. Not at all.

Ivy studied her for a long minute, and Selina kept her attention on the road, monitoring for any deer or wildlife trying to cross as she gave her space to reply.

Ivy said a bit softly, "I've never had many friends."

Selina was grateful for the road to distract her.

"And even though it's risky, this little trio of ours . . ." Ivy's voice remained soft. "It's more fun than I've had in ages." She swallowed. "I went through school so fast I never got the chance to, you know—be normal. Go to parties or hang out with kids my age."

"I could be forty-five for all you know." Selina often felt like she was. She certainly hadn't done anything society liked to call *normal* while growing up.

But she'd tried to give it to Maggie. As best she could. Making Maggie happy had made up for the lack of having a typical teenage experience. Mostly.

"You're not forty-five," Ivy said, snickering. "What I can see of you certainly doesn't look like it. And you don't talk like you are, anyway."

Selina laughed a little. "Harley complains about my fancy-talking."

"Harley is just being Harley."

Selina asked carefully, "What's up with you two—your history?" She'd been dying to know for weeks now.

Even in the darkness of the car's interior, Selina could have sworn she saw a blush spread on Ivy's face. "We hook up. Harley was one of the first people I met after all the school stuff was done and I started doing this. The Poison Ivy gig, I mean. And I fell . . . hard."

"And Harley?"

A shrug. "I'm a distraction for Harley, I think. From the things that haunt her." Ivy held up her hands, vines pulling away to reveal bare flesh. "It's hard to be together when one of you is literally *toxic.*"

"I thought you could control your toxins," Selina said, still mesmerized, despite the horrors of Ivy's past, by what she'd become.

Ivy let the vines cover her hands again. "I can. But sometimes, if I lose control . . . It's a risk. Skin-to-skin contact."

It had to be lonely as hell to be that way, to worry like that.

Perhaps it was one of the most unforgivable things those scientists had done to her.

Ivy waved away her own words. "It didn't matter, anyway. Harley has never wanted to put a label on us. After the Joker, she said she wanted to be free, but . . . I don't know if it's truly because she doesn't want to be tied down, or because she worries that the Joker will take vengeance on anyone who dates her."

Noble. "I thought he's her ex, though."

"He is. But I'm not sure if Harley is even entirely over him. The Joker speaks to some broken part of her, a part I can't reach." Ivy's eyes flickered.

A good friend—Ivy was truly a good friend. "Harley deserves better than someone like the Joker." *Someone like you*, Selina added silently.

Ivy drummed her fingers on the arm of her seat, the vines along her hands shifting a bit with the motion. "He's a monster. He's worse than a monster. I don't know if you ever met him, but he's . . ." Ivy rubbed her face.

"I've heard enough to know how awful he is." Cold licked down her spine at the thought of it.

"*Evil.* He is *evil*," Ivy insisted.

"And Harley wants to be with him?" The question slipped out before Selina could stop it.

After working with Harley and Ivy these past few weeks, it still baffled her. Ivy was smart, funny, and warm. Yes, her history was pained, yes, she was a criminal, and definitely a bit of a fanatic, yes, but . . . Selina didn't understand it. Why Harley would choose to run to the Joker. Especially when she could have Ivy.

"I've wanted to ask Harley that every day for the past year," Ivy said hoarsely.

"Why don't you?" It wasn't her business, Selina reminded herself, even as she tried to convince herself that she was asking only to better know her allies.

"Because if I confront Harley about him, it will only drive her away, and I'd rather be at her side and keep an eye on her than be shut out of her life completely." Ivy's laugh was low—sad. "It's pathetic, I know."

"No, it's not," Selina said, and meant it. "For the person you love . . . you find yourself making choices like that. Living in gray areas. It's not pathetic at all."

God knows she'd done plenty of that. Gladly. Still would.

Ivy stared out the window. "I'm not sure if Harley even knows—that I still feel this way. Still want more with her, more for us. She's better at hiding that sort of stuff than you realize."

Selina refrained from saying that Harley hadn't given any sort of sign about returning Ivy's intentions. She wasn't that cruel.

Ivy blurted, "Please don't say anything to her."

"I won't." Selina studied Ivy for as long as she dared to take her eyes off the road. She admitted quietly, "I've never had any friends, either. Doing this sort of thing?" She waved a hand to the car, their little joyride to the ley line. "Never done it before."

"Why?"

Selina debated lying. Wanted to lie. But she said, "Because I had something important that I needed to take care of. And it required all my time, my energy to do it. Friends were a luxury I couldn't afford."

Ivy's throat bobbed. "And what happened—to that something you had to take care of?"

Selina steered the car into the dark. "I made a sacrifice, and then I didn't need to take care of it anymore."

Ivy told Selina where to stop, pointing out an abandoned factory that loomed like an iceberg in the sea of blackness before them. A dusty service road led off the paved street to the warehouse, dirt crunching under the Range Rover's wheels as they approached.

"Did you bring me here to murder me?" Selina asked as she put the car in park.

Ivy laughed. "If I'd wanted to do that, wouldn't it have happened by now?" She threw open the door, stepping into the night, and Selina followed suit.

The night was brisk, the stars clearer above them. Calm and quiet and safe.

Ivy gulped down a breath of air. "I'd forgotten—what fresh air tastes like."

"Me too," Selina murmured. In the silence, they stared up at the glittering bowl of the sky.

Movement caught her eye, and Selina glanced to Ivy in time to see her tip her chin up, her face bathed in moonlight. All along the vines on her hands, peeking through her sheet of red hair, white blossoms began to bloom, as if opening up to the stars themselves. The petals nearly glowed, as if they were lit from within.

Ivy slid her gaze toward Selina, toward the mouth Selina knew was hanging open. "Not all the side effects of my *transformation* were awful or deadly." More flowers bloomed in her hair, until a crown of them flowed over her brow.

"It's beautiful," Selina whispered.

Ivy smiled, wide and warm. "Thank you."

She spoke with enough gratitude that Selina wondered when the last time was that someone had said such a thing.

Selina's chest tightened at the thought. Shoving that tightness away, Selina cleared her throat and asked, "So this ley line, where is it? Under the factory? I thought it would be more obvious."

Ivy nodded, those flowers furling up and slipping back into her hair. "People have been drawn to ley lines throughout history, without even knowing why or what they were. There's no scientific reason for them, for how ancient people *knew* those lines were there. All we have to go on is that many of the world's monuments are built atop them, Stonehenge being one of the most famous. You can feel the energy in some of the lines, in the stones on them."

"I can't feel anything."

Ivy beckoned, striding toward the wood-and-steel warehouse amid the barren field. Selina marked every detail as they approached: the one-story building, the high-up windows that seemed mostly shattered, the sagging tin roof. The wooden slats that made up the siding had been cracked or ripped away in spots, the gravel drive leading to the building mostly overgrown with weeds and grass. No one had been here in a long, long while.

"It might fall down on us," Ivy warned as they paused by the small antechamber that jutted out from the side of the building, the glass window in the steel door caked with grime, "so don't go inside, but the line cuts through right about . . . here." She pointed to a spot in the grass beneath her feet, moonlight shining on shards of glass scattered among it. "You feel it?"

Selina stood where Ivy indicated. Still nothing. "I think I'll just have to take your word for it." She pointed to the car. "No hill to try it on, it seems."

"I know. I just wanted to get out of the city for a while."

"I should have guessed as much." Selina chewed on her lip. "So no one has ever harnessed the ley line's power? Here or elsewhere?"

Ivy shook her head, red hair flowing like a silken river around her. "No. Why?"

Selina followed a straight path through the grass and debris, walking the ley line. "Have you ever heard of a Lazarus Pit?"

A beat of silence. Selina looked over her shoulder at Ivy as the woman asked, vines slithering around her wrists as if curious, too, "No, what is that?"

Selina went back to tracing inside the line with her steps. "There are only a few dozen in the world. They're naturally occurring pools with regenerative powers. All atop ley lines."

"I've never heard of them."

"Because their owners don't want you to."

"And you were making fun of *me* for the hocus-pocus earlier?"

Selina shrugged. "Legend claims that a Lazarus Pit can keep old age and sickness at bay. Even bring you back from death."

"Hence their owners protecting them. And the name."

Selina nodded, pivoting on one foot—just as she'd done so many times on the balance beam at the Y—and traced the line back toward Ivy. "Once used, though, the Pit's powers are drained forever. So it's a onetime get-out-of-jail-free card."

"How do *you* know about them, if they're so secret?"

Selina paused her steps. "In the place where I was trained . . ." Ivy tensed at that, at the implication of that word. *Trained.* She'd know from that word alone what Selina was. That she'd answered to deadlier powers than Falcone or the Joker. "They had a Lazarus Pit in the catacombs. It was guarded day and night. I first heard about it from the other students, who claimed they heard instructors whispering about it."

Certainly never from Nyssa or Talia.

Ivy crossed her arms. "I'm not surprised the rich and powerful want to keep such a natural wonder and gift to themselves."

Selina studied the ground beneath her feet. "Neither am I."

Ivy asked, "If you knew about ley lines, why act like you didn't?"

"I didn't know much, just rumors. And you're the science nerd," she said. "I wanted to see if you knew more." Selina toed the dirt. Not a thrum of energy to be found, at least not through the thick soles of her boots. "And . . . maybe I wanted to get out of the city for a night, too." While Harley was off doing whatever it was that Harley did in her spare time.

Ivy smiled, a few of those flowers blooming again. "You can just ask me to hang out the next time, you know."

Selina laughed. "I realize that now."

CHAPTER 24

Luke had thanked his parents profusely for the gala—and apologized for the broken glass afterward.

Just a drunk reveler who forgot to go home, he'd told his mom. She'd given him a look that said she highly doubted it, but asked no questions.

His dad didn't need to ask questions, however, when Luke had insisted his parents go to their château in Provence.

His dad had only said he'd have the private jet fueled up and they'd be on it by midday. How his dad explained it to his mother, Luke still didn't know. But his father had hugged him tightly before Luke left the estate. He wondered if his dad was worried he'd never get to do so again. If he was remembering the phone call he'd gotten in the middle of the night when that IED landed Luke in a field hospital.

A few hours later, his parents were gone, flying over the Atlantic. That had been three days ago. And since then, Luke had spent that time holed up over at Bruce's manor—well, beneath Wayne Manor, technically. Reading through any and all files on the League.

Tigris: deceased. He'd written that into the system himself. And then he'd combed through Bruce's archives, searching for any sign of Catwoman.

Luke found nothing. Not a whisper. She hadn't gone by Catwoman until she arrived here. And either she was young enough to never have made a name for herself at the League, or she'd been kept secret by Nyssa and Talia as they waited to unleash her upon the world.

Until she'd unleashed herself instead.

And whatever she was going to sell to Gotham City's underworld . . . He couldn't risk that happening. Gray as her morals might be—ready to kill a woman and then uttering a final rite for her the next—he had no doubt that she'd go through with her plan. Jeopardizing Gotham City in the process.

Or would she? He was still puzzling over it as he finally returned to his apartment that night. She'd warned him to *protect* Gotham City from the League. The good people here.

It made no sense.

And time was short. There was a GCPD event tomorrow night, honoring the police's service to this city. Every important cop, politician, and donor would be there. It was her ideal sort of target. The kind that packed a message.

Luke had no intention of wasting this chance to grab her. Stop this madness.

He'd already warned Gordon to have extra security: armed guards, bomb-sniffing dogs, metal detectors, snipers on the roofs of adjoining buildings. Every angle had been considered.

Back in his own apartment, Luke opened his fridge and frowned at the empty insides. Right—food. He had none. He'd been living on Alfred's mercy these past few days, the older man delivering him sandwiches and tea services and the odd slice of cake or stack of cookies.

But Alfred's care went beyond that. The level of trust between Alfred and Bruce . . . that was a one-in-a-million type of bond. Not easily found or built. Yet Bruce had paid a steep, steep cost for it, one that Luke couldn't imagine. One that still haunted Bruce, decades after his parents' murder.

Luke shut the fridge, the click nearly drowning out the sound of the elevator's ding down the hall.

Which meant—

Pathetic. He was really pathetic, he decided, as he rushed to the peephole in his door and watched Holly approach her apartment. She had shopping bags again—heavy ones.

He hadn't seen her since the party at his parents' house. Since their strange, tense conversation. But it was still normal. *She* was still relatively normal.

Not at all like that cool-voiced woman who made him grind his teeth, who took on assassins and walked away. Whose face he hadn't even seen, but that quiet laugh of hers haunted him.

Normal. He needed, *wanted* normal. Even if Holly herself had warned him that it was a cage, he didn't care.

Luke flung open his door.

Holly whirled, keys in the lock, eyes wide.

He cringed. Perhaps he'd been too enthusiastic with the door-opening.

A little too eager.

He leaned an arm against the doorframe. "Hey."

Smooth. Really smooth.

She flicked her eyes over him, body loosening as she opened her door and dumped her bags inside. They landed with a heavy thump. "Hey yourself."

Not the warmest greeting. It was probably Bruce-level, if he was being honest.

"How was shopping?" His mind was a vacant hole, and he scrambled for a question, any sort of sane thing to say to her.

She flicked up her brows. "Stimulating."

Luke tapped a bare foot on the ground. "You eat yet?"

A pause. A slight tensing of her shoulders. "No," she said warily.

He tried not to look too desperate as he asked, "Pizza?"

Holly considered. Glanced at her bags behind her, then toward him. "Give me five minutes to change." Luke avoided the urge to sag with relief. "And order two this time," she added with a hint of a smile.

And even with Catwoman's low, sultry voice still purring in his head, the ghost of a real smile on Holly's mouth made everything vanish.

"I can't move," Luke groaned to Holly forty minutes later, patting his aching stomach as they sat a conservative distance apart on the couch. The TV flickered atop the lit fireplace, his apartment cozier than he could remember in recent memory.

Holly set her pedicured feet on the leather ottoman, stretching out. "I sense a food coma coming on."

Luke smiled at her, scrolling through the channel guide. "You want to watch a movie?"

A casual, tossed-out-there question. One that might very well constitute a date, if he'd asked it at another time and place.

Holly paused again. He braced himself for the rejection, but she said, "Sure."

Luke eyed her. "You're being . . . nice."

"Would you prefer I not be?"

"No, I just . . . I wasn't sure where we stood after my family's gala."

She opened her mouth to speak, but his phone buzzed on the couch between them, and her eyes dipped down.

Bruce Wayne was displayed in big letters across the front of his phone. Christ.

Luke gave her an apologetic wince and hurried into his bedroom, shutting the door.

Luke picked up right before it went to voicemail. "Hey, man."

He could practically hear Bruce's frown through the phone. "Hey yourself."

Luke stepped into his walk-in closet, shutting the door there, too. Just to be safe. "What's up?"

Another pause, heavy and long. "What the hell is happening over there?"

And there it was. The call he'd been waiting for these weeks. "I've got it under control."

"Doesn't look like it."

Luke gritted his teeth. "I don't answer to you."

"No, but you answer to the people of Gotham City."

"I've got it under control," he repeated.

"You call three women wreaking havoc on Gotham control? Poison Ivy: she's been mostly harmless. An environmental fanatic, but harmless." Luke could have sworn he heard Bruce ticking the items off on his fingers. "Harley Quinn: not so harmless, but has been quiet since her ex-boyfriend went to Arkham. So the way I see it, this newcomer—Catwoman, whatever you call her—*she's* the ringleader."

"I know."

"She's the one you need to lock up," Bruce went on.

"I know," Luke snapped.

Another one of Bruce's Pauses. "I should come back."

"No," Luke growled. "You should not. One, I've got it under control; *two*, you've got your own mission to deal with." That Bruce still hadn't told Luke about.

Luke felt just a tinge guilty—just a tinge. Because aggravation aside, the idea of seeing Bruce go head-to-head with Catwoman . . . It made something in his stomach twist a bit. Just enough that he didn't want Bruce coming home anytime soon, mission or no.

Bruce sighed tightly. "Call if you need anything."

Luke debated reminding Bruce that he wasn't some underling, but only said, "Sure, man." Bruce terminated the call without further farewell.

Luke sighed, staring at the built-in oak shelves of his closet. No, he didn't answer to Bruce. Never had and never would. But he did owe this city some semblance of safety.

Taking a moment to gather himself, Luke loosed a long breath before heading back into the living room. "Sorry about that," he said, setting the phone on the coffee table before sitting on the couch once more.

Holly lifted a groomed brow. "Friend of yours?"

"He's my boss, so . . . yeah?"

"I thought your father was the CEO."

"He is, but it's the Wayne family's company."

"And I suppose you and Bruce Wayne are card-carrying members of the Rich Kids Club."

"And you're not?"

She blinked at him. "It's different for boys."

He leaned back on the cushions. "Yeah, yeah. Says the girl who told me Europe was *boring*."

Holly rolled her eyes. "A bit of posturing."

"Why did you come here, then?"

The amusement on her face died. Went quiet. Those green eyes again wary and distant.

Luke pressed, wondering if he sounded like an idiot as he asked as casually as he could, "Bad breakup or something?"

Holly swallowed. "You could say that. I wanted . . . a fresh start."

He tucked his hands behind his head. "Well, I'm glad you did."

"Was that a *nice* thing you just said to me?"

Luke chuckled. "Smart-ass." He pointed toward the TV with the remote. "Pick a movie. Any movie."

A challenge and dare. Her green eyes flickered with it. "All right. *Carousel*."

"The musical?"

"You know it?"

"I saw the revival on Broadway a few years back." He shrugged. "*Carousel* it is."

"No, no, let's watch something *you* want—"

"Backing out of it now that I called your bluff?"

Holly crossed her arms. Luke chuckled, switching over to his streaming service and finding the movie. But as the overture started, he could have sworn he saw her smiling.

There was sand, and blood, and screaming.

His body was on fire, shrapnel turning into claws that dug deep and shredded. Limbs rained, blood sprayed, and he could do nothing while they died and died around him, while the world turned over and his ears hollowed out, and he knew he was never going home, would never see his mom or dad, would never make it home—

"Luke."

He was going to die here, in this place where he'd come to prove something—to himself, his parents, the world. To prove he wasn't some spoiled brat, to fill some hole inside himself. Now he was full of countless holes, bleeding out—

"Luke!"

He couldn't stop it. The blood, the dying. Couldn't move to help his friends, screaming in pain. Or the ones so still—not screaming at all.

"LUKE!"

The shouting tugged at him, but it was the pain that slammed him home.

His face stung, and he blinked, blinked and gasped for air, trying to reconfigure where he was, in the blue-lit dimness—

"You are in your apartment in Gotham City," said a steady female voice. "You are alive."

Luke shook, unable to halt the tremors, the mortification now burning up his face, or the nausea rising up in him—

He ran. Not for the bathroom but for the balcony.

Fresh air. He needed fresh air.

He reached the door when two strong, slim hands grabbed his shirt. Tugged him into a stop. "Luke—"

"Fresh air," he got out.

Those hands loosened their grip, but remained steady on him. One slid around his waist.

Holly.

Holly Vanderhees.

She brought him to the railing. Let him brace his arms against it, head hanging in the brisk wind, peering toward the drop below as he rallied himself, steadied himself.

"You must have nodded off." Right. After the movie had ended, he'd switched to regular cable news and she'd stayed to watch, and he'd been so warm and comfortable.

"What can I get you?" Her voice was a low, steady purr. And familiar. That tone. That calm—

"I'm fine," he said, his voice raw. He must have been screaming. "It's just the . . ." He sucked in another lungful, working through his breathing the way the therapist had taught him. "This happens. Since I came home."

She was so silent that he glanced toward her.

He didn't find the pity he expected. Or the fear.

Only—surprise. Something else he couldn't place.

But it was gone with a few blinks. She brushed sweat from his brow with her bare fingers. She did it again on his other temple. Then his cheek. The other one.

Tears.

She said quietly, "I understand. My mother was . . . abusive."

The nightmares, the horror, eddied out of his head. "I'm sorry."

Her mother was dead, he reminded himself. If only so that he didn't contemplate hunting her down and putting her behind bars.

"I still remember it, too. When she'd come home drunk or high. Sometimes both. I still hear her . . . rants. Still remember shaking in terror because I knew what was coming."

Abuse happened at every level of society. Even the highest one.

It made him sick to be reminded of this by hearing what Holly had gone through.

"She broke my arm once. When I was ten. And it's such a stupid cliché, but I told the hospital that I fell while climbing a tree."

His stomach churned as he glanced at the arm she now touched, like she could still feel that broken bone.

"Did your dad . . . ?" Her parents were both dead; asking was dangerous territory, yet—

"He was never there. Didn't even know it happened." He stared at her, and Holly did not look away. "I know what it's like," she said quietly. "To have those nightmares."

Luke swallowed, his heartbeat at last calming, his breath evening out as he focused on Holly and her voice. "We both survived," he rasped. "We both made it out."

Again, that flicker of emotion in her eyes that he could not place. "We did," she replied, her arm brushing against his. That arm that had seen such pain, such ugliness.

He studied their touching arms. The fingers that had so gently wiped the tears from his face. He hooked a finger under her chin, lifting her head to find her eyes upon him.

Luke found himself not caring about who might be watching from the buildings around them, the street far below. He didn't really care about much at all as he leaned in and kissed her.

Or tried to.

Holly pulled away.

His gut dropped and twisted, his face heating instantly as she recoiled. Rejected him.

Bad breakup, she'd said. And from the grimace he'd seen when they'd danced to that song the other night, she still wasn't over whoever had broken her heart. "I'm sorry," she blurted.

"You don't need to apologize." Her choice—it would always be her choice if she wished to kiss him or not. "It's fine."

Those green eyes darted over him. "I'm not what you need, Luke."

"Don't assume you know what I need." The words burst from him before he could restrain them.

She backed away from the balcony, swallowing. Color high on her cheeks.

His voice was hoarse as he demanded, "Does it scare you?" *This nightmare I can't control?*

"No—never." There was enough raw honesty in her voice that he was tempted to believe her. She still kept backing toward the balcony doors. "My life is complicated. You are a good man, Luke."

And the way she said it . . . "Are you in some sort of trouble?" He'd find a way to help her; Batwing could find some way.

"My life is complicated," she repeated. "It's unfair to make promises."

And before he could find out what that meant, she was gone.

Luke was spoiling for a fight with some of Gotham City's worst. To do *something* to stop them.

He knew that the moment he woke up the next day. When he donned his tux for the GCPD event that night. When he arrived and danced his way through the party.

Waiting—for her. The one who could give him the fight he was looking for.

He'd seen her with Tigris. He knew that he could throw everything he was at her and she wouldn't break. Tonight it *ended*. No more fooling around, no more letting her edge past him. If she and her two *besties* showed up tonight, they would find themselves leaving in handcuffs.

Luke tried his best to focus on the job at hand, and not to glance at Holly. Holly, beautiful in seafoam green, who kept looking like she'd approach him all night.

Luke made a point not to get near enough to let her. To always have a dance partner.

He knew he was being a jerk. What Elise would call *immature man-baby bullshit*, but he didn't care.

He had bigger things to worry about than kissing his neighbor. Or failing to.

So Luke stood in the crowd, champagne in hand, while Gordon got up on the stage to make a toast. The time for Catwoman, Harley, and Ivy to strike would be *now*. When everyone was watching and the cameras were rolling.

Yet Gordon, clad in a tux, his auburn hair slicked back for once, got through his speech about the ongoing efforts of the GCPD to build bonds with the people of this city, saluting the men and women in uniform who worked tirelessly to make it a safer place. Some of what he said was bullshit, but most of it was born out of Gordon's genuine hope and belief that the GCPD could rise above its past and current history and become something *better*. Gordon paused only once to glance down at his phone, and then he saluted the assembled cops. Luke followed the crowd in lifting a glass to the officers as well.

Luke casually followed the men and women at his table—top city officials—toward where Gordon now stood to the left of the stage, speaking quietly to those gathered. No one noticed Luke standing off to the side as Gordon softly announced, "When I tell you what I'm about to say, I want no signs of panic. You act normal."

Luke's blood began to pound.

Gordon went on, "The chemical factory in Otisburg was robbed an hour ago."

Catwoman wasn't going to come, Luke realized as Gordon spoke.

She'd taken advantage of every top cop in the city, every resource, being focused here instead. Focused here because—

"Poison Ivy was spotted driving off with a semi full of chemicals." Shit. *Shit.* Gordon's throat bobbed. He said so quietly Luke had to lean in to hear it, "And Harley Quinn just used her extensive knowledge of explosives to blow up another wall of Blackgate Penitentiary. She's freed key members of the Joker's gang. His Numbers Two, Three, and Four."

Luke's blood went cold.

Gordon said, "We move now. Don't breathe a word. They need to be recaptured before the press knows."

Gordon's people began asking questions as Luke stalked toward the exit.

Holly caught his eye as he passed, her brows rising high. As if she'd spotted Gordon's little conference—had seen him listening in.

Luke gave her a cold, bored stare in exchange and prowled out.

Fast. He had to act fast.

Because if the Joker's top three guys were out of jail, then bad, bad things were about to happen.

CHAPTER 25

Luke knew their names, their long, long list of crimes.

Honestly, it might have felt like a joke, taking on three guys named Smiles, Bozo, and Chuckles. But these guys were far from well-meaning clowns.

He soared over the East End, his suit providing readouts of the people below. None matched the known height, weight, and description of the Joker's top three men.

His heart hammered in his chest, even as he tried to calm it. This rush, right before a fight, before launching himself into the fray. There had been some nights, when he first returned home, when this rush was the only *feeling* he'd had in days. It had made it easier, back then, to head out into Gotham City's shadows. To know this adrenaline pumping through him was waiting.

He'd found balance since then. But even now, as his wings caught an updraft and he *soared* . . . Yeah, he loved that rush.

Loved how it expanded, as if it would fill the entire world, and then narrowed—focusing right as he saw them.

Honing that rush directly on the three men who stalked down an alley, one with a baseball bat slung over a shoulder, one with what seemed to be a chain wrapped around his fist, and the other . . . What looked to be a long, wicked knife glinted in the dimness. They hadn't even bothered to ditch their jumpsuits.

Luke banked, checking his speed.

Three against one—not bad odds. But these weren't ordinary men.

There was a dark, wet stain on the back of the tall, slender one in the center—Bozo. Not his blood, the suit told Luke. But someone else's. The chain dangling from Bozo's hand had blood on it, too.

Jesus.

Chuckles's baseball bat, propped against his broad, meaty shoulder—those were nails sticking out of the tip. Big ones.

Luke lowered himself, closer and closer to the opposite end of the alley. Ambushing from behind would work in his favor.

It went against every bit of training in the ring, felt cowardly even against these men, but . . . It was Smiles, slender, average height, and the Joker's Number Two, who held that large knife.

Smiles hadn't become Number Two because of a pleasantness of personality. No, Luke knew that nickname came from *Smiles While Killing. Smiles While Robbing. Smiles While Doing Whatever Evil the Joker Commands.*

It was Smiles who Luke had to look out for. And Smiles who made him dim his suit lights to darkness, land near-silently on the alley floor, and free a Batarang from his suit. He'd modified the simple metal design in his lab. This, at a signal from his suit, would inflict as much of an electric shock as a Taser.

One of his friends overseas had been a sniper. Luke had talked with her countless times about how she calculated distance and wind and light and movement. She'd never missed a shot.

The three men reached the edge of the alley, still unaware of his presence behind them.

Luke lined up his shot, then freed two more Batarangs for his second and third, anticipating how the other two might scatter.

His job wasn't to kill them.

He'd seen enough of that overseas for a lifetime. Still discussed it in group therapy with the others.

The victims of these men deserved justice—*real* justice, through a court of law. Not vigilantism. And as screwed up and evil as these men were . . . they had some right to a trial, too.

Luke fired the Batarang at Smiles's wiry frame.

But the Joker's Second must have heard the buzz of the electric charge.

Faster than Luke had expected, Smiles grabbed Bozo and whirled, the Joker's Number Four pressed against his chest.

A human shield.

The Batarang hit Bozo right in the chest, stunning him. The chains jangled as they hit the concrete, Bozo following them. Utterly unconscious.

As Luke had anticipated, Chuckles whirled toward his companion, rather than run for cover. Luke fired his second Batarang, right where he'd calculated.

Chuckles and his baseball bat thudded on the ground.

Smiles sized up the alley, his pale face gaunt and sneering.

"Come out, come out," he whispered, his voice high and reedy. A poor imitation of the Joker's natural bone-chilling voice. "No one likes a party pooper." He beckoned with his long knife. It glinted, catching the light of the streetlamp.

One against one: much better odds.

Luke stepped out of the shadows, letting the insignia on his chest flare brightly.

Smiles grinned crookedly, dancing on his feet—an uneven, unbalanced move. Something he'd seen plenty of people do when they thought they knew about boxing. It only served to make his center of balance unwieldy. "Catch me if you can," Smiles whispered, and sprinted away.

Let him run. Luke was already dialing the GCPD. He had learned early on that he risked losing two unconscious criminals if he didn't make sure they were secure before going after a third on the run.

It was a matter of a few minutes to get Bozo and Chuckles tied to a lamppost, sirens sounding from a few blocks away.

Good.

With patrol cars swarming down the block, Luke leapt into the skies, scanning the streets below.

It had been five minutes max. But a great deal could happen in five minutes in Gotham City. There were sewer entrances everywhere—the preferred route of many of the city's worst.

There. Sprinting toward the docks, that knife shining in the dark.

Smart, yes, but untrained. Unaware that the glint was a dead giveaway.

Smiles turned a corner in the labyrinth of dockside warehouses. Heading for the small marina. Luke banked right and landed in the shadows just north of his route.

Only to discover that Smiles had found a way *through* the warehouses, rather than around them.

As Luke landed, the alerts on his helmet flared, and—

He ducked, falling back as Smiles slashed at him.

Not fast enough. The knife dragged along his side. Sundering metal plates. And flesh.

Luke swore, shutting out the pain, despite the warmth of blood filling his suit.

On an unarmored person, that blow would have gutted them like a fish.

Smiles smirked at the blade, the blood on it. "You know how much this DNA will sell for?"

Luke's blood leaked from him. Dangerously fast.

He had to end it now.

"Too bad you won't find out," Luke said, and moved.

His suit insignia flared, bright as the flash on a camera bulb. Blinding Smiles, throwing him off-balance—

Luke barreled into him. Slammed a palm into his elbow, forcing his fingers to splay and drop the knife, then blasted his fist into Smiles's face in a decimating right hook.

Bone crushed and blood sprayed.

Luke wasn't done yet. As Smiles reeled to the right, Luke swept his leg out, turning the criminal's already uneven balance against him.

Smiles went crashing to the wooden planks, groaning.

Luke was on him in an instant, his Batarang firing right onto his chest.

Smiles slumped against the planks, nose leaking. Unconscious.

Luke didn't dare pause and let his adrenaline wear off. Not with a wound leaking down his side, not with the pain barking through him at every movement.

He managed to make another call to GCPD before he hurled Smiles's knife into the dark river, sending his own DNA washing away, hoisted the slim criminal over a shoulder, and carried him out of the docks. Here, any manner of lowlife might easily find him.

Luke gritted his teeth with every step. But he made it.

And when Smiles was chained to a post office box, whimpering into consciousness as cops began arriving on the scene, Luke managed to leap to a nearby rooftop.

Gotham City had never seemed so large. Endless. He'd have to make it home before he could risk pausing to catch his breath. He could barely focus enough to land and tuck in his wings.

And find her waiting for him.

Catwoman let out a sultry laugh. "Did you wait for me at the gala tonight?"

He had. And she'd made a fool of the GCPD on a night in their honor.

Luke lunged for her.

But his body chose right then and there to remind him that it had its limits. And they had been reached and then some tonight.

His step forward turned into a sway back. Back, back, back as darkness closed in.

Clawed hands reached for him as the drop off the roof loomed.

Luke barely remembered how they got there.

How he didn't wind up shoved off that roof and splattered on the street below.

Everything was veiled in a pain-filled fog. The slice to his ribs must have been deeper than he'd realized. He had the vague sense of being half carried. Of a slender body holding him upright, helping him down and over things . . . But he had no idea where he was when she led him into a small, yet clean, apartment. Dark and quiet. All he knew was that it wasn't his apartment. A shiver skittered down his spine.

The bedroom she shut them in was also neat and tidy. Pretty, but not fancy—no sign of wealth in the aging paint, the chipped dresser. The mattress she plunked him on groaned softly beneath the weight of him in his suit.

She'd given him something before they'd started walking, he remembered. A shot injected through the small sliver of skin between his neck and shoulder. Adrenaline—or a compound like it. It had steadied him enough to move. And now it seemed to be kicking in more. Clarifying things.

A small light clicked on, dusting Catwoman's black suit in its golden glow.

She took a seat beside him and said, "Either I can patch this up for you here, or I can take you to the hospital."

Luke managed a half smile. "You offer me another option *now*?"

She didn't answer, instead opening a small pouch in her utility belt to remove what seemed to be bandages, a sterile needle, and thread. Along with two vials of what had to be antiseptic and some local numbing agent.

"You know how to use that stuff?"

"A skill I picked up at the League," she said, bending to examine the gash visible through his armor. "Can you remove this?"

Luke hesitated. The helmet and the suit were separate, but taking off the suit required more movement than he could muster right now, and being prostrate before her, his brown skin exposed—well, it'd certainly narrow any potential list she had for who Batwing might truly be. There were plenty of black guys in Gotham City, but ones who might have access to tech like this?

She didn't wait for him to decide. The drug she'd given him or perhaps his blood loss made him unable to react fast enough, to block her, as she flicked a steel claw free and carefully sliced away sections of bloodied metal. Carving out a hole in his suit, as easily as she'd sliced that circle in the glass display case at his family's estate.

Luke watched, his head heavy, while she removed the over-lapping metal scales, setting them on the bed. "You'll have to take those with you, or else the DNA might be a problem," she advised.

She was right. If someone analyzed it and matched it against the Marines database, his cover would be completely blown.

Catwoman adjusted something in her helmet's lenses as she examined the wound. "No signs of foreign objects inside," she said, more to herself than to him.

"Your helmet can tell you that?"

"Among other things."

He hissed as she dabbed the antiseptic onto the slice down his ribs. And just to keep himself from thinking about what she was going to do with that needle and thread, Luke asked, "Where did you get that suit?"

She stabbed him with a syringe, numbing the area. "I made it myself." Perhaps she had a shred of pity for him, because she went on, as if to distract him from the stitches. "I've always loved science and technology." A rasp of laughter, muffled by that helmet. "I won a state science competition when I was a kid. It probably put me on the League's radar long before I even knew they existed."

He tucked away those facts. *State*—she'd likely grown up in

America. He opened his mouth, then shut it. Admitting his own passion for science would only let her gather facts of her own on him. "That suit must have taken forever to make."

"The base model belonged to the League." Her needle glinted as it rose and fell. Luke shut out the strange sensation of thread passing through numbed skin. "I modified it to meet my specifications."

"Like the cat ears and claws."

Another rasp of laughter. "Like those."

"Why the cat stuff?"

"Why the bat stuff?"

She had him there. "It was part of a larger theme."

"Your . . . colleague's theme, I assume."

Luke avoided the urge to shrug, considering she currently had a needle in his skin. "Really, though: why the cat motif?"

Another few passes of the needle and she was done, tying off the stitches. Luke dared a look—and found a neat, precise line down his ribs. She leaned back, gathering up the needle and remaining thread in the plastic case they'd come in, along with the various needles and wipes. She handed them to him, and Luke blinked.

Right. They were covered in his blood. His DNA. And yet—there she was, handing it over. Dousing her own gloved hands in sanitizer once again, wiping away any trace of him from her.

"I had a stupid nickname at the League," she said at last. "So I took back the symbol for myself. Decided I liked it. The other assassins had their own personal touches, so I made this"—a wave of the hand to encompass her claws, her eared helmet—"to reflect my own."

"It's impressive work."

"Did you make your suit?"

The answer to *that* might lead to too many questions—and answers. "Parts of it." Not a lie, not entirely. Some of the tech *had* been made by others. Like the robots in the lab.

Her head angled, and Luke followed the line of her vision to his side. Not on stitches she'd made, but the scars he realized were showing.

The tail end of the big scar that sliced down his chest, ending right near the bottom of his ribs.

He didn't move as she traced a claw over it, leaving his skin prickling in her wake. He waited for the question about it, building the lie on his tongue: one of the underworld cronies had given it to him, not that piece of shrapnel that tore through his body. His very existence.

Instead, she asked, "Who hurt you tonight?"

The question was icy. The coldness not directed at him, but at whoever was behind the wound. As if she'd hunt him down and hurt him for it.

Luke was grateful for the mask covering his face as he blinked in surprise. He managed to say, "You should know. You freed him."

She went still for a heartbeat. "You caught him."

"I caught all of them."

Silence.

She stood, stalking to the windows and shutting the curtains over the blinds. Cutting off the streetlight. Then she opened up a drawer, fished out what seemed to be two sweaters, and shoved them in the crack between the door and the floor. She still managed to navigate the way back to the bed, as if she'd mapped the entire room already.

In the pitch black, he heard the hiss and click of her helmet coming off. Heard the soft sigh of her hair being freed. Felt the slight weight of the helmet as she set it on the mattress behind them. He waited, heart thundering in his chest.

She said, voice low, "Take off your helmet."

Luke couldn't help but obey. His side barked in pain at the movement, but he lifted his hands to either side of his head and pulled it off. Cool air kissed his skin.

Both of them utterly blind here in the darkness.

"I should arrest you," he managed to say.

"You should," she agreed, and he could have sworn he heard her smile. "But you won't."

"We shouldn't be doing this."

"We're not doing anything yet."

It was the wry humor in her voice that had him facing her fully. Had him lifting a hand to where he sensed her face would be and tracing her features. Soft, warm skin greeted him. And her hair, tied back from her face . . . Straight. Silken—thick.

Luke ran a hand from her hair down the column of her neck. Could have sworn her breathing became uneven. He brushed a finger over the line where her skin met her suit.

"Why did you bother saving me tonight?"

Metal and leather hissed as she removed her gloves. Slender hands found his hand resting on his thigh. Turned his hand over and brushed over the calluses on his palm. "Because we're two sides of the same coin."

"Really? You and I have a lot in common?" He couldn't stop tracing the line of her neck. His thumb found the hollow of her collarbone and settled, letting her pounding pulse hammer into his skin. "You're trying to destabilize my city. I'm trying to save it."

Through the barrier of his suit, he could barely feel her hands making a path up his leg, up his stomach, his chest. "Is there that much worth saving?"

"You said there are good people here, that I should protect them."

"What about the corruption, the broken systems? Are they worth saving?"

"They are a part of this city—and people like that always benefit from chaos."

"Not permanent chaos," she said. "Just . . . temporary."

"Just long enough for you to sell whatever you stole from Nyssa to the highest bidder?"

Again, he heard that smile in her voice. "Perhaps."

He opened his mouth, but she asked, "Don't you ever get bored of fighting for the *good* side?"

"No. It was a part of who I am long before I ever put on this suit."

Her hands explored down his chest, to the scar down his torso. Luke shuddered as her fingertips whispered over the thick scar tissue. "Such a noble hero."

She dragged a finger over that scar again.

"Why are you here?" Not in Gotham City—but in this room. With him.

Her fingers paused. And as her breath fanned over his mouth, he realized how close they'd drifted. Felt every inch of her thigh pressed against his, the warmth seeping from her. Not the cold-blooded creature of shadows that she appeared, but someone alive and burning. "I can *not* be here, if you want."

She started to rise, and Luke's body barked in protest as he lunged for her, grabbing her arm and dragging her back to the bed.

The suit beneath his hands was flexible, yet hard, some material he couldn't place. But the shape of her body beneath it—"Don't," he said.

"Don't what?" she purred.

"Don't leave me in the dark," he said quietly.

She knew he didn't mean the request as simply what it was: *Don't leave me alone in the darkness. This place where we both exist, yet serve different callings.*

Her fingers ghosted over his face. His nose, his mouth.

As she made to pull her hand away, Luke gripped her fingers in his, interlacing their hands, and kissed her.

The kiss was soft, yet left no room for questions.

And Selina realized she might very well have lost her mind as she leaned into it. Answering his kiss with her own.

Warm—he was so warm.

She could not remember the last time someone had held her.

When she'd seen him on the roof, when he'd swayed and she'd spotted the blood leaking from his side, it had been blind instinct to save him. Just as it was now blind instinct to slide her arms around his neck and press close.

Here in the dark, in the silence, she let him. Breathed him in.

His tongue traced the seam of her lips in quiet request, and a small noise came out of Selina as he tasted her. Gently—then deeply.

His scar, that brutal scar slicing down his chest . . .

She wanted to tell him. That she knew.

And that she also knew that they were as unlikely a pair as—

He nipped at her bottom lip.

Every thought eddied from her head.

She didn't care. Didn't care about any of it, anything beyond this room and this man before her, and—

No. That wasn't true. Would never be true.

He sensed the shift in her, and pulled back, his lips hovering over hers. "You okay?"

His breathing was a jagged, uneven rasp.

Not yet. She couldn't afford to make mistakes yet.

Selina leaned forward to kiss him. Once. Twice.

His hands buried themselves in her hair, his body shuddering as he seemed to yield to that kiss, to her.

She slid into his lap, his hands now grazing down her back, lower—

He didn't react fast enough, didn't seem to realize that the click in the forearm of her suit meant all was not well.

By the time the small needle punctured his neck, by the time he grunted in surprise, she'd leapt off him.

"You—" he started.

Stopped.

In the pure dark, she couldn't see, but she could hear as his breath left him in a rush and his powerful body fell back onto the mattress. Unconscious.

Selina scooped up her helmet, setting it on her head but opting to keep the lenses away.

It had been an unspoken promise of trust—not to look.

So she didn't. Even as she opened the bedroom window and vanished into the night.

CHAPTER 26

Harley's hideout in an abandoned underground subway station was precisely the sort of place Selina would have imagined for her: chaotic, colorful, and stocked with various weapons.

It seemed that the circus was the prevalent theme. Amid the various worn pieces of furniture were vibrant old posters of fireeaters and tightrope walkers, strands of lights strung up across the vaulted stone space, and what seemed to be an old red-yellow-and-blue-striped tent canvas had been converted into a curtain to conceal a tiny bathroom in the far back of the round chamber.

Selina didn't even know what she was doing here. It was past three, and they were likely asleep, but . . . She needed to talk. To someone. Anyone.

The thought of returning home to her apartment, to pacing across the immaculate floors for the remainder of the night, had been irritating enough that instead of heading north, she'd come here.

Ivy had answered thirty seconds after Selina knocked on the dented metal door.

Her red hair was up in a messy bun, black-rimmed glasses were perched on her pert, freckled nose, and an old sweatshirt with faded letters that read *Plants Are People!* dangled off one shoulder. "What's wrong?"

Selina had leaned against the grimy doorframe. "Can't a girl say hi?"

"At three-fifteen in the morning?" But Ivy beckoned her in, glancing around the dripping dark of the old train tunnel.

Selina surveyed the space again, noting the desk against one wall, full of piles of those little circus-ball bombs. Some were only half formed, left in pieces beneath a magnifying glass and light. On the desk chair, Harley's bandolier of throwing knives draped to the floor.

"She's certainly got the madcap villain's lair down," Selina observed.

"She views this as the ultimate form of self-expression." Ivy waved a hand toward a vine-covered table shoved against a poster of a lion tamer. The table was covered in papers, books, and—plants. "That's the only self-expression I'm allowed to have here," she said, chuckling. "The only place Harley *isn't* allowed to 'decorate.'"

The plants shimmered and writhed under the sunlamps humming above them. "Your pets?"

"My friends," Ivy said, padding over to the table and smiling at the seven potted plants. "Elizabeth, Emma, Fanny, Catherine, Anne, Marianne, and Elinor."

Selina's brows crossed beneath her helmet. "You named them after Austen heroines?"

Ivy beamed as bright as the twinkling lights strung overhead. "You're my new favorite person. No one ever gets the reference—even Harley asked me what the hell I was talking about."

Selina slid the lenses of her helmet up as she studied the seven plants. "I'm more of a Brontë girl."

Ivy waved a hand. "Ugh, Mr. Rochester is gross. Darcy all the way."

Selina grinned, nodding her concession. "Why are you up, anyway?"

Ivy pointed to the laptop half buried among the papers and books on the table. "Working."

"Where's Harley?" No sign of her in this underground circus.

Ivy slid into the swivel chair in front of the table and twirled around. "Don't know. She left a few hours ago in a hurry. Hasn't come back since." Worry darkened her eyes. "But she does that a lot. I try not to pry."

It seemed like Ivy never wanted to pry, to push Harley. Silence fell, and Ivy stared up at her. Waiting.

Selina blew out a breath. "I may or may not have made out with someone I shouldn't have."

Ivy grinned rather wickedly. "Oh, do tell." Selina knew the woman was well aware of who it had been.

Selina paced across the worn, star-flecked blue carpet, past the three large mallets leaning against the red velvet fainting couch. "It just . . . happened. I don't know."

"Was it good?"

Selina sighed at the vaulted stone ceiling. "Yes. God, yes."

Ivy scanned her from head to toe. "So you came here to tell me all the steamy details?"

"I came here . . . I don't even know." She glanced toward the metal door. "I should let you work." She grimaced, desperate for any way out of this. "What *are* you working on, anyway?"

"Refining the formula for that regenerative salve I used the other night. And don't try to change the subject."

But Selina asked, "That formula—are you going to sell it?"

Ivy waved a hand. "It would require so many stupid hoops with FDA approval that there's no way I could really sell it. Especially with who I am."

"You could have a third party represent you—stay hidden."

"And have them get all the credit? No."

"So you'll make this miraculous thing and not share it?"

Ivy frowned, propping her bare feet up on the table. One of the plants—Emma?—reached out a green tendril and tickled her. Ivy laughed, toes curling. But the smile faded again as she said, "I started down this road. I have to face the consequences."

"You can change lanes—change the direction. There are . . . there are a lot of people who could really use that salve. You should find a way to share it with them."

"I know," Ivy said, lowering her feet to the blue carpet. "I think it could be particularly successful with burn victims. At least, it's worked on me."

Selina raised a brow, scanning Ivy's expanse of smooth skin.

Ivy winced. "I may or may not have experimented on myself—"

"You *burned* yourself?"

Ivy waved a hand. "Just a little one."

"Jesus," Selina said. "You need to get into a real lab."

Ivy stiffened. "I *did* have a real lab. Until it was blown up."

"I mean with people. Other scientists to help you."

"You get a 'real' job, and I'll get one, too."

Selina smiled. "Fair enough."

Ivy gave her a sly look. "You still haven't told me about your make-out."

Selina glanced to the metal door behind her and started slinking toward it.

"Don't you even dare leave without telling me the details," Ivy said. She marched across the room, dodging everything from discarded fishnets to pink wigs to a cymbal-playing monkey toy. Plopping onto the red fainting couch before an old TV, she patted the worn velvet beside her. "Time for some girl talk."

"I don't know how to do girl talk," Selina admitted, approaching the couch.

"Good. Neither do I," Ivy declared, smiling up at her.

Luke groaned as he woke up, his head pounding, his side a throbbing, aching mess.

Daylight leaked in through the edges of the curtains.

Not his house. He didn't know *where* she was, only that she'd drugged him and left him here, a faint, floral scent—*her* scent—still in his nose.

Luke lunged for his helmet, biting down a shout of pain as the skin along his ribs pulled. He jammed the helmet onto his head, flicking the lenses over his eyes as he gathered up the scales of armor she'd ripped away, depositing them into his Utility Belt pouches, along with the stitching kit she'd used on him. No DNA left behind.

Luke opened the bedroom door, kicking away the wool sweaters she'd used to cut off any light. Any trace of her beyond the feel of her body, the heat of her mouth, the scent of her hair and skin—

He was grinding his teeth, buckling on his Utility Belt as he stormed for where he assumed the front door would be.

Right into the kitchen of Commissioner Gordon. Where Gordon, his teenage daughter, and his young son were eating breakfast.

Gordon's daughter let out a murmur of alarm, his son a cry of delight, and Gordon himself . . . He dropped his cereal-filled spoon right onto the small kitchen table.

"Good morning" was all Luke could think to say, and headed for the front door just past the table.

Gordon recovered enough to say, "Good morning to you, too."

His son whispered, reverent and overjoyed, *"Batwing."*

Luke smiled beneath his helmet and went so far as to ruffle the boy's dark hair as he passed.

Gordon's daughter spotted his ribs first. "Are you all right?"

Gordon's attention shot to the bare skin, the stitches. He rose from his chair. "Jesus—"

Luke knew Gordon would never say anything—none of them would—but it wouldn't surprise him if some of the shock on the man's face had to do with the brown skin peeking through Batwing's suit. "I'm fine," Luke said, reaching the front door. "Totally fine." He glanced toward Gordon's son. "Just making sure all is well in the neighborhood."

They just watched him, wide-eyed, as he unlocked the door and headed into the hall.

Oh, she'd known precisely whose apartment she'd brought him to. He didn't know whether to be furious or amused.

From the smile tugging on his mouth . . . Luke fought it and made a quick exit down the building stairs. As he headed for the nearest rooftop, Luke realized that he'd slept through the night. And hadn't been woken once. Hadn't had one nightmare.

CHAPTER 27

Harley was leaning against the brick wall of the alley when Selina and Ivy arrived the next night. No sign of the boy shorts and fishnets. Just two-tone leggings, boots, and a tiny ball-bomb in either hand.

"New outfit?" Selina asked, but Ivy had gone still at her side. Nervous.

"No more robberies," Harley said, her face hard and cold.

"Well, I'm sure the Gotham Antiquities Museum will be sorry to hear that our appointment tonight is canceled," Selina said, sizing up the space between Harley and Ivy.

When she'd called Ivy this afternoon with the time and location for their next rendezvous, she hadn't hinted at anything between them being amiss, but—

Selina halted a healthy distance away.

Harley's eyes remained on her, though. As if Ivy didn't exist. "I want the Joker out of Arkham *now*."

Selina kept her arms within casual distance of her weapons, not daring to let her claws slide free. Not yet. It'd signal a fight, and getting into it with Harley tonight would not be good for her plans.

She'd humiliated Gordon and the GCPD. Whether he'd figured out that Batwing had been dumped in his guest room by her didn't matter. It was only a matter of time until they came for Catwoman. And only a matter of time before Nyssa and Talia's army arrived, too. Bringing with it utter annihilation.

"Wait another day or two," Selina said calmly, her voice the portrait of boredom.

"We do it *now,*" Harley snapped. "We proved twice now that we can break someone out. And I have it on good authority that my man's aware of us—of our little shopping spree here in Gotham, and he's *pissed* we're taking so long."

Ivy flinched at the two words—*my man*. But Ivy countered coolly, "Arkham is a different beast than the city prison, Harley."

"You're siding with her?" Harley demanded.

Perhaps it was pity for the pain on Ivy's face, but Selina said, "We need to sell some of what we've stolen first. We need more cash to bribe the right people—"

"Get the damn cash. We do this *now.*"

Harley aimed both of her bombs toward Selina.

"*Harley,*" Ivy barked.

"Shut up," Harley snarled, not taking her eyes off Selina as she advanced, thumb on the small trigger atop each bomb. "Just *shut up,* Ivy."

Selina calculated the distance between them. Harley would not miss.

"Wherever you've been hiding all the stolen shit, we go there now. *Now.*"

Ivy's face had gone pale. *Use your gases,* Selina silently willed her. *Stop this—*

Harley kept a safe distance away. Knowing that if she got close enough for Selina to reach her, those bombs would be out of her hands. "Lead the way, Cat."

Selina looked to Ivy, who shook her head in warning. And in apology.

Love—as venomous as one of Ivy's plants.

"Let's go, then," Selina said, and started into a walk.

This particular warehouse in the docks was so decrepit even the lowlifes didn't bother with it. Didn't sniff around, or look at the hidden lower level, the trunks inside.

Harley kept her bombs at the ready the entire time Selina unloaded whatever smaller stolen items the duffel bag could carry, Ivy's hands shaking as she helped. And when they were done, Harley ordered, "Go find a buyer."

So Selina did. With Harley breathing unevenly behind her, she led them through the maze of the slums, to the abandoned fish-processing plant at the river edge of the Bowery. She'd placed the call with a burner phone to the number of the man who used this place to sell things that couldn't be traded in legal markets. And as they entered the cavernous, reeking space, Selina said, "Now we wait."

"How long," Harley demanded. Her eyeliner had smudged, some running down the side of her face in a mockery of tears.

"No more than an hour," Selina said calmly.

Ivy stepped up to Selina's side. "Harley—put the bombs down. We're here now. It's fine."

Harley only turned one of those bombs on Ivy. "The hell it is."

Selina let out a quiet laugh, temper straining. "What does that bastard have on you to get you to so easily turn on your friends?" *On Ivy, who loves you for whatever reason I can't see?*

Harley's own laugh was broken—jagged. "When we unleashed the Joker's men, you know what they did? They went right to my mom's house."

Selina's heart stalled a beat. "Batwing brought them in."

Harley mimicked, *"Batwing brought them in."* She spat on the ground. "Your little boyfriend didn't get to them fast enough. They had hours. And since *my* boyfriend knows who I am, he made sure those bastards went to my mama's house *first*."

Selina's stomach turned over. That's where Harley had been last night, why she hadn't been at the apartment. "Is she all right—"

"Don't pretend that you give a shit." Harley's chest heaved. "He told her to tell *me* that if we don't spring him free immediately, he'll make sure my mom receives his own brand of justice."

Bile coated her throat as Selina pleaded, "Put the bombs away, Harley. If they're dragging your mom into it, we won't mess around. He'll be out tonight. Just put those bombs away."

Panic flared in Harley's blue eyes, right beneath the rage. "He is going to *hurt* her—"

"I know," Selina breathed. "And I won't let that happen. I swear."

"Your promises are *shit*," Harley hissed. "You think we don't know where you went last night? Who you went with?"

Selina shot Ivy a look. So much for a code of not screwing over allies. Ivy mouthed, *I'm sorry.*

Selina said to Harley, "It's not what it seems."

"Part of the game?" Harley mocked. "Hooking up with the enemy?"

"Put the bombs away, Harley," Selina said.

Ivy was shaking beside her, looking like she'd vomit over the stained concrete. But she said, voice clear and steady, "If the Joker is out, Harley, you know how bad things might—"

"He *won't touch you*," Harley snapped at Ivy. "I *told* you that. You, my mom—you're safe."

"But what about the other people?" Ivy demanded, voice trembling. "What about them?"

"Who gives a shit?" Harley's left thumb shifted on the bomb.

"I do," Ivy breathed. "*I do*, Harley!"

Selina cut in, "If the buyer sees those bombs, you can say goodbye to the bribe cash."

Harley leveled a seething look at her. "How about we show him whatever's under that mask instead—"

The warehouse doors blew open in a cloud of smoke, the windows exploding a second later.

And a SWAT team from the GCPD stormed in.

CHAPTER 28

Selina had marked the exits and defensible locations in the warehouse. She rolled toward a hulking tower of machinery as Harley lobbed her bombs, swearing.

They detonated with a flash and bang that shattered windows and sent dust raining from the ceiling. Ivy sprinted for Harley's side, thumbing free a few of those beautiful flowers. She hurled them toward the police, smoke instantly filling the space.

But the GCPD had marked them, too. And the SWAT team that burst through the doors were all wearing gas masks. Ivy lobbed more flowers toward them anyway, vines snapping into the fog, the smoke now near-impenetrable.

The police had the exits guarded. Gordon was taking no risks.

But the window closest to them, twenty feet away . . . "Here!" Selina shouted through the smoke to Harley and Ivy. *"Now."*

Harley had slid on a gas mask courtesy of Ivy, and as she

emerged, throwing bombs blindly into the smoke, police shouting orders to fall back, to cease fire, a trickle of blood was sliding down her arm. She'd been clipped. Nothing bad, but Ivy was pressing a hand to Harley's wound. Blood coated Ivy's pale fingers, her wrists.

They slid to a stop behind the machine that Selina was braced against. Selina pointed toward the window. "Another squadron is outside, waiting. We make a run for it—we can surprise them if we leap through."

"They'll shoot us before we clear the window," Ivy said, sizing up the distance, the squad no doubt in the alley beyond.

"I'll buy you time," Selina panted. "You keep running. Don't stop."

Harley studied Selina as the shouts from the SWAT team across the factory floor grew closer. "What about you?"

"I didn't think you cared."

Selina could have sworn something like regret flickered in Harley's blue eyes. But Ivy ordered, "We need to move. Now."

Selina didn't give them another warning as she charged for that window. A trap—a big one—lay outside.

She drew the blade from down her back, bullwhip clenched in her other hand. At her side, through the smoke, green flashed— Ivy's own vine-whip.

Selina reached the window. "Blow it out, Harley!"

A bomb answered—Harley's last. Glass was still shattering as Selina leapt atop the crate beneath the window, grabbed the sill, and swung herself through and out.

An armed SWAT team waited by the back door a few feet away, guns pointed, masks over their faces as they whirled toward where Selina landed.

"DROP YOUR WEAPONS AND—"

Selina didn't hear the rest. She snapped her whip through the air, catching the nearest gun and ripping it out of the officer's hands.

The others hesitated, as if surprised at the unusual weapon, the movement—

Twin sets of feet landed behind her. Harley and Ivy.

They wasted no time, Harley hurling two throwing knives at the shocked officers in her way, a brazen charge that Selina half noticed as she snapped her whip again, knocking another gun to the ground—

Ivy and Harley were through the line of fire. A few leaps had them atop a dumpster, then jumping over another line of cop cars, Harley throwing another knife with lethal aim, Ivy's vine whipping through the air.

Selina didn't look to see if they made it beyond that—to where the Sprang River flowed past the warehouse at the edge of the docks. But she heard the twin splashes, barely audible over the shouts of the officers now before Selina.

The element of surprise gone. Guns now pointed at her face.

"Drop your weapons," the officer before her ordered, stepping closer. The door behind her slammed open, SWAT officers pouring out behind her, surrounding her completely. Thirty men. Armed. Granted permission to kill.

Selina took in the countless guns, the Kevlar.

Her sword clattered to the ground.

Then the whip.

And slowly, Selina raised her hands skyward as GCPD pressed in.

CHAPTER 29

Luke was up and in the gym before dawn. Just in time to turn on the early-morning news and see the headline that had him turning off the treadmill.

Cat Claws Way into Arkham Asylum

Luke couldn't move. Couldn't lunge for the exit, to his apartment and his closet, where his suit was, couldn't think of what to *do* as he saw the blurry footage.

Catwoman: thrashing and screaming, utterly wild as she was hauled into the armored police van. Not at all the calm, cool woman he'd known. No, this woman did not go gently into that van, her claws gouging deep lines into the metal as she was shoved in, handcuffed, chained down. Shrieking, *laughing*—

Arkham Asylum.

Some had tried to rename the facility and ditch its outdated title, but the name still hung around, the whispers of fear with it. A place where the criminally insane were sent—the worst of the worst. Its security systems and protocols were unmatched, even by Blackgate.

But there she was, the news footage now cutting to a live feed from Arkham. The media were invited to what seemed to be a small interrogation room. Luke knew that familiar, cold interior. The fluorescent lights, pale walls, and low ceilings that made everything look greenish, sickly.

Made even worse by all the press crammed in there, focused on the empty table, void of anything save an anchor for handcuffs. Chains.

There was nothing he could do. As Luke Fox or Batwing. Even if he called Gordon as Batwing right now, there was no way in hell that call would reach him in time. Stop him.

She'd made a laughingstock of the GCPD, and had pushed and pushed until—

Until the door to the room opened, and she was led in, still wearing her helmet and suit, cuffed and at gunpoint, a small army of SWAT team officers pushing her into the chair before that table.

Facing all those cameras.

The district attorney strode in after her. His face like granite.

And Luke knew. What was about to take place at this table. Why the media had been invited.

"Here in Gotham City," the DA said to the cameras, coming up behind where Catwoman was being chained to the table, "we don't tolerate those who threaten the security, happiness, and well-being of our people."

Arkham Asylum—it had to be a conscious choice to put her in there, too. To undermine her control over her actions these past few weeks.

"Are Harley Quinn and Poison Ivy in custody, too?" one of the reporters inquired.

The dark-haired DA stared down at Catwoman, sitting so still in that chair. Waiting. Ready.

Luke wished he could read her face. See whatever was going on beneath that mask.

"They remain at large, but once they see the example we set today, perhaps they will find it wise to turn themselves in."

Luke's stomach churned, his heart thundering in his chest. "Don't do it," he whispered into the whirring silence of the gym. "Don't do it, man."

"For too long," the DA said to the media, "the criminals of this city have hidden behind masks. Used them to garner fear and chaos. But they are not all-powerful. They are not gods."

The DA laid his light brown hands on either side of her helmet. "And today, we take a step toward revealing them for the mere mortals they are beneath."

Luke's feet were rooted to the gym floor, his breathing shallow and uneven.

The entire room seemed to be holding its breath as the DA lifted the helmet from Catwoman's head.

Luke saw the blond hair first.

Then the green eyes, full of cold emerald fire.

And his knees gave out from under him, sending him sinking onto the floor, as he found himself staring at Holly Vanderhees's face on the screen.

The DA recoiled in shock. Holly smiled slightly up at him. Then turned to smile at the camera.

Luke didn't wait for the media to realize who she was.

He raced through the gym, up the stairs, and into his apartment, his aching side protesting the entire way. He paused only to grab his tool kit from a kitchen cabinet and was out of his apartment in a few seconds. He stalked right up to Holly's door, some small part of him grateful that his hands held surprisingly steady as he picked the lock.

Her apartment, still shadowed in the early-morning light . . . Clean. Unremarkable. A mirror image of his own, though the furniture and art had a more feminine feel. She had probably rented the place furnished.

He stormed for her bedroom, barely hearing his steps over the roaring in his ears.

Holly—Holly, who he had danced with, laughed with, tried to kiss.

I'm not what you need, she'd said. Knowing what she was, the rich boy she believed him to be . . .

Living next door to him. All this time.

Her bedroom was clean, her large bed made, not a thing out of place.

But the closet . . .

Luke strode in. Scanned the racks of clothes and shoes until his eyes landed on the mirror in the back. He went right up to the mirror and slid his hands over the wood. There were no catches, no buttons like in his own apartment.

A mirror image of his own place. The button was on the other side.

He found it instantly.

A hiss and click, and the secret compartment door swung away. Revealing a dim room, lights flickering to life.

Revealing each detail as they warmed up:

The assortment of weapons on the walls.

The chrome worktable with her tool kit left scattered over the surface, wires and bits of metal everywhere.

The glittering heaps of jewels in the far corner. The piles of cash.

The shoe boxes full of gold bullion.

Shoe boxes.

How many times had he seen her walking into and out of this apartment with shopping bags full of them? They had always looked so *heavy*. And when he'd offered to carry them for her, she'd refused.

Knowing the weight would give away that she didn't have *shoes* inside.

Two sides of the same coin, she'd said.

She had to know that he was Batwing. That they were both pretenders, liars—one serving the light, the other the dark.

Holly, with that sad smile. Who seemed to hate the rich and powerful, and yet lived among them.

Luke racked his brain. He'd never heard of Holly Vanderhees until this fall. Never. She'd arrived on a private jet in August, as if she were a ghost emerging from the clouds. A wraith.

A ghūl.

Holly was a League *assassin*.

And—Holly had never really existed.

Luke was about to turn on his heel when a sliver of paper on Catwoman's worktable caught his eye.

Luke stepped farther into the space, her scent lingering—that same floral scent that he'd awoken with.

His name was on it.

Luke.

He picked up the slip of paper, heart pounding. His mouth

went completely dry as he flipped over the paper and beheld the three words there:

Protect this city.

Luke was moving before he could think it through. He was dressed and in his loaner car—a silver BMW i8—within minutes. Speeding down the streets of the city moments after that.

Heading to Wayne Industries.

It crossed the line to even *think* of getting her out of Arkham. Bruce would kick his ass for it. More than that, it was illegal. But . . . she'd wanted him to find that paper.

As if, should this ever happen to her, she wanted him to know. That she fully realized who had been living across the hall from her. And that her command from all those weeks ago still held.

Protect this city.

Luke's stomach clenched, as if recoiling from the ghost of the touch she'd brushed down the scar along his torso. Knowing it was shrapnel that had torn him apart. Bringing him to that room, kissing him, because she knew that as Holly, she couldn't start down that road, but as Catwoman . . .

What had been real?

A bad breakup had brought her here, she'd said.

Not with a guy, but with the *League*.

He had to know more.

Starting with finding out *everything* about Holly Vanderhees.

CHAPTER 30

It had been so easy to create Holly Vanderhees.

She wasn't particularly sad to see her go.

Selina knew that the world was wondering: *Who is this socialite crime queen?*

Harley and Ivy were probably wondering it, too.

And as she sat in her filthy solitary cell in Arkham, counting the hours and guards who leered at her, sorting through the shouting of prisoners down the three-storied cellblock, Selina herself wondered if Harley and Ivy would forgive her. For the lies. For being one of the rich assholes they so hated.

By now, the media would have found the social media profiles she'd crafted months ago: summers in Provence, winters in St. Barths, parties with her face seamlessly Photoshopped into group shots around gala tables or on yachts or in clubs. For a woman who'd never existed, Holly had led a remarkably public life.

The hours passed, one by one.

They'd taken her suit, her helmet. Shoved her into a white jumpsuit. In the changing room, even before she'd donned the long-sleeved shirt they gave her to wear beneath the pale threads, the female officer didn't comment on her tattooed arms. And in the chill cellblock, Selina hauled the rough wool blanket around her shoulders as she sat on her cot.

At least they hadn't put her in the sublevel below—the one for *intensive-treatment* inmates. But the cold, reeking air still seemed to reach her, rising up from the floor. As if it were a beckoning grave.

Selina blocked it out. She had suffered worse. Here in the enormous, vaulted space of the female-only east wing, she could watch. And listen.

Hour after hour.

Counting down the seconds, rallying her strength, her mind.

Because the moment Gordon had removed that helmet, baring her face to the world, Nyssa had begun to make her final move.

Selina slept. And ate. And braced herself.

It was nearing dawn when that final move came.

Selina knew within a few heartbeats of the shouting and chaos that exploded in the asylum that Nyssa hadn't dispatched one or two of her best assassins to finish the job.

Nyssa had sent a small army of them.

CHAPTER 31

The attack unfolded with textbook precision, exactly the way Selina had been taught to do it.

First the outer walls blew up. Or Selina felt they did, the enormous, U-shaped building shuddering, debris raining. Sending the guards running toward the explosions.

Right into the arms of assassins who executed them. All of them. Every leering, corrupt piece of shit who had rattled the bars on her cell these hours, ogling her, whispering the sorts of things that left no shred of pity in her heart as their screams went silent down the smoke-filled hallways.

Silent enough that Selina could clearly hear the click that filled the cellblock.

The doors to the cells swung open. An invitation and a challenge.

She had no doubt that in the west wing, the doors to the male prisoners' cells were doing the same.

Selina let the blanket drop to the floor behind her as she stepped into the hallway, smoke starting to fill the corridor. The escaped prisoners didn't look twice at her as they bolted in either direction, vanishing into the smoke.

They didn't glance at what Selina now approached, the item left hanging from one of the ceiling lights, near a disabled security camera.

Her suit.

No helmet. No gloves. No utility belt or bullwhip. Only her boots, set against the wall a few feet away.

Nyssa wanted her to fight this final battle as herself. No Death Mask. No additional tech.

Selina plucked the suit from its hanging place as the last of the prisoners in her cellblock vanished.

Quietly, she pulled off the white jumpsuit and slid into battle-black.

Her hair—her stupid dyed hair—she left unbound. No hair ties to be found.

Selina leaned against the wall of the hallway, watching the smoke-filled corridor that led out of the east wing.

The League arrived within seconds, wraiths in the smoke.

No individual markings. They were all in identical black, helmets on, their swords the same.

One unit, one avenging force of death. The League's brutal fist of justice embodied.

With the smoke, she couldn't count how many went past the ten filling the corridor entryway.

Selina pushed off the stark white wall, arms hanging loosely at her sides.

"You have betrayed your fellow living dead," the one at the front of the group said, accent placing the woman from somewhere in Australia. "And as such, we shall put you back in the ground."

Selina smiled. "Took you long enough to get here."

The assassin before her said, "You stand charged of theft and high treason. Do you deny this?"

"I do not."

The assassin to the leader's left tensed, as if yanking at the leash. The leader went on, "Return what you stole, what you have come here to sell to these godless fools, and the League will make your death swift."

The threat was clear: if she did not . . . oh, this death would last a long, long time.

Selina laughed quietly. "And what did I steal, exactly?" Beyond time. She'd stolen that. Too much of it.

"You will not delay this with foolish questions," the leader snapped, drawing a blade sheathed down her back, twin to the ones that had been removed from Selina's own suit. "You know what you stole."

Selina lifted a brow. "You can't mean to tell me that Nyssa doesn't remember her little formula?"

Silence.

Selina snorted. "Perhaps she should have paid attention to those scientists she kidnapped—and not had us execute them when they were done."

Selina had snapped one of their necks amid the gunfire of the other assassins.

A moment after he'd whispered to her, *begged* her not to. Explained what Nyssa had made him work on in secret for ten years, never seeing sunlight, never seeing his family. Knowing that if he disobeyed, she'd kill them. So he'd worked beneath the compound. Had done her bidding.

He and the two other scientists had found a way for the compound's Lazarus Pit to become self-regenerating. A formula to create one from scratch—and for the Pit to be used over and over again. The ability to grant immortality to the highest bidder. To bring back people from the dead.

The most valuable weapon on earth.

He had told Selina where the data was stored, his password. Begged her to help him get free. To keep Nyssa from unleashing this thing upon the world. Selling it to the worst of mankind.

Nyssa had entered the blood-splattered room a moment later, demanding to know why Selina hadn't finished the job.

Selina had broken the scientist's neck before Nyssa finished speaking.

And now, standing before the assassins who had trained her, tormented her, made her into this *thing* she'd become . . . Selina lifted her chin.

The leader snarled, "Give us the formula. *Now.*"

Selina smiled again. "It's too late."

The assassins began to advance, moving as one down the smoky cellblock hallway.

Selina went on, "Do you know that in the weeks I've been here, my crime spree has gleaned some *very* interested buyers? People willing to do *anything* not to die."

The approaching assassins halted.

Not at her words, but at the figure emerging from the smoke behind her.

The person she'd been brokering that formula to. He'd made it up from the sublevel. And right on time.

The Joker let out a hoarse laugh, his white jumpsuit baggy on his slim form as he stepped up to Selina's side and drawled, "Thank you for confirming the formula's existence." He sketched a mockery of a bow, the smoke obscuring his face, his body, as he said to Selina, "We have a bargain."

Then he clicked his tongue.

Even the League assassins seemed to recoil in surprise as the Joker's army of vicious criminals exploded from behind them and charged down the hall.

CHAPTER 32

———————

She had insisted Ivy bring Harley into their circle for this. All of it, every step—for this.

This moment, this gamble. This alliance with the Joker.

To have his army, *her* army now, fight for her when Nyssa's legion came to claim her head.

If the League assassins were cold precision, the Joker's people were scalding chaos. No rules, no lines.

In the madness, the Joker extended a slim hand to her. "The formula, if you will."

His reedy, light voice made her skin crawl.

Selina inclined her head. "Give me an hour, and meet me at the Statue of Saint Nicholas." Right before the city proper, if they followed the long road from the outskirts where Arkham lay, he would easily find the marble statue for the patron saint of repentant thieves.

She turned to go, but the Joker gripped her arm, his long, thin

fingers digging in hard enough to hurt. "If you aren't there"—
a breathy laugh—"you can imagine what I'll do to you and yours."

She peered down at the hand holding her, then up into the
pale, angular face just barely visible through the smoke. "Don't ever
touch me again," she said.

The Joker's dark eyes swirled with cruelty—and madness.
"We're going to have fun, you and I," he promised.

The words skittered over her, raking talons along her spine. She
shook off his arm. "Don't be late."

Down the hall, the shouting on both sides was rising. The assassins had the skill, but the Joker's men had the numbers on their
side. And the wild desperation.

Just as gunfire started breaking out, the noise deafening in
the tiny space, Selina prowled down the empty hall behind them.
Turned right and then stepped through the hole blown open in the
outer wall of the brick facade, revealing a sunny fall day, the dried-
out lawn beyond. The gaping holes in the Gothic-style fences.

Sirens wailed in the distance. Inmates still poured out, shoving
past each other to get through the spiked iron fences, sprinting
for the long road that would take them down the hill on which
Arkham was perched. And into the city itself.

She knew some weren't heading toward Gotham City to
escape.

Some were heading there to have fun.

Selina opened a panel in the arm of her suit and dialed a number she hadn't called in years.

She spoke as she walked out of Arkham, the towering Gothic
building looming above her, and then ran down that burnt-out
lawn, through the skeletal trees.

Time.

She had been living on borrowed time.

And it was about to run out.

All hell was breaking loose.

Luke got the alert midway through dissecting what and who Holly had been.

A lie. It was a *lie*, all of it.

But as he beheld the explosions at Arkham, as he beheld the inmates pouring down the bleak road, past the weather-worn Statue of Saint Nicholas, and into the city . . . He had a second suit at the offices. Changed into it and was out within minutes, soaring between the buildings. A veritable army of cop cars flew down the streets.

Faster. He had to be *faster*. Lives depended on it.

Luke caught a sharp wind, rising high, spearing for where smoke stained the horizon, gunfire already ringing out along the hill on which Arkham squatted, a hulking Gothic beast.

Chaos. Utter chaos.

And every criminal in the city would be heading there, to get their people out, to engage in what seemed to be all-out *war*—

She'd orchestrated this. Somehow he knew that "Holly" had gone into Arkham so that this melee could happen.

Weaving between buildings, he spotted Gordon's car and a small circle of police vans and armored trucks a few blocks from the road that would take them to the foothills—to Arkham. Luke soared for them, pushing his wings to the limit.

Gordon seemed to sag in relief as he landed. Startled, some of the other cops went for the guns at their hips. The commissioner motioned them to lower their weapons and pointed to the arc of video screens before him, the live feeds off of several city cameras. *"Shut that road down* now!" he barked into the walkie-talkie in his hand. Someone on the other end asked how to do it. *"Barricades!"* Gordon roared.

Luke scanned the screen, the feeds from the road. Too late. Too many of Arkham's worst had made it into the city. Into the streets. People were fleeing—into shops, into apartment buildings, going *anywhere* to escape their path.

"The hospital," Luke breathed, pointing to the building just a few blocks into the Coventry district, right in the path of the road. "Get them to the *hospital—*"

He braced himself to take off, suit humming.

But Gordon swore.

And Luke looked at the feed of the security cameras right outside the hospital.

They stalked around corners. Down the streets. Armed with baseball bats, brass knuckles, lead pipes. Anything they could get their hands on. Their *claws* on.

Luke's heart stopped as the Leopard girl gang prowled for the vulnerable, unguarded doors to the hospital.

"I need backup at GC Medical Hospital immediately!" Gordon roared into the walkie-talkie.

Luke stopped him with a hand on the shoulder.

Because the Leopards . . .

That was Mika Ikedo. Alpha of the Leopard Pack.

Taking up a defensive, guarding position at the hospital doors.

Flanked by Ani Hernandez, her Second.

Tiffany McBride, her Third.

And at every door, in front of every low-hanging window . . . Leopards stood watch.

Leopards held the line.

"These people are unbelievable," Gordon hissed. "They're guarding the drugs at the hospital for Falcone's men." He reached for his walkie-talkie again.

"No, they're not," Luke said softly as those girls, some as young as fourteen and some as old as twenty-eight, faced ahead, unafraid and unbowed as the chaos of Arkham barreled for them down the streets. "They're answering a call for aid."

Gordon blinked at him, walkie-talkie lowering. "Catwoman."

Luke nodded.

"Why?" Gordon scanned the screen for any sign of her. "Why not go to Arkham to get her?"

Luke didn't answer as Gordon began ordering his men into positions across the city.

A nickname, she'd said of her getup. The cat thing had come from a nickname the other assassins had given her.

Leopards inked their victories on their skin. If anything had led to a cat-based nickname . . .

He'd never seen Holly's arms. Even in the heat of early fall, she'd worn long sleeves. Every outfit.

To hide the tattoos.

The leopard spots inked there.

"I need your computer," Luke breathed, not asking for permission as he yanked the nearest laptop to him and had himself in the GCPD database in a few clicks. Had a web browser pulled up beside it.

A state science fair. She'd won a statewide competition.

A veritable glass slipper.

Articles scrolled past. Winners of every science fair, their photos—

And there she was.

Not Holly Vanderhees, socialite and heiress.

Selina Kyle, inner-city kid and gang member.

Fourteen years old, dark-haired and unsmiling as she held her statewide science fair trophy. More clippings of various gymnastics competitions. Victories. The dates matched, and the face . . . It was her. Fierce and focused.

He typed the name into the GCPD database. *Selina Kyle.* Her record had been scrubbed clean. Luke used a few backdoor hacking codes, and it reappeared.

Born and raised in the most dangerous, underprivileged part of Gotham City. Druggie mother, absent father. The mother who had *beat* her. That part of her story had rung true, at least. Currently serving a life term in prison for attempted kidnapping and murder, among other things.

But Holly—*Selina* . . . top of her class. Top percentile of all exams. Smartest kid in her school district. In *every* district. Skilled gymnast. And known member of the Leopards.

Theft. Aggravated assault. The charges went on and on.

Undefeated fighter in Carmine Falcone's underground ring. Vanished two years ago, at age seventeen, after a third strike to her record.

The reason behind the final, damning crime . . .

Luke's stomach dropped as he looked back at the hospital, the Leopards who had answered their former member's desperate plea. To guard not just those who could not defend themselves, but also to protect . . .

To protect . . .

Luke took Gordon's laptop with him and launched skyward.

* * *

Selina ran for the hospital.

Past the frantic, rioting inmates, past the cops who weren't dumb enough to stop her, past the panicking people of the city, Selina ran all the way from Arkham, her breath a sharp blade in her chest.

Mika and Ani were already there. Waiting at the doors.

They said nothing as they looked her over—the battle-suit and blond hair.

A new scar marred Ani's face, but they both seemed the same. They seemed the same, while Selina . . . She was a stranger in this body, these clothes. A stranger to herself.

Mika inclined her head, stepping aside from the glass doors.

Her old Alpha had picked up on the second ring. Had not asked any questions when Selina explained. When Selina had begged. Called in a favor as their undefeated fighter, who had never refused an order, who had done everything Mika had ever asked.

And so Mika had answered. Brought every Leopard she could.

Selina gave her former Alpha a nod of thanks, and one to Ani, too, before she stalked through the glass doors of the hospital and broke into a flat-out sprint.

CHAPTER 33

It had been two years since she'd last seen Maggie.

The young woman on the hospital bed before her was a husk. A shell of what her sister had been.

Machines hummed and chirped softly, the room dim and quiet. In the two chairs against the wall slept a pair of fortysomething men. Maggie's adoptive parents.

Camped here, with their daughter.

In her final days. Her final hours.

Maggie's skin stretched too tight over her delicate bones. Her beautiful curly hair lay limp and thin.

Selina's hand drifted to her chest, as if it could contain the cracking she now felt within. The feeling of the floor sliding out from beneath her as she stared and stared at her sister.

The cystic fibrosis had wrecked her.

The tubes and machines flanked her bedside, the IVs and

monitors standing like sentinels around her unconscious sister. So much technology. None of it could keep her alive.

Incurable.

And the two men sleeping at their daughter's bedside . . . They had known when they adopted Maggie that she was sick. Would not have long. That it would be expensive and hard and sad.

They'd welcomed her into their home anyway.

For two years, they'd fought for her sister. Every day. With every dollar they had.

And when the first of the anonymous donations came in a month ago, and all of Maggie's medical bills were paid off . . . they had cried.

Selina knew, because she'd been in the shadows outside their beautiful home in the suburbs the night they opened the letter in their kitchen.

But all the money in the world, all that stolen cash and jewels and art, hadn't been enough to stop the disease from ravaging her sister's lungs and stealing away her life. Stealing away that beautiful, lovely soul.

She'd known that, long before coming back. Before she'd given them the money.

She'd been keeping tabs on Maggie with the League's computers, hacking into Gotham City's social workers' reports on the status of her sister's new home, accessing her medical records to check up on the doctor's latest assessment and treatments.

It had been her secret rebellion, kept hidden from Nyssa and Talia's watchful eyes. Outside contact was forbidden, as were any tethers to their past lives. But if they'd caught on to the backdoor hacking she'd used to hide any trace of her history on the computer, they'd never called her out. So she'd waited until the dead hours of the night, when even assassins were asleep, and fired up the computer in the compound's subterranean workshop.

And then one night, six months ago, she'd sat down to do her regular check-in on Maggie.

She read the doctor's latest report as if through a long tunnel.

Life expectancy: a few months at best.

It was the doctor's note at the end—*It is now about making Maggie as comfortable as possible*—that broke her.

Selina had joined the League, their palace of assassins. She'd given everything, lost everything, to honor her bargain with Talia. Her life, her *soul*, in exchange for Maggie's safety and happiness.

But it was not enough. And no matter how much blood she spilled for the League, it could not save her sister.

But something else could.

She'd remembered what the scientist had spoken of: the Lazarus Pit.

Not caring about the consequences, or what might be demanded as payment, Selina had gone right to Nyssa the next morning. Had explained that Maggie was dying.

Selina had spent a year and a half training to bring down empires. She had dug her own grave, recited her final rite, and arose from the dead. She had done everything Nyssa and Talia had asked her to do. And yet when she had asked Nyssa to use the Pit on her sister, to save Maggie, Nyssa had laughed.

This is modern-day natural selection at work. The Pit cannot be used for such selfish purposes. Or on someone with so little value to offer. Even once the Pit is fully operational, I would not use it for such weaknesses as familial bonds.

Natural selection.

The words had sunk into Selina's brain. Burned there.

Perhaps you should go back into training, if such sentiments are still a concern to you, Nyssa had mused.

Selina let her face become cold, heard herself speak the distant, formal words that convinced Nyssa such a thing was unnecessary, that she *accepted* Nyssa's decision.

Then she had planned. With every hateful word out of Nyssa's mouth, she'd planned.

She remembered that scientist's password, his directions.

How to access the formula. How to steal it.

She had killed him. For this woman—this League.

And she would make up for it. To save Maggie and to honor the dying man's wishes.

No, it would not fall into the wrong hands.

Selina slid back into the obedient, quiet role they expected of her. Went on enough successful missions that Nyssa seemed to forget about her request. And the night before she was to leave on another mission . . .

She slipped into that lab. And she stole every file and note. All of it, everything the scientist and his partners had discovered, downloaded onto her flash drive, then deleted from Nyssa's own. Deleted from Talia's files, the League backups.

A few more commands had her gaining entry to Nyssa's bank accounts. Moving huge amounts of cash into a new Swiss account that she'd established on her last mission.

Money to start with. To get access to what she needed.

She left at dawn, right out the front door.

But not before she trashed the Pit. The scientist's files had shown her how to do that, too.

Part of her wished she could see the look on Nyssa's face when she entered that underground lab and found the pool to be dead. Forever.

Selina was long gone by the time Nyssa did. She knew, though, that they'd find her sooner or later. That Nyssa and Talia would use their usual methods to hunt her down.

So she'd come to Gotham City. Not because it had once been her home, but because it was the one place where a young, brilliant biochemist was an eco-vigilante by night.

The League had been keeping tabs on Poison Ivy, debating whether to recruit her. Nyssa wanted her for the Lazarus project.

Selina wanted Ivy to save her sister.

Worried whispers sounded down the hospital hall, and Selina slipped inside Maggie's room, shutting the door. Her sister's parents didn't stir. Maggie remained unconscious, breathing labored.

Selina's hands shook with every step closer to that bed, longing and terror knifelike in her chest.

Every question she had asked Ivy about ley lines . . . All of them were open gaps left by the scientists working on the Lazarus Pits, the ley lines on which the pools naturally occurred. Ivy had unknowingly filled them in. Just as she'd unknowingly helped steal those same chemicals the other night.

Some had been used to make explosives, yes. But neither Harley nor Ivy nor the GCPD had asked what happened to the semitruck containing the rest of the items Selina had demanded they take.

The chemicals inside, all needed to create a Pit from scratch. Right on that ley line outside the city.

She'd been *so* good to her source at the paper with her Cat-woman tips and photos. They hadn't voiced any questions when their anonymous benefactor asked that they indulge her request for an interest piece on ley lines in the paper. A conversation starter—

a way to make sure Ivy didn't question Selina's sudden interest when she asked her about them that night on the roof.

She regretted none of it. Using Harley and Ivy. Lying to them every step of the way.

None of it.

Selina crept up to Maggie's bedside. Her skin was sallow, her lips too pale beneath the breathing mask.

She carefully sent out a low electromagnetic pulse through her suit that rendered the machines and monitors silent and dead.

Gently, she slipped the IV from Maggie's arm, the breathing apparatus from her slender face, and scooped her sister into her arms.

She was light. So thin.

Selina hefted her sister over a shoulder in a fireman's carry, her free hand opening the door for them to slip out. Again, Maggie's parents didn't stir, and Selina didn't look back as she shut the door behind her.

The hospital halls were deserted.

Save for a woman at the desk by the elevator.

Selina remembered her. The pinched, overworked, hateful face of the receptionist.

It was pale with fear and shock as she watched Selina stalk by, Maggie over her shoulder. "Y-you can't—"

Selina's steps didn't falter as she passed. "I can."

The woman got a good look at her face. Her face, and Maggie's. Recognition flared there.

The woman reached for the phone on her desk.

"Go ahead," Selina said as she reached the stairwell doors. "Call them."

She didn't wait to see what the woman did as she kicked open the metal door.

The stairs were chaos. Doctors and nurses and patients and families rushed up and down, desperate to escape the bedlam in the streets.

The last piece of her plan: utter chaos in Gotham City to cover her tracks when she made her move. Courtesy of Arkham Asylum being sprung open by the League of Assassins.

Selina kept a hand free to hold any frantic people at bay as she hurried down the concrete stairwell to the ground level.

She had to move quickly.

Off the machines, Maggie's lungs might not be able to last long. It was forty-five minutes to the old factory atop the ley line and the Pit she'd built beneath it.

"Hold on," Selina breathed over the shouting in the stairwell. "Hold on."

The seven Leopards there were wide-eyed as she came barreling out the back door into the alley. The street beyond was filled with smoke and darting figures. There was already blood dripping off the bat of one of the Leopards at the door—an unconscious man in Arkham white sprawled on the pavement a few feet away.

The Leopards sized up Selina, Maggie draped over her shoulder, and one of them pointed to the street in the opposite direction. "We kept it quiet that way for you."

Gratitude crushing her chest, squeezing the breath from her, Selina could only manage a nod.

The Leopards would remain, guarding the hospital, until the GCPD had the city under control again. Mika had sworn it.

She didn't have the words to voice her gratitude for that, either. For the remnant of home that had come when asked.

Selina started for the clear street beyond, keeping her jog as even as possible to avoid disturbing Maggie. She'd stashed her Mercedes a few blocks away days ago, waiting for this.

No one stopped her as she crossed the wild street, cars honking at each other, some people abandoning them completely to flee. Not that way, then.

Selina hit another alley, sprint turning into a run. She could see it—the black Mercedes parked along the street, covered in a day's worth of tickets. The hidden keys taped to the chassis, just under the trunk.

"Hold on," she repeated to her sister.

Fifty feet. Forty. Thirty.

"Selina."

She had not heard her own name in over two years.

It rang through her, foreign and heavy. She didn't care how Harley had figured it out.

Selina. She almost mouthed her name, just to taste it. Hear it again.

Nyssa and Talia hadn't used it. The other assassins had called her kitty-cat or variations on it.

But there was Harley Quinn, striding from around a corner, her bleeding, swollen lips twisted in a sneer.

Aiming two throwing knives at her.

"Stop." Harley's order was a rough snarl. Blood covered her knees, her arm. "I said *stop*!"

Selina kept walking for the car.

"I SAID STOP!"

Selina paused, looking over a shoulder just as Ivy arrived at Harley's side. Blood leaked from Ivy's temple, her knuckles were raw, her vine-whip in shreds at her wrist. Her pallid skin saying enough about the depleted stocks of her toxins.

Harley kept the knives cocked toward her. "You lied. You are a *liar*."

Selina said nothing. Maggie's breathing was a soft rasp in her ear.

"You're in the League," Harley said. Those were tears streaking down her pale makeup. "And you used me, used *us* to get to him." The Joker. "You manipulated us into fighting for you—into doing *this* for you." She gestured with her free hand to the city in chaos.

Ivy was glancing between them, face ashen with pain.

"We rushed for Arkham when we saw the explosion. To get you out," Harley spat. "We went by the Statue of Saint Nicholas. Or tried to. And you know what we saw?"

Selina refused to speak. Maggie's raspy breathing rattled in her ear.

Harley was shaking—with rage. Utter and complete rage.

"We saw my man arrive, waiting for *you*. We saw the GCPD show up instead."

Selina had placed a second call on her way over here. Straight to Commissioner Gordon. Warned him who would be arriving at the statue.

Harley kept the knives trained on Selina. "They *hurt* him. His top men are *dead*. And they dragged him back to Arkham. They dragged him back after *you* set him up, you *liar*!"

The last words were screamed. Maggie stirred, a phlegm-filled inhale sounding, and Selina's temper went razor-sharp. At the words, at the delay, at Harley's twisted obsession with the Joker. At the pain and fear on Ivy's face.

It built and built, until it was a wave, a tsunami, cresting and crashing within her. Until she didn't bother to stop it. Not anymore.

"Then *let* them drag him away!" Selina snapped, her shout cutting through the chaos. "*Let* him stay in there! Do something for *yourself* and your family. *Get out* while you can—before it's too late, Harley!"

"You don't know *shit*," Harley spat. "You don't know *anything*, about me, or what I've been through—"

"You think I don't?" Selina pointed to the Leopard spot just visible on her wrist. "You think I don't know what it's like to feel like there are no options, no choices, no help coming to protect who I love?" She gripped Maggie harder, adjusting her slight weight on her shoulder.

Ivy spoke up, her voice steady. "She's right, Harley. You and me—let's walk away. Let's *help* her. Can't you see that little girl is sick?" She pointed to Maggie. "Let's help her. Then you and me, we can figure something out, get *you* some help—"

"*Shutupshutupshutup!*" Harley screamed. Ivy cringed, stepping back. Harley kept the knives aimed on Selina. "I don't need any"—her voice broke—"*help!*"

She did. Perhaps they all did.

"Put the knives down," Ivy pleaded, her voice edged in panic.

Maggie drew in another rough, mucus-filled breath. Time. Selina didn't have *time*. She had to risk it. Had no other choice.

Keeping her movements as smooth as possible for Maggie, she started walking again, heading for the car. She blocked out the devastation on Ivy's face as she turned her back, the surprise and pain. And Selina finally said without looking back, perhaps for Ivy's sake, perhaps for all their sakes, "The world is better off with him behind bars. And so are you, Harley."

Selina felt the impact in her shoulder before the pain splintered through her.

Saw her blood splatter on the car window.

Selina staggered, a low sound breaking from her as her body buckled—

She shut it out. Shut down the pain, the shock rippling through her body, her bones.

She stumbled one step—two. And kept walking.

Kept gripping Maggie. She left the throwing knife where it had embedded in her back, right into her upper shoulder, its tip jutting clean through her front.

She didn't hear Ivy's screamed words or Harley's answering ones. Selina grabbed the concealed keys, unlocked the sedan, and carefully laid Maggie across the back seat. Blood had spread all over Maggie's hospital gown and bare, too-thin legs.

Her sister didn't stir as Selina arranged her bare feet on the pale leather seats, made sure she was secure, and shut the door. The movement dragged a moan of pain from her gut.

Selina's hands shook as she reached for the knife, shock setting in, pain a dull roar.

She had been undefeated in the ring. She had learned to take hit after hit and never went down, never yielded.

Selina clenched her teeth, swallowing a scream as she yanked the knife out and clapped a hand to the front of the gushing wound, applying as much pressure as she could stand as she reached for the smooth black arc of the driver's door handle. She wasn't going down here. Not now.

Opening the door, she grimaced as her shoulder screamed at the movement.

Harley aimed her other throwing knife at Selina. "I'm going to kill you, you—"

A flash of red and green.

Ivy stepped in front of that knife. "Stop, Harley," she pleaded. *"Stop."*

"Get out of the way." Harley's voice trembled.

Ivy spread her arms, held her ground. "I am *begging* you. As your friend, I am *begging* you not to throw again. Not to throw that knife at *our* friend."

They had come for her. To Arkham. To save her.

Selina shut down the thought. Forty-five minutes. All that remained between Maggie and the Pit. Her sister might not even have that time.

Selina slid into the front seat, using the bloodied knife to slice up a long strip of the seat belt. A few brutal motions, a few grunts of agony, and it was wrapped around her shoulder. Stanching the bleeding. Or as much of it as she could manage.

Her fingers shook as she reached for the push-button engine ignition.

She could barely move the gearshift out of park and into drive.

But as the car grumbled to life, purring beneath her . . .

There was Ivy, pale green smoke—a lingering, last tendril—weaving around their feet. The few remaining flowers along Ivy's shredded vines closed up. Vanished.

And there was Harley, sobbing, reaching a hand out toward Ivy.

Ivy's shoulders shook. Crying—her friend was crying, too, as the toxins rose around them.

Selina pulled from the parking space, gunning the engine as she took off down the street. Through the rearview mirror, just before Selina turned down another street, she looked back.

Saw Ivy wrap her arms around Harley just as her toxins took effect, lowering her gently to the concrete, the knife clattering. Then there was nothing but green smoke.

CHAPTER 34

A trickle of blood still leaked from her shoulder.

She pressed her palm against the wound to stanch the bleeding, but the pain . . .

She pushed that Mercedes's engine to the breaking point.

Every bump sent agony burning through her, but Selina rerouted the pain, let it focus her. Over the roar of the engine, the road, even with the sound-canceling tech of the car, she couldn't hear if Maggie was breathing. Didn't dare take her eyes off the road for long enough to check. Not when the speedometer passed 100 . . . 110 . . . 120.

She wove through traffic, frantic and sloppy drivers honking in her wake, adrenaline honing her vision. Blood leaked down her front and back.

Now 130 . . . 140 . . . 150.

The quieter roads opened up, flat and steady. Selina pulled around cars in her way, dodging oncoming traffic, using the shoulder as a lane where she needed to.

Red lights, stop signs . . . She blew through them.

At last, the ruined, grassy plain opened up, the solitary road winding through it. Ten miles ahead lay the factory.

Time slowed and sped, warping and bending during those miles. Until she was pulling right up to the concrete barrier. Fifty feet of cracked asphalt pathway lay between the barrier and front door to the factory.

She didn't have the strength to swear, to beat the steering wheel into a pulp. Could hardly turn her head to look at Maggie.

Her sister's chest rose—slightly. As if she fought for every breath.

Not yet. Not now.

Selina could barely make it out of the car and walk the two steps to the back door.

Maggie was utterly limp on the seat.

A hundred steps. A hundred steps from salvation.

Selina rallied herself, trying to shove down the agony in her shoulder.

But the lightness in her head, the blurry vision . . .

She knew about the dangers of blood loss. Knew that the amount she'd spilled on the ride over here . . .

She was on borrowed time now, too.

And the Lazarus Pit she'd made only had enough in it for one use. One person.

It didn't frighten her. Not as much as Maggie's labored breathing. Nothing had ever scared her as much as that. Nothing ever would.

Fifty feet. A hundred steps.

Selina braced herself. Allowed herself three steadying breaths, the movement sending pain rippling from her shoulder, all the way down her body.

A hundred steps.

She reached for Maggie. Bit down on her scream as she hauled her sister's weight up and over her good shoulder.

One step. Another. Another.

Down that cracked path, the sky open, stars watching above them.

Any minute now, Nyssa's assassins would arrive. They'd probably stitched a tracking unit into the suit before handing it over at Arkham. She hadn't dared waste a moment to find something to change into.

Ninety steps.

Selina's blood dripped onto the brown dirt beneath her.

Eighty.

Maggie was still—so still.

Every impact and footfall sent sparks bursting behind Selina's eyes.

Seventy. Sixty. Fifty.

Everything she had stolen, all of it, had been for this.

It is now about making Maggie as comfortable as possible.

She refused to accept that. Forty steps.

Selina picked up the pace. If she could make it there and turn on the machine . . . she could finish before the League arrived. Give Maggie the Mercedes keys and tell her to *run*.

Thirty steps left. Twenty.

The derelict factory loomed, its entry point leading down a long, narrow corridor that ended in another door—which opened to the factory floor beyond. To the space she'd converted into the

Pit, the hollowed-out floor now filled with the chemicals and water she'd hauled in on those off-nights. The equipment she'd set up using machines she'd bought, forklifts and clever contraptions. No workers. She wouldn't risk their speaking about it.

Ten steps.

She slowed, her body starting to shake, strength seeping out of her like the blood now streaming from her shoulder.

Five.

She lifted her hand for the twisted metal handle of the heavy door.

Maggie's breath in her ear . . . Had it stopped?

Her own breathing halted in response.

The brink of death. Just at its doorway.

The Pit could draw her back from that threshold. It *would* bring her back. Even if—

Maggie's chest rose and fell. Slow and shallow.

Relief shuddered through Selina, threatening to buckle her knees.

Her trembling fingers closed around the handle. Right as the door opened—from within.

She found herself staring up at Batwing.

Staring up at Luke Fox, helmeted and the bat-symbol blazing on his chest, blocking her path into the factory.

He'd been too late to the hospital to catch her.

To do what, he didn't know. But she'd grabbed her younger sister, Maggie Kyle, and vanished. Maggie's adoptive parents were frantic. The girl wouldn't survive an hour without the various machines she'd been hooked up to.

The couple didn't know who had taken their daughter. They'd been asleep.

Luke opened Gordon's laptop and began hunting.

Hospital security footage showed Selina leaving the building, Maggie over a shoulder, ten minutes earlier. Then street camera footage of Selina in a Mercedes, speeding through a red light. But going *where*—

He'd found it, then. The deed of ownership. Of this factory, purchased by Selina Kyle over a month ago. Cash offer, but because of the factory's chemical history, the owner had to be listed should any environmental issues arise.

He'd soared here. Beat her here by twenty minutes.

Long enough to see the Lazarus Pit inside. He and Bruce had looked into them once, as a potential project for Wayne Industries' medical division. They'd both deemed them little more than myth, and likely impossible to ever create. Yet here one lay, exactly as the legends and rumors described.

She'd used a large, round vat the size of a swimming pool—once used for mixing some compound here. On a raised concrete platform above it, various machines had been gathered, cords draped and snaking along them.

And along the edge of the pool, dangling from pulleys anchored into the high, domed metal ceiling, a metal grate—a *bed*—swayed slightly. To be lowered into the dark, faintly iridescent liquid within. Liquid so dark that even the light leaking in through the grimy windows set high above didn't pierce it.

The Pit could change everything. Especially for wounded soldiers, both overseas and at home.

The implications for the larger world were enormous. It was

why he and Bruce had even considered investigating whether they could be made.

But in the wrong hands . . .

Luke had heard a car pull in and finished inspecting the machinery.

And when he hauled open the door, every word eddied out of his head. Every demanding question, every curse.

Her face was white as death. Blood covered her suit. A stab wound in her back, piercing through the shoulder. Still bleeding out.

Yet she still held her sister over a shoulder. Fingers white-knuckled as they clenched her.

She'd been stabbed, and yet Selina had *carried* her sister here.

Tears began sliding down her face. Her mouth trembled.

And the look in her eyes as those tears brimmed and slipped free—exhausted. Despairing.

She thought he was going to stop her from saving her sister.

Terminally ill. Incurable.

She'd built the Pit to save her sister. Had discovered and taken the chemicals to make it and the money to buy everything she required, including the chaos in Gotham City. She'd rallied the allies she needed to fight the army of League assassins who would come for it—what she'd stolen. What she'd pretended to broker to *gain* those allies: the formula for the Lazarus Pit.

"Please," Selina whispered.

One word. Just one, as those tears rolled down her face, through the dirt and blood.

Please.

Luke's chest cracked.

In the distance, a plume of dirt flowed down the road. And before it, barreling toward them . . . a black SUV.

* * *

Selina saw that car. The dust and the speed.

She was out of time.

"Who—" Luke asked, hand going to some weapon at his suit's side.

"League assassins. At least two." Her words were a broken rasp. "Nyssa's best."

He turned toward her and removed his helmet. Showed her the face beneath. The one she knew so well—the one she'd known was beneath that night on the balcony, when his PTSD had seized him.

"They'll kill you," Luke said.

Selina let out a low laugh. "I'm already dead."

And as if the words were a promise, her knees gave out. She felt Maggie's fragile form tumbling from her, tried to stop it—

Luke was there in an instant. Grabbing Maggie from her in one swift motion, before her little sister could hit the ground.

Selina's knees slammed into the dirt, the world spinning, pain clawing at her.

Luke straightened with Maggie limp in his arms, her curls a tumble over the metal plates of his suit. On her knees before him, Selina watched Maggie's chest rise—just a bit. Heard that car nearing.

For a heartbeat, Luke held her stare. Scanned her face.

And then he pivoted, Maggie in his arms, and headed into the factory. To the Pit.

She managed to claw her way upright. To stand again. Managed to put one foot in front of the other and follow Luke into the factory. Down the narrow hall. Through the heavy door that led onto the factory floor.

Getting every bit of equipment into place had been hell. But the factory had enough working parts that she'd been able to modify what was there. The raising and lowering platform, once used to dip objects into whatever chemicals had filled the enormous vat in the center of the room, was one of them.

Selina braced a hand on the doorway as Luke gently laid Maggie upon the grated bench of the platform, right where it hovered at the edge of the pool.

He turned toward her, the machines along the pool edge shiny and new. Built by Selina herself. "Tell me—"

Gravel crunched outside. A car engine rumbled and shut off.

They were here.

Luke was at Selina's side instantly, assessing the outer door down the hall. The car they could just barely glimpse through the tiny window in the metal slab.

Not now.

Luke whirled to her. Scanned her face, his brown eyes bright.

He kissed her.

Just once, swift and fast. A promise—and a farewell, she realized as he said, "I'll buy you whatever time I can."

Before she could say anything, he was gone. Shutting the factory door between them, throwing the heavy outer lock over it. Barricading her inside.

CHAPTER 35

Luke chose his battlefield carefully.

Donning his helmet again, he felt it whir to life, giving him a read of every advantage and pitfall in the narrow hallway. Not many of the former. Too many of the latter.

Right as three League assassins strode in through that outer door, sunlight leaking in with them. A ray of brightness, blinding him, before dark settled in again.

Luke marked their faces, his gut churning. Two women and one man.

Nyssa al Ghūl hadn't just sent some of her best. She'd sent her three top ghūls to execute Selina and get the Pit formula back.

Cheshire. Onyx. Rictus.

Cheshire—for that wild, wide grin that never faltered, even when the dark-haired assassin made her gruesome kills. And left similar smiles carved into her victims.

Onyx and Rictus, the two notorious killers identified by the intricate matching tattoos banded around their necks. And by the way the man and woman stood with utter stillness as they stared calmly at Luke. Living ghosts—that's what Onyx and Rictus were. Their list of victims too long for even Luke's brain to memorize.

He didn't have to fight for long. Just long enough.

Luke braced his feet apart, angling his head at the three assassins, all wearing Selina's black battle-suit. None bothering with helmets. They wanted Selina to see their faces when they executed her. Wanted her to know who it was that ended her.

From Cheshire's wide grin, Luke knew precisely what she'd do to Selina's body afterward. His own. Maybe even Maggie's.

The thought was enough to focus him. Steady him.

Three against one. He'd faced worse odds, but his opponents had not been lethal killers. His opponents had not been built to take lives.

Luke calmed his breathing. Readied himself as the assassins noticed the trail of blood down the hallway, leading to the door behind him, the door he'd go down swinging to defend. They exchanged knowing glances and gave him cold, clever smiles.

When the first attack came, he was ready.

Every breath was an effort.

Every movement of her hands on the three various machines, each step between them, required the entirety of her focus.

Selina recited the process, telling herself what to do as she worked.

Activate the ley lines first. She moved to the machine on the far left, flicking on three switches. *One to charge the machine. One to draw up the energy from the lines. One to direct it to the pool.*

She staggered toward the second machine. *Green button starts the chemicals mixing. Red stops it.*

Maggie lay so still on that grated platform. So still as the liquid just beyond her began to eddy and churn, deepest green and darkest black swirling and blending, faint flickers of light darting among it like minnows.

Selina stumbled for the third and final machine, the toggle stick. *Swing the platform outward. Lower it into the pool. Activate full charge of ley lines. Chemicals will drain as they are absorbed.*

Selina's fingers could barely clench the maneuvering stick as she pushed it to the left. Machines groaned, metal clanking. But the grated platform, Maggie unconscious atop it, slowly moved out over the center of the pool, the swirling liquid ten feet beneath.

From the locked door, the hallway beyond, shouts and thuds sounded. Brutal—the fighting had to be brutal. Something deep in her, buried in her chest, began to ache. Luke wouldn't last long.

Neither would she. But she wasn't the one who needed to survive.

Maggie reached the center of the pool, and Selina jammed the stick downward.

Slowly, so slowly, Maggie descended into the pool.

The dark water swallowed her up with barely a ripple.

Breathing became difficult. Impossible.

Her knees buckled, and Selina let them, sliding to the ground, still clenching the toggle stick.

It didn't matter. It didn't matter, none of it.

She was not afraid. Not as darkness crept into the edges of her vision. Not as she slid her hand from the toggle stick to the keyboard hovering right above her head. Punched in the final commands.

A low hum sounded through the room. Light flared within the water.

All of it, for this. All of it, for Maggie.

For Maggie.

Selina managed to push the toggle stick upward. Pushed with the tips of her shaking fingers.

The platform began to rise out of the Pit. Maggie's soaked hospital gown clung to her body—

A body that was not frail.

Not thin.

A body that was healed.

And a chest that rose and fell, deeply, evenly.

Luke knew he was screwed.

He'd taken out Cheshire on a lucky, quick shot of his electrified Batarang. The woman had dropped like a stone.

No twisted smile lingered on her unconscious face after that. He doubted one would return after the GCPD picked her up.

Focus. Breathe. He went through his therapist's instructions, even as he snatched up Cheshire's fallen dagger and raised it against the other two.

Onyx and Rictus had only laughed—and attacked.

And were now kicking his ass. Where he lunged for one of them, the other attacked. Where they darted away, the other was striking. Partners, equals in fighting style, too.

Their knives chipped away at his suit. His blood mingled with theirs.

They remained standing. Herding him back toward that door. They were toying with him, and they all knew it.

Luke feinted a jab at Onyx, lunging instead right for Rictus. They saw Luke's move, easily countered it. A left hook from Rictus to the ribs that had him yielding a step, a slash of Onyx's dagger that had him yielding another. Rictus let out a low chuckle.

A sound that ended quickly as light flashed over Luke's shoulder, flickering through the tiny window in the door.

The assassins' faces tightened, all amusement fading.

The Pit was in use.

He caught the look exchanged between Onyx and Rictus. Playtime was over.

As one, they freed twin short swords from across their backs. The same blades Selina bore.

As one, they assessed him.

He just needed to stall them long enough for her to finish and get her sister out of here. It didn't seem like a bad way to go.

To do right by his city, do right by those he cared about . . . It was all he'd wanted from the start.

So this did not seem like a bad way to go at all.

The assassins took a step, peeling apart.

They'd try to make it swift. To get to the door behind him as fast as possible.

He'd keep it going for as long as he could. Light died behind him.

As long as he could.

Luke managed to stand upright.

"Let's get it over with," he panted.

Rictus and Onyx smiled. Not one word. They hadn't uttered one word since they arrived.

Those blades angled, mirror images to each other.

Luke surveyed the injuries on each. Taking out one assassin

would mean being exposed to the other, but maybe if there was just one for Selina to face—

He sucked in a breath, legs bending, fighting past the pain as he prepared to lunge.

Something hissing and metal thumped and slid down the hallway behind the assassins.

Spewing smoke.

Instantly, the hall was full of it. The assassins whirled, daggers flying.

Onyx got a lungful and went down, crumpling to the cracked, blood-streaked tiles.

Rictus stayed up. He must have had some sort of toxin immunity as part of his training—that even Onyx had not received.

Rictus whirled, swords angled upright, as Poison Ivy emerged from the smoke. One of Luke's fallen batarangs in her hands.

The assassin glanced between them. Ivy didn't take her gaze off Rictus, her bloodied face pale as she said to Luke, "Help her."

He didn't object. Whirling toward the door behind him and throwing the lock, his body barking in agony with each movement, he got through the door. He locked it from within, glancing through the window in time to see Ivy beckon to the seething assassin. Rictus's sword lifted in answer.

Luke scanned the room.

The machines were on. The platform was dripping dark liquid at the edge of the pool. And the girl now sitting up atop it, soaked . . .

She rubbed at her face, made a small sound at the thick liquid coating it, her hands. Her hospital gown and body.

Luke said nothing, barely breathing as he compared the healthy girl now sitting up with the wrecked, wasted body he'd seen moments before. She started, as if realizing it, too, a hand going to her chest.

Maggie Kyle sucked in a long, deep breath. Marveling. Glancing at the pool, the factory around her, her brown brows knotting as she twisted the other way, toward the machines—

Luke spotted Selina at the same moment Maggie did.

A limp, lifeless body by the third machine. Her emerald eyes staring up at the ceiling. Unseeing. Unblinking.

Maggie's sob cleaved the room.

Cleaved Luke's chest apart.

Feet slipping on the tiles, skin slick with that liquid, Maggie hurtled for her sister.

For Selina, lying on the floor.

Dead.

CHAPTER 36

Maggie was sobbing as she shook Selina's shoulders. As she stared into those lifeless eyes, the bloodless face.

Luke's head was empty. Silent.

It hadn't been this silent since that day in the desert. The memories pushed in, swarming, his chest seizing—

She'd known. That she was running on empty. That this pool had only enough resources for one.

And this woman, through every lie she'd fed him, every taunt and deception . . . Luke pushed back against the panic creeping over him, the flashes of desert sun and blood. *Stay here.*

He wasn't sure if his silent order was to himself or Selina.

Maggie laid her head on Selina's bloody chest, as if searching for any hint of a heartbeat. Her green eyes—the same as her sister's—met Luke's. No shock or surprise filled them upon seeing him, seeing Batwing. Just that panicked, despairing grief.

Do something. Luke pivoted, scanning the warehouse. Basic training had taught him a few medical tricks, ways to keep injured soldiers alive until they could get to a field hospital or the doctors could reach them.

If her heart had stopped, he could pull apart the wires on one of the machines, somehow get a safe-enough current going, and maybe—

The door blew open, and Luke whirled, hand going to his remaining batarang. But it was Ivy. Panting, bloody, but—alive. No sign of Rictus.

Her attention went right to Selina. Then she noticed Maggie, who lifted her head, still unfazed by the company she now kept.

But Luke watched the realization dawn on Ivy as she behld Maggie's emerald eyes, her now-healthy limbs.

As she understood who Maggie was. What all of this had been for.

Ivy stalked forward as if in a daze. "A Lazarus Pit," she whispered, scanning the machinery, the pool, and the few feet of liquid remaining at its bottom.

Ivy stopped at his side. Luke breathed, the only explanation he could muster against the panic crushing his chest, "Maggie was dying. If we can get the wires on the machines exposed, we could restart her heart—"

Maggie faced them. The machines and the pool. "Use it to save her."

Luke studied the pool at the same time Ivy did. Ivy said, "There's not enough liquid in there."

"Try it," Luke said roughly.

"Please," Maggie begged.

The same word her sister had uttered. Her broken plea for mercy—to save the person Selina loved more than her life. Her very soul, it seemed.

Ivy glanced to the pool again, to the machines. With the lingering chemicals and toxins, the natural charge of the ley line . . . Ivy's eyes were darting, as if calculating it, too.

"It's a slim chance," Ivy said, but already strode to the machines.

"Take it," Luke said, Maggie backing away on her hands and knees as he scooped Selina's lifeless body into his arms. He'd have tried it himself, but his mind was spinning, his body barking in pain, every movement an effort—

Picking her up, the blood on her . . . He'd done this before. That day. He'd carried a dead friend—

He breathed and breathed, working through the memories, the way his body clammed up against him. Ivy flicked a few switches, studying and assessing.

"Hurry," Maggie whispered, rising to her feet and standing between two machines.

"I'm going as fast as I can," Ivy said through her teeth, hands flying over the machines. "Right," she declared. "Put her on the platform."

Clenching his jaw against the pain, forcing himself to take deep, soothing breaths, Luke did so. Selina's hair spilled over the edge, her too-pale face still staring up at the ceiling. Lips white as death.

As death—because she *was* dead.

The thought clanged through him. He barely noticed Ivy flying through the network of machines, flipping switches and pumping levers. "A manual charge for the depleted ley line," Ivy muttered. "Clever kitty."

Because, as Ivy hauled herself into the lever in the machine, pumping it once, twice . . . those were white sparks beginning to flicker in the liquid pool below.

Ivy finished, darting to the next machine. "Red or green?"

"Green," Luke said, struggling to remember words over the roaring in his head. "Green means go."

Ivy cut him a look that said, *Duh*, and hit the green button.

The pool shuddered and groaned. Maggie let out a low whimper.

"Is she secure?" Ivy asked him, jerking her chin toward Selina and the platform as she gripped a toggle stick that no doubt controlled the levers to move it into the pool.

Luke peered down at the lifeless face, gently closing Selina's eyes as a panel slid up to reveal the lower half of his face. He leaned in, brushing a kiss over her mouth before he murmured into her ear, "Please."

"I'll take that as a yes," Ivy said, and the platform swung away, Selina's body jostling with it. Her body—her *body*—

In and out, deep and calming, he breathed through the panic, the feeling of the walls pushing in.

Ivy shifted the lever, and the platform lowered. Farther and farther into the depleted tank, the rusty sides encompassing her. Heading for the too-shallow sliver of liquid at the bottom.

Dark liquid seemed to rise up to meet her. Swallow her whole. It covered her—barely.

"Now what?" Maggie breathed, coming to Ivy's side as she hovered over the machine. Light flared, bright and blinding, from the water.

"I don't know," Ivy admitted.

But the liquid was dissolving, as if Selina had absorbed it, as if its usage, the charge of the ley line, evaporated it—

Bit by bit, her body appeared. The blood had been washed away, revealing the hole in the shoulder of her suit.

Ivy slammed a hand into the lever, raising the platform up as the last of the liquid vanished. Closer and closer, Selina came.

The skin beneath that hole in her suit . . . healed. Smooth.

The color had returned to her face.

But her heartbeat, her chest . . .

His helmet scanned her.

No life signs.

None.

The platform swung toward them, groaning as it stopped. Luke moved, hauling her off it, setting her down on the floor, his body numb and distant.

He couldn't endure this again. He *wouldn't* endure this again—

"Selina," Maggie pleaded. *"Selina."*

She did not move. Her eyes did not open.

Ivy reached for her wrist. "No pulse."

The wounds had healed, but nothing else. His stomach churned and rose up his throat. *Not again, not again, not again—*

"She's not breathing," Maggie said, pushing past Ivy, kneeling at her sister's side. "She needs help!"

Without waiting, Maggie rose up on her knees, interlaced her hands, and set them over Selina's chest. Pumping once, twice—Luke lost count before she tipped back her sister's head, blew a breath into her mouth, waited. Went back to pumping her chest. Her heart.

Nothing.

Ivy was pale. Unblinking as she stared down at Selina. At Maggie, performing CPR. Giving her new, unfaltering breaths to her sister.

It hadn't worked. The pool—it hadn't worked. And Selina . . .

Maggie sobbed through her teeth. *"Wake up."* Her curls bounced with every frantic push of her hands on Selina's chest. *"Wake up."*

Luke didn't quite feel his arms, his hands, as he reached for Maggie. "She's g—"

"Don't you say it!" Maggie shouted, knocking his hand away. She breathed again into Selina's mouth.

Nothing.

And at Maggie's shouted words, something snapped into place. Settled and cleared in his head. Luke said to the girl, "Keep going. Don't stop."

He scanned for the nearest cord to split open, to expose the wires and get a charge. He could restart her heart, risk the electrocution—

Maggie went back to pumping, weeping as she spoke. "You fought for me every day, every hour." Over and over, her hands slammed into Selina's chest. "You came home with those bruises, you stole and you fought, for *me*. And when they brought me to Peter and Hiroki's house, when I saw how nice it was, how nice *they* were, when you never came back . . . I knew you'd done that for me, too. The police said you went to prison, but I didn't believe them. And I knew—I knew when the money came in last month, the bills all paid . . . I knew it was you. Somehow. *I knew it was you.*"

Maggie blew another breath into Selina's lifeless lungs.

Across from her, tears slid down Ivy's face as she silently watched. Luke lunged for the nearest power cord, opening up a panel on his suit arm to grab the small pair of wire-splicers.

Maggie's shoulders shook as she resumed pumping. "You fought for me, even when no one else would. You fought, and I love you." Maggie sucked in a shuddering breath, sitting back on her heels. "Fight back," she whispered. "One last time."

Selina's chest did not move.

Luke sliced down the plastic coating on the wires, revealing the tangle of metal beneath. A hollow, aching void filled him, silence pealing through his head.

Maggie lunged, slamming a hand down onto Selina's heart as she screamed, *"FIGHT BACK."* Another slam of her hand, right over that silent heart. *"FIGHT—"*

Selina's body arced off the floor, eyes flaring wide.

His helmet glowed with assessments and data that he ignored. Ignored as she gasped for breath, then coughed, curling on her side—

Maggie threw her arms around her, shaking with the force of her sobbing. For a heartbeat, Selina just lay there, and Luke looked then—at his helmet's monitors.

To make sure the sudden stillness didn't mean anything amiss.

But there was her heartbeat, hammering steadily. The wire tumbled from his hands.

Slowly, Selina's arm rose, gently resting on Maggie's back.

Her younger sister pulled away, and Selina stared up silently into Maggie's face.

Those green eyes scanned over every curve and freckle, along every wild curl and plane of healthy, glowing skin.

Tears began sliding out of the corners of Selina's eyes.

Maggie surged forward, hugging her again.

This time, both of Selina's arms came around her sister—and held tightly.

Ivy asked, voice thick but clear, "Does this mean you have eight lives left?"

CHAPTER 37

The oak-lined street was awash with reds and golds and oranges, the sky a crisp blue above the fall splendor.

Luke and Selina lingered in the shadows beneath one of the trees, monitoring the lovely white house across the way, the mums lining the path to the red-painted front door, the flower beds bursting with color beneath the wide windows and black shutters. As pretty a house as one could picture, on an equally beautiful street.

Quiet, yet humming with life. Families out and about, kids shouting as they played backyard soccer. Luke and Selina leaned against the hood of the black SUV of the League assassins that they'd taken here, and he brushed his fingers against hers as they watched Maggie run up to the door and ring the doorbell. Once, twice. Bouncing on her toes, curls bobbing with her.

Healthy. Healed. Whole.

The door opened, an Asian man filling the space.

He fell to his knees at the sight of Maggie. As she threw her arms around his neck and he grasped her tightly. A heartbeat later, a white man approached, tall and blond. He took one look at his husband, at the girl in his arms, and knelt, too. Wrapped his arms around both of them.

Luke glanced sidelong at Selina.

Silver lined her eyes, a smile, soft and yet full of joy, dancing upon her mouth. Full of *life*.

He'd removed his helmet, his suit—and stood in the black athletic gear he wore beneath. But Selina . . . She still wore her torn battle-suit. Clean, but they were still shadows in this neighborhood. Slivers of the night. They did not belong.

"You sure you don't want to say hi?" Luke asked as Maggie and her dads rose to their feet, the men now looking the girl over with utter shock—and gratitude.

Selina shook her head, focus never straying from the family that moved inside, the door shutting behind them. She and Maggie had made their goodbyes in the SUV moments ago. Maggie had tried to convince her sister to meet her adoptive parents, but Selina had gently refused. Her return would raise too many questions, potentially bring too many people sniffing around Maggie and her family.

Maggie had cried, asking when she'd see her sister again. Luke had tried not to watch through the rearview mirror as Selina had kissed her sister's cheek.

"I'll surprise you," Selina had told Maggie. He'd never heard that voice, the tone she used with her sister. The softness. The kindness.

"But when?" Maggie had frowned deeply.

Selina had brushed a curl from Maggie's face. "So bossy."

Maggie's eyes welled again. "In a week?"

Selina kissed her brow this time. "Soon."

"What about Friday night movies?"

Joy—that was joy in Selina's eyes. "Get settled again, Maggie. Then we'll figure it out."

"Just come meet Hiroki and Peter. You'll love them. Maybe they'll adopt you, too—"

Selina had chuckled. "You should go in. They're worried sick." She'd held her tightly. "We'll see each other again soon. I promise."

With that, Maggie had reluctantly left the car. She'd taken two trudging steps before she sprinted for the beautiful house. Where she was now safely ensconced.

"She's safer this way," Selina said, staring at the now-shut front door.

Luke studied her. "And what about Holly Vanderhees? What happens to her?"

Selina faced him at last, mouth tightening. She said nothing.

"When did you figure it out—who I am?" he asked.

"That night on the balcony."

When he'd kissed her—or tried to. He lifted a brow. "So you'll kiss Batwing but not Luke?"

He could have sworn color bloomed on her cheeks. "That's what you ask about? Not how death was, what I saw, but why I kissed one of your identities over the other?"

"How was death, *Selina*?"

"None of your business, that's how it was."

Luke grinned, rubbing his jaw. "I mean it—what happens to Holly?"

"Well, I'm sure she'll mope over not getting easy access to the shellfish platters at all the galas. . . ."

Luke laughed as Selina strode for the passenger-side door and pulled the handle. She angled her head, hair spilling over her shoulder. "What do you think should happen to Holly?"

"Well, her apartment is now a crime scene. . . ."

"Too bad." She opened the door and sliding in. "There was so much money stowed in there."

Luke laughed again, coming around to the other side of the car and getting in. "Oh, I know." He slid the keys into the ignition, but glanced over at her. She leaned against the side door, watching him. "So Holly Vanderhees vanishes . . . but what about Catwoman?" He lifted a brow. "Or does the cat become a Leopard again?"

She let out an impressed laugh. "You really did your research."

"Like you, my computer skills are . . . above average." She'd explained everything to him, to Maggie, on the drive here. What she'd done at the League, what she'd stolen. How she'd stolen it. He had a feeling she'd left out some gory, brutal details for her sister's sake, but he'd filled in the gaps himself.

"You've got the tats, don't you," Luke said, jerking his chin toward her arms.

She only zipped down the front of her suit a bit, just far enough to peel it off her shoulder to reveal two splotches of black-lined purple. Black-and-purple leopard spots.

"How many?" he asked as she settled her suit back into place.

Selina buckled her seat belt. "Twenty-seven."

He blew out a breath. "Undefeated champ, huh?"

"I hear you are, too."

Luke gave her a lazy grin. "Maybe."

Silence fell, thrumming and light. And his smile . . . Luke let it stay there. Felt it in his bones.

"So, are you taking me to the nearest precinct, or . . . ?"

"Considering how poorly the last time you were arrested went for everyone involved, we can take a rain check."

Wariness flashed in her green eyes. "I'm waiting for you to yell about Arkham."

Luke snorted, pulling the car out into the quiet street and slowly driving down it. "You died. I figure that's payment enough to settle the debt." He glanced sidelong at her. "But *are* there any more upcoming escapades I should know about?"

She considered. "Perhaps."

"What's a girl to do, now that she's rich and saved the day?"

Her brows rose. "I'm not rich." She watched the street passing. "The money went to Maggie—most of it. And the rest . . ."

"The rest?"

Selina sucked on a tooth and said, as if she didn't want to admit to it, "I gave it to the children's hospital. To pay off the bills for the families who can't afford treatment."

Luke slowed the car to a stop at the red light at the corner. Put the car in park. "Robbing the rich, Robin Hood?"

She cut him a glare. "If that is a new nickname—"

Luke grabbed her face in his hands and kissed her.

The light changed, and the car behind them began honking, but Luke didn't move, didn't really care about anything as her mouth opened to him and her hands slid around his neck.

When he pulled back, her breathing was just as uneven as his. Luke brushed his mouth over hers. Once, twice. Unable to stop himself.

"Let me take you out—a real date."

The words slipped from him before he could think.

Selina pulled back, studying him. Luke finally moved the car back into drive and continued on. "No pizza and *Jeopardy!*, huh?"

"You sound disappointed."

"I am."

Luke chuckled. "If you can sneak into the apartment building, then go ahead. Come over every night, if you want."

"You want a known criminal hanging at your place?"

"I've been thinking about it."

"Oh?"

Luke turned onto a broad avenue, the SUV blending with the cars around them. "Perhaps the future of Gotham City doesn't lie in crushing the underworld in some endless Whac-A-Mole game."

When she didn't answer, he looked over at her—found her face serious. Contemplative. But her eyes . . . full of light. The face beneath Holly, beneath that mask.

Selina.

Luke went on, "I'll take a gamble and assume that this crime spree . . . now that Maggie is safe, disrupting the stability of Gotham City isn't your endgame. Not while she lives here."

Selina said simply, "Yes."

"But the problem remains that you've made a hell of a lot of criminals think *you* are in charge. You tricked the Joker. They won't forget that. Neither will he."

"And?"

"*And*, in addition to this being a warning to you to be careful, I've been thinking that the future of Gotham City doesn't lie in trying to hunt them all down one by one. But in working with the underworld's new *Lady*." He nodded to her with a wicked grin.

She considered, chewing on her bottom lip in a wholly distracting way. "I would have pegged you for a hard-liner on the no-criminal-activity policy."

Luke reached over the console, offering his hand to her palm-up. "Oh, I am. But the darkness will always exist, in some form or another. Corruption is still rife—on both sides of the law. We could help fix it."

Selina nodded. "The GCPD has been overdue for some major changes for a while now." She arched a brow. "Commissioner Gordon won't be thrilled that you're making an alliance with me."

"I'd think that would be an incentive for you to say yes." When she didn't answer, Luke added, "Gordon's one of the good ones. He'd support us, want to improve things. The innocent need protecting."

Her green eyes danced. "They do." He knew in her own way, she would protect them. "A working relationship," she repeated, musing over the words as she eyed his hand.

"If the Lady of Gotham City wants one," he said, smiling broadly. "If she's not already taken."

And when Selina interlaced her fingers with his . . . her answer was all Luke hoped it would be.

CHAPTER 38

"Those sunglasses make you look like a terrifying Audrey Hepburn."

"It's the look I'm going for," Selina said, brushing her dark hair over a shoulder and being surprised—for the tenth time this hour—to find the color changed. Back to usual. Since everyone would be looking for the blond Holly Vanderhees, dark-haired Selina Kyle blended in far better. "And besides, you look like a drunken beekeeper."

Ivy was indeed wearing an enormous floppy hat that concealed her face, giant sunglasses that rivaled Selina's own, and a loose white tunic that fluttered in the autumn breeze alongside the river-front café where they sipped their drinks. A latte for Selina, a soy chai for Ivy.

No one paid them any heed—not that the hipster café would be a likely place for anyone to start looking for Catwoman and her cohorts.

Ivy gestured down at her attire. "It's my Sunday leisure suit."

Selina smiled and sipped her drink. Luke had slipped into her apartment last night to get her clothes, sneaking them down to where she waited with the League SUV. She'd dumped the vehicle hours later, but kept the bags full of stuff. And when she'd opened them . . .

A letter had fallen out.

Here's to a working relationship was all it had said. She'd smiled for a good while afterward.

She adjusted the lapel on her black blazer, then brushed an invisible bit of lint off her dark jeans, the outfit more casual than Holly's power suits and dresses. Certainly more casual than her League-issued suit. She'd deposited it in the Sprang River this morning, having already decided not to retrieve her Death Mask from Arkham.

It was time to create her own suit and helmet, designed exactly to her tastes.

"So, you didn't invite me to meet you here for overpriced drinks," Ivy said.

Selina looked up. Ivy had left the factory yesterday in her own stolen vehicle, missing her explanation to Maggie and Luke. But before Selina told her . . . "What happened to Harley?"

Ivy's eyes shuttered, and she swirled her chai in its cup as she studied the river. "I stayed until the GCPD showed up. Made sure they didn't hurt her. By the time she woke up, I think she realized what she'd done—to you. Risking Maggie in the process. It . . . it was a wake-up call. About a lot of stuff. She went willingly with the police, bought me some time to run to you. Arkham's a mess, so they took her to another facility. Where she's getting therapy for . . . for those parts of her that are drawn to people like the Joker. She *wants* to get some therapy. And is awaiting trial."

"I'm sorry." It was the only thing Selina could think to say.

"I don't blame you for what you did. And Harley . . . She is un-well. I've known that for a while, and she knows it now, too, but . . ." Ivy eyed Selina's shoulder, where that blade had gone through. "My enabling her behavior—I can't live with it. So even if it means her taking some time for herself, even behind bars . . ."

"I know someone who can make sure she gets in front of a good therapist, and a good judge," Selina offered. "Make sure she gets the right treatment and the support she needs." Luke had said as much last night. That he'd help with whatever sort of cleanup she needed. Get things in order so they could figure out how to handle this city.

Because he was right: with Maggie living here, going to school . . . Over Selina's dead body would crime lords rule the streets. There were innocent, good people in this city who needed someone to fight for them. And as Catwoman, as the Lady of Gotham City, *she* could help set the rules. Control the chaos.

"Thank you," Ivy said. She swallowed. "And you, with your sis-ter, I get it. All of this—" Ivy waved a hand toward the skyscrapers flanking the river, the café, the space between them. "It was all part of your plan to save her."

"It was."

At Ivy's expectant pause, Selina settled into her chair. And told her story.

The sun arced above them, their drinks were replaced by the waitress, and the chill autumn air had wrapped around them be-fore Selina finished.

Ivy blew out a breath and whistled. "Well, that's certainly one hell of a story."

Selina snorted. Ivy flicked her thick braid over a shoulder. "Was any of it real? What you—you felt for us. As friends."

"It wasn't supposed to be," Selina admitted. "But it was. It is."

Ivy finished her chai with a long gulp. "Will the League come after you?"

"Oh, most definitely. Especially now that I destroyed the formula, the data—all of it." What Ivy herself had gleaned, Selina knew she wouldn't tell. As far as the League was concerned, Ivy had never been in that factory. "But until then," Selina said, stretching, "I've got bills to pay."

"Oh?"

Selina smiled. "I got a cat." She'd found herself one, was more like it. That small gray alley cat. It had taken a heartbreakingly tiny amount of food to get her to jump into Selina's arms last night. And stay there, purring the entire way home. She'd named her Jane.

Ivy lifted a brow. "And cats are that expensive?"

Selina's smile turned into a grin. "Certainly. Especially when they live in the new hideout I plan to build with my villainous roommate."

She placed a set of keys on the table between them.

Ivy laughed, picking up the keys and jangling them.

"I got the idea from Harley's pad. Two underground levels in another abandoned subway station—the lower floor can be converted into lab space," Selina said. "Three bedrooms can be made out of the upper level."

"Three?"

"One for guests," Selina said. "Or another cohort. When the time is right for her."

A home. For all of them. To start living how they wished, on their own terms.

Ivy blinked furiously, ducking her head and hiding her face as she said, "Thank you."

It was the least Selina could do. If Harley got out, if that good judge let her off easy and she received the help she needed and now wanted . . . For Ivy's sake, Selina prayed Harley got better. Found some way to get beyond the Joker, the past that haunted and drove her. To see the woman right in front of her, who had been waiting for her all this time.

And maybe not try to kill Selina in the process.

But she'd think on that tomorrow. Another day. Another week.

Ivy straightened, her freckled face lighting. "Making that sort of lair is going to be expensive." She dangled the old janitor's keys from a crooked finger. The metal sparkled in the sunlight. "What will our next heist be?"

Selina looked toward the river, the sun just starting to set. And for a heartbeat, a calm, contented sort of quiet settled over her, wrapping around her bones, warming her blood. As if that sun sinking toward the horizon, the shadows growing . . . It was not an end. Not an end at all.

And the city now cast in light and dark—it was hers for the taking.

For the first time, all of it was hers. Open and boundless. A path to carve as she willed. As she dreamed it to be.

And a home.

Selina smiled. "There are a few museum exhibits I've been dying to see."

ACKNOWLEDGMENTS

Being asked to write Selina's story was such a tremendous honor, and from the start, it has been an absolute dream project. But it would not exist without several people. My deepest and eternal heartfelt gratitude goes out to:

My wonderful husband, Josh: Nine lives wouldn't be enough time with you. I love you.

To Annie, my faithful canine companion (aka the Batdog): You make every day a joy (even when you demand endless snacks and treats). I'm sorry for the thousands of photos I've taken of you while you were snoozing, but you're too cute to resist.

To Tamar Rydzinski, my badass agent, who works so tirelessly on my behalf: You are a queen.

To everyone at the Laura Dail Literary Agency for being the best group of people to work with. Ever.

To Chelsea Eberly, editor extraordinaire, who made this project such a delight to work on and who shaped it into something that I am truly proud of. Thank you for *everything*.

To the marvelous team at Random House: Michelle Nagler, Lauren Adams, Kerri Benvenuto, Hanna Lee, Kate Keating, Elizabeth Ward, Aisha Cloud, Kathy Dunn, Adrienne Waintraub, Regina Flath, Alison Impey, Stephanie Moss, Jocelyn Lange, Jenna Lettice, Barbara Bakowski, Tim Terhune, Mallory Matney, Felicia Frazier, Mark Santella, Emily Bruce, Becky Green, Kimberly Langus, and Cletus Durkin. Thank you all so much for your hard work!

Thank you to the awesome DC/Warner Bros. team: Ben Harper, Melanie Swartz, Shoshana Stopek, and Thomas Zellers, who provided such key input and guidance. To Afua Richardson: Thank you for the beautiful Selina artwork.

Endless love and gratitude to the marvelous Nic Stone for providing truly invaluable and thorough feedback. And a huge thank-you to Jason Reynolds for taking the time to offer such crucial insight.

Thank you, thank you, thank you to Cassie Homer for being a brilliant assistant. To Steph Brown, Lynette Noni, Alice Fanchiang, Jennifer Armentrout, Roshani Chokshi, Christina Hobbs, and Lauren Billings: Thank you for being such fantastic friends. To Louise Ang: Thank you, as always, for your infectious excitement and kindness. To Charlie Bowater: Your art never fails to inspire and move me, and I'm so grateful that our paths crossed.

To Jennifer Kelly, Alexa Santiago, Kelly Grabowski, Rachel Domingo, Jessica Reigle, Laura Ashforth, Sasha Alsberg, and Diyana Wan: You are all such special people, and I'm so lucky to know you.

To my family, who provide such unwavering love and support: I am blessed to have you in my life.

And lastly to you, dear reader: Thank you from the bottom of my heart for picking up Selina's story. I hope it inspires you to raise a little hell (preferably the noncriminal kind!)—and have fun while doing it.

ABOUT THE AUTHOR

SARAH J. MAAS is the #1 *New York Times* and *USA Today* bestselling author of the Throne of Glass series, as well as the Court of Thorns and Roses series. Sarah wrote the first incarnation of the Throne of Glass series when she was just sixteen, and it has now sold in thirty-six languages. A New York native, Sarah lives in Pennsylvania with her husband and dog.

sarahjmaas.com

 @therealsjmaas

THE NIGHTWALKERS
ARE HUNTING GOTHAM CITY'S ELITE.

BRUCE WAYNE IS NEXT ON THEIR LIST.

TURN THE PAGE TO SEE HOW
BRUCE'S ADVENTURE BEGINS,
IN THE BESTSELLING DC ICONS SERIES!

As Bruce rounded another bend, the wails suddenly turned deafening, and a mass of flashing red and blue lights blinked against the buildings near the end of the street. White barricades and yellow police tape completely blocked the intersection. Even from here, Bruce could see fire engines and black SWAT trucks clustered together, the silhouettes of police running back and forth in front of the headlights.

Inside his car, the electronic voice came on again, followed by a transparent map overlaid against his windshield. *"Heavy police activity ahead. Alternate route suggested."*

A sense of dread filled his chest.

Bruce flicked away the map and pulled to an abrupt halt in front of the barricade—right as the unmistakable *pop-pop-pop* of gunfire rang out in the night air.

He remembered the sound all too well. The memory of his parents' deaths sent a wave of dizziness through him. *Another robbery. A murder. That's what all this is.*

Then he shook his head. *No, that can't be right.* There were far too many cops here for a simple robbery.

"Step *out* of your vehicle, and put your hands in the air!" a police officer shouted through a megaphone, her voice echoing along the block. Bruce's head jerked toward her. For an instant, he thought her command was directed at him, but then he saw that her back was turned, her attention fixed on the corner of the building bearing the name BELLINGHAM INDUSTRIES & CO. "We have you surrounded, Nightwalker! This is your final warning!"

Another officer came running over to Bruce's car. He whirled an arm exaggeratedly for Bruce to turn his car around. His voice harsh with panic, he warned, "Turn back *now*. It's not safe!"

Before Bruce could reply, a blinding fireball exploded behind the officer. The street rocked.

Even from inside his car, Bruce felt the heat of the blast. Every window in the building burst simultaneously, a million shards of glass raining down on the pavement below. The police ducked in unison, their arms shielding their heads. Fragments of glass dinged like hail against Bruce's windshield.

From inside the blockade, a white car veered around the corner at top speed. Bruce saw immediately what the car was aiming for—a slim gap between the police barricades where a SWAT team truck had just pulled through.

The car raced right toward the gap.

"I said, *get out of here*!" the officer shouted at Bruce. A thin ribbon of blood trickled down the man's face. "That is an *order*!"

Bruce heard the scream of the getaway car's tires against the asphalt. He'd been in his father's garage a thousand times, helping him tinker with an endless number of engines from the best cars in the world. At WayneTech, Bruce had watched in fascination as tests were conducted on custom engines, conceptual jets, stealth tech, new vehicles of every kind.

And so he knew: whatever was installed under that hood was faster than anything the GCPD could hope to have.

They'll never catch him.

But I can.

His Aston Martin was probably the only vehicle here that

could overtake the criminal's, the only one powerful enough to chase it down. Bruce's eyes followed the path the car would likely take, his gaze settling on a sign at the end of the street that pointed toward the freeway.

I can get him.

The white getaway vehicle shot straight through the gap in the barricade, clipping two police cars as it went.

No, not this time. Bruce slammed his gas pedal.

The Aston Martin's engine let out a deafening roar, and the car sped forward. The officer who'd shouted at him stumbled back. In the rearview mirror, Bruce saw him scramble to his feet and wave the other officers' cars forward, both his arms held high.

"Hold your fire!" Bruce could hear him yelling. "Civilian in proximity—*hold your fire!*"

The getaway car made a sharp turn at the first intersection, and Bruce sped behind it a few seconds later. The street zigzagged, then turned in a wide arc as it led toward the freeway—and the Nightwalker took the on-ramp, leaving a trail of exhaust and two black skid marks on the road.

Bruce raced forward in close pursuit; his car mapped the ground instantly, swerving in a perfect curve to follow the ramp onto the freeway. He tapped twice on the windshield right over where the Nightwalker's white vehicle was.

"Follow him," Bruce commanded.

DAUGHTER OF IMMORTALS.
DAUGHTER OF DEATH.
THEIR FRIENDSHIP
WILL CHANGE THE WORLD.

TURN THE PAGE TO SEE
HOW DIANA'S BATTLE BEGINS!

You do not enter a race to lose.

Diana bounced lightly on her toes at the starting line, her calves taut as bowstrings, her mother's words reverberating in her ears. A noisy crowd had gathered for the wrestling matches and javelin throws that would mark the start of the Nemeseian Games, but the real event was the footrace, and now the stands were buzzing with word that the queen's daughter had entered the competition.

When Hippolyta had seen Diana amid the runners clustered on the arena sands, she'd displayed no surprise. As was tradition, she'd descended from her viewing platform to wish the athletes luck in their endeavors, sharing a joke here, offering a kind word of encouragement there. She had nodded briefly to Diana, showing her no special favor, but she'd whispered, so low that only her daughter could hear, "You do not enter a race to lose."

Amazons lined the path that led out of the arena, already stamping their feet and chanting for the games to begin.

On Diana's right, Rani flashed her a radiant smile. "Good luck today." She was always kind, always gracious, and, of course, always victorious.

To Diana's left, Thyra snorted and shook her head. "She's going to need it."

Diana ignored her. She'd been looking forward to this race for weeks—a trek across the island to retrieve one of the red flags hung beneath the great dome in Bana-Mighdall. In a flat-out sprint, she didn't have a chance. She still hadn't come into the fullness of her Amazon strength. *You will in time*, her mother had promised. But her mother promised a lot of things.

This race was different. It required strategy, and Diana was ready. She'd been training in secret, running sprints with Maeve, and plotting a route that had rougher terrain but was definitely a straighter shot to the western tip of the island. She'd even— well, she hadn't exactly *spied*. . . . She'd gathered intelligence on the other Amazons in the race. She was still the smallest, and of course the youngest, but she'd shot up in the last year, and she was nearly as tall as Thyra now.

I don't need luck, she told herself. *I have a plan.* She glanced down the row of Amazons gathered at the starting line like troops readying for war and amended, *But a little luck wouldn't hurt, either.* She wanted that laurel crown. It was better than any royal circlet or tiara—an honor that couldn't be given, that had to be earned.

She found Maeve's red hair and freckled face in the crowd and grinned, trying to project confidence. Maeve returned the smile and gestured with both hands as if she were tamping down the air. She mouthed the words, "Steady on."

Diana rolled her eyes but nodded and tried to slow her breathing. She had a bad habit of coming out too fast and wasting her speed too early.

Now she cleared her mind and forced herself to concentrate on the course as Tekmessa walked the line, surveying the runners, jewels glinting in her thick corona of curls, silver bands flashing on her brown arms. She was Hippolyta's closest advisor, second in rank only to the queen, and she carried herself as if her belted indigo shift were battle armor.

"Take it easy, Pyxis," Tek murmured to Diana as she passed. "Wouldn't want to see you crack." Diana heard Thyra snort again, but she refused to flinch at the nickname. *You won't be smirking when I'm on the victors' podium*, she promised.

Tek raised her hands for silence and bowed to Hippolyta, who sat between two other members of the Amazon Council in the royal loge—a high platform shaded by a silken overhang dyed in the vibrant red and blue of the queen's colors. Diana knew that was where her mother wanted her right now, seated beside her, waiting for the start of the games instead of competing. None of that would matter when she won.

Hippolyta dipped her chin the barest amount, elegant in her white tunic and riding trousers, a simple circlet resting against her forehead. She looked relaxed, at her ease, as if she might decide to leap down and join the competition at any time, but still every inch the queen.

Tek addressed the athletes gathered on the arena sands. "In whose honor do you compete?"

"For the glory of the Amazons," they replied in unison. "For the glory of our queen." Diana felt her heart beat harder. She'd never said the words before, not as a competitor.

"To whom do we give praise each day?" Tek trumpeted.

"Hera," they chorused. "Athena, Demeter, Hestia, Aphrodite, Artemis." The goddesses who had created Themyscira and gifted it to Hippolyta as a place of refuge.

Tek paused, and along the line, Diana heard the whispers of other names: Oya, Durga, Freyja, Mary, Yael. Names once cried out in death, the last prayers of female warriors fallen in battle, the words that had brought them to this island and given them new life as Amazons. Beside Diana, Rani murmured the names of the demon-fighting Matri, the seven mothers, and pressed the rectangular amulet she always wore to her lips.

Tek raised a blood-red flag identical to those that would be waiting for the runners in Bana-Mighdall.

"May the island guide you to just victory!" she shouted.

She dropped the red silk. The crowd roared. The runners surged toward the eastern arch. Like that, the race had begun.

Diana and Maeve had anticipated a bottleneck, but Diana still felt a pang of frustration as runners clogged the stone throat of the tunnel, a tangle of white tunics and muscled limbs, footsteps echoing off the stone, all of them trying to get clear of the arena at once. Then they were on the road, sprinting across the island, each runner choosing her own course.

You do not enter a race to lose.

Diana set her pace to the rhythm of those words, bare feet slapping the packed earth of the road that would lead her through the tangle of the Cybelian Woods to the island's northern coast.

Ordinarily, a miles-long trek through this forest would be a slow one, hampered by fallen trees and tangles of vines so thick they had to be hacked through with a blade you didn't mind dulling. But Diana had plotted her way well. An hour after she entered the woods, she burst from the trees onto the deserted coast road. The wind lifted her hair, and salt spray lashed her face. She breathed deep, checked the position of the sun. She was going to win—not just place but win.

She'd mapped out the course the week before with Maeve, and they'd run it twice in secret, in the gray-light hours of early morning, when their sisters were first rising from their beds, when the kitchen fires were still being kindled, and the only curious eyes they'd had to worry about belonged to anyone up early to hunt game or cast nets for the day's catch. But hunters kept to the woods and meadows farther south, and no one fished off this part of the coast; there was no good place to launch a boat, just the steep steel-colored cliffs plunging straight down to the sea, and a tiny, unwelcoming cove that could only be reached by a path so narrow you had to shuffle down sideways, back pressed to the rock.

The northern shore was gray, grim, and inhospitable, and Diana knew every inch of its secret landscape, its crags and caves, its tide pools teeming with limpets and anemones. It was a good place to be alone. *The island seeks to please,* her mother had told her. It was why Themyscira was forested by redwoods in some places and rubber trees in others; why you could spend an afternoon roaming the grasslands on a scoop-neck pony and the evening atop a camel, scaling a moonlit dragonback of sand dunes. They were all pieces of the lives the Amazons had led before they came to the island, little landscapes of the heart.

Diana sometimes wondered if Themyscira had called the northern coast into being just for her so that she could challenge herself climbing on the sheer drop of its cliffs, so that she could have a place to herself when the weight of being Hippolyta's daughter got to be too much.

You do not enter a race to lose.

Her mother had not been issuing a general warning. Diana's losses meant something different, and they both knew it—and not only because she was a princess.

Diana could almost feel Tek's knowing gaze on her, hear the mocking in her voice. *Take it easy, Pyxis.* That was the nickname Tek had given her. Pyxis. A little clay pot made to store jewels or a tincture of carmine for pinking the lips. The name was harmless, meant to tease, always said in love—or so Tek claimed. But it stung every time: a reminder that Diana was not like the other Amazons, and never would be. Her sisters were battle-proven warriors, steel forged from suffering and honed to greatness as they passed from life to immortality. All of them had earned their place on Themyscira. All but Diana, born of the island's soil and Hippolyta's longing for a child, fashioned from clay by her mother's hands—hollow and breakable. *Take it easy, Pyxis. Wouldn't want to see you crack.*

Diana steadied her breathing, kept her pace even. *Not today, Tek. This day the laurel belongs to me.*

She spared the briefest glance at the horizon, letting the sea breeze cool the sweat on her brow. Through the mists, she glimpsed the white shape of a ship. It had come close enough to the boundary that Diana could make out its sails. The craft was small—a schooner maybe? She had trouble remembering nautical details. Mainmast, mizzenmast, a thousand names for sails, and knots for rigging. It was one thing to be out on a boat, learning from Teuta, who had sailed with Illyrian pirates, but quite another to be stuck in the library at the Epheseum, staring glazed-eyed at diagrams of a brigantine or a caravel.

Sometimes Diana and Maeve made a game of trying to spot ships or planes, and once they'd even seen the fat blot of a cruise ship on the horizon. But most mortals knew to steer clear of their particular corner of the Aegean, where compasses spun and instruments suddenly refused to obey.

Today it looked like a storm was picking up past the mists of the boundary, and Diana was sorry she couldn't stop to watch it. The rains that came to Themyscira were tediously gentle and predictable, nothing like the threatening rumble of thunder, the shimmer of a far-off lightning strike.

"Do you ever miss storms?" Diana had asked one afternoon as she and Maeve lazed on the palace's sun-soaked rooftop terrace, listening to the distant roar and clatter of a tempest. Maeve had died in the Crossbarry Ambush, the last words on her lips a prayer to Saint Brigid of Kildare. She was new to the island by Amazon standards, and came from Cork, where storms were common.

"No," Maeve had said in her lilting voice. "I miss a good cup of tea, dancing, boys—definitely not rain."

"We dance," Diana protested.

Maeve had just laughed. "You dance differently when you know you won't live forever." Then she'd stretched, freckles like dense clouds of pollen on her white skin. "I think I was a cat in another life, because all I want is to lie around sleeping in the world's biggest sunbeam."

Steady on. Diana resisted the urge to speed forward. It was hard to remember to keep something in reserve with the early-morning sun on her shoulders and the wind at her back. She felt strong. But it was easy to feel strong when she was on her own.

A *boom* sounded over the waves, a hard metallic clap like a door slamming shut. Diana's steps faltered. On the blue horizon, a billowing column of smoke rose, flames licking at its base. The schooner was on fire, its prow blown to splinters and one of its masts smashed, the sail dragging over the rails.

Diana found herself slowing but forced her stride back on pace. There was nothing she could do for the schooner. Planes crashed. Ships were wrecked upon the rocks. That was the nature of the mortal world. It was a place where disaster could happen and often did. Human life was a tide of misery, one that never reached the island's shores. Diana focused her eyes on the path. Far, far ahead she could see sunlight gleaming gold off the great dome at Bana-Mighdall. First the red flag, then the laurel crown. That was the plan.

From somewhere on the wind, she heard a cry.

A gull, she told herself. *A girl*, some other voice within her insisted. *Impossible*. A human shout couldn't carry over such a great distance, could it?

It didn't matter. There was nothing she could do.

And yet her eyes strayed back to the horizon. *I just want to get a better view*, she told herself. *I have plenty of time. I'm ahead.*

There was no good reason to leave the ruts of the old cart track, no logic to veering out over the rocky point, but she did it anyway.

BEFORE HE CAN SAVE THE WORLD,
CLARK KENT MUST SAVE SMALLVILLE.

THE BESTSELLING DC ICONS
SERIES CONTINUES WITH A NEW
MUST-READ BLOCKBUSTER!